All To Play For

A Novel

By

William Rocke

All To Play For Published 2004 by Rocphil Publishing,
3 Hazelwood Drive,
Dublin 5, Republic of Ireland.
Telephone: O1 – 8475593.
Email: rocphil @ 02.ie.

This book is a work of fiction. Names, characters, places or incidents are
either the product of the author's imagination or are used fictitiously. Any
resemblance to actual events, locales or persons, living or dead, is entirely
coincidental.

A catalogue record for this book is available from
The British Library.

— 📓 —

ACKNOWLEDGMENTS

'All To Play For' is dedicated to my wife Phyllis for her support, also for her important role in co-signing the cheques. I wish to thank former Irish Press Art Editor Liam and his wife Eithne for being the first to advise me to 'go for it!; thanks also to Pat Ruddy of the European Golf Club for his invaluable contacts, and to television golf commentator, the incomparable Ewen Murray, for consenting to write the foreword.

Also by William Rocke

BOOKS

Operation Birdie (a novel)

Passion, intrigue and a bomb plot at the Open Golf
Championship.

'A rivetting read' – Golf World.

'An auspicious debut' – Irish Times.

'A powerful read' – golfer Christy O'Connor Jr.

Last Tango In Ibiza (a novel)

(With the Ardlea Writers' Group)

High jinks among a disparate group of holiday-makers on
Spain's island in the sun.

World Cup Wonders

(Dramatic highlights of soccer's World Cup)

PLAYS

Try Anything Twice! (comedy)

Family Affairs. (comedy)

What's A Promise In A Place Like This? (comedy/drama)

One-act plays for females

Summer Belles (comedy)

Neighbours (comedy/drama)

ABOUT THE AUTHOR: Journalist (semi-retired) author and
playwright. Married to Phyllis, lives in Artane, Dublin, Rep. of
Ireland. Father to four young adults. Founded his own
publishing company to foster his writing. Interests: people,
theatre, sport, reading, travel and playing golf badly. Person he
would most like to meet – Jesus Christ.

FOREWORD

by

Ewen Murray,
Golf Commentator.

Once every two years golfers throughout the world, not only in Europe and America, like to play at being Ryder Cup captains, selecting the pairings they
think will win vital points and make them a hero. The Ryder Cup was founded in 1926 by a rich English seed merchant named Samuel Ryder, and the trophy was first played for in Massachusetts the following year. It was an event initially mooted by rivals, American Walter Hagen and England's Abe Mitchell in 1926, to bring goodwill into the game through the meeting of the two most powerful forces in golf on a winner-take-all basis.

The Americans triumphed in that inaugural contest, starting a winning streak broken only by the occasional British victory. It all changed from those early days when, in 1979, golfers from the rest of Europe joined their British and Irish counterparts to take on the Americans. Since then the biennial Ryder Cup contests have been more evenly contested, resulting in edge-of-the-seat finishes that have thrilled millions of people – not all of them golf fans - throughout the world.

The Ryder Cup is a sporting spectacular where the great game reigns supreme, where the two teams battle over three days, not for huge prize money (there is none on offer), but for the sole honour of representing their respective countries. A Ryder Cup clash is sport at its best, sport in its raw natural state, sport the way we once knew and respected it.

The author is a man I have known for only a short time. He is obviously a person who loves the ancient game. Reading his novel, you will find yourself sometimes arguing, sometimes agreeing with the fictional events, both on and off the course, as his vivid imagination takes flight on this glorious journey. You will be drawn into this adventure and the only annoyance will be the fact that he had kept you awake later than desired in order to digest the fictional world he has taken you into.

Golf stories, in my opinion, have never been anything near as thrilling in telling as the real thing. That will change when you start turning the pages of 'All To Play For'. You owe yourself some quality time to unwind, to drift off into a world of seriously entertaining golf - and non-golf fiction.

Author William Rocke has created such a world – and believe me it's a compelling journey!

Good golfing,
Ewen Murray.

CHAPTER ONE

As they reached the approaches of the town the traffic became more congested and one sensed the air of excitement. Inside the Mitsubishi Ranger Katie felt the tension rise inside her and her mouth was dry. Sunday evenings were usually a quiet time of the day in Loughduff, with car spaces outside the local hostelries yet to fill up. Groups of teenagers and young adults gathered around street corners prior to heading off to the various centres of entertainment in the area.

This evening however, for the past hour there had been a steady stream of vehicles nosing their way around the lake under the shadow of the mountain range that towered majestically over the town. Their drivers were mostly men dressed in their Sunday best; tomorrow they would be back in the fields, having swopped their automobiles for the tractor or the combine harvester. Tonight there was some serious business to attend to. After the meeting they would gather in groups in local bars for further discussion over rounds of drinks.

Beside her in the driving seat Ben Gartland nodded in the direction of yet another poster nailed to a telegraph pole. 'They've got it well advertised. Someone's got the finger out.' When she didn't reply he glanced sideways at her. 'There'll be a big crowd in tonight to hear what you've got to say. Don't be a shrinking violet, you hear? Give it everything you've got. You should get a lot of sympathy after seeing your husband being dragged off his farm and slung into jail.'

Katie didn't reply, knowing this would annoy him. Instead she stared straight ahead. Holding a conversation with her brother-in-law had never been one of her favourite pastimes. Better to concentrate on the upcoming meeting, try to get her thoughts together. After the traumatic happening of yesterday morning she knew a lot would be expected of her. Katie hoped she would be up to the task. In the back seat of the Mitsubishi Ranger she could hear her two teenage sons converse in excited tones. Thank God both Garret and Jack didn't seem to be taking on their father's dour manner; they seemed to be enjoying being thrust into the limelight.

'Look Mom,' Jack the youngest exclaimed, 'there's another poster with your name on it. You're cool!' Beside her she heard Ben growl something under his breath.

They were inching along slowly now through the traffic. Many men had abandoned their cars on the outskirts of the town and were making their way to the meeting on foot. Katie had ample time to read the words printed in bold black script on the square of stiff white pasteboard:

IRISH LAND
FOR IRISH
FARMERS.
FOREIGNERS OUT!

Meeting tonight in Community Hall. 8pm sharp.

Principal Speaker: Katie Gartland.

'Pity Travis is not here to see that – the family name on a poster. After tonight the whole country will have heard of me and Travis.' Ben's voice cut through her thoughts. He swore again under his breath as the driver of the car in front stopped momentarily to exchange a greeting with a group of men making their way into the town along the narrow pathway bordering the road. When Katie didn't reply once more he said impatiently: 'What the hell is wrong with you? You're not talking.'

'I'm nervous. I don't feel like talking. I've never spoken in front of a big crowd before – ' She broke off. At least she would not have to face her husband when she returned home tonight. She took pleasure in thinking of him in a cell in Mountjoy Jail in Dublin. Thank God he wouldn't be arriving back from the town in the early hours, drunk as usual, groping for her in the bed…

'What the hell are you nervous about? They're all friends of Travis, aren't they? Tell them how much you're missing your husband.' Ben laughed at his own private joke.

Katie bit her lip, remained silent. She treated Ben Gartland the way she would treat an obscene telephone caller – by ignoring him. In her mind's eye she re-lived the scene when the Gardai had arrived early yesterday morning: the two police cars with lights flashing sweeping in through the gates and up the short driveway just after daybreak. Travis, who had been expecting the visit, had risen early and was dressed and waiting. Katie and the boys had dressed hurriedly and had gone down to the kitchen where the sergeant and three strange policemen with grim faces – obviously brought in from outside the area to carry out this distasteful task - were waiting. Travis had demanded his breakfast which she had cooked and which they had allowed her husband to eat.

Then it was out onto the open porch to face the members of the media, and the large number of locals who, despite the early hour, had shown up to lend Travis their support. They gathered in the August sunshine to witness Travis Gartland being taken off to jail. He had become a martyr by refusing in court the previous day to withdraw threats he had made in public, on behalf of local farmers, against any building company brought in by a Japanese consortium to begin work on an exclusive golf course and sports complex in the area. The controversy had been raging in the area since the plan for foreigners to build their hotel and golf complex on prime farm land had been announced last year. Local farmers had immediately opposed the multi-million Euro project by the Japanese.

Travis had paused on the porch steps, acknowledging the cheers of support from the locals, an unlikely hero in the eyes of many who had run foul of the truculent Gartland brothers over the years. Katie had looked on in surprise; gone was her husband's usual glowering, aggressive countenance. Now he was grinning, raising a clenched fist in the air, acknowledging the cheers of the crowd, enjoying his moment of glory.

Last night he had come in as usual from a late night drinking session in the town and joined her in bed without a word of greeting. She had got the smell of alcohol off him, heard him muttering to himself as he undressed. Thankfully he had dropped off into a drunken sleep almost immediately, albeit keeping her awake with his snoring.

The Gardai hadn't given Travis much time to work up the crowd. He had shouted his defiance to his supporters, then pulled Katie to him and kissed her clumsily on the mouth. It was as if he was performing a duty for his audience. Despite herself, Katie felt tears welling up into her eyes as they broke apart. She clung to the hope that Travis's last words to her might be something tender, but all her husband could manage was a hurried:

'Ben will hire in a man in to help him with the farm. The boys will help out too. Make sure they do their share.' He was bundled into the back seat of the police car between two constables as the crowd pushed forward. Several men rained blows with their fists on the roof of the squad car as it was driven through the jeering mob, down the short drive and out onto the road. Travis did not turn to look or wave at her through the back window of the vehicle.

Then it was her turn to face the newspaper reporters in the crowd. With Garret and Jack by her side she had done her best to cope with the barrage of questions fired at her by the eager members of the media. The clicking of cameras and the glare of the television lights unnerved her. But the news people sensed a good story and were determined to make the most of the opportunity. The questions had come rapidly.

'Do you think you can persuade your husband to give up his protest, Mrs. Gartland? I'm told he's a stubborn man – '

'Does he plan on going on hunger strike?'

'Is he determined to stay in jail until the foreign investors in the land project pull out?'

Katie had answered each question as best she could. Ben had arrived in just in time to see his elder brother being hustled away. He had pushed his way forward and joined Katie on the porch, determined to impose his presence on the proceedings.

'You can be sure my brother will remain in jail until these foreign land-grabbers clear out,' Ben shouted to the crowd. 'Our farmers are angry that large tracts of land are being sold off and turned into golf courses for the rich. Travis and myself are calling on the full support of the United Farmers' Organisation. You crowd from the newspapers and television - if you want to hear how we plan to bring our fight to the attention of the world, bring along your television cameras to the meeting in Loughduff tomorrow night!'

An excited buzz gripped the crowd as Ben finished speaking. He looked pleased with himself, his unshaven face, with the scar from an earlier battle running down his left cheek, breaking into a grim smile. He had certainly caught the attention of the onlookers, especially the members of the media.

'What plan is that, Ben?' a reporter asked. The cameras began whirring again.

'Come on Ben, give us a clue,' another shouted.

Ben Gartland was really enjoying the attention. But he was no fool. His big occasion would be tomorrow night. 'I've said enough already,' he shouted back. 'Come along to the meeting. We farmers are not taking this plan to grab our land lying down.'

When the cheers had died down a reporter with an English accent shouted: 'This is a relatively minor land row in Ireland. How do you plan to get it picked up worldwide?'

Ben knew he was getting into dangerous territory. But he was anxious to keep the interest level high. He could sense that the reporters were hanging onto his every word. Maybe he would throw them one more titbit; he was enjoying his new-found power.

'You know that the land at the centre of this row is being bought over and turned into a golf course. And you all know that the Ryder Cup is being staged in Killarney in a few weeks time…' He paused. 'We farmers aim to use that rich man's game to highlight our cause.'

His reply sparked off another buzz of excitement among the journalists. After a few moments one of them shouted out: 'Are you planning a protest at the Ryder Cup, Ben?'

The question hung in the air. Everyone knew that the bi-annual clash between the top professional golfers of America and Europe was scheduled to take place next month in nearby Killarney. Was this small-time farmer serious? Was he aiming for a rumble at the Ryder Cup, one of the most hyped-up international events in world sport? This was shaping up into a fairly useful story after all!

The clash between the two great golf powers raised national passions to unprecedented levels and was beamed by satellite to practically every country in the world. What a platform to use to escalate a minor land row in Ireland to global proportions! This Ben Gartland fellow had to be listened to.

Angry at having been goaded into revealing more than he had intended, Ben shouted to his inquisitors: 'I'm not saying any more about this right now. If you want to hear more come along to our metting in town tomorrow night. Now clear off our land the lot of you!' He had ushered Katie and the boys into the house after that. When she had sought further information about the planned protest he had brushed her aside.

Katie had only a vague idea what the Ryder Cup was about. She remembered watching television some years ago when the triumphant European team had arrived back in Dublin from America after defeating the Yanks and seeing the Irish hero of the hour – she could not recall his name – holding aloft the coveted trophy after the Europeans had alighted from their flight home by Concorde. She had envied the smiling Ryder Cup wives that night, they had all looked so happy and glamorous. She had gone to bed, dreading the drudgery that faced her on the morrow.

Of course she knew that the Ryder Cup was being held this year in Killarney, a mere twenty miles from Loughduff. Every hotel and guesthouse for miles around had been booked out for practically the past year. A lot of wives in the area had converted their establishments into temporary bed and breakfast houses to cater for the huge demand from golf fans all over the world wanting to see the three day Ryder Cup clash.

As the Mitsubishi Ranger nosed its way into the centre of the town Katie wondered if the plan of action that her brother-in-law had mentioned really had the backing of the United Farmers' Organisation. She knew that Ben was a bit of a hothead, prone to explode when he didn't get his way. Now that his elder brother was off the scene she would not be surprised if Ben was already taking matters into his own hands.

'You'll come for a drink after the meeting – ' Ben's voice cut across her train of thought. 'You'll not be wanting to rush back to that lonely house. You could do with a few drinks and a bit of company.'

It was not so much an invitation as an order. Out of the corner of her eye she saw Ben, stopped in traffic, taking the opportunity to study her. Ben Gartland had always regarded his sister-in-law as a fine looking woman. Her long dark hair, high cheekbones, and slim figure owed a lot to the work routine she had to put in on the farm. Katie had excited him from the first night that Travis had brought her home, a teenage slip of a girl not long out of the convent orphanage in the town. Not that she had much of an opportunity to show off her sexuality married to someone like Travis! In the twenty years they had been married Ben had never seen his brother take his wife out anywhere socially. Work on the farm and looking after the two boys was her lot. Ben wondered what she would be like with a few drinks on her.

'If you don't mind I'd rather go straight home after the meeting.'

'Would you now – ' Ben blared the car horn in a fit of anger. 'Then you and the boys will wait until I'm fit and ready to go.' When she didn't reply he went on, 'I'm not good enough to be seen in your company, eh?'

He was getting angrier. Better humour him. 'It's not that, Ben – '

'What's it, then?'

'I just don't think it's a good idea to be seen drinking in a bar with a crowd of men so soon after my husband has been taken away to jail. People will talk.'

'Let them talk – ' He swore at her. 'Who the hell cares!'

Katie didn't reply. Avoiding local gossip was only part of the reason why she didn't want to be seen with Ben Gartland. Personally she didn't care what the locals said about her. She hardly ever mixed with any of them. She knew that when Ben drank to excess, as he usually did, he had many of the ill-mannered traits of his elder brother. Besides, the Loughduff Inn was the last place on earth she would socialise. It and the treatment meted out to her at the hands of the childless couple, Benjy Duff and his shrewish wife, who owned the hostelry had evoked bad memories within her since her teens. She had been farmed out to them from the convent orphanage and it was in the town's hostelry that Travis Gartland had first set eyes on her. She had never been inside the door of the place since her wedding day.

Her marriage to Travis had not prevented Ben, over the years, when his brother was not around, from displaying a sexual urge for the new arrival in the household. He seemed to regard her as a chattel, a piece of the furniture to be shared between himself and his brother. Ben's advances usually came about through not very subtle mumblings, or brushing up against her. It was after one such episode that Ben moved out after she threatened to tell her husband.

She had never actually complained about Ben to Travis. Katie simply didn't see the point; herself and Travis never spoke in intimate terms, their short conversations invariably centred around farm routine with Travis grunting instructions to her either in the kitchen or the bedroom. When she had threatened Ben about telling Travis of the carry-on behind his back he had just grinned and invited her to go ahead. He had said Travis wouldn't believe her anyway and he was probably right. He had moved out nevertheless.

Ben found a parking space just off the town square. 'You still refusing to come with me for a drink?'

'Yes, Ben, and that's final. Can't you get it into your head that that I'm not interested?'

She was glad that Garret and Jack had already climbed out of the Mitsubishi and were not privy to the conversation.

'Does that go for Travis too? I see the way he treats you – '

'That's different. I'm his wife.'

'What happens if he wants to become a martyr and stay in jail – maybe even starve himself to death, eh? You'll be depending on me a lot then. I might even give up my place in town and move back into the house.' He cast another glance sideways at her. Katie was in no doubt what he had in mind. 'Now wouldn't that be interesting…'

She got out of the car and, flanked by the two boys, joined the throng of people entering the community hall. Out of the corner of her eye she was conscious of some of the men nudging each other and staring. Travis Gartland's young wife didn't often come into town at night, more the pity as far as they were concerned. She had certainly grown into a fine looking young woman from the slip of a girl whom they remembered working behind Benjy Duff's bar.

Walking behind her as she entered the hall, Ben Gartland noted the admiring glances and overheard some of the whispered comments of the locals. Although her demeanour and dress were not geared to attract male attention, his sister-in-law certainly had the air about her to turn men's heads. Ben took pleasure in studying her trim figure as she climbed the few steps onto the stage where a microphone and tables and chairs had been set up. The thought of her lying in bed alone at night aroused him. Katie would learn that his desire for her was not going to be brushed aside that easily.

● ● ● ●

Ben Gartland was not the only man experiencing trouble with a woman at that particular moment. As he lined up a straightforward 8-iron shot to the 10th green at the Placid Lakes Golf and Country Club on the outskirts of Chicago Wayne Folen, veteran professional golfer and captain of the American Ryder Cup team, knew he was in for a tough session with the media when he finished his round.

That was why right now, competing in the TriStar Banks Classic, he was shooting one of the worst 18 holes of golf in an illustrious career. At 51, and after a distinguished and lucrative twenty-five years on the regular pro tour during which he had won two majors – the Masters at Augusta and a U.S. Open – he was well on his way to making another million dollars on only his second year on the over-50s Seniors tour. He had looked like winning this tournament until he had received that phone call from Marcia early this morning.

The call had woken him up at precisely 3.20am. As soon as Wayne heard Marcia's voice he sensed trouble. It had long been a rule that his wife would not call him in the middle of a tournament unless it was really urgent. Professional golfers do not relish being troubled by trivia from home at any stage, even from a spouse who had not seen her husband for two weeks.

'Wayne? Hello Wayne - ' The tone was a mixture of anxiety and sharpness.

'Marcia! Is that you Marcia?'

'Who the hell were you expecting to call you in the middle of the night.' There was no mistaking the anger in her voice. Very unlike Marcia, his ever-loving wife.

Wayne glanced at the travelling clock on his bedside locker. 'Hello, honey. Good to hear your voice,' he lied. 'Something wrong?' Beside him in the bed Angie stirred, turned towards him, blonde hair falling across her sleepy green eyes.

'You bet there's something wrong. Have you been watching the tv news?'

'Not tonight I haven't.' Jeez, she's rumbled him. 'Marcia honey, you realise I'm leading this tournament with only one round to go. I got into bed early last night - '

'No doubt you did – and I bet you weren't alone!' Holy

Jesus – This wasn't his ever-loving Marcia talking. She obviously suspects something. Her next words confirmed his worst fears. 'Tell me it's not true, Wayne, - ' Her voice softened, trembled slightly.

'What's not true, Marcia?' He had a terrible feeling that the game was up.

'About you – and that blonde actress. It's on all the newscasts. That you've picked up with a young blonde and you're talking about a divorce so that you can marry her. CNN broke the story and now all the other stations have picked it up.'

He paused for a fatal second, trying to figure out what to say next. He could tell Marcia that this wasn't the time to be discussing their marital problems, in the middle of the night and just when he was leading a big tournament….

Marcia took his hesitation as an admission of guilt. 'I see, so it is true. I can't believe you'd do this to me, Wayne. Not after all our years together. You of all people, America's Ryder Cup captain, the man the whole country is admiring, looking up to…'

He thought he heard a sob. 'Now wait a minute, honey. I can explain. It's not as bad as those reporter guys are making out – '

Beside him in the bed Angie had turned into him. He could feel her warm, young body pressing into his back. Underneath the duvet she was doing things to his lower body that Marcia had stopped doing years ago. He was going to have to end this conversation or else his wife was going to hear the kind of noises at the other end of the line that would confirm everything she had heard on the news.

'Marcia honey, I can't talk right now – ' Wayne stopped. The line had gone dead. He looked at the telephone in his hand. Should he call his wife back and try to explain the situation more fully? It would not be easy. Better wait until he got home and they could discuss it calmly with Shiralee, their married daughter.

'Trouble, honey?' Angie asked.

'Yeah. That was Marcia. She says the story about us is on all the networks.'

'No kidding. Surprise, surprise.' Angie didn't seem too worried. Indeed she appeared quite happy with the news. She had nuzzled the back of his neck. 'We'll talk about it tomorrow.'

Now, as he stood over the ball and surveyed the shot to the 10th green, Wayne tried to shut out from his mind the early morning conversation with Marcia. Concentrate! You haven't blown the tournament yet, he told himself. But three over par for the first nine holes had seen him slip down the leader board into joint fourth place. He was now four shots behind the new leader, Ken Kenwright, his playing partner today. Hell, Kenwright was 60 years of age for God's sake. Wayne knew he would be the butt of a lot of jokes in the locker-room if he lost the tournament to an old man today!

He swung the 8-iron and the ball took off towards the distant sward of green 140 yards away. But he had cut across the ball on impact and it was tailing off, heading towards the trees to the right of the green. There were shouts of 'fore' and he could see spectators ahead ducking low as the ball flew over heads and crashed into the branches of a tree. Wayne swore under his breath, thumped his club into the fairway in frustration.

He caught a glimpse of Angie among the spectators lining the fairway. It was difficult not to notice her; the day was hot and humid and it had given her an opportunity to show off her curvaceous figure. Her white trainers, ankle socks, tank top and matching white pleated skirt, rising halfway up her tanned thighs, showed off her long, shapely legs to perfection. Between the skirt and her tank top several inches of her perfectly proportioned midriff was on display. Her blonde shoulder-length hair was held in place by a white band, framing a face guaranteed to make any male casting agent offer her a second audition – at a price, of course.

They had met by sheer chance not long after he had been named non-playing captain of the American Ryder Cup squad. What a week that had been – given the job of leading the team with the huge task of bringing back the coveted trophy to America, and meeting a girl like Angie Wilde, all in the space of seven days.

If Wayne's meeting with a beautiful actress half his age had come out of the blue, his being picked as Ryder Cup captain had not been unexpected. After the humiliating defeat on home soil by the Europeans two years previously, the American nation had been outraged. In the newspapers and on tv talk shows there had been calls for those behind the U.S. Ryder Cup committee to resign – or get tough and pick a captain who would imbue his players with a steely desire to win.

'We want a guy who will cross the Atlantic, kick some European ass, and bring back the Ryder Cup!' was the cry from red-blooded Americans, many of whom had never been on a golf course in their lives. And guys with a will-to-win didn't come any tougher or more fired-up than Wayne Folen, the ex-U.S. marine who had fought his way to the top of the golf game through sheer determination and talent.

The austere members of the U.S. Ryder Cup committee, mindful of the extreme nationalist feelings whipped up at previous clashes between European and American golfers, had baulked at such outspoken sentiments.

But another Ryder Cup defeat in a tournament they had at one time dominated was unthinkable. Under pressure, the committee had reluctantly given way to public opinion and selected Wayne Folen as their captain. Not without some misgivings, however.

Wayne knew that he was not the unanimous choice of the U.S. golf hierarchy. He knew they feared his gung-ho, no nonsense approach as non-playing captain would arouse unwanted passions on both sides of the Atlantic. It didn't worry the man who had seen action in Vietnam; when the seven man committee had invited him to a meeting in the U.S. Professional Golfers' headquarters in Florida before announcing his appointment. He had not flinched when it had been made plain to him that the men who ran American professional golf abhorred some of the extreme comments that were already being bandied about in the media.

'Let's make one thing clear, Wayne,' chairman Cord McCallum had explained in his southern drawl. 'We have excellent relations with our friends in the European P.G.A. Where the Ryder Cup is concerned, we intend to keep it that way.

Cord McCallum had paused, waited while his fellow committee members nodded in agreement, then continued: 'In other words we are not in favour of ' - he coughed dryly, making it clear that he found his next words distasteful – 'to use an expression attributed to you, 'kicking European ass.'

Wayne had not responded immediately. Instead he had fixed them all in turn with one of his renowned steely glares. Then he took up the challenge. 'Gentlemen, I appreciate your sentiments. But let me ask you all one question…. come September, when we face the Europeans in Killarney with the Ryder Cup at stake, do you want me to bring that famous trophy back to America where it belongs, or do you want us to suffer another humiliating defeat?' He had paused, letting his words sink in.

McCallum had waved a dismissive hand that was as brown as his wrinkled face. 'But of course we want to win the Ryder Cup. Dammit we are all Americans – '

Wayne had stood up, thumped the table hard . 'If you are as American as you claim, then act like an American! I'll bring back the Ryder Cup even if we have to repeat the

War on the Shore scenes at Kiawah Island in 1991, or stoke up the players to display the naked nationalism that we showed when winning at Brookline in 1999. But I'll do things my way or not at all.' Wayne paused, said softly… 'Now gentlemen, make up your minds. Do we have a deal?'

He could see they were taken aback. This governing body of respected men seated behind the polished desk in the large oval room redolent of golf's glorious times past, were not accustomed to being given an ultimatum by anyone. There was an angry buzz as several of them spoke at once.

One of the seven raised his voice above the others. 'Now see here, Wayne, there are limits to which our respected members will go to achieve victory in the Ryder Cup – '

Wayne rose to his feet. 'Thank you gentlemen. We obviously don't see eye to eye. I'm afraid you're going to have to find a new captain!' With that he had turned on his heel and made for the door.

'Now wait a minute Wayne, don't be so hasty – ' Cord McCallum's voice had halted him. When he turned he saw the chairman had risen to his feet and was gesturing to the empty chair. 'Sit down, sit down. You're our man. I'm sure we can both – ' McCallum checked himself. Compromise was a word that he found distasteful. ' – I'm sure we can come to some arrangement – '

Half-an-hour later Wayne Folen had walked out of he U.S. P.G.A headquarters with a smile on his face. He had fought for and got everything he wanted. Hell, he was determined to bring the Ryder Cup back to America – and no group of wizened old guys in tailored blazers was going to get in his way!

Wayne chipped out from between the trees onto the 10th green. He knocked his approach putt four feet past the hole, missed the one back, dropping another shot. He grimaced as he walked towards the 11th tee. The pressure, plus the thoughts of Angie and the energetic sessions in bed with her before and after Marcia's early morning telephone call, was getting to him. The tournament was being televised so he had warned Angie not to approach him during the round. No doubt half the nation – including Marcia, would be tuned in hoping to catch a glimpse of the Ryder Cup captain's new girlfriend. The situation wasn't helping his golf.

Things didn't improve over the final eight holes. At the end of the tournament he was down in joint 14th place after shooting a closing 78. Wayne stormed off the 18th green and into the recorder's hut to sign his card, brushing aside several reporters who were asking the kind of questions he didn't want to hear. But when he exited ten minutes later they were waiting for him – and the group had grown. He noticed Angie on the fringe of the crowd. Their eyes met and she gave him a smile and a wave. Hell, he might as well get it over with. He approached her and took her hand, then turned and faced the reporters.

'Ladies and gentlemen, I'd like you to meet Angie Wilde – '. Wayne paused. He was making an effort to be polite. 'Angie and I are good friends, okay? Now if you want to ask some questions make it fast. I haven't got all day'

The reporters could hardly believe their luck. They knew and respected Wayne Folen as a fearless, no nonsense individual, both on and off the golf course. They had not expected him to be so upfront about what was happening in his personal life.

A female journalist was first up. 'What exactly do you mean by good friends, Wayne?' She had a cute smile on her face that he didn't like.

He fixed her with an icy glare. 'Do I have to spell it out for you. You're a big girl, I think you get the drift.'

'Does your wife know about your relationship with Angie?', the same reporter asked, obviously unphased by Wayne's curt manner.

Again that icy stare. 'Yes, I spoke to my wife by telephone during the night – '

'And?' She was playing with him now. He would liked to have wiped that smile off her cute face.

'I'm not going to divulge our conversation.'

After that the questions came thick and fast from the other reporters. 'How did you and Angie meet?'

'At a golf tournament recently. By accident – I spilled my drink over her dress and in return I offered her a golf lesson as compensation.'

'Are you and Miss Wide planning on getting married?'

'Give us a break. We only met a short time ago.' The reporters laughed and the tension eased. Wayne looked more relaxed.

'What do you do for a living, Miss Wilde?' Before Angie could reply another reporter fired a follow-up question. 'Where are you from, Angie?'

She gave the assembled members of the media one of her brightest smiles as cameras clicked. 'I'm from New York and I'm an actress.'

'An actress? How come we never heard of you. Have you done any movies?'

'I've been in a couple of small budget films,' Angie replied. 'Nothing that would win an Oscar,' she laughed. She hoped they would not probe too deeply into her movie career. Maybe she could steer them off the subject…'I've done a lot of stage work in New York.'

'How about Broadway? Have you appeared on Broadway'

'Er, well, not exactly on Broadway itself…'

'You mean in a play off Broadway then? Or maybe you mean off-off-Broadway, huh?' There were a few sniggers from the media.

Her agent, Mervyn, had warned her that there would be awkward questions. He had instructed her how to handle them but she was finding it tough. Still, looking around at the tv news crews and the newspaper photographers clicking away, Angie consoled herself that with Wayne's high Ryder Cup profile she would feature on every major newscast and grab a lot of newsprint. Not a bad price to pay for worldwide publicity!

Mervyn's plan was working like a dream, just like he had said it would. Angie dragged her mind back to the present.

'Exactly how far off Broadway have you played, Miss Wilde?'...'

A mental picture of some of the crummy little theatres she had played in New York flashed across Angie's mind. She smiled sweetly. 'Let's just say they weren't four-star productions. But I'm a determined girl. I'll make it someday – with the help of you guys, of course.' Angie gave them another of her dazzling smiles.

They had to admit that she was some looker. Wayne Folen sure knew how to pick them. Angie was relieved when the questions switched back to him.

'What about the Ryder Cup, Wayne. You still expect to lead the team next month against Europe?'

'You gimme a good reason why I shouldn't.'

'Well, with your domestic problems just now – '

America's Ryder Cup captain silenced his inquisitor with a glare. 'Are you insinuating I can't handle my own life?' The threat behind the question hung in the air.

The reporter held his ground. 'The word is that you might be asked to resign the captaincy by the P.G.A. – '

'If the committee want my resignation they know where to come for it. Right now I'm still captain. My private life is my own business and anyone who tries to stir up something up between me and my wife and Marcia will have me to reckon with. Do I make myself clear?' His glare swept the gathering.

The reporters took the hint. The next question went

off at a tangent. 'When will you be announcing your two wild card choices to the team, Wayne?

Wayne was tiring of the impromptu press conference. 'I'll finalise the team when I'm good and ready. The two guys I pick as wild cards will hear it from me and not read it first in the newspapers. O.k?' He took Angie's arm. 'Come on, honey, I think we've answered enough questions – '

One newsman wasn't quite finished, however. 'How about you, Miss Wilde – will you be accompanying Wayne to Killarney with the American squad? You know that the partner of the Ryder Cup captain has an important role in looking after the wives and girlfriends of the other members?'

Angie was pleased that the spotlight was focussed on her again. 'I'd love to go to the Ryder Cup with Wayne to help out. I feel I would have something to contribute – '

'Really? In what way?'

Before she could reply Wayne grabbed her arm and steered her through the crowd. 'Like I said, honey, we've answered enough questions. Let's get out of here' He was anxious to catch an early flight back to San Diego before Marcia saw the interview on a late night newscast.

CHAPTER TWO

Ben Gartland shifted uneasily on his hard seat on the platform of the Loughduff Community Hall. Below him the sea of faces were looking up and listening with mild interest as Dan Collins, president of the United Farmers' Organisation, finished his speech.

Ben's glance took in the two rival television cameras that had been set up in the centre aisle. He reckoned that so far the tv crews had little to get excited about.

Dan Collins is useless, a wimp, Ben thought. He had no right to be the leader of the country's biggest farmers' body. Collins's speech to the assembly had been of the milk-

and-water variety and had hardly raised a murmur from the overflow meeting. Ben reckoned he would have no problem in outshining the opposition and whipping up some support. He couldn't wait to get hold of the microphone and let loose some of the anger and frustration that had been building up inside himself since the meeting had begun almost two hours ago.

'So while our sympathies are with our colleague Travis Gartland as he faces his time in jail, and of course also with his wife Katie – 'Dan Collins turned from the microphone and gave a sympathetic nod towards the woman who was seated at the long table beside Ben – 'we must refrain from any drastic action that would bring our organisation into disrepute – ' the murmurings from the floor was a warning that not everybody in the audience agreed with him.

Sensing this, Dan decided to show some steel. 'But let the word go out that we, the farmers of Ireland, will not stand idly by indefinitely while the land which is rightly ours is being sold off to foreigners for their exclusive pleasure. I advise we await further developments.' He paused, waited for the mild applause to die down. 'And now I hand you over to Travis Gartland's brother Ben....'

The lukewarm applause that had greeted the president's final words grew in volume as Ben strode to the microphone. The crowd sensed that they were in for something special.

Ben Gartland didn't disappoint them. 'Ladies and gentlemen I'm going to keep this short and to the point – ' His gaze swept the hall and his voice was so loud as he shouted into the microphone it made that instrument redundant. 'We've been listening to some very wishy-washy guff from our president here this evening. My brother has been dragged off his farm and is in jail. His wife and young children have been left to fend for themselves. I want some action!'

The roar that greeted his words from the body of the hall fuelled Ben's fire. He grabbed the microphone. 'I want action – and I want it now!' he roared. 'Let's not sit on our backsides like our president wants us do. Let's show the people of Ireland, and the government itself, that we mean business!'

Another roar from the crowd. A burly man seated in the centre of the hall jumped to his feet. 'We're with you, Ben. Farmers have been pushed aside and ignored for far too long while foreigners have come in and bought land that is rightfully ours. You called for action...What do you have in mind?'

Ben waited while everyone quietened down. 'I'll tell you what I have in mind,' he roared back. 'I want our members to take part in a protest that will show our government, the European Union – and the whole world

– that we aim to fight for what is rightly ours by taking the law into our own hands – '

More applause. As it died down the burly man jumped to his feet again. 'Okay Ben. So what do you want us to do?'

Silence fell as they awaited Ben's next words. 'We're going to target the Ryder Cup, the big golf tournament between the superstars of Europe and America that's being held in Killarney next month. It's an event that gets worldwide media coverage – and we'll use it to highlight our cause.'

There was a moment of stunned silence, then loud applause broke out. Groups of men jumped to their feet, some waving their fists in the air. Ben Gartland's plan seemed to have massive approval. Katie glanced sideways at Dan Collins. He looked worried. Slowly the hubbub in the hall died down.

Ben raised his hand for silence. He knew that eye in the hall was on him. 'I'm not going to outline the plan of action I have in mind,' he announced. 'This meeting is being covered by the media and I don't want to tip off the authorities. But I guarantee you this…' he paused, raised his voice for added effect. 'If my brother Travis is not released from Mountjoy Jail in Dublin within the next few days I'll be calling on each and every one of you for support for the immediate plan of action I have in mind. Do I have that support?'

A roar of approval showed he had. Ben turned, looked at Katie and Dan Collins, his face flushed with success. Katie averted her eyes. She sensed that Ben was getting carried away in his role. He had the crowd worked up now and she felt sick at the prospect of having to stand at the microphone and make a speech.

Dan Collins leaned across to her, whispered above the din. 'Ben is dangerous, talking about taking the law into his own hands. He's working up the hotheads in the crowd, hinting at violence. Look at him, he's enjoying it all…'

'Why don't you get up there and stop him,' Katie said.

'I think you're the one who can do that. You've got to calm things, Katie. Are you ready?' Dan Collins rose, approached Ben from behind and grabbed the microphone.

'I'll take that,' he said. Before a startled Ben could recover, the leader of the farmers' organisation turned to the crowd and announced: 'I want to make it clear that as your president I do not agree with what Ben Gartland has been saying. We must settle this dispute through peaceful means, otherwise - '

He didn't get to finish. A growl of disapproval rose from certain sections of the assembly. When other factions demanded that their president be heard the meeting was in danger of breaking up in disorder. Dan Collins reckoned it was time to introduce Katie. He shouted for order and after the din had died sufficiently he said:

'Right – if you won't listen to me perhaps you'll pay attention to what Katie Gartland has to say. Give her a big welcome….'

Katie felt a knot in her stomach as she walked across to the front of the stage. It was hot and humid in the crowded hall and her mouth felt dry. Male eyes took in the shapely figure of Travis Gartland's wife which the cheap summer dress and the rather dowdy pink cardigan failed to hide. Her dark shoulder-length hair framed a striking finely sculpted face with its wide mouth, high cheekbones and dark eyes.

Dan Collins handed her a glass of water and gave her an encouraging smile. She swallowed some of the liquid before she began to speak.

Katie started off hesitantly, glad that her audience was attentive. She grew in confidence when she realised that everyone in the hall was listening intently to what she was saying. There was sympathetic applause when she described the early morning arrest of her husband by the local Gardai, witnessed by herself and her two sons. Then she called for support for the stance advocated by Dan Collins. Behind her Katie sensed Ben's anger as she made a plea for non-violence and called on the members to support their president by not engaging in a protest coming up to or during the Ryder Cup. She returned to her seat on the platform and sat down to generous applause.

But Ben Gartland wasn't finished yet. He strode purposefully to the dais, his face a mask of anger as he picked up the microphone. 'I want to say that I think Dan Collins and my sister-in-law are talking absolute rubbish,' he bellowed. 'We want action, not words – and I want you all to give me your backing.'

Ben's outburst had the desired effect. Groups of men jumped to their feet, overturning chairs, shouting and demonstrating their allegiance. Amid the chaos Katie noticed a man leave his aisle seat in midway down the hall and make his way to the stage. She recognised him immediately as the Englishman who had moved into the area some months ago, an artist she believed. He had bought a derelict cottage on a patch of land overlooking the sea. She had seen him a few times in Loughduff, always alone, a stranger with a trim beard whose bohemian style of dress made him a stand-out among the local community.

Her near-neighbour Nell Flavin, her only real friend in Loughduff, who read romantic novels to combat the drudgery of farm work, had told her the Englishman's name but Katie had forgotten it.

She kept her eyes on him as he approached, climbed the short flight of steps at the side of the stage and approached the dais. Unnoticed amid the din, he picked up the microphone and in a firm voice called for attention. Slowly knots of people began to stop arguing and look towards the stage. Ben Gartland glared at the intruder but did not interfere.

The Englishman waited for the hubbub to die, then

began to speak. 'Ladies and gentlemen, most of you don't know me. My name is Jeremy Walker. I'm English, I'm an artist, and I recently moved into your community – ' A smile broke across his lean features. 'As a foreigner who has just moved in and bought up some Irish land I'm possibly being a bit presumptuous in voicing my opinion in this dispute, but for what it's worth I believe you, the farmers of the area should pay attention to what your president Dan Collins and Katie Gartland has just said. I reckon both of them are talking sense – '

The noise in the hall started up again. While some of the audience was applauding, it was obvious that Jeremy Walker's words had angered the hardliners.

Ben Gartland was one of those. He strode angrily across the stage, grabbed the microphone from Jeremy Walker and shouldered him aside.

'Do we, the farmers of Loughduff, need a foreigner to tell us what to do?', he bellowed. 'Of course we don't. Tonight one of our members – my brother Travis – is in jail. We see good farm land being sold off from under our feet to foreigners to build build luxury golf courses and big hotels which, I assure you, none of us will ever see the inside of……' Ben paused for the were roars of approval.

'Are we going to stand by and do nothing? Of course we're not! – '

He was interrupted momentarily by a huge roar. Ben's voice carried above the noise. 'We'll take whatever course of action we feel is necessary. And those who disagree with us – ' he glared at Jeremy Walker who was standing at the side of the stage – 'had better keep their noses out of our business. Or else…' This was greeted by thunderous applause.

Ben slammed the microphone down on the dais and stormed off the stage. He was immediately surrounded by a large group of supporters and several tv reporters and cameramen. Dan Collins endeavoured to get the crowd's attention once again, but the meeting was now out of control and he wisely brought it to a close. It had not been a good night for reason.

Katie looked down over the crowd and spotted Jack and Garret at the back of the hall where they had been listening to the proceedings. She was making her way towards them when she felt a tap on the shoulder. She turned to see Jeremy Walker smiling at her.

'Hello.'

'Hello.' She stared at him, surprised by his presence.

'I hope you weren't annoyed when I spoke up on your behalf,' he smiled. 'But if you don't mind my saying so, you did look in need of support.'

'Thank you. Making that speech was an ordeal. I'm not used to that sort of thing.'

'Neither am I. I don't know what came over me. I – I just felt I had to say something.' Katie felt uncomfortable. The hall was now emptying out and she noticed a few wives staring at them as they passed with their husbands.

'I suspect you have made an enemy of Ben, my brother-in-law. He won't have liked what you did.' Katie blushed as she spoke. She wasn't accustomed to speaking to strange men.

'I suppose you know I bought a cottage a few miles from your farm. I'm a painter, an artist.'

'Yes. I know. My friend Nell Flavin has told me about you. Her husband's place overlooks your cottage…' For the past few weeks Nell had been going on about the handsome Englishman who had moved into the area whenever she dropped in for their weekly mid-morning coffee and chat. Katie had to admit her friend hadn't exaggerated when, in her usual effusive manner, Nell had described the newcomer as 'very attractive.'

'I saw the cottage advertised in my local newspaper in England and came over and bought it. Beautiful country around here, ideal for painting….' He paused. 'I was outside your house yesterday morning when your husband was taken away. It was a bad business. I'm sure you and the boys will miss him…'

'Yes,' Katie lied. She was feeling uncomfortable under Jeremy Walker's gaze. 'I'm sorry but if you don't mind, I have to go. The boys are waiting…'

'Of course.' As she turned away he said: 'Would you like to go for a drink in the Loughduff Inn? I'm sure the boys wouldn't mind waiting – '

'No!' The vehemence of her refusal surprised him. She saw the look of hurt in his eyes. 'I'm sorry. It – it has nothing to do with you. It's just that I never go to the Loughduff Inn. Too many prying eyes for one thing.' She couldn't tell the real reason why the mention of the town's most popular hostelry sent a shiver down her spine.

'Can I at least offer you a lift home then?'

'I'm sorry. I came with Ben – '

She saw him glance across the hall to where Ben Gartland was being interviewed on camera. A group of friends were waiting for him to finish. 'I doubt if your brother-in-law is going to be free for some time. Besides if you listen, I think the weather has turned nasty – '

Katie could hear the rain beating down on the roof of the community hall. No doubt Ben would adjourn with his cronies for a long drinking session to the nearest hotel or pub, not worrying how herself and the boys would make their own way home.

'In that case. Yes, I would appreciate a drive home.'

'Good.' He seemed genuinely pleased that she had accepted his offer. He put his hand on her arm and guided her towards the exit. Jack and Garret joined them, staring at Jeremy Walker shyly. She introduced them and the shook his hand before falling in behind, whispering to each other.

Outside the late August evening had turned nasty and the rain was pelting down. Katie and the boys waited in the doorway while Jeremy fetched his car from the parking area in the town square. Garret and Jack piled into the back seat while Katie sat in the front, acutely conscious of the Englishman sitting beside her.

She had never met an artist before, which wasn't surprising since her social life revolved mainly around the monthly meetings of the local Irish Countrywomen's Association group in Loughduff, an activity which her husband made plain he considered a waste of time. She went with Nell Flavin to the meetings, lingering with her in the car afterwards, praying silently that Travis would be in bed asleep when she returned home.

Katie waited for Jeremy Walker to start up a conversation. She knew she could not remain silent for the entire journey home, short as it was. She was relieved when he broke the silence.

'How are you going to manage the farm now that your husband is in jail?'

'Travis left Ben in charge. He'll probably hire a man in while Travis is away. The boys and myself will also do our share of the work.'

'I'd like to help out if I could.' She stole a glance sideways at him as the lights of the town disappeared behind them. 'I'm from Norfolk and came from a farming background before I took up painting.' His bearded face broke into a smile. 'I'm pretty handy at milking cows, that sort of thing. And I can handle a tractor - '

He was serious, Katie could see that. Her heartbeat quickened at the prospect of having someone like him around the farm, unlikely though it was after his outburst against Ben. The last time someone had shown an interest in her was the night Benjy Duff had sidled up behind her in his bar, that perpetual leer on his face, and informed her that Travis Gartland was asking after her. She was aged seventeen at the time, a teenager pursued by an older man, desperately seeking a way out of the hell into which she had landed from the convent orphanage. Twenty years on she was little better off, looking at life from the inside of a loveless marriage. Jeremy Walker's offer excited her, but instinct warned her she would have to be wary.

'Well?' Jeremy was awaiting an answer.

'Thanks for the offer, but no doubt Ben has one of his cronies lined up.'

'The offer is still there. If you are short-handed you know where to find me. And do feel free to drop into my place anytime you want. I'd like to show you some of my paintings - as long as you're not shocked by some of my female nudes –' He laughed.

Katie brushed a strand of dark hair back into place, scolding herself for not having paid more attention to her appearance before she had left the farmhouse. But then she hadn't known she would be driven home by Jeremy Walker!

'Yes, I'd like that.' Maybe she should tell him about her talent for painting when she was in the convent. She decided against it; it was unlikely that someone like Jeremy Walker would be interested in what she had done years ago.

'Do drop in anytime you feel like a chat,' Jeremy said. 'I haven't made too many friends in the area as yet …'

They completed the rest of the journey to the farmhouse mostly in silence. Katie was mortified that she found it so difficult to sustain a conversation. She wondered what this handsome Englishman thought of her, if he was as uncomfortable in her company as she was in his. Jeremy drove slowly up the winding driveway, switched off the ignition. She speculated that maybe he was waiting for an invite to go inside. Jack and Garret had said a hurried 'good night' to Jeremy and were waiting at the door for her.

'Thanks for the lift Mr. Walker. It was very kind of you – ' She turned, saw the outline of his face in the gloom.

'My pleasure. But shouldn't we be on first name terms? After all we're practically neighbours – '

'I'd ask you in for something except it's getting late.' Ben lived with a girlfriend in town but she was afraid he might call out when he finished drinking in the Loughduff Inn. If he had not seen her leaving the hall with Jeremy Walker someone would be sure to tell him.

'Not to worry, Katie. Now that we've got to know each other there will be other opportunities. Maybe you'll show me around the farm sometime,' he replied cheerfully.

'I'd love to – ' she heard herself saying. The words were out before she could stop them. 'Only problem is,' she added hastily, 'I'm not sure I'll be at home. I'll have to go to Dublin soon to visit Travis – '

His eyes lit up. 'Hey, I'm going to Dublin myself soon. I have an exhibition opening up there shortly and there are some things I have to arrange…Perhaps we could drive up together?'

Katie's heart pounded. The prospect of spending practically a whole day in Dublin with Jeremy Walker sounded exciting. Deliciously dangerous no doubt, but exciting all the same. If the word got out the local gossips would have a field day. Imagine what Nell would say when she dropped in for coffee later in the week!

'You're very kind – ' Oh God, she was repeating herself!

'Phone me whenever you're ready to go. Here, I'll give you my number – ' He reached into an inside pocket of his suede driving jacket, took out a card. Katie took it and slipped it into her shoulder bag. 'Now I must go in to the boys – ' She fumbled for the door handle in the dark.

'Allow me…' He reached across her, his leg brushing hers, his dark hair close to her face. She caught a whiff of aftershave. She couldn't recall Travis ever used a lotion like that.

The car door on her side opened and she slid out into the semi-darkness. 'Good night, Jeremy,' she said. He had just time to return the greeting before the door closed and she began to walk towards the house. She could feel his eyes on her as she walked up the steps. In the porch she turned, waved, and watched the lights disappear out onto the road. She wondered if Jeremy Walker was married. He hadn't mentioned a wife, or a partner for that matter. He hinted he had come to this scenic part of Ireland to paint. Was that the only reason? Maybe he was running away from something – or somebody.

As Katie lay in bed later she found her thoughts more on the handsome Englishman than on her jailed husband. It was some time before sleep overtook her.

● ● ● ●

Angie Wilde pressed the seat release, closed her eyes and relaxed back into a reclining position. After the day's happenings she reckoned she would enjoy the American Airways Flight 101 back to New York.

Right now things were looking up. Half an hour ago she had kissed Wayne Folen goodbye at Chicago's O'Hare Airport, leaving him to fly east to San Diego and a confrontation with his wife Marcia while she journeyed back to Brooklyn, congratulating herself on the fact that she was no longer an unknown actress. Her 'accidental' meeting with the gung-ho captain of the U.SA. Ryder Cup team had seen to that. Angie smiled to herself. It had all been so easy....

Trust Mervyn Lazlo to come up with a crazy idea like that. But then that was his job, figuring out ruses to get the names of his struggling would-be showbiz stars into the news. She had arrived back in his office from yet another fruitless audition for a small-time production so far off-Broadway that it was nearly in the next borough. Disillusioned, dispirited, Angie had needed a shoulder to cry on and that's what agents were for. She had entered

Merv's office, plopped down in the chair opposite, kicked off her stilettos and glared at him across his desk.

'No luck honey, huh?' He didn't have to ask. The look on her face said it all.

'Right first time. The place was crawling with wannabes like myself. I got two minutes up on stage and that was it. 'Thank you, honey…we'll be in touch.' Like hell they will. Bastards!'

'Not to worry. How about some lunch?'

'I don't want a lunch, Mervyn. I want a job. Any kind of job, a walk-on even. I'm desperate.'

'Sure, honey, sure. I understand. But don't worry, something will turn up – '

She hated being told not to worry and that something would turn up. It rarely did. 'Don't give me that, Mervyn. I'm sick listening to you saying that. When will something turn up…come on, you tell me….'

Mervyn leaned back in his black swivel chair. It was the most expensive item of furniture in his office, bought because every agent seemed to have one. It made him feel big-time.

'Who knows? Maybe tomorrow I'll send you along to an audition for a walk-on part, a one-line role. So what happens? The director likes you, the guy backing the show fancies getting you into bed, you're offered a lead role and suddenly you're big-time with your name up in lights on Broadway.' Mervyn beamed at her. 'How about that for a scenario?'

'Bullshit! You're talking crap, Mervyn, and you know it. I've worked my ass off, slept with fat, balding guys. I've even gone nude in a couple of blue movies that I want to forget. And I'm still nowhere – ' Angie paused, looked angry. 'Maybe I need a new agent, huh?'

Mervyn stopped swivelling. Jeez, the broad is really disillusioned. She needs a lift, a verbal massage. He didn't have all that many clients that he could afford to lose one. Leaning forward across the desk he said: 'Don't talk that way, honey. Look on the bright side. You've got me, one of the best agents in the business, working for you. You're an actress with a great talent. A nice light touch. Like Meg Ryan, or Goldie Hawn maybe. Know what I'm getting at?'

Angie had glared at him. 'Are you trying to tell me something, Mervyn? Like get out of the business or something?. Goldie Hawn…Jeez! That the best you can do? Goldie Hawn is ancient, for Chrissake. Me – I'm twenty-four – ' She was actually twenty-seven, but her cv didn't show that. 'Besides, you've tried that Goldie Hawn stunt on me before.'

'I mean you're a young Goldie Hawn, Angie.' Mervyn explained patiently. Telling an actress how young she was always worked, made them feel good. 'You're on your way, Angie, believe me – '

'Okay Mervyn, so you've convinced me yet again that I'm Tony Award material, with a sure-fire Oscar waiting when I break into Hollywood. So how do you plan on getting me a walk-on part? Come on, you tell me.'

Mervyn looked at her, contemplated for a while. Finally he said, 'What we need, Angie, is for me to come up with an idea, something that will get you noticed, get your name into the headlines…'

Angie rolled her eyes skywards. 'Brilliant. How about my jumping off Brooklyn Bridge? You think that might do the trick?'

Mervyn laughed, rubbed a stubbly chin. 'You're a howl, Angie, always good for a laugh. But maybe, just maybe, I got a better idea..'

'Yeah? This had better be good. .'

Angie waited while he opened a drawer in his desk, rummaged inside. She was tired, hot and bored. Still, she had to stick with Mervyn. He was her only chance. She had been bluffing when she had talked about finding a new agent. Would it make any difference to her career? Who the hell would take her on?

She watched as Mervyn took out a half-smoked cigar, studied it, struggled to light it without singeing his eyebrows. Angie groaned inwardly. She was signed-up with a guy who couldn't even afford a decent cigar. That just about summed up Mervyn Lazlo; no wonder she was a struggling actress! She managed to contain her anger as he leaned back and blew a column of smoke towards the ceiling. Jeez! The guy thinks he's Spielberg!

'Know anything about big-time time golf, Angie?,' Mervyn asked.

She groaned again, outwardly this time. So this was his big idea! Big deal! 'The only thing I know about golf is that it's played by a lot of people. Didn't Kevin Costner and Renee Russo made a film called 'Tin Cup'. That was about golf, wasn't it?' She had seen the movie, had found it mildly entertaining.

'How about the Ryder Cup?' Mervyn asked. 'Know what that is?'

'Haven't a clue.' Angie was losing patience. 'Mervyn, will you stop playing quiz games and get to the point! What I know about golf could be written on the head of a pin and stuck right up your ass!'

Nevertheless, she listened patiently as he explained what the Ryder Cup was and how American golfers would soon be battling with Europe in a highly publicised encounter in Ireland shortly to regain it. 'The whole thing is televised worldwide and everyone connected with it – wives and girlfriends of the golfers included – get a helluva lot of publicity….' Mervyn tapped the ash off his cigar. 'Especially the captain's lady…'

'Yeah? So what?'

'See this guy – ' Mervyn had pushed a newspaper across the desk, sports page upwards. Angie saw a picture of a square-jawed man, tight-cropped hair, 50-ish she reckoned and handsome in a rugged sort of way. 'That's Wayne Folen. He's the captain of our team. A tough, no-nonsense guy by all accounts.' Mervyn had paused. 'You're going to meet him, Angie. You and him are going to get acquainted, get up close and personal. Know what I mean?'

'I think I get the message. You want me to sleep with the guy.'

Mervyn winced. Did she have to be so up-front? 'That's the deal. It doesn't have to be forever if you don't want it. Just so we get lots of publicity in the newspapers and on television…'

'Doesn't he have a wife?'

'Yeah. But I'm sure you won't let that trouble you. It hasn't before – '

'Don't be a smart-ass, Mervyn. I'm having a bad day. What's her name?'

'Marcia. They've been married a long time. Too long maybe. I read she's had a hip replacement operation recently so you can bet Wayne's sex life is not exactly hectic.' He blew another stream of cigar smoke towards the ceiling. 'Like I just said, Angie baby, in showbiz notoriety is the name of the game. You gotta do something to get noticed, get people talking about you –

Mervyn leaned on the desk, waved the remains of his cigar about. 'Madonna and Britney Spiers share a kiss and they make headlines all over the world; Jennifer Lopez keeps announcing she's getting married and doesn't; Britney gets married in Las Vegas and has it annulled next day. And how about Janet Jackson – she unveils her breast while singing at the Superbowl, she gets so much publicity around the world that suddenly her career is back on track….'

'So what's it all about? – ' Mervyn was enjoying himself. 'I'll tell you what it's all about honey. Publicity, that's what…Their publicist thinks up a stunt, gets them to do something outrageious and bingo! - their pictures are all over the place. It works a dream. You want proof? That dame Monica Lewinsky was a nobody until she caught Bill Clinton's eye and they both started fooling around with a cigar. She made history – and she doesn't even have your looks.' Mervyn broke off philosophising, leaned back in his chair. 'Time for you to grab some of that action, baby.'

Angie stared at the newspaper picture again. Wayne Folen looked interesting. At least he appeared in better shape than some of the fat, out-of-condition director creeps she had rolled in the hay with. A roll in the hay with him wouldn't be the worst thing in the world. And if it got her into the movies.... 'Okay Mervyn, I'm convinced. You'd like me to get this guy Wayne Folen into bed. That what you got in mind?'

Her agent winced again. That's what Mervyn had in mind but he wished Angie had put it a little more delicately. 'Something like that. Do something to make him want you around.'

'How do I meet Wayne Folen?'

'Leave it to me. Let me make a few phone calls, find out what his golf schedule is over the next couple of weeks. Wayne is playing on the Senior Tour right now – '.

'The what?' This was all foreign to her.

'I'll explain later. Right now, Angie, I want you to read up on golf over the next few days so you know a little about the game. I know a guy on the sports desk of the New York Post. I'll get him to send me over some clippings on the Ryder Cup so you'll know something about it before you accidentally bump into Wayne Folen. After that it's up to you.'

Mervyn eased himself out of his chair, came around her side of the desk. He leaned over her shoulder and ran his finger along her thigh. 'Now that I've put your career back on track, how about that lunch I promised you. We could go back to my place afterwards and talk some more. My secretary will take care of things here...'

Angie had given him one of her cute smiles. 'I'll take you up on the lunch offer, Mervyn, but – ' she had then removed his hand which was becoming disconcerting – 'if you don't mind, darling, I'll skip the afters!'

'Accidentally' bumping into Wayne Folen presented no great problem for Angie Wilde. She reckoned a middle-aged guy who spent a considerable time away from his wife would be a sucker for her charms.

Merv had done his homework as promised. He checked that the Ryder Cup captain's next tournament on the American Seniors Tour was the million dollar Rolling Hills Classic, played over a three day weekend at the Greenbrier Golf and Country Club in West Virginia. He booked Angie a plane ticket and hotel accommodation adjacent to the course.

On Friday, the first day of the tournament, suitably attired in an all-white outfit of sneakers, short white socks, neatly tailored shorts, shirt-blouse and Raybans, Angie took a taxi to the course and joined the multitude of spectators scrambling over the hillocks and hollows of the exclusive country club. It was a very hot weekend in mid-Summer and the surrounds of the clubhouse was ablaze with a cornucopia of flowering borders. Angie paraded around, conscious of the many admiring glances she was attracting from the large number of male spectators, the majority of them middle-aged, attending the event.

She caught her first sight of Wayne Folen that morning on the putting green behind the clubhouse where he was practicing before his mid-day tee-off. She was pleasantly surprised at what she saw; sure he was twice her age, but physically he looked in a lot better shape than many of his contemporaries on the Senior Tour. Not bad, not bad at all, Angie reasoned.

When he teed-off an hour later she joined the large crowd that followed his threesome. But watching grown men belting a little white ball around a golf course wasn't exactly her idea of fun and she quit after a couple of hours to return to her hotel. She had a short nap, showered, and changed into a simple white cotton dress with a scooped neckline and set-in waistband that ensured a figure-hugging fit.

It was late evening by the time she finished her preparations. Again she took a taxi to the Green Golf and Country Club where play had finished and the bars were doing good business. Time to put the next part of Merv's plan into action....

Wayne was turning away from the bar, about to rejoin a couple of his buddies at their table, when he brushed against the young lady. She had been standing directly behind him trying to catch the bartender's eye and now most of his drink was making a not very pretty pattern on the white cotton dress she was wearing.

'Oh, sorry lady. I – I'm afraid I didn't see you – '

'That's alright. Please don't apologise. It was my fault. I guess I was standing too close – '

Wayne smiled, his eyes flitting momentarily to her bosom. 'If you were standing that close how come I didn't notice!'

Smart ass! Angie allowed herself a smile. She wasn't crazy about his sense of humour and thought maybe she should slap his face. She decided against it.

'Let me buy you a drink. You're wearing most of what was in my glass – '

'It's okay. Thanks all the same – ' Angie gave him a dazzling smile, turned away. She knew she was taking a chance. If he doesn't call out after her she was in trouble. Merv would be angry with her for messing it up.

'Hey, hold on! Come on young lady, let me buy you another drink. I really want to – '

To her relief she felt his hand on her arm. She turned back, paused a moment. 'Well, okay, if you insist. It's very nice of you....' It wasn't often she was called a lady twice in one day!

'Good. What'll it be?' His eyes were appraising her again.

'A vodka martini. On the rocks.'

While he gave the order Angie took a handkerchief out of the tiny shoulder handbag and dabbed at her dress where the liquid stain was showing. 'I hope the stain comes out when you get it cleaned,' she heard him say. 'I'll give you my address. Send me the bill.'

'That won't be necessary,' she said. Confident now, she decided to push her luck.

'Thanks for the drink.', she raised it, smiled. 'It was nice meeting you – ' She turned away again, held her breath.

'Hey, hold on – ' Again Wayne put a restraining hand on her arm. Jeez, she was a stunner. And she seemed to be alone. He couldn't see a handsome hunk hovering in the background.

'Yes?' She gave him the full treatment with her eyes.

'Look, you can tell me to get lost if you wish, but…' He hesitated. 'Are you alone?' Wayne paused, feeling uncomfortable. He had never done anything like this before. It was new territory for him. Marcia had accompanied him on tour until her hip had started acting up. The blonde with the stunning figure was smiling at him. 'Why don't you and I sit down, talk for a while….'

Hell, was he out of his mind! This girl was only about the same age as Shiralee, his daughter. Besides, he was the U.S. Ryder Cup captain. If he was photographed chatting up a young blonde there would be hell to pay. But he wanted to take that risk.

Angie played it cool. She hesitated, sipped her drink before replying. 'I'd love to sit down. I've had a pretty busy day…'

Wayne lead the way to an empty table, conscious that the eyes of every one of his Senior Tour buddies in the bar were on him. He was glad when they were seated at a secluded table. 'What's your name?', he asked. When she told he said. 'What do you do for a living? Are you a model or something?'

'An actress actually, but I do some modelling on the side,' Angie replied. She had her story well prepared. 'I'm here to shoot a tv advert. For golf equipment. It helps pay the bills while I wait for my big break.' She gave him one of her special smiles. 'You're Wayne Folen, aren't you?'

He looked pleased. 'That's right. How did you know?'

'Easy. You're famous right now. I've seen your picture in the newspapers and on television.' Flatter the guy, Merv had said, as if she didn't know already. She was used to doing just that with casting directors. A long time ago she had learned that the best way to a man's heart was through his ego.

Sitting opposite her, toying with his glass of Bud, she had to admit he looked pretty cute in his expensive, open-necked light blue shirt and dark tailored slacks. Wayne Folen may be old enough to be her father, but with his rugged, tanned face, close cropped grey hair and a body that looked more muscle than fat, Angie figured he could be her sugar daddy any day – for as long as it suited her at least.

'Tell me more about this golf advert you're shooting,' Wayne said.

'It's to do with selling a range of ladies' fashionable golf outfits,' Angie replied. Time to play her ace. 'Problem is I'm no golfer. I was hoping to meet someone who might show me how to swing and hold a golf club – '

Wayne Folen took the bait so quickly that Angie reckoned maybe she was Oscar material after all. If only Mervyn was here to see her performance. 'Honey, say no more. I'll give you all the golf tips you need – and for free.' He was beginning to think this was his lucky night.

'Oh, I couldn't expect someone famous like you to take time out – ' She broke off. 'I mean you've so much on your plate right now, with the Ryder Cup and all that – '

He waved his hand 'Not to worry. You leave everything to me. I'll make time for you, Angie. It's the least I can do after spilling that drink over you.'

Wayne ignored the warning bells that were ringing in the back of his mind. So what if he was married. Here was a girl, smart, outgoing and attractive, practically begging him to do her a favour. Sure, at his age and in his position being pictured showing a shapely young blonde how to swing a golf club was asking for trouble. But what the hell, it would probably be only a once-off golf lesson anyway; Marcia had nothing to worry about. After giving her the few tips he would probably never see Angie Wilde again.

'I'm not due to tee-off in the tournament tomorrow until early afternoon. How about if you and me were to meet before that. Say 10am – '

'I'm really grateful – '

'But not on the practice ground, that'll be too crowded.' By that he meant too many nosy photographers.

'I'll do anything you say.' Angie reckoned this rated her wide-eyes Marilyn Monroe look. 'I can't believe it, me getting golf tips from our Ryder Cup captain. How can I ever repay you, Mr. Folen?'

Wayne could figure one way straight off, but he let it pass. Instead he said, 'You can call me Wayne for a start – and let me buy you another drink.' This would be his third drink tonight. He never took more than two during a tournament. But tonight was something special.

They stayed chatting for the rest of the evening, enjoyed a couple more drinks each. Wayne told her how he had worked as a caddie at his local club in Iowa as a youngster before joining the Marines and serving three years in Vietnam. After he came out of the service he had decided on a pro golf career, married his childhood sweetheart Marcia, and spent the first two years on the circuit with her travelling in a camper before he had hit the big-time.

Angie managed to suppress a yawn as he recounted how his tough training in the Marines had helped him mentally and physically during those early years. 'My big break came when I won the Masters at Augusta in 1985, then the U.S. Open a couple of years later. That's when I really began to make big money – ' Wayne broke off. 'Sorry, I'm probably boring you to death – '

'No way,' Angie lied. 'I know what's it's like to struggle for something you want so badly, dreaming of the big breakthrough…'

The bar was emptying out. Wayne wondered about the girl sitting opposite him. Angie says she's an actress but maybe she's a high class hooker? How come a good-looking girl like her was on her own? If she was in town to make a golf commercial how come nobody had approached her all evening?

'Don't you have a photographer with you? I mean if you're shooting a commercial…'

'Oh sure. I got a photographer who has a very good-looking assistant. They're off having a good time…'

'Oh.' Jeez, everybody's at it these days, Wayne thought to himself. Hell, what was he worried about? His tour buddies had already retired to bed. If they had been chatted up by a good-looking young blonde they wouldn't be too worried about her background. Wayne knew of several golfers on the Senior Tour who looked for some off-course action wherever they played. He had never done it so far, but one had to start sometime. He still found Marcia attractive but she had been out of action since her hip operation. On tour, it got lonely in a strange hotel bedroom sometimes….

As though reading his thoughts Angie said, 'It must get very lonely for you guys on tour.'

'Yeah. Sometimes.'

'Don't you have your wives travelling with you?'

Wayne shrugged. 'Some do. I used to, but not right now…'

'Oh. So…you're alone, Wayne?' Her eyes were lowered, her finger was circling the rim of her vodka martini. He watched her red-painted fingernail, found the movement very sensual. She looked up, her eyes meeting his.

'I'm going to bed.' Her voice was almost inaudible. 'How about you, Wayne?'

Angie pushed her glass aside, her eyes still locked into his. 'I'm in a hotel five minutes drive from here.' She gave him the name. 'Room 404, fourth floor,' she whispered. 'Give me fifteen minutes…,' She rose from the table.

Wayne looked after her, savouring the vision of a shapely pair of legs and an equally shapely posterior showing through the thin fabric of her dress as she wended her way through the tables. Several pairs of envious male eyes followed her progress.

He also rose, went outside, strolled around under the trees, savouring the cool of the night. Fifteen minutes later he was walking down the carpeted corridor of the fourth floor towards Room 404. He felt slightly guilty that he would miss his nightly telephone call to Marcia.

CHAPTER THREE

'**D**arling, come in here a moment. There's something on the telly that I think will interest you.'

Sally Cartray paused in the open french windows and called out to her husband who, having completed a practice putting session on the smooth mini green which he had had laid out in the corner of his extensive garden, was now throwing a stick for Sampson, their playful Scotch terrier, to retrieve.

'Pardon – what's that you said, darling?'

Sally sighed in exasperation, noting with annoyance a patch where Sampson had mangled some of her prize rhodedendrons. 'I said come quickly. There's something on the television news about Wayne Folen. I think he's in a spot of bother again.'

Bruce scampered across the well-cut lawn, careful to kick off his overshoes before entering the elegant drawing room. He was just in time to hear the final minutes of an impromptu Sky News interview between a group of reporters and America's Ryder Cup captain which seemed to have taken place at the completion of a Seniors' tournament in America. Probably over the weekend, Bruce reckoned.

The stunning looking blonde standing beside Wayne Foley caught his eye immediately. Probably Wayne's daughter, was Bruce's first thought. He was gob smacked when he picked up the trend of the interview and realised who the girl referred to as Angie Wilde really was.

'Good heavens, a mistress! Wayne has gone and picked up a lady friend – and a beauty at that,' Bruce mused aloud. 'What has happened to dear old Marcia, I wonder…'

'SShhh! Do be quite dear!' Sally was listening attentively, her expression changing to one of disbelief as the interview unfolded. Finally she exploded. 'An actress! The man must be out of his mind. He's surely not expecting me to liaise with a bimbo actress during the Ryder Cup!'

Sally and Bruce watched the rest of the interview in silence. They saw Wayne whisk Angie away from the eager reporters. The Sky News announcer came on screen again.

'That interview with American Ryder Cup captain Wayne Folen and actress Angie Wilde was recorded yesterday in Chicago. Since then members of the American Ryder Cup committee have again summoned Wayne Folen to a meeting. It is expected they will want assurance from their captain that his present marital problems will not interfere with his commitment to the run up to the Ryder Cup – '

The presenter paused momentarily, then continued. 'Meanwhile it is believed that the European Ryder Cup committee will be in touch today with their captain Bruce Cartray. The European and American Ryder Cup captains and their wives have already had a preliminary meeting about the protocol surrounding this year's event…' The presenter paused. 'At that meeting three weeks ago Wayne Folen was accompanied by his wife Marcia….'

Bruce and Sally exchanged glances. He hid a smile. This extraordinary move by the U.S. captain was not going to help the American players in the build-up to The Shoot-Out By The Lakes, as the media had dubbed the upcoming sporting clash in Killarney. Nothing like a high-profile marital bust-up to take one's mind off the business at hand, Bruce told himself gleefully. Advantage Europe!

'Poor old Wayne. The fellow just can't keep out of

trouble.' Bruce tried to sound sympathetic. 'Bit of a rough diamond, really. Always had my doubts about him as America's Ryder Cup captain. Looks like I'm about to be proved right.'

Sally nodded agreement. They made a good team, herself and Bruce. She made sure of that. Two years ago during Europe's victorious clash in America she had basked in the publicity of being the captain's wife, in charge of organising the off-course social and cultural activities for the wives and girlfriends of the team members. She had not put a foot wrong and and had garnered fulsome praise for the way herself and Bruce gelled in their respective roles. Two years on it had surprised nobody when Bruce was elected to again captain the Europeans.

Sally had enjoyed the hype first time around and had been a respected figure in their golf club and a popular speaker at captains' day dinners and on the Women's Institute circuit. She had been looking forward to jousting with Marcia Folen at the upcoming Ryder Cup, putting her skills as a hostess up against her American counterpart. And why not…Sally reckoned that Wayne Folen's wife, homely, down-to-earth Marcia, would not provide too much opposition to her in the publicity stakes. When it came to dress sense and organising a range of social events to exercise the minds of the Ryder Cup wives in her charge, Sally had reckoned she was way out in front of her American rival.

Now however, with the arrival of Angie Wilde on the scene, the whole scenario had changed as far as Sally was concerned. Vying for publicity with that scene-stealing actress Wayne Folen was now escorting was something Sally had not bargained for. Compared to Marcia this budding actress, with her hour-glass figure – no doubt due to a couple of silicone implants, Sally reckoned - and an eye for publicity and would pose much more of a threat than arthritic Marcia. Still, Sally Cartray told herself, she liked a challenge. She aimed to do her duty and help her husband bring the Ryder Cup back to Europe and no bimbo actress was going to get in her way.

This latest development was the second happening to annoy Sally. Earlier that morning Bruce had received a fax from the European Ryder Cup headquarters stating that due, to the threat from a group of Irish farmers who were planning to stage a protest during the event, the players, wives and officials of both teams would now be accommodated, not in a luxurious hotel just outside Killarney as planned, but in an equally luxurious hotel complex called the Parknasilla Palace, thirty miles from Ireland's most famous beauty spot.

'What a nuisance!', Sally had snapped when Bruce had read out the fax message. 'Never heard of this place Parknasilla. I do hope it's suitable.'

'We'll find out soon enough. We're going over there later this week to inspect the place for ourselves – the captains, their wives and some officials.' Bruce had informed her.

'I presume Wayne Folen will be bringing his new girlfriend with him instead of Marcia when he comes over to inspect the new hotel arrangements,' Sally said as Sky News moved on to the next item on the schedule.

'I think Wayne's bosses, the members of U.S. Ryder Cup committee, may have something to say about that. Knowing Wayne, he'll face them down. Pity, I rather liked Marcia. Think you'll get along with Miss Angie Wilde, my dear?'

'Frankly, I'm not looking forward meeting her. Blonde bimbos are not my cup of tea.'

Bruce winced. 'I do hope you won't refer to Wayne's bit on the side as a blonde bimbo, my dear. For all we know she could have an I.Q. of one hundred and sixty – '

'With implant boobs like those we've just seen – I

doubt it!' Sally snorted. 'Take it from me all that young lady's assets are on show up front. Now fetch me a drink before lunch, darling. And make it a stiff one.'

• • • •

Sergeant Martin Gilhooly paced up and down his tiny office in Loughduff Garda Station. He stopped now and then to glance out of the window which gave him a view of the road leading into the town. Out in the public office he could hear Garda Jerry Carney talking to someone on the telephone.

The Sergeant paused, looked at his watch. It showed 1.25pm. He knew that in five minutes precisely Chief Superintendent Kieran Clarke's car would arrive outside the station entrance. Better check one last time that everything was in order.

As he entered the outer office Garda Carney muttered something in a low voice into the telephone and replace the receiver. 'That girlfriend of yours checking up on you again, Jerry?' the Sergeant laughed. 'She has you in handcuffs already, and the two of you not even engaged.' He glanced around. 'Everything in order?'

'Yes, Sergeant. Look at the place. You could eat your dinner off the floor it's so clean.'

'You might be doing just that if the Super is in a bad mood today!' Gilhooly glanced at himself in the small wall mirror. 'He left Killarney on schedule so he'll be on time – as usual.' He walked towards his office, turned. 'Remember the instructions…no telephone calls unless it's absolutely necessary. The Super and I are not to be disturbed – this Ryder Cup protest by the farmers is serious.'

'I have you, Sergeant. Leave everything to me – ' They both heard the sound of a car. Garda Carney looked out of the window. 'Speak of the devil. Here he comes…'

Sergeant Gilhooly paused at the door, turned. 'What

was the name again of that young American golfer whose father is a politician and whose ancestors are supposed to come from around here?'

What Sergeant Gilhooly knew about golf could be inscribed on the head of a creamy pint of Guinness, his favourite drink. But he did know that the Ryder Cup was a huge sporting event that would be shown on tv in roughly 200 countries around the world and would bring thousands of visitors crowding in the Killarney area. With a group of farmers from his area signifying their intention of staging a protest during the event, and the son of a high profile U.S. Senator included in the American team, Sergeant Gilhooly knew he was in for a busy time. The Irish Government was anxious that maximum security be put into force. Nothing was to be left to chance.

'Joey O'Hara is the young fellow's name,' Garda Carney informed his superior. 'He's the world's No.1 golfer – a superstar. Not married, known to fancy the women – '

'Right, right!' The Sergeant waved Carney to silence. 'I've got the picture.'

The Sergeant stepped outside, advanced as the uniformed driver opened the car door and Superintendent Clarke stepped out. 'Welcome to Loughduff, sir – '

'Thank you, Sergeant.' The Super shook the extended hand brusquely, strode through the open door into the three-roomed station. He nodded curtly to Garda Carney, entered the inner office, placed his gloves and gold-braided cap on Sergeant Gilhooly's desk and sat down in the chair. He came straight to the point.

'Sergeant, that protest meeting those local farmers organised in town the other night is causing no end of concern within Government circles. If these farmers succeed in disrupting the Ryder Cup the whole world will be watching and there'll be hell to pay.'

'I understand, sir.'

'I presume you're keeping on top of the situation?'

'Very much so, Superintendent. My men and I are watching everything.'

'Good, good.' The Super leaned forward, flicked an imaginary speck of dust from his cap. He was the youngest of his rank in the force. Still in his late forties, ambitious, he saw a high-powered event like the Ryder Cup as an opportunity to showcase his potential to his superiors in Dublin. The challenge of the local farmers' protest must be successfully dealt with.

'This man Travis Gartland and his brother Ben, the ringleader of the protest. What do you know about them?'

'Tough boyos, both of them. A right pair of rogues. Both have short tempers which have got them into trouble in the past...fistfights, damage to property, threats to anyone who gets in their way, that sort of thing. Travis, the eldest, inherited the family farm when their parents died. He's married to a lovely young woman and they have two kids – she came out of the convent orphanage in her teens to work in the Loughduff Inn where Travis put his evil eye on her. He's is a surly bastard, a bully like his brother. Ben lives with a woman in town and works with Travis on the farm.'

The Super pursed his lips. 'Tell me more about Ben. He's the one in charge right now, isn't he? The one organising the protest. I believe he's been in serious trouble a few times.'

Gilhooly nodded. 'He gets violent when he's had too much to drink. He's beaten up his woman a few times but she won't charge him. Afraid probably – '

'What I really want to know is this – is Ben Gartland capable of giving us big trouble during the Ryder Cup?'

The Sergeant paused for a moment before replying. Better to play it safe now than have the finger pointed at himself later. 'Yes. I wouldn't underestimate Ben Gartland, Superintendent. He got big support at the meeting the

other night. Poor old Dan Collins from the IFU didn't
stand a chance. The farmers' anger is understandable - a
bunch of wealthy Japanese coming in to buy up land
around here for a luxury golf course is bound to get them
angry. You know yourself that, in the past, men in these
parts have been known to kill for land – '

'Yes, yes,' the Super said sharply, looking worried. He
didn't need to be reminded the value local men put on
land. 'But exactly how many men can Ben Gartland
muster? What's his next move? If this protest is as serious as
you say it is I presume I'll have to bring in extra men from
outside?'

'Ben has called another meeting for tomorrow night in
the upstairs room of the Loughduff Inn. He'll be drawing up
a plan of action. He's enjoying being in charge and the
attention he's getting so I expect he'll talk to the media
afterwards. We should learn something more after
tomorrow night.

'Hhmmm…I don't like the sound of a hothead like Ben
Travis running a protest like this. He's obviously enjoying
the hype he's getting. It could easily get out of control….'

'My sentiments exactly, sir.'

'He's been up to Dublin to visit Travis in jail, probably
seeking some advice. I suppose you know that, Sergeant?'

'Oh yes.' It was news to Gilhooly, but he wasn't going to
tell the Super that.

'We believe Ben may be urging Travis to go on hunger
strike to whip up sympathy for the farmers. It would also
get headlines worldwide. The last thing the Government
wants is for the Ryder Cup to be moved from Ireland. It
could happen even at this late stage.'

Sergeant Gilhooly was beginning to wish the Ryder
Cup had never come to Ireland – and Killarney especially.
He had a feeling that the next few weeks were going to be
pretty hectic.

'I've recommended that the European and American

Ryder Cup teams and officials be moved out of their Killarney base and accommodated instead in the Palace Hotel in Parknasilla. It's more secluded there and easier to maintain security.'

'A splendid idea, Superintendent!' The latter looked pleased. 'How did you manage that at this late stage?'

'On my recommendation the Government requisitioned the Palace, moved all the guests out for the required time. It created a bit of chaos but it had to be done. The two Ryder Cup captains, their wives and officials from both sides are flying in later this week to inspect the new set-up. We can't leave anything to chance, Sergeant. Which reminds me...'

'Yes, Superintendent?'

'These top golfers who are coming for the Ryder Cup.....they'll be guarded day and night, especially that young American O'Hara. Joey's father is Senator John O'Hara, a close friend of the President. The word is that the Senator and the President will be flying in for the last day of the Ryder Cup. That's a Sunday if I'm not mistaken. The President is taking the opportunity to drop in on his way to a G8 meeting of the world's top finance ministers scheduled for Germany the day after the Ryder Cup.'

'Really? The President of America coming' The Sergeant managed a smile. Inwardly he wasn't pleased. Holy God, more trouble, as if they hadn't enough on their plate already! Gilhooly swore to himself.

'You're aware by now Sergeant, I'm sure, that Senator's forebears emigrated to America from this part of Ireland. He's particularly anxious to know if any trace of them can be found. Distant relatives, ruins of the old family home, that sort of thing.....'

'Ah, I doubt it, sir – '

'You'll put a man on it anyway, won't you, Sergeant?' It wasn't a request, it was a command.

'Of course, sir. Right away.'

'Good. Keep me informed of everything that happens in this area – I want a report especially on Ben Gartland's meeting with the farmers in the town tomorrow night - '

The Sergeant was relieved to see his superior rise, pick up his cap and gloves. In the outer office Garda Carney came out from behind his desk and he and the Sergeant saw the Superintendent out into the street. They both stood watching as the Garda car took off up the slight incline leading out of the town.

'How did it go, Sergeant?'

'Pretty good. I let the Super know we're on top of everything. He was impressed.' As they turned to go inside the station he said, 'By the way, I want you to check out all the O'Hara families in the area. Find out if any of their forebears emigrated to America in the past and if by chance they're related to the Senator. I doubt it myself but if any of them do they'll have a superstar golfer on their doorstep shortly.'

Sergeant Gilhooly looked at the station clock. 'Where's Garda Glynn?' He was referring to Pauly Glynn, the third member of the force stationed in Loughduff. 'He should have reported for duty by now.

'I haven't seen so far this morning, Sergeant.'

'I believe the lazy sod was drinking after hours in the Loughduff Inn last night. I'm told he was with Ben Gartland and his cronies. Get on the phone and have him report to me immediately.'

●　●　●　●

'I'll be honest with you, Katie. I think Jeremy Walker is just gorgeous. And sexy into the bargain. I think I'm madly in love with him this minute!'

Katie smiled and jocosely 'tut tutted' at her friend across the kitchen table. 'You're a married woman, Nell Flavin. Stop talking like a schoolgirl – '

The reference to her marital status failed to dampen Nell's ardour. 'I'm finding it madly exciting having an artist living next door to me. I can look across into his yard from my bedroom and see him coming and going in that lovely car of his – ' This time Katie smiled. Nell's over-romantic nature even extended to cars! 'You'll never guess what Marty Kerrigan told me about Jeremy Walker...' Nell's voice was conspiratorial. She was referring now to the local postman who was in on everybody's business.

Katie put a plate of her friend's favourite chocolate biscuits on the table and poured the tea. 'What was that old gossip whispering to you?'

'He said there are painted pictures of a naked young woman all over Jeremy Walker's living room. Not a stitch on - naked as the day she was born!'

Nell was surprised at how calmly Katie took this latest bit of gossip. After all, not every household in Loughduff had a picture of a naked lady adorning their walls!

'Jeremy Walker is an artist, isn't he. That's the type of painting that interests artists. The lady is probably a professional model.'

Nell started on the chocolate biscuits. 'He won't sell many pictures of naked women around here, I can tell you!' They both laughed uproariously. 'And he won't get too many females willing to pose for him, either!'

'Why don't you offer yourself as a model to him, Nell?', Katie teased. 'You seem very interested in Jeremy Walker and his work.'

Nell looked suitably startled. 'Me! A married woman with two growing teenagers, not to mention a growing waistline! Imagine what the neighbours – and my Tom – would say. Besides – ' she looked slyly at Katie, 'it was you he showed an interest in the other night. Has he dropped in to see you since?'

Now it was Katie's turn to smile. 'Yes. He came by yesterday...' Nell stared, a biscuit halfway to her mouth.

'Did he now….' She studied Katie closely. There was something different about Katie Gartland this morning. She was smiling for one thing – and Nell rarely saw her friend do that often during her weekly visit. There was a perkiness about her that Nell had not noticed before. Obviously the absence of her husband wasn't impinging too much on her just now!

Also, Katie had done something to her appearance. True, she was still wearing the same faded jeans which she invariably wore on the farm. But now she had a crisp, white blouse tucked in at her slim waist. Her long, sleek dark hair was tried in a neat pony tail, giving her a young girl look. She certainly wasn't looking or acting like a wife whose husband was languishing in jail in Dublin, threatening to go on hunger strike.

Nell helped herself to another chocolate biscuit and said, 'Well, out with it. Are you going to tell me what you and Jeremy got up to around here yesterday?'

'We didn't get up to anything. He wanted to see the farm, so we strolled around – '

'Hand in hand, I suppose!,' Nell cut in mischievously.

'He does know a lot about farm work, actually' Katie continued, ignoring the good-humoured jibe. 'He arrived about noon and afterwards we came back here and we had something to eat.'

'Where was Ben all this time?' Nell asked.

'He had gone to Dublin to visit Travis. I phoned Jeremy and invited him over, told him this would be a good time to visit…'

'Did you now…So you spent the whole day alone with Jeremy Walker – ' Nell was almost drooling. 'Is he coming to help out on the farm?'

'He offered to, but I told him I'd rather he didn't. Not with Ben around. I told Jeremy he'd be asking for trouble.'

'God, that's a pity. Did you tell you were a bit of an artist yourself when you were in the orphanage?'

'As a matter of fact I did.'

'And?' Nell was all agog again.

'He was very interested. He said I should take it up again - and even offered to give me some lessons…'

'Oohhh,' Nell rolled her eyes in ecstacy. 'I think I'll take up painting! Why not ask him to start up art classes in Loughduff…' Her eyes sparkled with excitement at the idea.

'Why don't you ask him yourself, Nell. I mean you're living practically next door to him.'

'You know, Katie, I might just do that!' Nell helped herself to another cup of tea.

'Go on, tell me what else happened between you two'

'I'm going to Dublin with Jeremy tomorrow –' Katie heard Nell's intake of breath. 'He has an exhibition opening up there shortly and he has some arrangement to make. I was going to visit Travis anyway and Jeremy suggested we drive up together.'

Nell looked suitably impressed. No wonder Katie looked so different this morning. So alive. Nell was sure she could even detect a sparkle in Katie's eye. She couldn't suppress a pang of envy.

'That was very convenient. Will you be staying overnight?'

'Nell Flavin, how could you ask such a question! Of course not. We're coming back tomorrow night.'

'Oh, pity. What a waste of a lovely day!' They both had a fit of girlish giggles.

Katie didn't dare mention it to her friend, but the he mere thought of the trip to Dublin in the company of Jeremy Walker was sending a frisson of anticipation through her very being. She was looking forward to it more than she cared to admit. He had promised to bring her out to dinner before driving back to Loughduff tomorrow night. What if he suggested staying overnight? Katie tried not to allow herself to think of what she would do in that situation…

'I suppose you heard how he angered Ben at the meeting

the other night?'

'Yes. Tom told me that Jeremy stood up in the packed hall and spoke up for you in front of everyone.' Nell closed her eyes. 'I wish I'd been there to see it…You a damsel in distress, he the knight in shining armour riding to your rescue…'

Katie laughed. 'I think you're reading too many of those romantic novels, Nell. Jeremy was merely voicing his opinion like a lot of others who spoke up at the meeting.'

'Ah yes, but he was the one who volunteered to drive you home afterwards. Tom saw the two of you leaving together – and he wasn't the only one to take note, let me tell you.'

Katie sighed. Nell was her best friend – indeed she was her only friend – but she was like a lot of farm wives in Loughduff, bored to death with the drudgery of their daily work and starved of any real excitement. All of them only too willing to read too much into minor happenings.

'It was raining heavily when the meeting ended. Jeremy was only being polite,' Katie said as she poured another cup of tea for them both.

'Do you know what I think, Katie Gartland, I think Jeremy Walker has his eye on you. And fair play to you. You've been cooped up on this farm for far too long, with only Travis and Ben and the two boys for company. Do you know what I'd do if I was in your shoes – ' she didn't wait for Katie to reply – 'If Jeremy Walker invited me to go to Dublin with him I'd jump at it - and I'd make sure I'd be looking my best. Take my advice and go for it!'

'Go for what, Nell? What are you suggesting?'

'I'm suggesting nothing. But if I were you I'd nip into Killarney this afternoon, have your hair cut, styled and shaped, and buy yourself a new dress. You owe it to yourself, Katie.'

Katie didn't reply. She sipped her tea thoughtfully. Nell was right….she could hardly go off to Dublin for a day with

Jeremy Walker without doing something about her appearance. She had difficulty remembering the last time she had splurged on a new outfit – probably when Jack had made his Confirmation – and that was all of three years ago. Why shouldn't she spend money on herself, make sure she was looking her best? Nell was right – she had a duty to look to herself – and the future!

'Why don't you come with me, Nell?' Katie asked, excited.

'I'd be delighted! It'll get me away from my place for a few hours. I'll be back in plenty of time to have Tom's dinner ready. We'll go to Killarney -there's a great selection of boutiques there. We'll surely find something suitable in one of them after you've been to the hairdressers... Upstairs quick girl and grab your purse – and to hell with the expense!'

Katie dashed upstairs to the bedroom, stood in front of the old-fashioned full-length mirror and ran a brush frantically through her hair. She grabbed a jacket from the wooden wardrobe in the corner and, on the way out, glanced at the big double bed with its faded coverlet which invariably groaned with the weight of her husband, usually when he climbed the stairs after a late night drinking session in Loughduff.

She quickly banished the vision from her mind as she slammed the bedroom door and hurried downstairs to the waiting Nell.

● ● ● ●

Wayne Folen moved the curtains of the upstairs window aside cautiously and scowled when he saw the group of reporters and tv cameramen gathered outside the locked gates at the end of the driveway. He was grateful for the curving row of neatly trimmed cypress trees that blocked off their view of the house.

He swore under his breath. He had arrived home from

Chicago late last night, having seen Angie off on her flight
back to New York. As soon as the cab had stopped outside
the house it had been surrounded by reporters shouting
questions and blinding him with arc lights as the television
cameras whirred.

The shouted questions had come thick and fast as he
stepped out onto the pavement and prepared to unlock the
gates to allow the cabbie to drive right up to the house.

'Hey Wayne, what's the latest with you and Marcia?
Are you splitting up?'

'How about your new girlfriend…Will you be taking
her to Ireland with you for the Ryder Cup?'

'Is is true you've been asked to resign as Ryder Cup
captain?'

'What's the latest on the domestic front? Has Marcia
moved out?'

This last shouted question had come as a shock. Marcia
moved out…what the hell were they on about? Stone-
faced and staring straight ahead, he had unlocked the gates
and climbed back into the vehicle after the cabbie had
entered the driveway. He was glad when he finally reached
the sanctity of the silent house.

When he entered he realised why the members of the
media had asked about Marcia. She had indeed moved out.
A note, signed by his daughter Shiralee, propped up
against a vase over the fireplace in the spacious living-
room explained it all. He read it swiftly:

> Dad   how could do such a terrible thing to Mom?
> Burt and I have taken her over to our place away
> from the media until all this has blown over. Hope
> you come to your senses soon! Shiralee.

He had sat down last night, read the note several times. He
visualised the newshounds surrounding the house as soon
as the story broke, making Marcia's life a misery. He
reckoned she would have a lot more privacy with Shiralee

and her husband in the exclusive suburb of Redondo on the other side of San Diego.

Wayne had telephoned his daughter's house and Marcia had agreed to speak to him. The conversation had been terse and difficult for both. He had tried to explain how he felt about Angie, but Marcia had cut him short, told him she still loved him and implored him to come to his senses.

'Can't you see how difficult you're making it for yourself, Wayne? That young actress is only using you to further her career.' When he had argued with her his wife had refused to listen and had put Shiralee back on the line.

'Do you know that Mom has been incredibly loyal to you despite what you have done to her?,' his daughter had said.

'What do you mean?'

'She has been offered a lot of money to tell her side of the story by some newspapers – and she has refused them all. Most of the talk shows have been on to her too – Oprah Winfrey included. She has said no to them all.' Wayne had wiped his brow. He could do without that kind of publicity right now! Before he could say anything in his defence Shiralee had slammed the phone down.

Cord McCallum and his committee members were also on the warpath. When Wayne checked his fax machine before going to bed the first message on it was from the head of the U.S. Ryder Cup committee. It read:

> Myself and my committee are deeply disturbed at your marital problems and the liaison you had struck up with a young actress. We feel these developments could impact not only on you personally but also on team morale leading up to and during the Ryder Cup. Please get in touch immediately.

Wayne read the message, crumbled it into a ball and dispatched it into the waste paper basket. So once again he had outraged the old guys in blazers. To hell with them! They had no right to interfere in his private life. He had faced them down before and he would do so again.

He had gone to bed and telephoned Cord McCallum at the PGA headquarters the next morning. He had not slept well and having to prepare his own breakfast and eat it alone in a big empty house had put him in a bad mood. McCallum had come straight to the point. 'What the hell are you up to now, Wayne? This is not the behaviour we expect from our captain – '

'I take it you're referring to myself and Angie?' Wayne had asked mildly.

'You know damn well that's what I'm referring to,' McCallum thundered. 'Ditching your wife Marcia for someone half her age. You're projecting a bad image, Wayne, and myself and my committee members don't like it. We expect exemplary behaviour from our Ryder Cup captain.'

'My job is to bring the Ryder Cup back to America and that's what I aim to do, Mr. McCallum,' Wayne had answered levelly. 'There are millions of Americans out there who don't give a damn what I do in my private life. All they want is to see that trophy in our hands when we step off the plane back home. I aim to give them something to cheer about.'

Of course McCallum wouldn't understand. He was a bachelor, a rich and respected former big-time banker who had made a fortune on Wall Street before he had brought his business acumen into the world of professional golf. Hell, the old guy hadn't even made it to the top as an amateur! Now here he was, the strong man of the U.S. Ryder Cup committee, telling Wayne how he should live his life. It just wasn't on.

What would a wealthy old guy like McCallum know about love, sex and the whole damn thing? How could he envisage a man in the prime of life in a marriage gone off the boil being rejuvenated by a chance meeting with a warm, bubbly young woman like Angie Wilde? Wayne reckoned that McCallum would never understand that he still loved Marcia and always would. But right now he wanted to be around Angie.

McCallum was speaking again in a cold, measured voice. 'I'll give it to you straight, Wayne. If the decision was mine alone I'd fire you as Ryder Cup captain right now – '

'That so?' There was open animosity between them now.

'Yes. Unfortunately I alone don't have that power, but I will be recommending it to my committee when we meet shortly. However, right now you're still our Ryder Cup captain and we've got a problem....'

Wayne sighed. 'What's it this time, Mr. McCallum?

He listened while his boss outlined the details of the Ryder Cup protest planned by a group of angry farmers in Ireland. Then McCallum dropped the bombshell about the Irish authorities moving both teams and officials from their base in Killarney to a place called Parknasilla.

Wayne had secretly breathed a sigh of relief. The news wasn't good but at least it was taking the heat off himself and Angie. 'Can those Irish officials switch us around with the Ryder Cup so close?'

'They can and they have. I want you to begin preparations for yourself and our team members to go over to Ireland to inspect the new arrangements. It will give the guys an opportunity to play the Killarney course. I'll be going over also with some members of the committee. We're meeting the European delegation, including captain Bruce Cartray and his wife, at Shannon. We'll be taken from there to Parknasilla by helicopter. The visit will last two days, three at the most. Got that?'

'I got it.'

'As I mentioned the European captain, Bruce Cartray, is

bringing along his wife Sally whom we were acquainted with at the Ryder Cup two years ago....' A pause. 'What are your plans in that field, Wayne?'

Wayne decided to bite the bullet. 'Sounds like an ideal opportunity for everyone, the media included, to meet my new partner Angie Wilde...'

He could sense Cord McCallum's anger. 'You're making things very difficult for yourself, Wayne. I just hope you know what you're doing.' The line went dead.

Two minutes later Wayne was speaking to Angie by phone in New York. She was surprised to hear from him again so soon. 'How would you like a quick trip to Ireland?', he asked, 'for a couple of days – and a couple of nights, of course!'

The innuendo wasn't lost on her. Angie's laughter trickled down the line. 'Ireland? Great! You just won't believe this, Wayne darling, but my agent Mervyn Lazlo has just been in touch with me. Guess what – a couple of film offers have come in for me – one of them involving a trip to Ireland!'

'No kidding! That's great, honey. Big-time at last – '

Big-time, small-time, who the hell cares, Angie wanted to shout. Mervyn's plan was working. Once she had made it onto the news pages with Wayne Folen things had begun to happen. It was an opening, something she had been working her ass off for. Now she was going to grab it with both hands.

'Ever hear of an Irish film director called Patrick Mannion?' she asked.

'Can't say I have. Who is he?'

Angie was ecstatic. He could tell by the way the words poured out. 'He's only one of the most exciting new directors around. Outside of Hollywood that is. Patrick Mannion was nominated for an Oscar last year. Everybody's talking about him right now. And he's interested in me. Oh Wayne, I'm so excited!'

'Maybe he's interested in you for his next film.'

'That's what I'm hoping. He had planned on flying to New York to meet me, but now that we're flying to Ireland soon I'll get Mervyn my agent to arrange for him to meet me there. What did you say the name of that place we're staying in is?'

'Parknasilla. It's not far from Killarney. In Co. Kerry somewhere.'

'Jeez! I hope I can remember that name. I'd write it down only I wouldn't be able to spell it!' She giggled. Angie was really on a high. She sounded like she'd had a few vodka martinis to celebrate her good fortune.

Wayne waited until she had control of herself again. 'I'll fly to New York day after tomorrow, pick you up there, and we'll head for Shannon together. How's that?'

'Fine, fine. How long will we be in Ireland?'

'Three days I expect.'

'Hmmm – and three nights! Oh, Wayne honey, I can't wait!'

He clicked off a few minutes later, drained the last of his coffee and went back into the living-room. Upstairs, he peered out of the bedroom window across the sunshine dappled lawn. Over the trees he could see small groups of media people gathered outside the high front gate. They were obviously awaiting the next big story in the saga of America's beleaguered Ryder Cup captain.

He would give them that story. Why should he wait for Cord McCallum and his comrades to decide his fate? Time to go on the offensive. Why wait around to be fired; he would try to get the American public worked up and on his side before that happened.

The happenings at Kiawah Island and Brookline had shown how the American public liked to see their guys win the Ryder Cup. Time to cash in on that patriotism.

Faces turned in anticipation as Wayne approached down the winding gravel driveway. A few photographers shot off some film and tv cameras whirred as he strolled purposefully down the avenue between the cypress trees.

'You guys interested in a good story?' He got his answer in the excited buzz of conversation that started up. 'I suggest you headline it: 'We're going to Killarney to kick European ass!...'

CHAPTER FOUR.

T he Loughduff Inn was suitably crowded approaching 8.30pm when Ben Gartland entered and made his way through the tables towards the counter. He caught Benjy Duff's attention and the rangy proprietor joined him at the end of the bar.

'Everything ready for us upstairs?', Ben asked.

'Aye. The room is set out and you won't be disturbed. I'll send one of the lounge girls up to take orders.'

'Good.' Ben glanced around the bar, nodding to several of his supporters who had arrived early and were enjoying a drink before the meeting began. There were also a few unfamiliar faces in the bar; Ben reckoned they were either tourists or members of the media who had got wind of a story.

'How many are you expecting?', Benjy asked.

'Enough to give them bastards of Gardai something to worry about,' Ben replied gruffly. 'Some of the lads are busy with the harvest but there'll be plenty from other counties to give us support.'

'Good luck anyway. Anything I can do to help just ask.' Benjy was pleased that the protest group had made the Loughduff Inn their meeting place. Since Travis Gartland's arrest and Ben's planned Ryder Cup protest Benjy's bar was doing overflow business.

'And how is Travis?'

'He's fine.' Ben took a long pull of his Guinness. 'I was

up with him earlier in the week. He's started his hunger strike.' Ben tapped a newspaper under his arm. 'We got a lot of publicity out of it.' That seemed more important to Ben than his brother's hunger strike.

'Aye. It made the tv news the other night.' Benjy's watery eyes twinkled and his Adam's apple moved into view and then disappeared below his collar as he laughed and said, 'Bejaysus Ben, you're becoming a celebrity! The media can't get enough of you.'

Ben tried not to look too pleased. But Benjy was right. For the past week or so the Loughduff farmers' Ryder Cup protest had featured in newspapers and on television, accompanied usually by a picture or an interview with Ben Gartland. He had had several camera crews up to the farm, Irish and foreign, to film him and get him to point out the local area where the Japanese planned their golf complex. It had been a good move on his part to talk Travis into going on hunger strike; apart from the publicity there was always the possibility that his brother could suffer everlasting damage from a prolonged hunger strike. Maybe even die in the process. That slut Katie wouldn't stand in his way of his hands on the farm.

Benjy Duff moved off on other business. Time for him to check on Tina, see how the young lass he had taken on last week was progressing with the washing-up in the kitchen behind the bar. Ben's wife served only snacks, coffee and sandwiches from lunchtime until early evening. Tine would be in the kitchen on her own, bending down and stretching her supple young body as she stacked plates and cutlery away. Benjy would enjoy watching her.

The young ones nowadays would teach you a thing or two about sex, Benjy ruminated as he headed towards the kitchen. The convent no longer had an orphanage and he recruited young girls from the locality. They were independent and shared an apartment, either with a boyfriend or one of their pals. He liked offering young girls like Tina a lift home in the early hours, enjoying their company and their talk, not to mention their physical presence. Not like the good old days though, when the hired help stayed in a room over the bar and he could visit them during the night.

Tina didn't have a boyfriend and was still living with her parents. Tonight he would offer to drive her home. Sit in the car chatting to her in the half darkness. The idea excited him...

Ben Gartland drained his pint and was about to head through the doorway leading upstairs when he felt a touch on his arm. Looking around he saw Pauly Glynn leaning close. Pauly wasn't wearing his Garda uniform so Ben reckoned he was off duty. He got the whiff of alcohol off Pauly's breath.

'A quick word in your ear, Ben...'

'What is it, Pauly? – ' Ben stepped aside to allow some of his buddies to go upstairs. 'Can it wait till later? I'm on my way upstairs to a meeting – '

Pauly grinned. 'Stirring up more trouble, eh?' He had already had several drinks too many. 'Be careful, Ben – I might have to arrest you!' Pauly laughed.

Ben shook his arm free and was about to follow the others upstairs when Pauly's whisper stopped him. 'Not interested in hearing what that sister-in-law of yours is getting up to, eh? ...'

Ben paused. The last man on the stairs turned to see what was keeping him. Ben waved him on, turned. 'You talking about Katie?' He didn't like the way Pauly was grinning.

'Who else?'

'What about her?'

'Ah shure maybe you're not interested – ' That was as far as Pauly got. Ben grabbed him by the front of his jacket with his two hands and pulled the Garda towards him and

out through the door. The door into the bar swung closed
and they were alone at the bottom of the stairs.

'Don't play games with me, Pauly. If you've something
to tell me about Katie out with it quickly or damnit, Garda
or no, I'll beat it out of you!'

Pauly was frightened but he fought to remain calm.
'Get your hands off me, Ben, if you want me to tell you
what I saw.'

Ben released his grip. He was breathing heavily and
Pauly could smell the Guinness off his breath. 'Out with
it.'

'I saw Katie parking the car outside the railway station
in Killarney early this morning…'

'She was going up to Dublin to see Travis. I thought she
was driving up.'

'She was all dolled up. Looked lovely. I hardly
recognised her.'

Ben's eyes glinted. 'I'm sure Travis was pleased.'

His companion gave a sly smile. 'Well now, I don't
think she was dolled up for Travis….'

'What do you mean. Out with it, Pauly – '

' She was meeting Jeremy Walker, the Englishman.'

A figure appeared at the top of the stairs, shouted down
to Ben that they were waiting for him to start proceedings.
Ben swore loudly, bellowed that he would be up shortly.
The man disappeared and Ben turned to Pauly. When he
spoke again his voice was a mere whisper. 'I suspected that
painter boyo was interested. What happened?'

'Katie got into his car and they drove off together – up
to Dublin I suppose, unless they were going to his place….'
Pauly was secretly pleased at how angry Ben looked. Time
to exit. 'Now if you don't mind, Ben, I'd like to go back in
and finish my pint. See you later.'

Ben Gartland stared at the closed door. It was all falling
into place; Katie in the kitchen this morning looking like
he'd never seen her before. Her hair shining, not a strand

out of place, denoting a visit to a hairdresser. And wearing
an outfit that would catch any man's eye. It had certainly
caught his eye as he gulped down a mug of tea before going
outside to work on the farm. He had secretly admired the
long slip skirt that fell away provocatively to show a length
of shapely leg whenever she walked across the kitchen. He
might have known she wasn't going to all those lengths to
please someone like Travis His stupid brother wouldn't
notice if his wife walked nude into Mountjoy Jail!.

Ben was in a foul mood as he climbed the stairs. He
would check again with Pauly when the meeting was
ended. Then he would decide what action to take....

The room was buzzing with talk and half filled glasses
littered the large table in the centre. As he sat down
someone asked, 'Well Ben, what's our plan of action for
tomorrow?' The roomful of expectant faces turned in his
direction.

Ben waited until everyone was silent. He enjoyed being
the centre of attention. 'I'm sure ye all know by now that
some of the Ryder Cup crowd are arriving in Parknasilla
tomorrow. We'll be there to give them a warm reception!'

An excited buzz of voices greeted his words. 'What's the
plan, Ben?', Mikey Donnelly, a bachelor who lived with
his aged parents and who farmed 50 acres in the area,
asked.

'We'll stage a protest – a mighty big, noisy one. Right
outside the Parknasilla Palace. We'll blockade the place
with cars, tractors, harvesters – all types of farm machinery.
I want it as rowdy as the one the farmers staged in
Killarney a few years ago when the EU bigshots had to be
rescued from the hotel by Gardai. I want everyone in
Parknasilla by noon at the latest.'

'It doesn't give us much time, Ben,' one of the group
spoke up.

'To hell with that – it's too good an opportunity to miss.
We'll alert the reporters down in the bar. A blockade of

the Ryder Cup organisers will show everyone – the Government included – that we mean business. It'll get massive publicity.'

A murmur of approval went up from his listeners. Ben looked around, satisfied at how his plan had been received. He banged his fist on the table for attention, read out telegrams and fax messages of support that had arrived in Loughduff from farming organisations in the United Kingdom, France and other countries in Europe. There was even one from the farmers in Australia. Each message was greeted by a burst of cheering as he read it out.

They spent the next hour arranging the details of tomorrow's protest. Ben kept an eye on his watch. He was anxious to get back to Pauly Glynn and get more details about Katie. He was finally able to wrap up the meeting and go downstairs. As he opened the door into the bar he blinked in the glare of the lights set up for the tv cameras. Ben spent the next half hour giving an impromptu press conference then doing short sound-bite interviews for the individual networks.

Finally he was free to elbow his way to Pauly at the bar. 'Jaysus Ben, they'll be wanting you out in Hollywood next!'

Ben was in no mood for jokes. He ordered two pints of Guinness. 'Enough of your sarcasm, Pauly. Get back to what you saw this morning.'

Pauly, his voice slightly slurred from drink, repeated what he saw. 'Katie got into the boyo's car and they drove off. She fooled you, Ben, she wasn't going up to Dublin by train.'

'And you're sure it was Katie?'

'Oh, it was her alright. Looking better than I have ever seen her before.' Pauly had driven the six miles into Killarney for a few early morning drinks. It was a habit of his now when he was off duty; you couldn't be seen drinking in Loughduff before noon, not if you were a Garda, even out of uniform. The whole town – especially

Sargeant Gilhooly, would be in on it. Killarney was a much safer haven to enjoy a jar.

'I had just parked my car outside the railway station and there she was, getting out of hers. I didn't recognise Katie at first with the style she had on.'

'And you're sure it was Jeremy Walker she was meeting?'

'Definitely. He was out of his car waiting for her. She didn't exactly run into his arms but you could tell she was happy to see him.' Pauly paused, smirked. 'He kissed her on both cheeks, they exchanged a few words, then he opened the car door for her.'

'Did he now.' Ben's voice was almost inaudible.

Pauly drew on his pint. 'I wouldn't say Katie was used to having car doors opened for her – or being kissed like a lady for that matter! He has breeding, that English fella –' He knew that would annoy Ben.

'What the hell would you know about breeding!' Ben retorted. He was glaring ahead, his eyes fixed on a spot behind the bar. A silence fell between them, finally Ben said, 'You don't say a word to anyone about this Pauly. Understand? I'll take care of it.'

'Watch yourself Ben. Don't get into trouble – '

'Shut up!' Ben was angry 'When I want your useless advice I'll ask for it.' With that he drained his drink, slammed the glass down on the bar counter. He turned and left without another word.

• • • •

Katie had deliberately arrived ten minutes late into Killarney, wanting to be sure that Jeremy Walker would be there before her. If she were seen hanging around the town by someone she knew it might set tongues wagging.

She was relieved when she saw Jeremy standing in front of the line of parked cars as she drove up. He was dressed in a well-cut green corduroy jacket and dark slacks, with a green open-necked shirt and silk scarf tied loosely around his throat. She thought he looked very elegant, flamboyant even. With his neatly trimmed beard and close-cropped dark hair it was easy to see why her friend Nell thought him 'madly attractive.' No wonder he turned heads whenever he walked down the main street of Loughduff.

He watched her park the car and she was conscious of his gaze as she approached. 'Morning, Katie – ' He surprised her by kissing her lightly on both cheeks – another flamboyant gesture which both pleased and surprised her. 'I'm delighted you could come.'

'Sorry I'm late – ' She could feel her face burning.

'Not to worry. Looks like a good day for a drive to Dublin.' He was opening the car door, but his eyes were on her. 'Would it embarrass you if I told you you're looking extremely pretty for this time of the morning?'

'Thank you'. She slid into the seat, conscious of her new wrap-around dress exposing a length of bare left leg past her knee. Katie quickly pulled the dress into place as Jeremy turned the key in the ignition and eased the car through Killarney's early morning traffic and onto the Dublin road.

She was pleased that she had allowed Nell to talk her into getting her hair done and buying the new dress. It had lifted her spirits. It was a long time since she had spent any real money on herself. Not only had she bought the dress but much to Nell's delight she had also splurged on a white silk blouse, a slim-line skirt and also a well-cut sky-blue jacket with gold buttons.

Back home she had brushed aside the curious stares of Garret and Jack and rushed upstairs with her fashionable shopping bags. In her bedroom she had flung off the faded jeans and shirt top, kicked off her shoes and took out a pair with high heels. She had tried on the skirt and blouse first, then the dress, admiring herself in the full-length mirror of the old wardrobe and looking at a new woman. Nell had always told Katie that she had a good figure and had often hinted that she should show it off more. Well, once again she was following her friend's advice!

'We must stop somewhere later on and have something to eat,' Jeremy's voice brought Katie back to the present. 'I'm afraid I didn't have time for a breakfast before we left…' They had left Killarney far behind by now and were traversing Tipperary.

Katie nodded. She was enjoying the drive. It was good to get away from the farm, away from having to answer questions to reporters who were now beginning to telephone or call in during the day for whatever news she had on Travis. Despite her reticence she found Jeremy Walker was lively company, easy to talk to. He had a way of drawing her out of herself.

They stopped at a hotel in Cashel for a mid-morning snack of coffee and sandwiches. 'We haven't known each other very long but already I see a change in you,' he remarked. She blushed but didn't answer. 'You have a very interesting face, Katie. Unusual bone structure. I'd love to do a portrait of you sometime.'

'I thought you specialised in nudes?', she half-joked. 'I believe you have some interesting ones of a certain young lady on display.

He looked surprised. 'That's right. I do. How did you know?'

'Local gossip. Someone who saw your paintings…' Katie didn't mention Marty Kerrigan. 'It's not everyday paintings of nude ladies appear in Loughduff.'

Jeremy laughed. 'I suppose the locals think I'm depraved. Yes, I do specialise in nudes, the female nude particularly. That's why I'm going to Dublin. There's an exhibition featuring paintings of the nude form opening there shortly and some of my work will be on show –'. He broke off. 'I hope I haven't embarrassed you?'

'Of course not.' The waitress came with the sandwiches and coffee. Jeremy waited until she had departed. 'When I talked about painting you a few moments ago, Katie, I didn't only mean your face, interesting and unusual as it is. You also have an extremely good figure. Will you do me the honour of posing for me sometime?', he asked earnestly.

'You mean – ' She let her voice trail off. Now she was embarrassed.

'Yes. Nude. It would all be done tastefully, I assure you…' When Katie didn't reply he went on. 'Don't decide now, but promise me you'll think it over.'

'Yes, I will,' Katie heard herself say, her heart pounding.

'Drop by the cottage sometime and see some of my work. I'd like to know what you think it. It might also help you make up your mind about posing. Will you promise you'll call in?'

'Yes, I'd like that.'

'Good.' His hand found hers across the table top. 'I want you to enjoy the day, Katie. I know you're probably worried about your husband in jail, especially now that he has begun a hunger strike. Relax and try to forget about Loughduff.'

Katie felt guilty. Her thoughts weren't on Travis in Mountjoy Jail and his hunger strike. She wasn't even looking forward to visiting him, trying to discuss things with him. If she were honest with herself she would admit that she was more excited about Jeremy Walker and their blossoming relationship. Suddenly since their fateful meeting that night in the Loughduff community centre she had something to look forward to every morning. It was if somehow a door had opened and she had emerged from darkness into bright, warm sunshine.

She daren't tell Jeremy Walker how excited she was about the prospect of visiting his cottage, looking at those naked portraits, pondering about becoming one of his subjects. Last night she had tossed and turned in bed, her thoughts not on her jailed husband, but on the meeting with the handsome English artist and their journey to Dublin together. When Ben had arrived for work and was eating his breakfast she could see his eyes studying her over his mug of tea. She knew he was intrigued by the way she was dressed this morning, but he never asked, just sipped his tea and stared. If only he had known she was meeting Jeremy Walker…!

Jeremy paid the bill, removed her chair and as he guided her through the tables towards the exit. Katie was conscious of several pairs of female eyes being cast openly in their direction. It felt good to be the centre of attraction!

For Katie the main part of the journey to Dublin passed all too quickly. The initial awkwardness had passed and she was surprised at how at ease she was in his company. Inevitably the talk turned to Travis; she told him about her early life in the orphanage and how she had met her husband through working at the Loughduff Inn and how she had come to marry.

'It was a very young age to marry.'

'Too young, you could say. I didn't have much choice.'

'Did you love him?' When she didn't answer he said: 'I'm sorry, I shouldn't ask you that question. It's really none of my business…'

'I'm glad you did ask the question, Jeremy – ' Katie paused, stared straight ahead. 'No, I didn't love my husband then and I don't love him now. I know I shouldn't be telling you this, but I want to. Nell Flavin is the only other person I've spoken to about Travis and me and our life together. Although I suspect the boys sense all is not well between us…'

Now it was Jeremy's turn to fall silent. They were now on the Naas dual carriageway approaching the outskirts of Dublin. He feared if he didn't broach the subject the chance might be lost forever. 'You're not happy, are you Katie? I've heard the local gossip. Nobody has a good word to say about either Travis or Ben....'

'Travis Gartland is the only man I've ever been with. The farm means everything to him and Ben. More than me or his boys. I had to accept that.'

'I understand - '

A deep silence fell between the two of them. For no particular reason Katie found herself was staring at Jeremy's hands on the steering wheel as he guided the car through the city's midday traffic. His fingers were long and slim, the nails clean and neatly trimmed. An artist's hands, not the hands of someone who works the soil. Sensitive hands she imagined, those of a sensitive man, someone to whom she could relate. She wished Jeremy would talk about himself rather than discuss the relationship between herself and her husband. Perhaps in the not too distant future she would have an opportunity to learn more about Jeremy Walker.

It was a long time since Katie had last been to Dublin and she did not know the city particularly well. Jeremy pulled over to the kerb and asked directions, then had to do so once more before they found themselves on the long thoroughfare that was the North Circular Road off which Mountjoy Prison was situated. The entrance to the jail was approached along an avenue. Jeremy eased the car to the kerb a short distance from the avenue and said, 'Good luck, Katie. I hope you have some success with Travis.'

She thanked him and alighted from the car. They had already arranged a meeting place in the bustling, artistic Temple Bar area of Dublin where the gallery which was holding the exhibition was situated. Jeremy planned on taking her to dinner that evening before they drove back to Loughduff.

As Katie turned into the avenue the large, grey-bricked building that was Mountjoy Prison loomed over her. She stopped at a checkpoint halfway down the avenue, gave her name to a young Garda in the security hut. 'I'm afraid you have a reception committee waiting for you,' he said sympathetically.

The group of reporters, photographers and those manning tv cameras spread out as she approached. Most of them had expected a middle-aged, dumpy farm housewife to come visiting her husband, instead they saw a slim female figure walking towards them, the sarong-style dress blowing open in the slight breeze to reveal a shapely leg. Photographers couldn't believe their luck - Page One potential….Cameras clicked and whirred and followed Katie all the way to the main gate. A door in the huge gate had opened and another Garda with a clipboard checked her name before she entered. Reporters were shouting questions at her but Katie merely smiled politely and remained silent.

Inside she was escorted by a female Garda across a courtyard and into a building. Down several corridors, through another door and into a long room divided by a high wire mesh with chairs spaced out on either side at intervals. Several couples were already holding muted conversations with each other through the wire mesh, watched by a male and female Garda at each of the room. Katie sat down on the chair indicated by her escort and waited for Travis to appear.

When he did so shortly Katie thought he looked a bit thinner than usual. He hadn't bothered to shave and looked rather unkempt. He didn't attempt a welcoming smile as he sat down.

'Hello.' It was more a grunt than a greeting.

'Hello Travis.' Neither of them ever used verbal endearments. 'How are you?'

'How do you think I am? How would you feel if you were locked up in a jail and not eating?'

A silence. Katie felt uncomfortable. There wasn't much

privacy in the room. She was sure every word being exchanged between them could be overheard. 'Where are the boys? Are they not with you?', Travis asked.

'No. They're in school. I didn't want to bring them into a place like this – '

'You had a right to being them up to see their father.' Travis's voice was loud, aggressive. Heads were turning in their direction.

'I didn't want them to see their father in prison – '

'What's wrong with me being in prison? I'm proud to be in jail – ' His voice was rising.

'I'll bring them next time - .'

'Don't bother. I don't want to see them.' She knew he meant it. As in her case she could not recall the last time he had spoken civilly to his two young sons.

Another silence. Katie knew on the drive up that it was going to be like this. She saw that the other three couples were talking to each other animatedly through the grill. She would die of embarrassment, just sitting there staring, if Travis didn't make conversation.

Finally she said, 'I bought a new outfit.' Travis barely raised his eyes. 'I hoped you might like it.'

Now he stared directly at her. 'You sure it was for my benefit – ' When she looked blankly at him he went on: 'Ben tells me you were talking to that English fella at the meeting. Says you left together – '

'Yes, it was raining. Jeremy Walker offered to drive me home. Ben was going off drinking with his cronies – '

'So you went with the Englishman then   ' Travis let out an expletive. It blew away the whisperings of the other couples. 'Why was that English bastard sniffing around in the first place?'

'I told you, Travis, it was raining. I was grateful for the lift home. Nothing happened. We just talked. I had Jack and Garret with me – '

'I don't fucking believe you! – ' Travis crashed his fist

down on the wooden bench. 'You tell that English fucker to stay away from my wife, you hear!' Katie saw the male Garda at the end of the room take a step forward. 'If he comes sniffing around you again I'll get Ben to take care of him. Understand?'

'Please, Travis – ' Katie tried to placate her husband.

'You're not fooling me, you ungrateful bitch – ' Travis was shouting now, rising to his feet. 'I took you from that orphanage, married you and gave you a good home. And I can throw you out just as quick. Remember that, you slut –'

Katie prayed he would calm down. She was beginning to panic. Her husband's eyes were filled with hatred and she knew that only for the wire mesh between them he would probably have struck her. She was grateful when the two Gardai approached. Each of them grabbed hold of Travis's arms, restraining him.

'I think it would be better if you left now, Mrs Gartland,' the female officer said. Katie rose from the chair, tears welling in her eyes. Everyone in the room was not staring.

'Get off home. I don't fuckin' care if I never set eyes on you again!,' Travis shouted as he was escorted away, flanked by the two Gardai.

Katie could feel the eyes burning into her back as she turned and left the room, glancing neither to right nor left. It wasn't as if she deserved such treatment from her husband; she had gone to great lengths to look her best and he had called her a whore. Ben had obviously given his own interpretation of her brief encounter with Jeremy Walker on the night of the meeting. He would have taken great pleasure in relaying it to Travis.

At the gate she asked the Garda on duty if he would phone for a taxi. The officer looked at the attractive woman with the tear-stained face and reckoned he had lost count of the number of times he had witnessed the scene; the young wife tied to an erring husband, missing him and unable to come to terms with the enforced separation. He always admired how well the womenfolk managed to look when they came to visit. This lady looked particularly smart in her figure-hugging pale blue jacket and slit dress. Lucky the husband with a wife like that waiting for him to be released...

When the taxi arrived Katie pushed through the throng of reporters waiting outside, again ignoring the questions fired at her. Meanwhile the cameras captured the tear-stained face of the woman whose husband was on hunger strike inside. It would make a great human interest picture-story on tv or in the newspapers.

During the short taxi ride into town in the afternoon traffic, Katie did a quick repair job on her make-up. She wouldn't let what had just happened spoil her day. She tried and succeeded in blanking completely the memory of the visit to Travis from her mind. The door was opening once again to her new world.

'Here you are lady, right to the door!' The taximan's smiling face and cheery demeanour lifted Katie's spirits even further. She had read in the newspapers about Dublin's bustling Temple Bar area and she stood on the footpath outside the Sapphire Gallery for a few moments, savouring the atmosphere before entering. The gallery was surrounded by a panorama of trendy pubs and chic shops and restaurants, the people a mixture of smartly-dressed tourists and Dubliners alike. It was a delight to see so many happy, smiling faces.

The Sapphire Gallery was a modern edifice; large, airy with sunshine streaming in through the glazed windows in the roof. When Katie entered there were quite a few people moving about, gazing with interest at the sculptures and some rather odd looking fixtures that took up space in the middle of the floor area. The pictures hanging along the walls on two sides of the gallery ranged in size from miniatures to large landscapes and were also attracting a fair share of admirers.

Katie spotted Jeremy talking to a man in a lightweight suit and with a red handkerchief dangling languidly from a breast pocket. Jeremy saw her, said something to the man and crossed to greet her.

He clasped her hands in his, gave her a welcoming peck on the cheek. 'Welcome to the Sapphire Gallery, Katie – ' He broke off, looked at her closely. 'Something wrong?'

She raised a smile. She didn't want to cry again, make a scene in front of all the people in the gallery. 'It's nothing important – '

'Something happen between you and Travis?'

She nodded. She was determined that she wasn't going to spoil his day. She wouldn't let that happen. 'Travis was upset about something. He – he started shouting…'

'What was it that upset him, Katie?'

She hesitated before replying. 'Ben had told him about you leaving me home after the meeting the other night. Travis is very jealous, he thinks there's something going on between us – ' She broke off. 'He called me a whore in front of everyone. It was awful…'

Jeremy reached out and drew her to him. Katie's head rested on his shoulder and she could feel the comfort of his arms around her. If only there weren't so many people around….After a while he eased her away, wiped a tear from her face with his handkerchief. 'Look, I know you've had a terrible time in that jail, but we mustn't let it spoil your day. Maybe it's the wrong thing to say, but try to forget about what happened with your husband. And forget about Ben too. You're away from the farm for a day, why don't we both enjoy it – '. He looked at her earnestly. 'Will you do that for me, Katie?'

She smiled despite herself. Jeremy was right. She was allowing things to get on top of her. Nell would be angry with her if she saw how she was letting Travis spoil her day with Jeremy. She had better snap out of it.

'There, that's better,' Jeremy enthused. 'Now, come with me, there's someone over here I want you to meet. After that I'm going to take you out to dinner. How's that?' He noted how the smile lit up her face, made her look younger. Not for the first time he wondered how the hell someone as attractive as Katie had fettered herself to a brute like Travis Gartland. He made a mental note not to bring the subject up during dinner…

'Henry! – ' Jeremy called out. The man in the white suit came over and joined them. 'I want you to meet Katie Gartland. Katie, this is Henry Mackintosh, owner of this splendid gallery – '

'Katie, my dear, it's a real pleasure to meet you. Jeremy hasn't stopped talking about you since he arrived.' Katie flushed as Henry's artistic eyes ran over her from head to toe. 'Now I see why,' he added admiringly.

Henry took her hand in his, but instead of shaking it he made a great show of raising it to his lips and kissing it elegantly. Katie was amazed, tried not to look too embarrassed. No one had ever kissed her hand before – certainly not Travis! She thought it was very romantic.

She knew instinctively she was going to like Henry Mackintosh. He was fiftyish, tall and slim with wispy brown hair that kept sliding sideways on his forehead. His eyes were full of merriment and Jeremy seemed to find everything he said amusing. Henry invited her on a tour of the gallery and, with Jeremy by her side, she listened attentively as Henry Mackintosh moved slowly around the exhibits, giving a racy rundown of each and making the occasional acerbic comment. Despite not understanding half the things Henry was saying Katie found him immensely entertaining.

Whey they had finished the tour he invited them into an inner office where he opened a bottle of white wine and poured some into three slim glasses.

'To lasting happiness, Katie. And to you, Jeremy, may

your paintings bring you fame and fortune.' Henry drank from his glass, dabbed at his lips with another handkerchief which he pulled and replaced after use up the sleeve of his jacket.

'Thank you Mr. Mackintosh – ' Katie sipped her wine. If Nell could only see her now!

'Oh, tut, tut. You must call me Henry. Everyone does. Besides, I expect we'll be seeing a good deal more of each other in the near future, Katie my darling…' He waved his glass of wine in the direction of Jeremy. 'Do you know that this young man has tremendous potential. I'm very pleased to have him under my wing.'

'Does that mean he'll be famous someday?', Katie asked.

'Possibly,' Henry replied. 'When I show his paintings I expect to sell a lot of his work. Jeremy will be good for me – just as I venture to say he could be good for you also.' His eyes twinkled mischievously.

Behind him Jeremy looked pleased. What had he been telling Henry about herself, Katie wondered? She had obviously been a topic of conversation between them. 'You must come to Dublin for the exhibition, Katie,', Henry's voice cut across her thoughts.

'She certainly will. I'll see to that,' Jeremy said.

'I'd love to see some of Jeremy's work, I really would,' Katie enthused. In the convent she had always come out tops in the art class. Sister Rita, the art teacher, had implored Katie when she was leaving the orphanage to go to art classes. Of course it had never happened. Now she felt her interest being rekindled. It was thought she was entering into another world other than the one she had been inhabiting for so long.

Henry Mackintosh finished off his glass of wine, glanced at his watch and said: 'Now if you both excuse me, I'm off to meet someone. Do finish off the wine between you if you wish.'

With that Henry breezed out. Katie thought it rather unusual that the gallery owner would leave two people whom he hardly knew alone in his office but Jeremy didn't seem surprised. He poured more wine into her glass.

'Henry likes you,' he said.

'I like him too. He's very witty.'

'He made you laugh a lot. That was good for you.'

'Yes. I'm pleased to have met someone like Henry Mackintosh. He makes me feel good about myself.'

'I hope I do that too, Katie…' Jeremy moved close, his eyes searching her face, awaiting her response.

'You do, Jeremy,' Katie said, her voice almost a whisper. She was conscious that the departing Henry had closed the door behind him and that they were now very much alone in the room.

Jeremy suddenly bent forward and kissed her full on the lips. Katie was taken by surprise. Her first reaction was to break away, but instead, after the initial shock, she found herself responding to him. When she did break away she was slightly breathless and she knew her cheeks were burning.

'Wh-what made you do that?', she asked. It was a silly question but she felt she had to say something.

'I've wanted to kiss you ever since we met,' Jeremy replied. 'I know it was wrong, Katie, but I'm not sorry I did it. Tell me you're not sorry either.'

She looked into his eyes for what seemed an age. Then she stepped forward, moved her hands up along his shoulders and around his neck. Katie kissed him like she never thought she would kiss any man. Jeremy responded by putting his two arms around her and crushing her body to his. When at last he released her she stepped back and had to steady herself against the desk.

They stared at each other, each of them unwilling to speak. Katie picked up her glass of wine, went to the window. She had to stop looking into Jeremy Walker's eyes. She felt powerless when she did so, although she wasn't accustomed to drinking during the day and two glasses of wine on an empty stomach didn't help! From the window she gazed with unseeing eyes out onto the narrow street below. After a few moments she sensed Jeremy behind her. He brushed her hair aside, began kissing her on the neck. Katie could feel her heart pounding. She was sure he could hear it also. Did he realise what he was doing to her? She could feel her resolve weakening by the second. She moved away again, said, 'Look at the time. Shouldn't we have something to eat.....'

If he was disappointed in her opting to feed a hunger other than the one he wanted to assuage he didn't show it. Instead he said, 'Of course, I'm sorry, Katie. You must be starving. Henry recommended a restaurant just up the street...'

They walked the short distance in silence, each of them wrapped up in the enormity of what was happening between them. The restaurant was comfortably crowded and they were lead to a table for two by a smiling young girl. The numbing memory of her encounter with Travis earlier had long been erased from Katie's mind. Now she looked around the restaurant, savouring the atmosphere, enjoying the buzz of conversation emanating from the tables, admiring the outfits of the smartly-dressed women and their escorts. She couldn't remember ever having been in a restaurant with her husband. They never went out together. Why couldn't she be a part of this world?

Jeremy had ordered a bottle of red wine and was pouring. 'Happy?', he asked. Her smile said it all. 'You look lovely, Katie. Tell me more about yourself. I want to know everything about you – '

Before she could reply the girl who had shown them to their table returned with a menu. Katie sipped her wine; the list of dishes were in a mixture of French and English and she did not have experience of sitting in posh

restaurants, choosing what to eat. She was grateful when
Jeremy read from the menu and took care of the ordering.
No man had ever looked after her like Jeremy Walker was
doing. Katie sensed she was getting involved in a
dangerous liaison. She had never really discussed her past
in detail with anyone, apart from her friend Nell. She had
never told anybody, not even Travis, of the abuse she had
undergone at the hands of Benjy Duff during her teenage
years working for him in the Loughduff Inn. No doubt
Travis would have accused her of leading the slimy bar
owner on. She had harboured an inherent fear of men for
a long time after that.

Now Jeremy had come into her life and she felt herself
being drawn to him. He was treating her like a woman,
saying things to her that she had never heard before,
arousing feelings in her that had long been dead or
suppressed. Katie was both thrilled and scared at the same
time.

'Now, where were we? – ' Jeremy had finished ordering
and was smiling across the table at her. 'Ah yes, you were
about to tell me all about yourself...'

'But I hardly know anything about Jeremy Walker,
except that you're an artist who specialises in painting
nude women,' Katie countered, hoping this would fend off
his questioning for the present. 'Are you married? I'm sure
your work brings you into contact with a lot of very
attractive women...' She smiled beguilingly.

Jeremy shrugged. 'Married no. But I'm not denying
there have been a few...liaisons. Painters are like doctors,
sometimes it's difficult not to get emotionally involved
with one's subjects.'

'But women are your favourite subject?'

He laughed, his white teeth showing against the
darkness of his beard. 'I'm not denying that. I paint
whatever subject I find interesting. It just so happens a lot
of those subjects are women. I find painting the female

form very exciting. Some women have an aura about them that will inspire an artist. You do that to me. Do you understand what I'm saying, Katie?'

She nodded. She realised that she had emptied her glass and that he was refilling it. Dear God, if she wasn't careful she would lose all control! How delicious that would be! She noticed him studying her intently. It was a long time since she had drunk so much wine and she was feeling rather light-headed. It was also making her more relaxed, more daring in her conversation. She hoped this day would never end; already she was dreading the long drive back to Loughduff.

He had already expressed a desire to paint her. Another in his long line of female nudes, perhaps – or could she be someone special? The prospect made her catch her breath. Fired perhaps by the wine she said, 'What if I said I was seriously considering posing for you, Jeremy?'

She saw the delight in his eyes. 'I'd be delighted. Honoured. Will you, Katie?'

She heard herself giggling. 'Let me think about it.'

'Promise you'll let me know soon?'

'I promise.' Wait till she told Nell Flavin about this!

She knew she would agree to do what Jeremy wanted. Having him looking at her body, studying her, gave her a certain pleasure. Maybe posing for him would exorcise the memory of those terrible nights in the room over the bar in the Loughduff Inn when she would lie terrified in her bed, dreading to hear the doorknob turn and in the semi-darkness, see the tall figure approaching...

Katie shuddered. Jeremy noticed and put his hand over hers on the table. 'I won't hold you to posing, Katie. You must want to do it yourself.'

'Yes, I know. I trust you, Jeremy.'

'Thank you. Let's drink to it then.'

She enjoyed the lunch. Several times during it she remembered fleetingly what had happened in the Sapphire

Gallery, Jeremy's lips on hers, the surge of passion of a kind she had never experienced before. And the day wasn't over yet…

'It's almost four o'clock,' Jeremy said. They had finished with two creamy cups of coffee and now hey were sipping the last of the wine. 'Would you fancy a stroll before we go back?'

'I'd love it,' she enthused. She didn't want this day to end. Besides the fresh air would clear her head. Outside, he took her hand in his and they retraced their steps along the busy street. As they passed the Sapphire Gallery he paused and pointed across the street. 'Henry lives in one of those apartments above the gallery.'

'They look very elegant. Like Henry himself. Is he married?'

Jeremy laughed. 'No, Henry isn't the marrying type.' He squeezed her hand. 'He left the key to his apartment with his assistant in the gallery, said if we wanted to use it later…' Jeremy looked at her, his voice trailing off.

Katie caught her breath. It was obvious what he had in mind. No doubt Henry Mackintosh's bedroom was open, empty, waiting to be used. Probably there was even a bottle of chilled wine on the table for their pleasure…

Jeremy was still holding her hand, awaiting her response. People were brushing past by them on the pavement, strangers oblivious to the drama taking place in their midst.

'What would you like to do, Katie? Henry won't be back until tonight. We can enjoy several hours together, alone, before we start back…'

Katie knew what she wanted to do. Her whole being ached for his touch, feel his lips on hers, his hands undoing the zip of her dress. But she couldn't give herself to him, not this time. It was too soon. So much had happened today already… 'Please Jeremy, don't ask. Not right now. There'll be another time, I promise…'

He forced a smile. 'Of course, I understand. It was inconsiderate of me to even think of it – '

'No it wasn't. It's just that I'm not used to this. I'm afraid of what I'm getting into. Things have happened to me in the past that you don't know about. Right now I'm not sure what I want – ' She was very sure of what she wanted, but something was holding her back.

'I feel that you're unhappy, Katie, and I want to do something about it. But you're right, getting involved sexually isn't always the answer.' He stopped and his face brightened. 'Come on, let's enjoy the rest of our time together.'

They walked the length of fashionable Grafton Street, laughing and whispering together like lovers as they strolled window-gazing from shop to shop. Almost a decade had passed since Katie had been to Dublin and she was amazed at the changes that had taken place in the city. Now there was an abundance of restaurants offering international cuisine, and trendy shops and fashionable apartment blocks seemed to have sprung up everywhere.

Jeremy spotted a sign pointing to the National Gallery and they both thought it was too good an opportunity to miss. They spent an hour browsing through the gallery, Jeremy studying some of the more famous paintings on display and explaining them to a spellbound Katie.

Afterwards they strolled hand-in-hand into the sylvan setting of nearby St. Stephen's Green. It wasn't long to closing time. The late evening sun was filtering through the trees and sparkling on the lake. It was an oasis of peace set right in the heart of the city and Katie could have spent hours there. But all too soon it was time to stroll arm-in-arm down Grafton Street and back to where Jeremy had parked his car. Darkness had fallen as they began the long drive towards Killarney.

'Tired?', he asked as they sped southwards as the night closed in. She smiled in reply. 'Relax and get some sleep,' he advised.

Katie closed her eyes, let her mind run back over the day's events, speculating on what might lie ahead. Meeting Jeremy Walker had turned her life around, given her something new to live for. But she had responsibilities to her boys, and even to a husband she did not love. Up to now she had never had to make decisions because she had accepted everything that had come her way in life. Now at least she had options.

Katie allowed herself to drift off into a fitful sleep, wakened only occasionally by the bright lights as they passed through some large town or other. It really had been a marvellous day and she was sorry it was drawing to an end. It seemed no time before she felt Jeremy shaking her awake. 'Hey, sleepy head. We're almost there.'

Kate's mind focused slowly. Then she saw her car parked a short distance away. Theirs were the only two vehicles in the car park. 'What time is it?', she asked.

He gestured to the clock on the dashboard. 'Fifteen minutes to midnight. The drive took longer than I thought.'

'Oh my God!' Katie was shocked. She hadn't meant to be back so late. The boys would hopefully be in bed. And Ben? She prayed he would have gone back to his own place in Loughduff and not be at the farm waiting for her.

'Thanks again for a lovely day, Jeremy.' Not for the first time in the past twelve hours she surprised herself by leaning over and kissing him lightly on the cheek. She would have to get used to showing affection to a man.

'I'll drive behind you to the crossroads. Stop there for a minute or two.'

Katie got into her own car. The warmth of the September day had faded now and there was a slight chill in the air. She was grateful that the car park was deserted; no prying eyes. She drove carefully through Killarney, past the dark mass that was the cathedral and out into the country, Jeremy's car lights reflected in her rear view mirror. A short while later she was at the crossroads where Jeremy would turn off for the two mile drive to his cottage. Katie stopped the car, left the headlights on. She got out and closed the door, holding her skirt in place against the breeze. She waited for Jeremy to approach, his figure silhouetted against the glare of his car's headlights.

He said nothing, just swept her into his arms and kissed her passionately. Katie felt herself being eased back gently against her car, his body pressing into hers. She put her arms around his neck, not resisting as he unbuttoned her new linen jacket and slid his arms inside, his hands on her back, sliding down her body onto her buttocks, squeezing gently, sending delicious sensations through her. Katie opened her lips wide and his tongue moved over them, seeking to enter her mouth.

Katie fought her emotions, pushed him aside, her breath coming in short gasps. 'Jeremy, stop. Please.'

'Come back to my place,' his voice was hoarse with passion. 'I want you so much, Katie – '

'No. I – I can't.'

'Why not?'

'The boys will be waiting. They'll be worried I'm not home – '

'Phone them from my place. Tell them that you're okay and that you'll be home first thing in the morning.'

Was this the first time he had put such a proposal to a woman?, Katie wondered. She doubted it somehow. She mustn't give in too easily to his demands.

'No, Jeremy. I'm going home.' She pushed gently against him. He took a step backwards. Katie buttoned her jacket, pulled her dress into place. 'Thanks again for a lovely day,' she said. 'I never thought I could enjoy myself so much.'

'My pleasure. I enjoyed myself too, Katie. I look forward to hearing from you about your portrait,....' He watched her drive away, waited until the tail lights of her car had vanished around a curve in the road. He got into his car and drove the two miles through the darkness to his cottage, his mind still on Katie Gartland. As he passed the Flavin house he noticed that the lights there were still on.

Jeremy saw the shattered window as he approached his front door. He stopped, inspected the damage. Someone had thrown an object through the main front window, leaving a large hole with shards of glass showing. He turned and looked around before opening the door. Was there someone out there watching? It was past midnight now and there wasn't a sound in the darkness save the wind rustling through the trees. Maybe the Flavins had heard or seen something? It was too late to disturb them now. He would check in the morning.

Inside, he switched on the light and saw the large stone lying on the carpet in the middle of the floor. Trinkets of glass glistened on the window-sill. Rough twine had been used to tie a sheet of white paper around the stone. He closed the door and pulled the curtains before lifting the stone and retrieving the paper. Printed on it in crude capital letters were the words: YOU HAVE BEEN WARNED! He stared at the words before placing the note on the table.

He glanced at his watch, wondering if Katie would be in bed yet. Maybe he should wait until the morning to call her. No, better fill her in now on what had happened, check that she was alright. Maybe something similar had happened at her place.

He lifted the receiver, dialled. 'Katie?'

'Yes?', her voice was low, suspicious.

'Jeremy here. Something has happened that I think you should know about. ‐ ' She listened in silence while he gave her details.

'Oh my God.' He could sense her shock. 'Ben…'

'You think so?'

'I think so. He's capable of anything. He has such a vile temper. He would have remembered you speaking out against him at the meeting...'

'Do you think he knows anything – about us, I mean.'

He heard Katie's sharp intake of breath. 'Oh God, I hope not.' Now there was fear in her voice. If Ben thought someone was getting involved with his brother's wife...

'How could he have found out?' Jeremy asked.

'Someone may have seen us together at the station this morning – '

'Be careful, Katie. I don't want anything to happen to you.'

Katie felt like crying. She didn't know whether it was from the shock or because at last someone was worried for her. 'You take care also, Jeremy. Goodnight.'

She replaced the receiver and went upstairs to the bedroom. The boys had not been wakened by the call. She had been preparing for bed when Jeremy had telephoned and now as she slowly removed the rest of her clothes she caught a glimpse of herself in the full-length wardrobe mirror.

Yes, she had a good figure, she could visualise herself as Jeremy Walker's model, languishing seductively on a chaise-longue in his studio, or perhaps posing in a shadowy glade with a diaphanous veil draped strategically across her body, his eyes on her as he committed her image to canvas...

He cared, that was all that mattered. Katie slipped on her nightdress and got into bed. It was a long time before sleep finally came.

CHAPTER FIVE.

The helicopter took off vertically into the late morning air, did a full circle over Shannon Airport, then headed southwards across the estuary, sweeping towards the wild beauty of County Kerry.

Inside the 'copter Angie Wilde leaned sideways and gazed out of the window, getting her first view of Ireland. After a couple of minutes she reckoned that the late Johnny Cash had exaggerated when he sang about the country and its forty shades of green. All she could see were patchwork fields with farmhouses and a river meandering its way through the countryside. All the fields looked the same colour of green to her. Mr.Cash had gone over the top with his lyrics.

Beside her Wayne Folen had opened his briefcase and was poring over a sheet of paper with the twelve names of his Ryder Cup team on it. Angie yawned. Doesn't he ever relax, take time to chill out? He was old enough to be her father but he had energy to burn; unfortunately it was being directed in the wrong direction! The guy was so obsessed with winning the Ryder Cup for America he was beginning to discuss team formations with her in bed before getting down to real business!

The fact that Cord McCallum had included himself on the reconnaissance trip to Ireland hadn't done much for Wayne's peace of mind. McCallum had shown up at Kennedy Airport last night with two other U.S. Ryder Cup officials for the three day scouting trip to survey the new team accommodation set-up for the big event. Relations between Wayne and McCallum were deteriorating. The Ryder Cup captain and his boss just weren't hitting it off. Back home the conflict between the two was making big headlines and had entered the public arena, due mainly to the impromptu press conference which Wayne had held in his home in San Diego yesterday, emphasising his determination to do things his way and accusing McCallum of interference.

Even the White House was said to be concerned at the continuing verbal battle which was seen to be damaging the prospects of America regaining the coveted trophy from Europe's golfers. Behind the scenes the President, a keen golfer himself, had hinted at both sides to forget their differences and put the nation first. Relations between the U.S. PGA chairman and his captain remained distinctly chilly however.

At Shannon Airport, the European and American Ryder Cup parties had been welcomed by representatives of the Parknasilla Palace Hotel and by members of Irish Tourism. The threat to golf's prestige tournament by a group of Irish farmers had made big news all over the world and when the topic was raised in front of a group of newsmen who had arrived in Shannon to cover the arrival of the American and European parties it was quickly brushed aside.

Angie was bored by a lot of what was going on. She had other things on her mind. Film director Patrick Mannion for instance. She was looking forward to meeting the wildly talented Irishman who had taken Hollywood by storm. Her agent Mervyn had labelled the Irish guy 'the new Quentin Tarantino.' Trust Mervyn go to overboard like that.

She wondered what Patrick Mannion would look like. Good-looking hopefully. Didn't all leading actress get into bed with the director – especially if it was their big breakthrough film? She wouldn't play too hard to get with the Irishman, not if he looked anything like those other handsome Irish hunks Pierce Brosnan and Liam Neeson. Sure Wayne Folen satisfied her in bed – whenever he could forget about the Ryder Cup.

One person who Angie wasn't eager to get too close to over the next few days was Sally Cartray, the snooty-looking bitch-wife of Bruce Cartray, captain of the English team. She didn't like the look of Sally the first time she saw her after the American delegation had disembarked at Shannon. Bruce Cartray and Wayne had greeted each other cooly, doing the ritual shaking hands and posing for the cameras together, but it was obvious that there was no love lost between them. When Bruce had introduced his wife, Sally had given Angie a frosty reception; instead of the usual ladylike warm embrace they had shaken hands formally. While Angie had smiled, Sally's gaze was cool and restrained.

Angie had to admit that Sally was an attractive looking woman, but when she spoke she reminded Angie of a schoolmarm, maybe even the Queen of England. It was obvious from their body language that the two women were not going to be best mates. Sally was dressed immaculately in a beautifully cut trouser suit and her hair was coiffed, in anticipation for the photographers who were buzzing about. It didn't help matters when, much to Angie's delight the photographers, anxious to get a picture of the American Ryder Cup captain's new girlfriend, made a bee-line for her in her figure-hugging outfit.

Sally was practically ignored as her worst fears were confirmed. She was going to have her work cut out to make her mark during this Ryder Cup campaign. Inwardly fuming, she excused herself and took refuge in the ladies' toilet.

When she emerged she was glad to see that both delegations were being ushered onto a waiting helicopter. As they waited to board Sally addressed Angie. 'Tell me, my dear, are you planning on coming over with Wayne for the Ryder Cup?'

'Oh yes. Wouldn't miss it for the world! I'm really looking forward to it.'

Sally hoped that her disappointment didn't show. Still, better set up some lines of communication with Angie, put the blonde bimbo in her place, let her know how far she was getting out of her depth. 'In that case, my dear, we must liaise with each other, formulate a calendar of social events for the ladies.'

'Social events? Of course. You mean a few nights on the town?'

Sally gave a tight smile. 'That's not quite what I had in mind. I mean now that you are, er, taking over Marcia Folen's duties, you will be expected to organise some social events for the wives and girlfriends of the team members. We ladies have a lot of time to ourselves when the men are practising, you know...'

'Oh yeah. Wayne did mention something about that. I must say I haven't given it much thought. I've got other things to think about right now – '

'Take my advice, my dear, and start thinking about it. It's a very important role for a Ryder Cup wife - ' Sally broke off, smiled sweetly – 'or even someone in your position, to play. No doubt with your showbusiness background you will come up with some interesting outings for your American ladies.'

You bet your sweet life I will, honey! Angie thought to herself. Aloud she said, 'What kind of social engagements are we talking about?'

'Well, at the Ryder Cup two years ago I organised some sight-seeing tours around the English countryside which I think were very popular. We visited several stately homes, went to a couple of very interesting art exhibitions.' She paused, arched an eyebrow at Angie. 'I take it you're interested in that sort of thing.'

'Yes, sort of.' Angie reckoned it was time to give this upperclass English bitch a shock. 'Sounds like a male strip show is out of the question…' Sally had the grace to smile. She decided not pursue the matter further. On board, she was pleased that Bruce had reserved her a seat away from Wayne Folen and his lady.

The intercom on the 'copter clicked into life. 'May I have your attention please…' It was the pilot speaking. 'On behalf of Tourism Ireland may I wish all on board Cead Mile Failte – that means a hundred thousand welcomes in our language. We should be in Parknasilla in approximately half-an-hour. On the way I'll fly over the Killeen golf course in Killarney to let you see the Ryder Cup layout – '.

There was a pause. 'That's the good news,' the man at the controls continued. 'The bad news is that, right now, there's an anti-Ryder Cup protest by local farmers taking place in Parknasilla – ' Groans all round on the 'copter. 'The farmers have driven a convoy of cars and farm machinery into the area and are endeavouring to block the entrance to the hotel. Fortunately the Parknasilla Palace has a helipad and we'll be landing there some distance from the protest -' Another pause. 'Welcome to Ireland!' the pilot finished dryly.

Angie yawned again, closed her eyes and tried to get as comfortable as possible in the cramped seat space. She was glad now that, in between posing for the photographers, she had gulped down that double martini vodka at Shannon. She felt nice and relaxed. Across the aisle she could hear Sally Cartray's voice raised in annoyance at something. Stately homes and art exhibitions…Angie smiled to herself. She would come up with something much more exciting than that to keep her ladies happy!

She let her thought drift to the more pleasurable delights of meeting Patrick Mannion in the Parknasilla Palace shortly. Her anticipation had been heightened by what Mervyn had told her when he had driven her to the airport earlier.

'Watch your ass with this guy Mannion, Angie. He's a talented director, hot with the money guys in Hollywood – and hot with women. Know what I mean?'

'So what else is new, Mervyn,'

He had filled her in also on the various offers that had come into his office in the wake of America's Ryder Cup captain having ditched his wife for her. 'My telephone has hardly stopped ringing and my fax has gone crazy. The talk shows are queuing up for you.'

'No kidding. Like who?' Angie had asked breathlessly.

'How about Oprah for starters.'

'Oprah wants me on her show?'

'As soon as you come back from this trip. She wanted to get you and Wayne Folen's wife together but Marcia turned her down flat.' Angie could hardly believe what she was hearing. Not so long ago she was unknown; now she was big news. 'Oprah's only the start,' she heard Mervyn say. 'We've got to keep the publicity going.'

'What else have you got lined up, Mervyn?'

'I'm working on a couple of things…' He was silent for a moment. 'How are things between you and Wayne.'

'Don't worry, I'm keeping him interested. Why do you ask?'

'Keep your eyes open for any publicity opportunity. The more outrageous the better.'

'Will do. Fill me in on this guy Patrick Mannion. How did he make it big?'

Mervyn had concentrated on the New York traffic flow before replying. 'He struck it lucky with a small budget movie he made in Ireland last year. Wrote a screenplay about a small-time Irish drugs baron who fights his way up from nowhere and bumps off a lot of people on his way to the top. It was off-beat, violent – got a distribution deal over here and made big bucks at the box-office. It even got

Mannion nominated for a best screenplay Oscar. Now the guy is on a roll and Hollywood is throwing money at him for his next film project.'

'Tell me about it, Mervyn.'

'In this business, Angie, if you hit it big and make millions you repeat the formula. Only this time you get a couple of big names, move the location, hype up the action and spend zillions on publicity. The slobs paying at the box-office will lap it up.

Mervyn had paused again. 'Mannion's next movie – surprise, surprise – is about a group of Irish gangsters in New York and Chicago operating under the umbrella of the IRA. He has these Irish guys take on the Mafia. And guess what, and here's the big sell – the leader of this Irish mob is a woman – a glamorous, ruthless broad who'll bed a guy as easily as she pumps him full of lead. How crazy can you get, for Chrissake! But it's what Hollywood wants right now – '

'How do you know all this Mervyn? Have you seen a script?'

'Mannion faxed me over a synopsis. But that's not all, honey. Listen to this…the IRA broad has the top Mafia guy kidnapped and guess what – she falls in love with him! Wants him big time. How about that? Isn't that something?'

'Mervyn, do you think….' She hardly dared ask.

'Right first time, honey. Mannion's interested in auditioning you for the part!'

'Jeez!' She was silent, letting it sink in. 'But why me, Mervyn, an unknown - '

'Don't you see, honey, you're big news right now, that's why. You're making headlines, Angie baby. And besides, by-passing all the big names and taking a chance with an unknown like yourself generates its own hype. Mannion's no fool; I just hope you can handle him.'

'You leave this guy Patrick Mannion to me. He'll be

putty in my hands.' Mervyn doubted that very much. But he let the remark pass without comment .

Now, while the others on board the helicopter craned their necks to catch an aerial view of the manicured fairways, specially cultivated rough and terrifying expanses of water that promised to make the Killarney Golf and Fishing Club a good Ryder Cup test, Angie kept her eyes closed and contemplated stardom .

'You not interested in the lay-out below honey?' Wayne asked.

Angie opened her eyes, suppressed a yawn. 'I've already seen all the forty shades of green that I want,' she retorted.

Wayne laid his briefcase aside and glanced at her. Angie was some looker, but a pro golfer's companion for life she wasn't. If it were Marcia who was sitting beside him she would be interested in his problems, encouraging him, anxious to give him the much needed back-up for the Ryder Cup tussle that lay ahead. He had to accept that Angie Wilde was an actress, caught up in her own career, rather bored with his. Still, she had her own way of easing his tensions in a way that Marcia wouldn't have dreamed of. Angie knew how to take his mind off golf and that was what he needed right now. Wayne was looking forward to the next few nights in the Parknasilla Palace.

● ● ● ●

Katie was in the kitchen preparing breakfast for the boys when she heard the sound of Ben's jeep crunching the gravel in the yard. A minute later he entered the kitchen. Katie looked up from the stove and nodded a greeting which was not returned. Ben sat down at the table, waiting for her to dish him up some breakfast. She could feel his eyes boring into her back.

After a while he said, 'You went up to Dublin to see Travis yesterday?'

'Yes.'

'How is he?'

Katie hesitated. She didn't want to fill him in on yesterday's details. 'He's a bit depressed.'

'Is he now. I wonder why.' His tone was more truculent than conversational.

'Being in prison, I suppose. It can't be easy being on hunger strike – '

'Didn't you ask him how he was?'

'Of course. We didn't have much time to talk.'

'Why not. You left early enough.'

Katie sensed danger. Why was Ben asking all these questions? Does he suspect something? Was he behind the incident at Jeremy's cottage last night. She turned and faced him. 'If you must know Travis wasn't very talkative. He – he became very aggressive. I – I had to leave.'

Ben rubbed his chin. He was glaring at her. 'So Travis was annoyed. Why was that now, I wonder?'

'You know Travis. He can be very moody sometimes…'

A silence. His eyes never left her.

Katie tried to deflect him from the topic. 'Your breakfast will be ready soon. Pour yourself some tea while you're waiting – ' She was on edge. More than ever she suspected that Ben knew something about herself and Jeremy.

'My breakfast can wait,!' Ben shouted angrily. 'I want some answers from you first.' Turning back and facing the stove again, Katie heard the chair scrape the floor as Ben rose to his feet. 'Tell me now, did you travel to Dublin on your own, or were you with somebody?' His voice was just above a whisper, which made him sound more frightening.

'Why are you asking? I don't know what you're talking about – '

'Why were you all dolled up going off yesterday morning? Was it for Travis – or somebody else, eh?'

Oh God he knows. Somebody must have seen her before she left Killarney yesterday morning, saw her meet Jeremy, told Ben. She turned around again. Ben had come up behind her and was standing close. She eased herself sideways, away from the heat of the stove, out of the danger area.

'Answer me, you fucking whore!', he shouted. He raised his hand as if to strike her. Katie moved away, cowering in terror.

'What if I did meet somebody before I travelled to Dublin? What business is it of yours?'

The fact that she was standing up to him made Ben even more angry. His face reddened. 'It was the Englishman, that painter fella, wasn't it? You bought yourself a new outfit so that you would look good for him, didn't you?'

'Who told you all this?' Katie shouted back. 'I bought that outfit because I need it. I wanted to look good for Travis – ' That last part wasn't true.

'You're telling lies, you bitch! You wanted to show yourself off to the Englishman. Play around with him while Travis is risking his life in jail.' Ben reached out, grabbed her, pulled her to him. Katie could feel his foul breath hot on her face.

'It was late when you got back last night. What kept you? Was he mauling you, screwing you somewhere – in the back seat of his car maybe!'

Katie struggled to get free but he was holding her in a vice-like grip. Their bodies were close together. Suddenly his lips were seeking hers, the bristles of his unshaven face feeling like sandpaper against hers. 'I want you, you bitch. And by Christ I'll have you if Travis can't– '

She made a superhuman effort and pushed him away. Katie moved quickly, putting the table between herself and him. She was panting with fright, her breath coming in short gasps. 'Stay away from me, Ben Gartland. You hear! Stay away from me or I'll tell Travis – '

He laughed and it wasn't a pretty sound. 'You tell Travis what you want. I'll let him know you've been seeing that

Englishman. See if he'll believe you then - ' He made a dash at her but she avoided him. 'You and Travis never got on. Everyone knows that. You hate him 'cos he treats you like the whore that you are – '

'I hate you too. You hear that, Ben. I hate you! You're just like your brother - you're a bully and you're disgusting! And next time I go to see Travis I'm going to tell him I'm leaving him. I've had enough of him and you – and this filthy farm - '

'It's that Englishman, isn't it? He's turning your head – '

He broke off. He could see her looking over his shoulder. Jack and Garrett had come downstairs after hearing the shouting and were standing in the kitchen doorway, staring, fear in their eyes.

Katie realised that she was trembling but fought for control. She put her hand to her hair, straightened her blouse, closing the several buttons that had come undone during the short scuffle.

'Are you alright, Mom?' Jack asked. The two boys edged their way into the room, their eyes flitting from their mother to Ben.

'Yes, I'm fine.' She went to them, put her arms around their shoulders. 'Go upstairs. Your breakfast will be ready soon. I'll call you. Everything is alright.'

'You sure? We'll stay if you want,' Garrett volunteered.

'I know that. But do as I say. Your Uncle Ben and I are having a talk, that's all.'

The two boys hesitated, unsure if they should disobey their mother for her own good. Katie forced a smile and they turned and went upstairs again. She suspected that they would be listening on the landing outside their bedroom.

She turned back to the stove, ignoring Ben, and finished cooking his breakfast. He watched her in sullen silence as she turned the bacon, eggs and sausages out onto a plate, put a pot of tea before him on the table. She was exiting to go upstairs when he growled:

'Wait. I'm not finished with you yet.'

She hesitated. 'Say what you have to say.'

'I'll be watching you and that Englishman – and others will too. And if I hear that you're with him again he'll have more than a broken window to worry about....' He turned to his breakfast, began to stuff the food into his mouth.

Katie bit her lip. She felt like crying, but didn't want to give him the pleasure of seeing her distress. It wasn't the first time Ben had grabbed her like that, but it had frightened her. Now that Travis was in jail Ben was getting more aggressive towards her.

'You have no right to tell me who I can and who I can't see,' she responded with spirit.

Ben paused with a forkful of food halfway to his mouth. 'I have every right. My brother took you into this house when you had nothing. You were nothing more than a skivvy, an orphan nobody wanted, working behind a bar. I had to move out of the family home because of you. Remember if anything happens to Travis you'd be a widow, here on her own. We'd see how bossy you'd be then.' His grin was a half leer.

She turned to go upstairs and he shouted after her, 'You tell that Englishman to keep away. If he doesn't there'll be more trouble. He's already got one warning...- '

Despite Ben's warning Katie knew she would have to drive over to Jeremy's place, alert him to the danger he was in. It would be risky but she must do it. He was alone, a stranger in the area, and vulnerable. If she was honest she would have to admit that she could telephone him, but she really wanted to see him again, feel wanted. Ben would be involved all day in the protest at Parknasilla; it had been on the early morning news and by all accounts there was going to be a huge turnout of farmers.

Katie went into her bedroom, sat on the bed, still

shaking from her ordeal. After a few minutes she heard the telephone ringing down below and Ben answering it. She tiptoed out onto the landing, listened, heard him telling whoever was on the phone that he would be leaving immediately and would be in Parknasilla ready to lead the protest at noon. Good! That would mean Ben would be away until at least late afternoon.

Katie's heart leapt. It would give her plenty of time to pay a visit to Jeremy Walker and be back in plenty of time. Suddenly the sun was shining again.

• • • •

In Loughduff Garda Station Sergeant Dan Gilhooly was also just finishing a telephone conversation. His two young assistants, Gardai Jerry Carney and Pauly Glynn, could tell by the expression on his face that something serious was in the pipeline.

They both had an idea what the telephone conversation was about; the demonstration by local farmers from the Killarney area had been on all the news bulletins since late last night. The word was that the Minister for Tourism was very concerned that the Gardai take control of the situation. He had gone on television to appeal to the farmers to call off their protest, stating that any demo against such a prestigious international sporting event like the Ryder Cup would do untold damage to the country's booming tourist industry. Ben Gartland and his cohorts had ignored the Minister's request and a crisis situation was building up.

'Well lads, you're going to have your work cut out for you today,' Sergeant Gilhooly paused, let his words sink in. 'You've heard most of that, I expect; the Chief Superintendent has ordered us over to Parknasilla to join our colleagues at that protest by the farmers. He's expecting big trouble there.'

The two young Gardai exchanged glances. Garda

Glynn spoke up first. 'How many of of us will be on duty?' he asked. Pauly was suffering from a hangover after a late drinking session in the Loughduff Inn last night and was not looking forward to anything vigorous.

'The Super has called in reinforcements from all the big stations in the area, Sneem Killorglin, Kenmare and others. He's also been in touch with his colleague in Cork requesting men be sent in from Millstreet and Macroom. All leave has been cancelled.'

'What sort of trouble are we expecting, Sergeant?', Garda Carney asked.

'Hard to say. Hopefully it will be a peaceful demo, but with the likes of Ben Gartland behind it I won't be surprised if some violence breaks out. You'll be issued with protective clothing, riot gear in other words' The sergeant looked suitably solemn.

'It could get ugly then?'

'I expect so. Like the protest in Killarney a few years ago when a delegation from the European Union was hemmed into one of the hotels by angry farmers. The Government doesn't want a repeat of that sort of thing – ' The sergeant turned to Pauly Glynn. 'I believe you were in the Loughduff Inn last night – as usual. Talking to Ben Gartland. Did he say anything about today's protest?'

Pauly swore under his breath. That Gilhooly, he doesn't miss a thing. If someone turns sideways in Loughduff Gilhooly knows about it. He had cronies everywhere. 'Ben was bragging that there will be a big turn out today. Everybody heard him.'

'Hmmm....' The Sergeant studied himself in the miniscule wall mirror and adjusted his cap. It wasn't often that the world media arrived in his neck of the woods and he aimed to be ready for them.

'Come on lads. Better be on our way. And re-member – ' he turned to them, his face stern – 'be careful how you re-act if any violence breaks out. There'll be plenty of tv cameras there. Don't be caught on camera throwing your weight around!'

• • • •

As the helicopter swooped in over the spacious grounds of the Parknasilla Palace Hotel those on board had a bird's eye view of the protest demonstration by the farmers. On both sides of the main road outside of the hotel, behind barriers manned by uniformed Gardai and well away from the main entrance, long columns of cars and farm vehicles were lined up. So far the protest had been noisy but peaceful.

From the air the 'copter passengers had a good view of the hotel's private lake and nine-hole golf course laid out behind the imposing edifice. Out front the well-manicured lawns were bisected by a tarmacadam driveway leading from the roadway to the hotel entrance. On the steps of the hotel, groups of guests and some staff members were observing the action on the roadway off in the distance.

'Looks like there's a reception committee waiting for us,' Bruce Cartray was heard remarking to his wife.

'What did you expect, darling,' Sally replied archly. 'After all this is Ireland of the Welcomes!' She considered it a witty riposte and was disappointed when nobody laughed.

Seated together, Cord McCallum and his European Ryder Cup counterpart Major David Mackenzie looked down on the scene, distaste etched across their faces. It was not the type of reception that they wished to see associated with their great sporting event. This type of protest had never happened at any previous Ryder Cup. Rivalry among the two teams and their partisan spectators, yes, but golf's premier team event had always been made welcome wherever it was played. The two representatives from Tourism Ireland were also looking unhappy.

The man from the Parknasilla Palace who had met

them at the airport was talking frantically into a radio telephone. He ended the short conversation and shouted to make his voice heard above the road of the whirring 'copter blades:

'May I have your attention please. I've been speaking to our manager Norman Spencer and he has asked me to apologise for this disturbance which is entirely out of our hands. The local police superintendent is negotiating with the leader of the protesting farmers and we expect the demonstration to be over soon.'

The hotel representative had not told the passengers the full story. In fact the situation down below was deteriorating. The farmers' leader was bullish and adamant that his men were going to drive their vehicles across the manicured lawns fronting the Parknasilla Palace. The Garda Superintendent was under orders to prevent this happening. Any moment now the bullish farmers' leader was expected to urge the convoys forward....

Angie Wilde was not unduly worried by the situation. Even from this height she could make out men with tv cameras on their shoulders. Some were pointing them at the descending helicopter. All this – and a multi-talented young Irish film director waiting down there to offer her a part in his next blockbuster film! Angie checked her make-up. Could a girl ask for more!

The 'copter hovered over the hotel helipad, steadied, then landed with scarcely a jolt. The passengers' exit from the craft was well covered by the mass of photographers, Angie's exit in particular receiving the full treatment. A couple of reporters shouted questions at her but she couldn't hear what they were saying. She was ushered with the others towards the hotel entrance by staff. A distinguished looking Norman Spencer in pin-striped trousers, dark jacket, starched shirt and wearing gold cuff-links waited to greet them.

But just as the manager began his well-rehearsed

welcoming speech all hell broke loose from the road. The angry farmers had been waiting for this moment and began hooting vehicle horns, waving banners and shouting.

The irate farmers had come to Parknasilla well prepared. Ben Gartland, fired up by their success so far, activated his walkie-talkie radio and got in touch with his colleague in charge of the other convoy several hundred yards away.

'Get ready to rumble!', Ben shouted into the instrument, using a phrase he had heard on television. 'Let's go!'.

The relatively small force of policemen behind the barriers didn't stand a chance. Large groups of burly farmers surged forward, pushing the barriers and the uniformed men behind them aside. At the same time engines roared into life and the two convoys of tractors, combine harvesters and milk trucks lumbered forward, with farmers in ordinary cars bringing up the rear. TV cameramen pointed their cameras to record the action.

Ben Gartland jumped onto the steel step of the lead milk truck and waved everyone forward. He turned to the whirring cameras and gave a triumphant wave. A short while earlier he had been interviewed by reporters from the international media about his Ryder Cup protest; now he was ready to give the eager cameramen some action that would be shown around the world!

On the hotel steps, in the early September afternoon sunshine, guests watched fascinated as the two lines of farm vehicles converged along opposite sides of the main road, met, and turned into the hotel entrance. Halfway along the tarmacadam they broke ranks and fanned out across the manicured lawns of the hotel.

On the steps of the hotel Norman Spencer watched in horror as the noisy cavalcade trundled towards him, leaving scars across the well-kept lawns. He had already endured the trauma a week ago of having had his establishment commandeered by the Tourism Ireland authorities at the behest of the Government. Now his beloved hotel was being besieged by angry farmers – and the Gardai seemed powerless to prevent it!

Norman shuddered, horrified at the type of publicity his prestigious establishment would receive from this shameful episode. He tried not to think about it.

He turned to the assembled guests. 'Inside everybody quickly. We are serving free drinks to everybody at the bar.' He waved his arms about, a smile pasted on his face. 'The Gardai will deal with the situation.' Damn! - the photographers and tv cameramen were having a field day!

Norman hurried to the rear of the hotel, took personal charge of the new arrivals, guiding the Ryder Cup party of Europeans and Americans towards the reservation desk. The quicker he got them to their rooms the better.

'Not quite the welcome we expected, Mr – er – Spencer.' The lady in the smart trouser suit said in an upper crust English accent. 'We've had an exhausting journey and I was hoping for a rest before lunch.'

'I do apologise, Madam – er – '

'My name is Sally Cartray. My husband Bruce is the captain of the European team. It's disgraceful that this noisy protest is being allowed to take place.'

'I agree with you entirely, Mrs. Cartray,' Norman replied diplomatically. 'My humble apologies to yourself, your husband and to all of the Ryder Cup party.' He smiled at the tall gentleman by her side who was looking rather embarrassed at his wife's sharp outburst. Norman's gaze swept the assembled group. 'Please follow me to reception and we'll have your rooms sorted out quickly.'

As the group moved to follow Norman Spencer, Angie grabbed Wayne's arm. 'Do me a favour, honey. Take care of my luggage and sort out our room number. I've got some business to attend - '

Wayne looked past her to where a group of

photographers had gathered, cameras at the ready. A couple of them approached and took pictures of himself and a smiling Angie. Damn! This wasn't what he wanted right now. He forced a smile…might as well make the best of the situation.

'Angie,' he said through gritted teeth as the cameras clicked away. 'For Chrissake be careful how you handle these reporters – '. He broke off as Cord McCallum and his two Ryder Cup associates approached.

'We have some important business to discuss Wayne. Could I have a quick word with you – if you're not otherwise engaged, that is' Cord McCallum said brusquely.

'Sure Mr. McCallum, I'll be right with you, – ' Wayne was glad to get away.

'Hey, Miss Wilde, how about you coming outside for some shots,' a cameraman shouted above the din of car horns from the farmers' demo out front. 'We'd like to get some of you on the back veranda with the lake in the background…'

'Whatever you say, boys…' Angie strolled across the hotel foyer, conscious that she was the focus of everyone's attention. Turning from the reception desk, Sally Cartray's eyes narrowed at the sight of her rival leading the group of eager photographers outside. The blonde bimbo was grabbing all the attention, with her stunning figure and the fact that she had caught the eye of America's captain. Sally sensed she had a battle on her hands to maintain her high profile among the Ryder Cup wives.

Half an hour later, still on a high after a very productive session with the media, Angie went to the bar and ordered a double vodka martini. She was happy; she reckoned her arrival in the hotel had created as much excitement among the media as had the protest outside. She sat alone, sipping her drink and watching the noisy departure of the convoy of farm vehicles from the hotel entrance, their drivers satisfied that their protest had made a big impact on the international media present. Last to depart down the tarmacadamed driveway was a big milk truck with a man standing on the steel step, shouting and waving a banner at the Gardai in a last gesture of defiance.

Angie felt a tap on her shoulder, Turning, she found herself staring straight into the eyes of a redheaded female about her own age. Beside the redhead was a short, bearded man staring up at her.

'Excuse me, are you Angie Wilde? I've been waiting for you to show up - ', she heard him say. She noticed that his shoulders were very wide and he had a mass of dark curls. He had dark, piercing eyes which at present were taking in her figure as she sat on the bar stool.

'Yes, I'm Angie Wilde.' She paused, taken aback. 'You – you're Patrick Mannion?' She tried not to sound too surprised.

'That's right. Pleased to meet you.' He extended his hand.

Angie shook it, felt his strength. Jeez, a midget! This guy Mannion was certainly no Pierce Brosnan! Trust Mervyn to tie her into something like this!

'Let's sit down at a table. We have to talk – and I need a drink,' Angie heard the little guy say.

'That's fine by me.' She drained the last of hers, rose from the stool. His head barely

reached to her shoulder. Lucky he hadn't suggested sitting at the bar - he'd have had a hard time make it onto a high stool! The redhead was already leading the way towards a table in the corner of the lounge.

'This is Naomi, my secretary.' Patrick Mannion said, pulling out a chair for himself and omitting to do the same for Angie. 'You two get acquainted while I visit the gents.' She watched him scurry across the foyer, noting again the width of the little Irishman's shoulders.

She joined Naomi at the table. The redheaded girl was dressed in a loose-fitting, ankle length green dress and matching cardigan which was doing its best to hide her shapely, well-proportioned figure. Secretary, eh? Naomi looked like someone who had walked straight off a film set.

Naomi ordered the drinks, which included a large Irish whiskey on the rocks for her boss. 'You'll like working with Patrick,' she volunteered. 'He's talented – and unusual.'

You can say that again! Angie thought. Aloud she said, 'How do you know I've got the part. He hasn't even auditioned me.'

'He will,' Naomi smiled, 'I probably shouldn't be telling you this but it's only a formality. From the first time he saw you on television he was anxious to have you in his film.'

Angie was puzzled. 'How does he know I can act? Has he seen anything I've done?' She doubted that he had seen any of her work; Hell, she hadn't done much up to now!

'Instinct,' Naomi said, a smile playing about her lips. 'Patrick is one of those directors who works by instinct. He has to – he hasn't been in the film business long enough to have worked with any of the big names. He's done only two low budget films, both of them shot in Ireland, but already he's been hailed in Hollywood as a genius.' Naomi sipped her drink. 'You're very lucky that he saw you on television at that golf club with Wayne Folen – '

'Yeah, wasn't I. I suppose you could say Patrick Mannion and I have something in common – we both got a lucky break.'

'Tell me, Angie, what sort of films have you done? I've tried to find something you were in but so far I'm afraid I haven't been at all successful.' Angie couldn't quite figure out whether Naomi was being sarcastic or genuinely curious.

'Oh – ' Angie tried to sound casual, 'I haven't done anything major. Like your friend Patrick I've been involved in a couple of low budget flicks. Mine didn't get me anywhere – '

'Art house films, like?' Naomi arched an eyebrow.

'Well, yes, I suppose you could call them that.' Naomi doesn't want to call them for what they really were, Angie reckoned. But she knows, no doubt about that. Okay, so what if they were porn; every actress, big-time or not, was doing nudity nowadays. It was no big deal. Still, they weren't the type of movies she wanted to be reminded of right now.

'I think you and Patrick will hit it off together,' Naomi opined.

'Why do you say that?'

'Because you want to make it big and he can help you achieve that. You both know what you want and are prepared to work for it.'

'Is he married?

Naomi waited until the waiter had brought the drinks and departed. 'If he is he hasn't told me anything about it. But let me warn you he likes women, and a lot of women seem to find a little guy like him irresistible. Maybe they're tired of screwing all those handsome hunks – '

'How did he get into the business?' Angie asked.

Again Naomi smiled. 'You won't believe it - pure Hollywood. He was born into an Irish itinerant family in England – '

'What's kind of family is that?' Angie looked puzzled.

'Gypsies. Mother, father and eight kids all lived in one caravan – what you Americans call a camper. They travelled around England scraping a living. When Patrick was in his mid-teens they were camped in a village where a film was being shot on location. The way Patrick tells it he met a woman, much older than him, the director's assistant. They got chatting over a few drinks and spent a couple of nights together – '

Naomi paused. 'I told you how women fancy him. And he knows how to keep them coming back for more – ' Angie wondered if Naomi was speaking from experience or quoting from one her publicity handouts. 'Anyway this lady got him a walk-on part in the film and he was hooked on the whole set up. He couldn't believe he was actually getting paid for what he was doing! She got him work on her boss's next film – '

'So he got himself paid and laid – ' Angie cut in. She knew the feeling.

Naomi didn't smile. 'That was ten years ago. He's worked his way up the ladder. It wasn't easy, not with his background, although Patrick did have other things in his favour.

'Like what?'

'You'll probably find out for yourself what I mean.'

'Whatever happened to his family?'

'As far as I know he hasn't been in touch since.' A shrug of the shoulders. 'No need to, I suppose. Now that he's hit the big-time he has all the booze, the money – and women he wants. Like a lot of little guys he has a very active libido.'

Angie toyed with her drink. It sounded like Naomi saw it as part of her job to give every leading lady about to work with Patrick Mannion a warning like this. 'About the film. I'd like to see a script?'

Naomi's mood changed. 'Come off it, Angie baby. When did you last get lucky enough to be given script approval?' She looked straight at Angie. 'Maybe you've won an Oscar or a Tony I don't know about?'

Angie was about to reply when she saw the object of their conversation approached across the lounge, walking quickly on his short legs, his long curly hair flopping about. Despite herself Angie had to admit that there was an air of dynamism about him. He looked like a guy who could make things happen. Mannion sat down, knocked back half of his double whiskey in one gulp. 'Has Naomi been filling you in on how I work?' he asked.

'Yeah. Sort of.'

'The finance for Roll Of The Dice is all in place and I want to get moving as soon as possible, right?' He didn't have the thick Irish accent Angie had expected. 'Can you do a Northern Ireland accent? I'd like to hear you read the part of Maria.'

'I'll have a good shot at it.' Bet your life she would make a good shot at it. Angie would have a go at speaking Swahili if it meant her getting the role.

'Good, good. Not to worry. We'll get you a voice coach and Maria is Irish-American anyway.' He stopped, downed the rest of his drink. Naomi immediately signalled for another. 'Want to hear the storyline? I wrote it myself' When Angie nodded he went on: 'Maria is a hard-line IRA terrorist who quits Belfast for New York with some of her henchmen. She has a run-in with the Mafia when she tries to move in on their territory. She kidnaps the Mafia boss's son, but instead of killing the guy she falls madly in love with him! Like it?' His dark eyes were dancing wildly, awaiting her reply.

'Sounds interesting,' Angie replied coolly.

'Interesting? – ' Patrick Mannion exploded, It's a lot more than that – it's fucking brilliant!. It's got everything Hollywood wants… violence, sex, car chases, shoot-outs – everything! And you'll be showing off your body. I mean nudity. Got anything against that?'

The little guy had a big voice. Heads were turning at tables within earshot. Angie thought of the crummy porn flicks she had done, thanked her lucky stars they had disappeared without trace. Roll Of The Dice would be different. But hell, she had better let this little guy see she wasn't a pushover.

'I've nothing against nudity if it's done in good taste – '

'Nice to hear that from an unknown actress. Very original,' Naomi smiled sweetly.

'When can you do the reading?', Mannion asked. Before she could reply he asked, 'How about tonight? In my room. Nine a.m.' He grinned, as though reading her thoughts. 'Don't worry, Naomi will be there.'

'Fine by me.' Angie hoped that Wayne would be tied up with Ryder Cup business. Tough luck on him if he wasn't.

'How are you fixed tomorrow.' Naomi coughed slightly. Angie wondered if it had any special significance.

'What have you got in mind?'

'We'll have to talk. Discuss Maria.'

That all, she wondered? The little guy's eyes were unashamedly sizing her up. He was moving fast alright, knew she was desperate for the role. 'I'm available for whatever you have in mind.' Two could play at this game.

'We'll sort a few things out between us and I'll get in touch with your agent later. We can take a boat out on the lake, talk about the film in private…'

Like hell we will, Angie thought to herself. Aloud she said. 'I'm looking forward to it. I'll find something nautical to wear.' At least it was a variation from the casting couch. 'I suppose you'll be bringing Naomi along to take notes?', Angie asked innocently.

'Naomi will have other things to do tomorrow, won't you, my sweet?' The little Irishman drained his second drink. 'Here, girl, how about getting me a refill from the bar –' .

Naomi rose obediently. He waited until his assistant was out of earshot then went on quickly: 'I like you, Angie. You've got looks and talent. The money men behind Roll Of The Dice are happy to have you on board.' It was a lie; the two of the biggest backers behind the movie had objected to an unknown actress being cast in such a demanding role. He had convinced them that with her sudden fame as girlfriend of the U.S. Ryder Cup captain she would generate enough publicity to make the movie a winner at the box-office.

'Does this mean I've definitely got the lead in Roll Of The Dice?'

He put his head back, roared with laughter. 'I'll tell you after our trip on the lake tomorrow.'

'Good. Now if you'll excuse me, Mr. Mannion, I'm

going to my room to rest – ' She rose to her feet, straightened her skirt.

He remained seated. 'Forget the Mr. Mannion bit. Call me Patrick.'

'Okay, Patrick. See you tonight.' She could feel his eyes devouring her as she exited the lounge.

Upstairs in the room Angie reached into her handbag, took out her mobile phone. Wayne's suitcase was on the bed, some of his clothes unpacked. She looked at her watch, checked the time difference to New York. Hopefully she would catch Mervyn before he left for lunch. Out on the balcony she punched in the numbers, admired the September sun dancing on the lake.

'Mervyn, it's me – '

'Angie baby! How are you?' She would imagine him swivelling in his beat up leather chair.

'I'm fine, Mervyn.'

'How is Mr. Mannion? Have you two met up.'

'We're both fine. You could have warned me that he looks like Danny de Vito.'

She heard him laugh. 'Sorry, baby. I didn't want to scare you off'. He didn't sound too contrite. 'How are you two getting on?'

She filled him in on the details. 'He has invited me out boating on the lake tomorrow. Just the two of us. So what do I do if he comes over all amorous?'

'Simple, baby. Just lie back and think of Hollywood!' Mervyn's laugh floated all the way across the Atlantic.

• • • •

Nell Flavin was cleaning her upstairs bedroom windows when she noticed the car turning in off the main road, easing its way along the narrow laneway then turning in through the gateway into Jeremy Walker's drive. She recognised the car; it belonged to her friend Katie Gartland.

Nell stepped back, watched from behind the curtains as Katie alighted. Jeremy had come around from the back of the cottage and was observing her. Nell saw Jeremy walk to Katie, give her a peck on the cheek. She saw her friend smile shyly. God! she had never seen Katie Gartland look so happy - or so nicely dressed for that matter.

Nell glanced at her watch. It showed 9.45am. 'Good on you, Katie girl,' she mused aloud, 'I only wish I had reason to call on a handsome man so early in the morning – and be greeted like that into the bargain!'

Katie had never been to the cottage before, even though it was within a couple of miles of her own home. Travis had never encouraged her to get too friendly with the neighbours; she knew the cottage was originally owned by an elderly childless couple who had decided to sell up and spend their last years in the luxury of a modern convalescent home on the coast. The cottage had lain vacant for months before Jeremy had moved in.

As she drove in through the gateway she had noticed the narrow gardens on either side were overgrown, although there were signs that Jeremy was endeavouring to bring some order after the neglect of the previous owners. She also noticed the broken window, the jagged shards of glass still in place, and a pile of burnt out rubbish on the grass.

Katie had been pleased at Jeremy's welcoming peck on the cheek, thrilled by his closeness of his greeting. He made it seem so natural, but she wasn't used to such effusiveness. Besides, Nell's place overlooked Jeremy's and she didn't miss much! Jeremy was dressed casually in check shirt, cuffs turned back above his wrists, a pair of faded jeans and dark tan leather boots.

'Hi. Nice to see you, Katie.' He nodded towards the pile of rubbish. 'I'm doing some cleaning up after last night...'

'Jeremy, I had to talk to you. I think I know who was responsible for this – '.

'You do?' He looked serious. 'Ben?'

'Yes. I'm sure of it. Something happened this morning…'

For the first time he noticed her distraught look. He gestured. 'Come inside, have some coffee.'

He followed her in. The room wasn't very big; a living-room with a big open fireplace with a baskets of logs and turf at each side. The rough wooden table and the four chairs had been left by the previous owners as had the large square of well-worn carpet that covered most of the polished wooden floor. There was a small kitchen immediately off and a stairs at the other side of the room leading to the bedrooms.

Paintings of various shapes and sizes, colourful landscapes, portraits, including several female nudes, were lined up against the living-room walls. She presumed they were Jeremy's. At least two of the nude portraits, Katie noted, were of a stunningly beautiful girl, painted outdoors and with shafts of sunlight flickering through trees and playing on her sculpted body, her breasts obscured by a mass of golden hair. One of Jeremy's models? Katie speculated. Or one of his lovers….

He noticed her roving eye. 'I suppose you're wondering who she was….Someone I met in Norfolk. French actually. I think she went back there.'

'She's lovely.'

'Yes. Now let's have that coffee…' He didn't seem anxious to pursue the topic. He disappeared into the kitchen. 'Now tell me why you're so sure it was Ben Gartland that vandalised the cottage last night.'

She told him about Ben's outburst at breakfast this morning. 'Someone must have seen us together, probably before we left Killarney, and told Ben. He was mad with rage. He's dangerous when he's like that – '

Jeremy exited from the kitchen with two steaming mugs of coffee. They sat down at the table. 'But what makes you think he came here and vandalised the cottage?'

'He hinted that you had already got one warning. And that next time it would be more serious....' Katie paused. 'I'm worried about you, Jeremy. You'll have to tell Sergeant Gilhooly. Have you reported it yet?'

He shook his head. 'No. But I will. I'm worried for you, Katie. Are you safe, alone with Ben in that house? You'll have to talk to Sergeant Gilhooly too, tell him that Ben has threatened you – '

Now it was her turn to show dissent. 'I can't do that. It would only make things worse. Don't worry, Ben won't dare touch me, not while Travis is still around. We'll both have to be careful, Jeremy. You especially. You're a stranger here, an outsider. This protest involves land – and things have happened to outsiders before...'

'Don't worry. I can look after myself.' His face brightened. 'Now let's forget about Travis and Ben. You want to be an artist, don't you? Come on and I'll show you some of my work...' He was earnest now, his tone inviting.

They strolled around the living-room, gazing at the various portraits, Jeremy filling Katie in on their origin, his technique, what he was trying to achieve with each one. She found it all fascinating. She remembered Sister Rita in the convent saying some of the things that Jeremy was explaining now and she felt an urge to try her hand at being an artist again.

When she expressed her wish to Jeremy he didn't burst out laughing and brush her hopes aside as she knew Travis would have done. She had never mentioned her yearning to paint to her husband; it would have been a waste of time. He would never have countenanced her doing anything artistic; Travis would have told told her there were more important things to do on the farm than sit in a field all day painting scenes of trees or rivers.

'Of course I'll help you, Katie. When would you like to start?'

'Right away. Now. Today!'

He laughed. 'You don't believe in wasting time, do you my sweet?..' His voice trailed off. His eyes were fixed steadily on hers. The silence in the cottage was awesome, broken by a bird chirping in the tree outside. 'You didn't really come over to tell me who broke my window, did you, Katie?'

They had been standing close together but he moved even closer. 'No, not really,' she replied softly. 'But I am worried about you, Jeremy.'

She watched in silence as he very deliberately put down his coffee cup, took hers from he hand and put it beside his on the table. 'We both know what really brought you over here, Katie. I want you'. His voice was a whisper.

'I want you too, Jeremy,' she heard herself answering in like tone.

He raised his hand, stroked her face, then he put his arm around her waist, drew her gently to him, and kissed her. Katie didn't resist. It started as a gentle kiss and became more intense as desire took hold. She closed her eyes and surrendered to the delicious sensation taking hold of her very being. She slid her arms up and around Jeremy's neck, surprised herself by audaciously arching her body into the curve of his. She was enjoying a level of desire which she had never thought existed. Jeremy's hands moved slowly down her back, pressing her body to his, sending delicious sensations in their wake.

Suddenly he bent down, swept her into his arms. Katie shrieked with laughter and delight as he strode across the kitchen and carried her upstairs. She knew she should protest, a married woman with two teenage sons allowing herself to be treated in this manner. She knew she should struggle, shout stop! , but what prevented her from doing so was the prospect of what lay beyond the bedroom door; sex with Jeremy would not be a sordid coupling of a man demanding his marital rights – and taking them with scant respect for his partner. She could not remember a time when Travis had not performed the sex act in a peremptory manner; accompanied with grunts and impatient movements, falling noisily asleep immediately afterwards, oblivious of her anguished tears. And Travis certainly did not give off the delicious scent of aftershave which she could detect right now!

Jeremy reached the top of the stairs, eased the bedroom door open with his foot. Katie opened her eyes. She saw the old-fashioned bed, looking rather incongruous under a green and white coloured duvet. It reminded her fleetingly of the scene from the film 'The Quiet Man', handsome John Wayne carrying a redhaired Maureen O'Hara into the marital bed in a room something like this. The nuns had brought all the girls in the orphanage to a showing of the famous Irish film in Killarney as a special treat and had been mortified during the scene. The girls had all giggled….

Apart from the bed the low-ceilinged room was sparsely furnished; a wooden wardrobe, a dressing-table with a mirror, the centre of the floor covered by a circular carpet.

Jeremy crossed the room, laid her gently on the bed. She released her arms from his neck and awaited his kiss. It was as hot and as passionate as she had hoped it would be. She was delighting in the touch of his tongue on her lips and she trembled when she felt his hand searching for the zip on at the back of her dress. The sensation of the zip sliding downwards made her tremble. Then his hand was inside, fondling, caressing, sending her into paroxysms of delight.

Just when she thought her whole body would explode

he stopped. Then he began to undress her, ever so slowly…

Two hours later Nell Flavin, having already rubbed her bedroom windows spotlessly clean, decided nevertheless to go upstairs and check them once again. She had already made several forays into the bedroom during the morning, glancing out to check if Katie's car was still parked outside Jeremy Walker's house. She did the same this time also. Yes, it was still there.

'Well, I never,' she muttered to herself. She spent so much time alone while Tom worked on the farm, that she was used to talking to herself. Like that other bored housewife of the screen, the fictional Shirley Valentine. Nell had really enjoyed that film.

She was turning away from the window, about to go downstairs again to tackle another household chore, when she saw the door of Jeremy Walker's cottage open and Katie came out. Katie paused on the doorstep, turned and called out. She was looking happier than Nell had ever seen her before. Then Jeremy Walker appeared, carrying an artist's easel and a large folder. Nell watched as Katie opened the boot of her car and Jeremy put the easel and folder inside. He entered the cottage again, reappeared almost immediately with some artist's brushes and what looked like a palette in his hands. These he also deposited into the car boot. He and Katie stood chatting for a few moments.

'Well, I never – '! Nell repeated herself. 'Looks like Jeremy is going to give her a few painting lessons.' She wondered what Travis Gartland will say to that!

Nell watched wide-eyed as Jeremy stepped close to Katie and kissed her. She saw Katie respond. Nell caught her breadth. It didn't take much imagination to guess what had gone on between those two in the cottage, their body language said it all. She saw Katie get into her car, waving to Jeremy before driving off down the laneway and out onto the main road.

Nell sat down on the bed, stared unseeing at the wall. She felt a bit guilty, spying on her friend like that. It wasn't really spying, she consoled herself. Just curiosity. One thing for sure – her next visit to Katie Gartland's house for morning coffee would be very interesting indeed!

CHAPTER SIX

Wayne Folen woke up in a foul mood as the memory of last night's events came crowding in. The long, drawn-out and acrimonious discussions in a private room on top floor of the Parknasilla Palace Hotel, between the American and European officials over Ryder Cup protocol and procedures, had taken its toll. When he did finally retire not even the sight of Angie sashaying in and out of the bathroom in a short towelly robe could lift his spirits.

Damn that guy Bruce Cartray and his snob of a wife. The English Ryder Cup captain was being awkward, endeavouring to swing the advantage towards his European team. Among Cartray's many demands was that the national anthem of every European Ryder Cup member on the team be played at the opening ceremony. Wayne had objected; his guys would hear the Stars and Stripes played only once. He had been overruled and lost the argument.

Then there was the matter of the captains' wives and the roles they would play in the proceedings. Europe's Ryder Cup chairman Major David Mackenzie – Wayne suspected at the behest of Bruce Cartray – suggested that wives only and long term partners of the players be allowed to attend official Ryder Cup dinners, also other social functions, and press conferences.

'Over the years the wives of the respective captains have played important roles in the lead up to the actual Ryder Cup contest itself, without the ladies imposing themselves in any way or benefitting publicity-wise from the event,' the Major had said. 'Myself and my captain fear, however, that there is a danger this year the same sense of good taste and decorum may not prevail.'

Wayne had seen this as an obvious slight on Angie. When Cord McCallum and his U.S. Ryder Cup committee members had appeared to be going along with Major Mackenzie's suggestion, Wayne had thumped the table and demanded that the 'wives and long term partners only' suggestion be withdrawn.

'I don't know who instigated this idea – ' he had thundered, glaring at Bruce Cartwright, leaving everyone present in no doubt that he knew who the instigator was, 'but I want to make clear that if it's proceeded with, even at this late stage, I will resign as U.S. captain!'

Only after some more heated discussion and a withdrawal of Major Mackenzie's suggestion was peace restored, although further arguments arose over what Wayne considered to be niggling matters brought up by the European delegation. When the meeting had finally ended and Wayne had enjoyed a drink alone at the bar before retiring to bed exhausted.

Now as he watched Angie in the towelling robe doing things in front of the mirror he asked: 'How did your session with that guy Mannion go last night, honey?'

'Pretty good. After I'd read the part he insisted on going into a heavy discussion about Maria, the character I'm playing.'

'Sounds like you got the part. You're on your way - ' Wayne decided not to say anything to her about last night's discussion on the roles of the Ryder Cup wives. No sense in hurting her feelings.

'It's not signed and sealed yet. But I'm working on it.' What an understatement that was, Angie thought. 'I'm meeting him again today. It could be another, er, heavy session.' And how!

She was glad when Wayne said that he was facing a hectic day also. 'Myself and the guys are playing a practice round over the course in Killarney today. The team is flying into Shannon this morning and they'll be helicoptered to the course.' Wayne sighed. 'Doesn't look like we'll be seeing much of each other on this trip – '

'What about later? What say we have dinner - and an early night...' Angie smiled at her reflection in the bedroom mirror. She had come to Ireland to work on Patrick Mannion and get that lead role in his film, not to traipse around a golf course after Wayne Folen and his teammates, or listen to him and a bunch of old guys like Cord McCallum wrangle about the protocol surrounding the Ryder Cup. Last night she had been pleasantly surprised at how business-like and professional the little Irish director had been during the reading in his room, although she had sensed a chemistry between them too. Patrick Mannion had big plans for her; Angie was sure of that – and they included more than a part in his upcoming film. She would have to play him along slowly and not rush things.

While he watched Angie at the mirror, Wayne ran over in his mind the sequence of last night's events. He had long been convinced that in recent Ryder Cup clashes the U.S. had lost too many verbal battles around the negotiating table – before the action had begun on the golf course. When he had been made captain he had determined that he would take a hard line with the Europeans. It had been some time now since the U.S. team had brought the Ryder Cup back in triumph across the Atlantic. He was determined to achieve that and give the American people something to cheer about!

He had to admit that, compared to himself, Bruce Cartray was a smooth operator and an experienced Ryder Cup captain. His wife Sally too exuded style, even if her snooty English manner left a lot to be desired. She was full of her own importance, accustomed to being obeyed, polished at giving interviews and getting her picture in the newspapers as the wife of the captain of the European team. No doubt coming up against Angie had been a bit of a shock; Wayne was certain it was Sally who had urged her husband to push the 'wives and long –time partners only' at Ryder Cup functions through.

Wayne watched fascinated as Angie raised her leg and put her foot on the arm of a sofa preparatory to painting her toenails. It reminded him of what he had missed by being so exhausted last night. He would make sure it wouldn't happen again tonight!

'Where are you seeing that guy Mannion today, honey?' Wayne asked.

'I'm not too sure yet,' Angie replied evasively. Why was Wayne so curious? Did he suspect there was something going on between herself and Patrick Mannion? She didn't want to tell him the next audition would take place in a boat on the lake. Wayne had enough problems already!

Haggling over protocol with the asshole English captain went out of Wayne's mind as he observed Angie. She had one foot propped up on the stool; her robe had slid sideways, exposing enough leg to suggest that she was wearing nothing underneath. Propped up in bed with his hands folded behind his head, Wayne groaned inwardly. Dammit, he had brought her over to Ireland with the express purpose of mixing business with passion; he sure wasn't having much success at either level!

The bedside telephone rang. Wayne picked up the receiver, his eyes still on Angie. He groaned inwardly when he recognised Cord McCallum's voice.

'Wayne, you got the television news on in your room? Or have you read the morning newspapers yet?'

'No to both questions, Cord. I've just woken up – ' Trouble, big trouble. He could tell from the tone of McCallum's voice. 'What's the problem?'

'It's all over the papers – '

'What is?'

'Your verbal bust-up with Bruce Cartray last night. You thumping the table in anger….it's all there.' McCallum was annoyed. And rightly so. 'There's a picture of you leaving the meeting. The expression on your face says it all.'

Wayne swore outright. So what if he looked angry leaving the meeting. 'How the hell did they get the details? The media were excluded'

'You sure you didn't say anything to anyone about what went on?'

'Of course not. Someone did, though.'

'Yes, and I have my suspicions. That woman, Cartwright's wife. Like that young lady you're with she'll do anything for publicity…'

Wayne wasn't going to let that one pass. 'Aren't you being a little unreasonable, Cord?'. McCallum seemed to hate all women. 'Far be it for me to defend that snobby lady, but Sally Cartwright wasn't even at the meeting – '

'Maybe not – but her husband is under her thumb and my bet is that she insists on knowing everything that goes on at. She saw an opportunity to keep on the right side of the media and took it.'

Wayne pondered this for a moment. At least McCallum wasn't accusing Angie of any wrongdoing. Let Bruce Cartray take the rap. 'Are you going to say what you've just told me to Bruce Cartray?'

'And give the media more ammunition?' McCallum growled down the line. 'No way. The Ryder Cup is too important an event to get involved in these minor squabbles. I'll have a quiet word with Major Mackenzie, tell him to give his captain a ticking off it it's true.'

'Good idea. You do that, Cord.' Wayne was studying Angie. She was still busy painting her toes. He sensed she was putting on a show for him. His mood was changing.

He was feeling better by the minute, especially now that his rival was in was in for a reprimand.

'Trouble honey?' Angie asked in her little girl's voice. She had finished painting her toenails and was now scrutinising herself in the mirror.

'Nothing I can't handle.' Wayne growled. He hoped he wasn't being over optimistic. He watched as Angie rose, crossed the room with that provocative walk of hers, sat on the side of the bed and smiled at him. She pulled the cords of her robe, slid the garment from her shoulders....

Wayne gazed, mesmerised at what was unfolding before him. He looked at his watch. His guys weren't due to fly into Shannon for another couple of hours. Time to catch up on what he had missed out on with Angie last night....

• • • •

Garda Pauly Glynn got into his car, and although it was a warm, slightly overcast morning with a September sun peeping through the clouds presaging another fine day, he pulled up the collar of his raincoat to cover the uniform he was wearing underneath. He didn't want to drive past either Sergeant Gilhooly or his colleague Gerry Carney and set them wondering why he was wearing his uniform on his day off.

He headed the car in the direction of Killarney ten miles away, cursing himself for having revealed to Ben Gartland in the pub last night how disappointed the Sergeant was that so far neither Gerry Carney nor himself had been able to uncover any long-lost Irish relatives of American golf superstar Joey O'Hara. Sergeant Gilhooly had reckoned it would be an honour for Loughduff, and a feather in his cap, if someone in the local station could uncover an Irish connection to the U.S. Senator and his son in the area.

Pauly had been ensconced in his favourite corner of the Loughduff Inn last night when Ben had come in and joined him. Ben was cock-a-hoop after leading the successful farmers' protest at the Parknasilla Palace Hotel earlier. Everyone in the bar had watched the action on the tv news earlier and Ben was the hero of the hour. Whenever his image appeared on television the whole pub erupted into a crescendo of cheering.

If some of the locals were surprised at Pauly Glynn fraternising with a man whom he had faced across the steel barriers earlier, nobody passed comment. But both of them were drinking companions from away back and always had some topic or other to talk about.

Ben had mentioned that he would be travelling to Dublin again tomorrow to visit his brother in Mountjoy Jail. He informed Pauly that Travis was feeling fairly weak now due to his hunger strike. 'The doctors are keeping an eye on him. I'll ask them to move him to a hospital if he gets worse '

'It wouldn't help Travis any if he was to hear what his wife is getting up to with that Englishman,' Pauly muttered. 'Are you going to tell him?'

'Do you think I'm a fool or what?' Ben shot back. 'You keep quiet about what you saw the other morning at the railway station in Killarney, you hear?' Ben gulped his Guinness, wiped his mouth with the back of his hand. 'I'll sort out that Englishman my own way.' .

Pauly didn't like the sound of that. 'Be careful what you say or do, Ben. Somebody threw a rock through the Englishman's window a few nights back. He was in the station this morning making a report. I don't suppose you'd know anything about that?'

Ben signalled for two more drinks. Pauly saw that he was smiling. 'How could I? I've been in bed early every night this week. Slept like a log. Check it out with my girl friend if you like. She'll tell you the truth.' He laughed outright.

'There was a note tied around the rock. A warning, like.'

'Was there now? I hope the Englishman takes heed of what it said. If I catch that artist fella sniffing around my brother's wife again I won't be responsible for my actions.'

Pauly glanced around nervously. Nobody seemed to have overheard. 'Jaysus Ben be careful what you're saying. I'm not supposed to hear those sort of threats!'

He had changed the subject quickly, trying to push Ben in revealing what he and the farmers might be getting up to next in their campaign against the Ryder Cup. 'You know the Americans are coming in tomorrow to play a practice round over the Ryder Cup course. This young fella Joey O'Hara is creating quite a lot of interest,' Pauly remarked.

'Who the hell is Joey O'Hara?', Ben asked.

Pauly smiled to himself. He wondered if Ben ever read a newspaper. 'He's only the best golfer in the world this minute. A superstar. Earns millions of dollars a year just for hitting a little ball into a hole - '

Ben had sworn under his breath at what he reckoned was yet another example men in sport being grossly overpaid for doing what was a relatively simple task. But he suddenly looked interested when Pauly mentioned that Joey was the son of a well-known U.S. Senator and that he and his father were going to be disappointed when they learned that none of their long-lost O'Hara forebears could be traced to the Killarney area.

'And why should they be disappointed?' Ben had asked as he paid Benjy behind the bar for the two drinks.

'I've just told you, Ben,' Pauly explained patiently, 'of the several O'Hara families in the area none had any family connections in America – '

'Is that right now?' Ben absorbed that bit of information. 'Young Joey and his Da won't know that, will they?', he said slowly. He seemed really interested now.

'Not unless Gilhooly gives myself or Jerry Carney the job of telling them – ' Pauly broke off, was suddenly on his guard. He didn't like the way Ben was asking so many questions.

Ben was thinking again. Pauly could almost hear the machinery at work. After downing a few mouthfuls of Guinness Ben said: 'I want you to do me a little favour, Pauly....'

'A favour? What are you up to now?' Little favours for Ben Gartland inevitably had a whiff of danger.

'I want you to meet up with this Joey O'Hara superstar fella tomorrow. You'll be in your uniform – '

'But I'm not on duty tomorrow, Ben,' Pauly cut in, relieved. 'It's my day off – '

'You're day off has just been cancelled, Pauly.' Ben growled without looking at him. 'Go to the golf course tomorrow in your uniform, get talkin' to superstar Joey, spin him a yarn that you have found some of his long lost relations. Got that, Pauly?'

'I told you there are no O'Haras with relatives in the States in this area Ben – '

'I'm telling' you to invent some. Are you stupid or what, Pauly? Listen to me carefully. Tell your friend Joey that when he comes back to play in the Ryder Cup later this month you'll personally take him to see them – '

'He probably won't believe me – '

Ben had brushed his protestations aside. 'Course he will. You're a Garda, aren't you – '

'And what do you want me to tell Joey O'Hara a lie for?' A silence. 'You've got something in mind, Ben? What is it?'

'Don't ask questions. Just do as I say Pauly. A little favour for a pal...'

'You know the regulations, Ben. A Garda is forbidden to wear his uniform when he's off duty – '

'Fuck the regulations!,' Ben hissed. 'Regulations never bothered you in the past – '

Pauly didn't like the sound of it. Ben was planning

something crazy by the sound of it. 'You'll have to tell me what you're up to Ben -'

'I don't have to tell you anything. Just do as you're told.'

'I can't Ben. You're asking me to provide false information –'

'So what!' Ben had cut in harshly. 'It wouldn't be the first time you provided false information for me, Pauly – '

'Forget it, Ben. It's too risky - . There'll be massive security at the Ryder Cup, particularly around Joey O'Hara – ' If Ben was stupid enough to try something crazy let him do it on his own. The Gartlands were no saints. Ben had a vicious temper and had been in the courts before on assault charges. Nothing had ever been proved, of course – Pauly had always been able to cover things up.

Ben had turned slowly, stared Pauly Glynn straight in the eye. 'You'll do as I say, Pauly, or else. You do what I want or that stupid sergeant of yours will be tipped off about a few things…' Ben knocked back his pint. 'Any further questions?' When Pauly hadn't replied Ben had smiled. 'Good. Now how about buying me another drink…'

● ● ● ●

'What the hell has been keeping you, Wayne?' Cord McCallum asked impatiently as Wayne came downstairs into the foyer of the Parknasilla Palace Hotel.

'Sorry – ' It wasn't often that Wayne Folen looked embarrassed. 'I – er – went back to sleep after you phoned - '

McCallum glared at him. 'We've been waiting for you for over half-an-hour. The cars are outside. We're behind schedule, dammit!' McCallum held back his anger. With that blonde bimbo sharing Wayne Folen's bed he wasn't surprised his captain was behind schedule. The other two U.S. Golf Association members within hearing tried to hide their amusement. Wayne noticed, grimaced… That

Angie, phew! He'd have to plan things a bit more carefully in future.

'I got a phone call a few minutes ago,' McCallum said brusquely as they hurried across the foyer. 'Our fellows have arrived at Shannon Airport. I expect they're already on their way to Killarney. We'd better get a move on.' A couple of chauffeurs, their gleaming limousines at the ready, jumped to attention as the American group exited from the hotel into the sunshine. Two smiling officials from Tourism Ireland greeted the American party which included several journalists.

'Good morning, gentlemen,' the older of the two chauffeurs gushed. 'Or cead mile failte as we say in Ireland. That means – '

McCallum waved his hand impatiently. 'We know what it means,' he growled, not breaking his stride. 'Let's get moving. We're in a hurry – '

'Yes, of course,' the man from Tourism Ireland was undeterred. 'It's such a beautiful day we've decided to take the scenic route to Killarney and show you some of the lakes and scenery for which this part of Ireland is famous – '

Wayne saw McCallum grimace. America's top Ryder Cup official exchanged a glance of annoyance with his two colleagues. 'I appreciate the offer but like I said we're in a hurry,' he said brusquely. 'Can't we take the shorter route?'

'Actually Mr. McCallum, going around the lakes is the shorter route. The roads are narrower, not built for speed, but we'll make good time I promise.' The Tourism Ireland man was persistent. His organisation was determined to extract every ounce of publicity from an international event like Ryder Cup. The plan was to show off the beauty of Ireland to millions around the world and no crusty old American was going to disrupt that.

'Oh, alright,' Cord McCallum growled. 'Let's get a move on.' Wayne made sure to avoid McCallum's company when they were getting into the limos. He had bought a pile of newspapers at hotel reception and whether the Irish tourism guy was pleased or not he wouldn't be spending the journey to Killarney admiring the scenery.

After the session in bed with Angie earlier Wayne had watched some of the news re-runs on tv while dressing. Sky News had what the station claimed was the inside report of last night's stormy meeting between the American and European Ryder Cup delegations in Ireland, focusing on the exchanges between the two captains and Wayne's virulent outburst.

The tabloid newspapers had concentrated mainly on the burgeoning rivalry building up between the female partners of the Ryder Cup captains. Angie had been interviewed about her audition with Patrick Mannion for the lead role in his new film; Sally was pictured beside a story that named her as the possible source of the inside story unveiling last night's verbal battle. The Ryder Cup event itself was playing second fiddle to trivia. No wonder Cord McCallum was in a foul mood!

'Bitter Battle of the Ryder Cup Women!', screamed one headline. Others were 'Angie and Sally Upstage the Ryder Cup' and 'Ryder Cup Ladies Grab The Headlines'. The media was having a field day.

Wayne eyes narrowed when he read what Angie was quoted saying when one reporter asked her what social programme she had lined up for the wives and girlfriends of the U.S. golfers. 'Let's just say you won't see us girls going around staring at all those ancient Irish monuments. I'm told wives and girlfriends at Ryder Cups in the past have complained about having to attend too many boring functions and listen to too many boring speeches – mainly by men. I aim to think up a more exciting programme for my girls.'

Wayne winced, groaned inwardly as he read the story. Hell, why couldn't Angie be more diplomatic? Marcia would have been more discreet. He folded the newspapers and put them away, staring out at the wild scenery as they wound their way through the mountains towards Killarney.

At the crossroads at a place the tourist official announced was Moll's Gap the cavalcade, including the cars carrying the ever-present members of the media, stopped and everyone alighted. They joined groups of sightseers from tour buses that had also stopped to allow their occupants to buy goods and admire the view. Wayne found himself getting impatient and was glad when, before any of the Ryder Cup party could make their way into the tourist shop to inspect what was on offer, Cord McCallum cut short the eulogy about the scenery from the tourist official and ordered everyone back into the limos.

But the Tourism Ireland guy got his own back and Cord McCallum almost exploded with wrath when, a few miles later there was another stop was called along the winding mountain road.

'This spot gentleman, is world famous and is known as Ladies' View,' the tourism official announced proudly. 'It is so called because when the Queen of England visited Killarney in the middle of the nineteenth century she and her entourage were passing this spot and her Majesty and her ladies-in-waiting were so enchanted with the view that the Queen insisted on stopping – '

'Look mister,' McCallum snapped, diplomacy forgotten and turning his back on the spectacular view of the blue-tinted lake nestling in the valley amid three-lined mountains rising on either side, 'we're here on a Ryder Cup mission. We're not interested in this bullshit about the Queen of England and your so-called spectacular views! For Chrissake get us to Killarney!' For once Wayne Folen was in agreement with his boss.

• • • •

Garda Pauly Glynn halted the car at the police roadblock outside the Killarney Golf and Fishing Club and was waved through by the two uniformed officers who were manning the obstacle. He drove slowly along the winding tarmacadamed driveway circling the waters of Loch Leane, the lake that formed part of the famous course, glancing at the several boats moored at the jetty, and drove into the car park overlooked by the imposing glass-fronted clubhouse. Across the lake he saw two helicopters parked, and assumed that the American Ryder Cup team members had arrived from Shannon Airport. He noted the large number of Gardai strolling around in short-sleeved shirts in the bright mid-day September sunshine.

On the drive into Killarney Pauly had seen for himself the effect the advent of the Ryder Cup was having on the town and the surrounding area. Even with over a week still to go to the big event Killarney was buzzing. Flags and bunting were flying and Ryder Cup posters were everywhere. At both entrances to the famous town two huge 'Killarney Welcomes The Ryder Cup Teams' arches with banners had been erected across the road. Every hotel and guesthouse within a fifty mile radius had been booked solid for the past two years. Practically every restaurant and pub in the area had been given a facelift.

Local tourist interests were ecstatic that the golf world's most popular team event had come their way. It was estimated that golf fans from throughout Europe and America crowding into Kerry during the next couple of weeks would spend an estimated ten million dollars in the area. Also, the tourism spin-off to Ireland would be enormous. The Irish Government was determined that no local group of disaffected farmers was going to spoil the party. As he surveyed the scene Pauly Glynn hoped that whatever Ben Gartland had planned wouldn't do so either!

He reckoned he didn't have much time. The Americans would be teeing-off shortly and even he knew enough about golf to know you don't engage a player in conversation when he is practising. Especially not with the Ryder Cup in the offing!

He observed the two small groups of men, bronzed, impeccably togged out in branded sports shirts and slacks, standing chatting and laughing in the vicinity of the first tee. A group of caddies hovered around in charge of bulging golf bags, several of their superstar owners' names emblazoned on the side.

'Excuse me, which one is Joey O'Hara?', he asked a man standing beside him. The man was wearing a blazer bearing the Killarney Golf and Fishing Club crest. He turned to see who had asked the question, saw the Garda beside him, smiled and said:

'Not a golf fan, are you?'

Pauly secretly wished he could arrest a person for giving smart answers. Had he not been wearing his uniform he would have told this know-all where to get off. He kept his cool, just smiled.

The blazered one pointed. 'See that fella, the tall, blond one with the dark shades, red pullover and navy blue slacks…He's your man.'

'Thank you. Why aren't they tee-ing off?'

'They're waiting for their captain and some of the Ryder Cup committee members. They're on their way from Parknasilla. Should be arriving shortly…' The man turned, saw two limousines accompanied by a Garda escort on motorcycles winding their way around the lake. 'This is probably them now…'

A burst of applause rang out as the cars drew to a halt near the clubhouse and groups of people emerged from them both. As cameras clicked, handshakes were exchanged between the Minister for Tourism, the captain and committee members of the club, and Irish and European golf officials. Pauly saw a burly, athletic looking middle-aged visitor with tightly cropped grey hair join the groups of golfers, some of whom were signing autographs.

Pauly reckoned it was now or never if he was going to talk to Joey O'Hara.

He tapped his quarry on the shoulder. 'Excuse me – ' The young man turned. 'You're Joey O'Hara, aren't you. Could I have a few words with you…'

'Sure – ' Joey's smile faded when he noticed the uniform. 'Something wrong, officer?'

'No, everything's fine,' Pauly grinned to reassure him. 'I'm Garda Pauly Glynn and I'm stationed in Lough-duff – ' He shoved out his hand. The young American shook it. 'Loughduff is where your Irish ancestors come from, isn't it?'

'It sure is.'

'I believe both your father and yourself anxious to trace them – ' He saw the interest in Joey's eyes. 'I've got some good news for you.' He had rehearsed what he was going to say with Ben Gartland last night.

Joey was all attention now. 'You mean you found some of them?'

'Yes, we think so. We're just checking out the details – '

'Great! This is fantastic! Wait till Dad hears – ' he broke off. 'Sorry, what did you say your name was?' When Pauly told him Joey grabbed his hand again, shook it enthusiastically. 'Great work, officer, Congratulations' The young fellow was really excited. 'Hey, I must tell my buddies that you guys have found my Irish forebears – ' Before Pauly could stop him Joey had turned, shouted, 'Hey, you guys, guess what – '

'No! Wait!', Pauly jumped in, frantic. Holy God! Joey was about to draw the attention of members of the media who hovering in the background. Already some were staring, wondering what the Irish cop was saying to the young American Ryder Cup star. 'We're not one hundred percent sure yet,' Pauly hissed desperately. 'We're still checking it out. Top secret like.'

Joey turned back, looked disappointed. 'Oh, sorry.'

'Don't say anything to anybody yet. Not even your father. Understand? Sorry I can't give you any more details just now - ' Pauly looked suitably apologetic.

Joey brushed his blond hair back from his forehead. Wayne Folen was leading the team members into the clubhouse. 'I don't have much time to talk right now, and that goes for later also. After we play eighteen holes we have dinner, followed by a team talk with our captain Wayne Folen. We leave for Shannon immediately and catch the ten p.m. flight back to New York'.

'Not to worry. When you come back to play in the Ryder Cup I or one of my colleagues will contact you. We'll have checked everything out by then.'

'That's fine by me, officer. We're back in Parknasilla in ten days time. The Ryder Cup doesn't start until the following Friday morning. Plenty of time for that trip to the old homestead – '

They shook hands. Pauly breathed a sigh of relief. So far so good. 'I'll proceed with investigation, Joey, and I'll keep in touch.'

Just in time. There was a flurry of excitement as Wayne Folen exited from the locker room and called his team around to announce the day's pairings. Joey O'Hara was in the first pairing with his captain and Pauly stayed to see the young superstar and his captain drive off. They were followed down the first fairway by their caddies, several photographers, and a couple of vigilant Gardai.

Nobody gave the lone Garda a second glance as he walked in the opposite direction towards the car park. A cool breeze was blowing in off Loch Leane as Pauly Glynn drove out onto the Killorglin Road and headed back towards Loughduff.

• • • •

For Nell Flavin the days had dragged interminably until at last the morning finally arrived when she could pay her weekly visit to her friend Katie. For the past couple of days she had replayed in her mind's eye the scene she had witnessed between Katie and Jeremy Walker outside his cottage; their passionate embrace had spoken louder than words.

Much as she had been dying to she had not mentioned the episode to Tom, her husband. Tom would probably have said that she was reading too much into the situation, that her over-active imagination was working overtime. Imagine, their friend Katie having a torrid love affair with a handsome English painter while her husband languished in gaol. Things like that just didn't happen in Loughduff.

Nell helped herself to a chocolate biscuit, sipped her coffee and studied Katie over the rim of her cup. No doubt about it, Katie Gartland was a changed woman these days. It was obvious that something – or someone special – had entered her life.

'What are you staring at?', Katie asked accusingly.

'I'm admiring the new Katie Gartland. You look so – er – different.' Nell knew that wasn't quite the right word. 'I can't ever remember seeing you so alive. Radiant I think is the word. You look gorgeous, Katie.'

Katie flushed. 'Thank you, Nell. I went into Killarney yesterday. One of the boutiques was selling their dresses off at a ridiculous price – '

'You got something done to your hair, too. What's it all in aid of, that's what I'd like to know!'

'Jeremy said – ' Katie broke off, embarrassed. She had not meant to mention his name. It had come out naturally, maybe because she had been thinking so much of him lately. There was an awkward silence.

'I saw you when you visited Jeremy a few days ago,' Nell said, adding quickly, 'I couldn't help it, I was in my back bedroom at the time...' She paused, decided to go for it. 'Tell me honestly, Katie, are you and Jeremy Walker having an affair?'

The question hung in the air for a few moments. Katie flushed, lowered her eyes. 'An affair…?' She gave a shaky laugh. 'Wh-what on earth are you saying, Nell?. I – I don't know what you're talking about ⌐'.

'Oh yes you do. Like I said, I saw the two of you the other day. You were both kissing – and it wasn't just a friendly peck on the cheek. It was a real passionate kiss! Like two lovers – ' Nell paused. 'Well, are you? People are beginning to talk you know…'

Katie still didn't answer. She ran her finger around the rim of her cup, her head lowered. Slowly she replaced her cup in the saucer, rose to her feet. She needed time to think Outside the sun had disappeared behind a black cloud and rain was beginning to fall. Katie stared at the raindrops on the window pane. Should she tell all, let Nell in on her secret?

Nell was sure she could hear her heart beating. She had to say something, anything.

. 'I'm sorry, Katie, I suppose I shouldn't have asked. Go on, tell me to mind my own business ⌐' Still no reply. 'I know you don't want to talk about it…'

'But I do, I do!' Katie turned from the window. She was smiling, although Nell saw that there were tears in her eyes. 'I want to talk about it, Nell, because it's the best thing that has ever happened to me – '.

Nell rose, crossed to Katie. The two of them embraced, hugged each other. 'Oh Katie, I'm so happy for you – '

'Are you really, Nell?' The two of them were crying now.

'Yes, of course. Why wouldn't I be? I know you're happy. You've been a different person these past few weeks.

'I know that – and it's wonderful! Does it show?'

'I've seen it with my own eyes. I knew something was happening between you and Jeremy Walker. I envy you, Katie Gartland.'

'What do you mean?'

'Oh, I'd love to be having an affair. With someone like Jeremy, of course! – '

'Nell Flavin! What are you saying? And you a happily married woman – '

'I know. Sure I was only joking!' They hugged each other again, laughing this time. When the broke apart Nell said, 'Go on, Katie. Tell me all about it. How did it happen?...' They were sitting down again, sipping their coffees.

'I don't know how it happened, Nell. It just did.

'Like I've already said, I'm so happy for you. I know you've been unhappy. Everyone around here knows. They gossip about it sometimes – '

'Promise me you won't tell anyone, Nell.'

'I won't!. I won't! Cross my heart.' Nell was beside herself with excitement. 'Go on, Katie, tell me how it happened. Please!'

'I went to visit Jeremy, see the damage to his window. We went inside – '

'I know. Didn't I see you. Hand in hand – '

'We talked for a bit. I knew something was going to happen between us. Jeremy put his arm around me. We kissed. Something came over me, Nell. I had no control over my emotions...'

'Oh God. It must have been very romantic.'

'We sent upstairs – '

'To his bedroom?' Nell asked breathlessly.

'Yes. He carried me up – '

'Jesus! Like Rhett Butler and Scarlett O'Hara in 'Gone With The Wind'! Nell had read the book, saw a re-run of the film on television only last week. Loved it!

Katie laughed. 'I can't remember what happened after that. All I know is that it was wonderful – ' She broke off. ' I'm madly in love with him, Nell. I know you'll say it's ridiculous, that I hardly know him – '

'I'm not going to say any such thing! I'm delighted for

you, Katie. You're a grown woman and you know your own mind. I mean it's not as if you've had any sort of a life with – with that husband of yours…God knows you've tried.' .

After a short pause Katie said: 'I don't feel like I've done anything wrong – '

'You've nothing to feel guilty about, Katie. Not so long ago in Catholic Ireland a young wife like yourself would have had to put up with her bad marriage, face a lifetime of unhappiness with a husband she didn't love. Not any more. You're doing the right thing, Katie.' Nell paused. 'Are you sure you're in love with Jeremy?'

'I've never been more certain of anything in my life. I want to spend the rest of my life with Jeremy Walker – '

'Be careful, Katie. We live in a small community where everyone knows everyone else's business. If it ever gets out you'd have to leave Loughduff… '

'I don't care. Jeremy would come with me.'

'What makes you so sure?'

'I know he would. He loves me too, Nell. He told me so. Funny, I sensed it from the very beginning, that night after the meeting in Loughduff when he drove me and the boys home…'

'You changed from that night. But it's an awful big step to take. Are you sure it's what you want, Katie?

Katie nodded. 'I've never met anybody like Jeremy Walker before. I just can't help myself ' Her voice was low, her eyes dancing with joy.

Nell looked thoughtful. 'I hate to be a spoilsport, but what happens when Travis gets out of Mountjoy, comes home. And what about Ben? What if he finds out?.'

'Like I've already said, I don't care. I'll go away with Jeremy, start a whole new life. Myself and the two boys. He's even got me interested in painting again. Wait till I show you, Nell! – ' Katie jumped to her feet, disappeared upstairs.

Nell sat alone, sipping her coffee, hardly able to believe what she was hearing. My God, it's true, Katie means what she says. She's found love and she's so besotted with Jeremy Walker that she's willing to give up everything for him – run off with him and leave her husband, no less. Nell was thrilled and envious at the same time. What if something like that had happened to her – not that it ever would! Would she be able to resist the charms of someone like Jeremy Walker?

Katie came into the kitchen holding a large folder. Nell recognised it as the one that Jeremy Walker had put into the boot of Katie's car the other day. Obviously the new man in her life had bequeathed it to her.

Katie flipped the folder open. 'Well, what do you think?'

Nell looked at a drawing, in bold, bright hues. It showed an outdoor setting; Nell recognised it as the old fort on the hill about half a mile from where they were now sitting. Only it looked different on canvas, more alive. Whoever had painted it had caught it in a shaft of sunlight filtering through the leaves of a tree. The artist's skill had enhanced what was essentially a mundane setting.

'And this – ' Katie put aside the old fort painting. This time the scene was a view across a river, with a man riding a bicycle in the background, a satchel over his shoulder and a fishing rod protruding over the handlebars of the bike. The artist had caught the setting in all its relaxed, sylvan beauty.

'I'm sure you'll recognise these two – ' A line drawing this time, a head and shoulders sketch of Katie's two sons, Garret and Jack, heads bent over a chess board. The artist had caught in full the fierce look of concentration in both their profiles. Nell was suitably impressed with all she had seen.

'Are all those yours?' she asked. When Katie nodded Nell continued. 'I didn't know you were so talented. You never let on you were that good – '

'I didn't know I had that much talent either, until I caught the bug again - thanks to Jeremy.'

While she poured more coffee Katie told a wild-eyed Nell about Sister Rita, how through her former nun/tutor she had first discovered her artistic talent in the convent; how that talent had, through her years with Travis, lain dormant until she had visited the Sapphire Gallery in Dublin a few days ago with Jeremy Walker. Now so many things were happening, a whole new life opening up for her…

Katie paused, breathless, her eyes shining with a light Nell Flavin had never seen there before. 'Nell, you're my best friend. In fact my only friend. Tell me you understand this thing that is happening between myself and Jeremy…'

'Of course I do' She laughed. 'I only wish it was happening to me!' Then Nell became serious again. 'You've slept with him then?'

'Yes.' The word came out softly.

'Oh God how I envy you! Some women have all the luck!' The two of them laughed. 'I'm delighted that you're happy,' Nell said. 'After the life you've had you deserve every moment.'

Katie clasped her friend's hand in both of hers.'Thanks, Nell. I knew you'd understand. I simply can't believe that this is happening to me.'

Nell groaned. 'Oh, stop it for God's sake! You'll have me climbing in through Jeremy Walker's bedroom window next!'

Katie rose from the table again, gazed out of the window at the fields beyond. 'All I know now is that I want to be with Jeremy Walker. Now and forever.' It was as if she was speaking her thought aloud. 'Travis never loved me, you know that Nell. My husband doesn't know the meaning of love, never has. I married him thinking there was nobody else. Now I know there is.'

'You've been given another chance, Katie. Take it, girl. I know I would.' Nell rose, joined her at the window. 'But be careful before you commit yourself.'

'What are you hinting at now?'

Nell didn't want Katie to think that she was envying her the happiness she had found. 'How much to you know about Jeremy?,' Nell asked, looked slightly uncomfortable. 'His background, for example. Like is he married for instance.'

'All I know is that he's an artist – and a very good one according to his agent in Dublin. He's from somewhere in England, Norfolk I think. And I know that he's kind, and caring – and that he loves me – '

'Has he told you so?'

'Yes.'

'Was he in a relationship before? Did he say anything about that? How do you know he's not running away from a wife – or a mistress with a few kids.' Nell paused. 'I'm sorry, Katie, but these things are important – '

'I know – but I don't care. Jeremy has hinted that he's been in a few relationships – '

'What man hasn't,' Nell cut in. Then she asked. 'Did he say why he left England to live over here?'

Katie shrugged. 'Like I said, he's an artist, isn't he? Artists like to travel. It fires the imagination – ' That's what Jeremy had said when she had asked. 'Look Nell, Jeremy Walker has changed my whole life, made me feel wanted, something I'd never felt before. He's promised to bring my work to Dublin to show to his agent Henry Mackintosh. I can't believe all this is happening to me. And guess what?', Katie finished excitedly.

'You mean there's more?'

'He wants me to pose for him!'

Nell looked amused. 'Pose for him? Go on! What exactly has he got in mind?'

'I mean really pose. Nude!'

'Jesus!' Nell's eyebrows shot up. 'You mean with nothing on?'

'Of course.'

'Oh God, I'd be mortified. What did you say? Are you going to do it, Katie?'

'Of course. Why not. Jeremy said I've a good body. It'll be so exciting!'

Holy God, Nell thought, all this happening in little Loughduff! She stared at Katie in disbelief. The gossips who were already whispering about Travis Gartland's young wife and the English artist who had moved into the area recently would have a lot more to whisper about in the near future!

• • • •

'Jeez Mervyn, the things I do for my art!'

Angie smiled into her mobile phone, glad that Mervyn couldn't see her expression. She was alone, relaxing in the lounge of the hotel.

The images of the sizzling afternoon session on the lake with Patrick Mannion was still vivid in her mind. Best not to let Mervyn in on just how much she had enjoyed herself; agents were supposed to earn their ten per cent, not envy their clients a good time.

'I take it you and that guy Mannion had a swell afternoon, Angie. My heart bleeds for you.' Then the banter disappeared. 'I just hope you didn't get so carried away that you let that little Irish guy talk you into a bum deal?'

'Don't worry, Merv darling, everything is taken care of. Wayne and I fly back to New York tomorrow. Patrick Mannion plans to go to L.A. to start pre-production work on the movie. He's stopping off in New York on the way and calling in to see you so that you can okay the contract. How's that?'

'Excellent, baby. This may be your first feature film but you don't come cheap. Your price is at least a million dollars. We'll let this guy Mannion know we mean business.'

Only a million! Mannion had got a million's worth out of her already! Couldn't the schmuck Mervyn show some sensitivity? Didn't he have some idea what she had to do to get the part? Mannion maybe new to Hollywood but he was no fool; like most film directors who knew what aspiring actresses like Angie would do for a shot at the big-time. And how! What an afternoon on the lake; The little Irish guy was no Arnold Swartzenegger but his equipment was well up to standard, she could vouch for that!

'Listen good, Mervyn. Patrick and I have already opened negotiations. Take my advice and push for two million.'

Mervyn could hardly believe his luck. Two mil! That would be the biggest deal he had ever pulled off. He decided to treat himself to some decent cigars when he went for lunch. Maybe he should move into a new office, get out of the current dog house from which he operated.

'Nice going, Angie. Hey, you must have showed that guy Mannion a good time?'

'You'd better believe it, Mervyn. The guy was so horny I thought he'd drill a hole in the boat!' She heard him laugh. No doubt he would enjoy hearing the details of her off-screen performance...

It had been past midday when the diminutive Irish film director, with powerfully executed strokes, had pulled away from the jetty. On shore the athletic-looking youth in charge wished he was in the boat with the busty blonde bombshell. Angie had taken a seat in the bow, her eyes on the squat body of the little Irishman, the muscles under his short-sleeved silk shirt threatening to split the garment. She was dressed in a white polo neck top and a matching short skirt with white sneakers and ankle socks. It was the outfit she usually wore on her weekly visit to the tennis courts in her local park back home.

Angie had stretched her shapely legs out after she had gingerly sat down in the boat. On the jetty, the red-headed young man's eyes were almost popping out of his head. As they pulled away she decided to make his day by blowing him a kiss.

At the far end of the lake, out of sight of other craft, Mannion had shipped his oars and let the craft drift. Since they had departed the jetty his smouldering eyes had hardly left hers. Now she watched with not a little excitement as he deliberately spread the rug out along the bottom of the boat. When he had finished he looked at her. It was obvious what he had in mind. Angie was under no illusion; her chance to make it in the movies depended on what she did next. Without saying a word she lay down, her head disappearing from view beneath the gunwale. It was a little uncomfortable but what the hell; she could feel the fissures of the small craft through the rug.

What was it Mervyn had advised? Ah yes, lie back and think of Hollywood!

For the next hour or so Patrick Mannion indulged himself with her. There was nothing subtle or sophisticated about his lovemaking, no preamble or complimentary words. In her time Angie had played host to her share of wannabe film moguls and small-time stage directors, in offices that reeked of cigar smoke or in impersonal out-of-town hotel rooms, trying not to think of the guy's wife probably sitting at home watching tv with the kids. Invariably the jousts began with her erstwhile mentor telling Angie how beautiful she was, that he was going to make her a big star, that this for him was something special. Invariably the storyline was that he was not in love with his cold, uncaring wife back home. But Angie was different, she was sensitive, had potential to make it into the movies, and they would be good for each other. Let's have one more drink, it'll help us to relax...

Mannion had gotten down to business straight away, helping her to remove her sweater and unzipping her skirt with a dexterity that belied his sexual hunger. She lay supine, her arms entwined around his neck, hearing his breath coming in short gasps. He was much more gentle at removing her bra and panties, sliding both garments off her body slowly, pleasure showing in his eyes as her surveyed her body. He clawed at his own clothes, and when he removed his pants Angie caught a fleeting glance of an enormous, erect penis. Then he was on top of her, caressing her, watching her respond to his every touch.

Three times during the next hour, between short periods of rest, their bodies locked and moved in unison, before they would pull apart, sated and spent. Such was the activity that at one stage Angie felt that the boat was in danger of overturning. Jeez, the guy was an animal, but he certainly knew how to make a girl happy!

'Tell me, honey, where was Wayne when your audition with this guy Mannion was taking place?' Mervyn's voice over the mobile brought her back to the present.

'Relax Mervyn. Wayne was away all afternoon in Killarney with his golfers. Who the hall cares about Wayne Folen anyway. Hollywood here I come!'

'Be careful, baby. At least until we sign the contract. And remember even when we do sign the deal with Mannion we can still use your guy Wayne and the Ryder Cup to keep you in the spotlight.'

Angie promised to be a good girl and switched off. She felt really tired. Hell, it had been a busy day. Wayne wouldn't be back from Killarney until late evening; time to soak in a hot bath, catch up on some beauty sleep.

She was crossing the hotel foyer to the elevator when the colourful poster caught her eye. Angie studied the glossy picture of the quartet of hunky, handsome young men, oiled muscles glistening and standing out in their bare torsos. The script with the picture was even more interesting.

'Ladies – See The Celtic Tigers In Action!' it proclaimed in bold, black print. Underneath was the name of the venue and the date of the show – Symie's Pub Lounge, Glengariff. One Night Only Sept.18th at 8.30pm. Doors open 7.30pm. Admission 10 Euros. Don't Be Disappointed. Come Early!'

Angie stared hard at the eye-catching poster, reading it
through a second time. An idea began to form in her head,
so outrageous that it brought a smile to her lips. Looking up
she saw the uniformed hotel porter at the pillar studying
her. He was obviously awaiting further developments.

'Interested, lady?'

'Yeah, I think so...' He strolled across.

'What can I do for you, Miss?'

'What if I want to take a group of ladies to see that show
when we come back here in about ten days time – '

'No problem. I promise you'll enjoy yourselves to be
sure.' He smiled broadly beneath his gold-braided cap.
'Those lads The Celtic Tigers are very entertaining.
Extremely popular with the ladies.'

'I'm not surprised!' They both laughed. 'What kind of a
show is it exactly? I mean is it – you know – ' She didn't
want to mention the four letter word.

'Sexy? Oh yes. Very'

'How sexy?'

'Male strippers.' He gave what passed for a sly wink.
'The local newspaper describes it as raunchy. Definitely
suitable for ladies looking for a good night out.'

'Nudity?'

'Oh yes. In good taste, of course. Depends....'

'On what?'

'On what they ladies in the audience get up to. If they're
enthusiastic they could be in for a great night altogether.'

'That place Glengariff....How far is it from here?'

'No distance at all. Just a skip and a jump as we say
down here.'

'How far exactly is that?'

'Seventeen miles or thereabouts.' Some skip and a
jump, Angie thought. 'Beautiful drive. You and the ladies
would enjoy that too. I can arrange everything.'

'We'll need transport. Taxis maybe, for a party of about
fourteen, maybe a few more...?' Angie was counting the

twelve wives and girlfriends accompanying the players on the U.S. Ryder Cup team. She might even rope in a few of the European ladies who no doubt would no doubt be bored with Sally Cartray's set-up. Angie reckoned The Celtic Tigers offered a welcome change from the schedule of formal dinners that preceded the Ryder Cup.

'Why not a luxury coach – with a mini bar included?' The helpful hotel porter offered. 'I have a friend who organises top of the range nights out for tourists' His commission on this one would be substantial.

'Great! Sounds perfect. Could I have your name?'

'Just ask for Seanie, Miss. I'm the head porter.'

'Mine is Wilde, Angie Wilde. I'm with the American Ryder Cup party – '

Wilde by name and wild by nature, Seanie thought to himself. Aloud he said, 'By the way, Symie's Lounge isn't very big. And the Celtic Tiger lads have a huge following. I'll need to book in advance for your fine bunch of ladies…'

Angie smiled, searched in her bag, took out a fifty Euro note. Seanie made sure nobody was looking before accepting it. 'Get working on it immediately, Seanie'. She gave him her room number. 'We leave here tomorrow. I'd be obliged if you could fix up things before then. And not a word about this to anyone, okay?'

'No problem. Leave it to me, lady'. Seanie touched his cap in salute. He watched in admiration as she headed for the elevator, admiring her shapely rear. A tip-off to the local newspaper on the night the Ryder Cup ladies were going to see the Celtic Tigers in action would pay rich dividends.

In the elevator Angie Wilde reckoned that it had been a good day's work. Mervyn had asked her to keep a look-out for publicity opportunities. She reckoned that the Celtic Tigers would fit the bill.

CHAPTER SEVEN.

The two cars containing the CNN and RTE television crews arrived within minutes of each other, easing through the front gates, gliding up the gravel pathway before pulling up outside the house. Ben eyed the occupants as they alighted from the vehicles with the assurance of a man now accustomed to having the international media call on him every day.

Katie stood beside him, silent. They had only exchanged a few curt sentences since the episode in the kitchen the other morning. Yesterday, while Ben was working out on the farm, she had taken the telephone call from RTE, the home tv station, requesting an interview with herself and Ben. It was one of the several such requests that they had dealt with yesterday. Was it only because her husband's hunger strike was connected with the upcoming Ryder Cup that she was in the news, Katie wondered? She hoped the media had got a whiff of the gossip of the relationship between herself and Jeremy.

Ben knew they would ask him about the condition of Travis, now into the third week of his hunger strike. His brother's condition was deteriorating and giving cause for concern. The media would also want to know details of the big farming rally he had called for in Killarney in two days time to highlight his brother's worsening condition. That had been a good move, Ben reckoned. Travis was so ill that last night he had been moved from Mountjoy Jail in Dublin across the road to a room in the Mater Hospital where he was under 24-hour surveillance.

'In view of your brother's worsening condition are you going to ask him to give up his hunger strike?', an RTE reporter asked.

'No way,' Ben retorted. 'We didn't ask Travis to go on hunger strike. It was his decision. He's a very stubborn man is my brother.'

'What if he dies, or damages his body permanently by his action?'

'If Travis dies the Irish Government will be responsible. They make the laws.' Ben glared at the assembled media. 'Small farmers are losing out when it comes to buying land because they can't compete with the cheque book power of wealthy foreigners.'

'Do you have any statistics to back up that statement, Ben?' the American reporter with CNN asked.

'We have proof. Our records show that in one year recently over fifteen thousand acres of Irish land were sold to non-nationals – and most of that land was in the scenic areas of Cork and Kerry. It began with the Americans and the Europeans, but now the Japanese are moving in. We will fight to stop them building a luxury golf courses on prime land that should rightly be sold to Irish farmers,' Ben roared.

'Is the sale of land in this area to a Japanese consortium worth your brother's life?', the American reporter insisted.

'Ask the Minister for the Environment that,' Ben snapped back.

'What do you think of your husband's action?, Mrs Gartland,' the RTE man asked.

The cameras focused on Katie. 'I don't want my husband to die,' she said softly. 'But the decision is his and yes, he is a stubborn man. He won't listen to me. Whatever I say won't make him change his mind.'

She could have elaborated and said that her husband

had never asked her opinion on anything, that they had never really communicated as a couple. She could also have told them that while she genuinely did not want Travis to die or suffer permanent injury, whatever happened to him really made no difference to her. She had a new focus in life, there was no going back to the old ways. She and Travis were finished as a couple. That was something she could not confide to the members of the media gathered in the farmyard.

'When are you planning on visiting your husband again, Mrs Gartland?'

'I don't know....'

'Soon?'

'Yes. In the next few days.

'Could I ask you about something else, Mrs. Gartland...A window in Jeremy Walker's house was broken the other night when a warning note thrown through it. Do you know anything about that?'

'Why should she know anything concerning that Englishman?'Ben shouted. 'What are you getting at?' There was menace in his voice.

'I was merely asking a question,' the RTE man replied evenly.

'Then stick to what the farmers around here are fighting for. Don't you want to know about the big protest rally we are staging in Killarney the day after tomorrow.'

'Will it be as big as the one in Parknasilla?'

'Bigger,' Ben boasted. 'We aim to bring Killarney to a standstill. With all this action and the Ryder Cup starting soon the government will have to listen to us. They'll have to take some action to save my brother's life.'

'Aren't you worried about all the bad publicity if the Ryder Cup is disrupted?'

'I don't give a damn about the Ryder Cup!.' Ben roared, glaring at the American reporter who had asked the question. He was getting more angry by the minute. 'My brother's life is in danger and you reporters come asking questions about why someone broke an Englishman's window – ' He paused for breath. 'Now clear off the lot of you. The interview is over!' With that Ben turned on his heel and disappeared from sight around the corner of the farmhouse.

Katie went inside, stood by the window and watched as the camera crew members climbed back in their cars and drove out through the front gate. She hoped that Ben would drive up to see Travis today. That meant he would be away until late tonight. It would give her an opportunity to drive over and see Jeremy, show him the latest drawing she had completed. Besides today was the day she had decided to pose for him.

• • • •

'We're on our way baby. Big time! 'Roll Of The Dice' will put your name way up there in lights. Hollywood here we come! Julia Roberts and all those other babes had better look to their laurels!'

Mervyn Lazlo took out a fresh cigar, admired it, lit it and looked across the desk at Angie Wilde. She smiled too. She had never seen Mervyn so upbeat. The guy was positively beaming. He rose to his feet and strolled around the office, thumb hooked into the pocket of his colourful waistcoat, his other hand holding the fat cigar.

'My next move is to get you onto the A-list for all those big Hollywood parties. You sure handled things well in Ireland, Angie.' He leered at her. 'You must have given that little guy Mannion a swell time!'

Three days earlier Angie had flown back to New York from her sojourn in Ireland

with Wayne Folen.and the other members of the U.S. Ryder Cup delegation. Wayne had left immediately for the training camp in the Catskills where he aimed to subject the 12 members of his Ryder Cup squad to a gruelling physical and mental preparation for the task ahead. This move by Wayne to get his men into shape for their upcoming tilt against Europe's best golfers was unprecedented and had received a lot of media attention. It underlined clearly his determination – some were calling it an obsession – to bring the Ryder Cup back to America.

While Wayne Folen was thus engaged Angie took the opportunity to call into Mervyn Lazlo's fifth floor office, eager to sign her name on the contract to appear in Patrick Mannion's next blockbuster. The dynamic Mr.Mannion had also been in attendance and a beaming Mervyn had opened a couple of bottles of champagne while a hired photographer had recorded the historic occasion.

Also keeping an eye on the proceedings was Naomi, Mannion's redheaded P.A. Ensconced in a the only other deep leather chair in the cramped office, she had looked on, a smile on her lips. The smile had frozen somewhat when, signings over, the little Irishman had given his latest film protege a congratulatory kiss that had somehow lingered a little too long. Later Mannion and Naomi had left for the airport to catch a plane to Los Angeles to continue pre-production work on the film.

Angie wished the Ryder Cup was out of the way so that she too could fly out to L.A. and get a taste of some real action before the cameras.

She was looking forward to seeing Patrick Mannion again as soon as possible – and it wasn't all to do with 'Roll Of The Dice'. Angie had fond memories of their afternoon on the lake in Parknasilla. She wondered what the new man in her life would come up with for an encore!

'That Mannion guy has the hots for you, Angie,' Mervyn opined when they were alone.

'Isn't that what you want?' Angie replied coolly. 'For me to keep him sweet.'

'Sure, sure, honey.' He paused, then asked, 'You happy

with the contract?'

She shrugged. 'What do you think!' Angie couldn't believe she was going to receive so much money, even after Mervyn had taken his cut. A few weeks ago she would have sold her soul for this chance. What the hell – she had sold her soul!

'I've been through it line by line several times. A million dollars now, another million bucks when the movie is completed.' Mervyn exhaled a cloud of blue cigar smoke towards the ceiling. 'Didn't I tell you I'd make you a star, Angie. Forget about those couple of pornos you made. They're buried in the past. Forgotten. After 'Roll Of The Dice' you'll be up there with the best. Who knows – maybe even in line for an Oscar.'

'I gotta hand it to you, Mervyn.'

'Thanks, baby. But we still got to keep you making headlines. What's with Wayne Folen lately? Has he been in touch?'

'He phones me every night from that training camp where he has taken the team. I don't think things are going too smoothly. He hinted at some problem or other.'

'He's probably missing you like hell. And yeah, you're right about Wayne having problems. Here, read this – '

Mervyn picked up a copy of the New York Post from his desk, passed it to Angie. The headline on the sports page jumped out at her: 'Ryder Cup Men Revolt' it read. Underneath was a sub-heading: 'Folen's Training Camp Regime Too Tough for Ryder Cup squad.'

Angie read quickly through the story. The U.S Ryder Cup squad, having reluctantly agreed to Wayne's training camp plan, had objected strongly after he had brought in a former U.S. Marine buddy as physical trainer to get them into shape. The revolt had taken place after Wayne's buddy had insisted on taking the squad members out on a five mile dawn run in the Catskills. After they had staggered back to their hotel, the golf pros had called a meeting among themselves at which they had agreed, under duress, to continue with the afternoon physical training sessions, but had given an ultimatum to their captain that unless he dispensed with the morning training runs that they would pull out of the Ryder Cup. Apparently Wayne had backed down and agreed to the team's demands.

Angie looked up, smiled. 'Poor Wayne. Maybe I should drive up there and see him. Give him moral support – '

Mervyn suddenly stopped pacing. 'Say honey, that's not a bad idea. I'd tip off a couple of the press guys, get them to send photographers along...' His eyes glinted. 'Yeah, why don't you arrange with Wayne for a visit, suggest you bring up the other wives and girlfriends...'

'D'you think he'll go for it?'

'So what if he doesn't. I'll still get a couple of photographers along. Leave it to me.'

'That's not all the good ideas I've had Mervyn. If it's publicity you want listen to this....' She told him about the Irish male strippers called The Celtic Tigers and how she planned to bring the American Ryder Cup wives along to see them perform during the build-up to the Ryder Cup. When she finished she could see that Mervyn was interested.

'Hunks in jocks! What a great idea! Angie, you're a genius.' He was almost beside himself with enthusiasm.

'Thought you'd like it.'

'I do, I do!'.

'Apparently these guys are a sensation. Hot stuff. The women really go for them.'

'Great. I can just see the headlines – ' Mervyn gazed at the ceiling for inspiration. Angie smiled. The guy saw everything in headlines. He jabbed every word into the air with his cigar. 'Ryder Cup women enjoy male strip show!' He broke off, looked at her. 'Hey, any chance you getting some of the European girls along too?'

'I'm already working on that, Mervyn.'

'Angie baby, you're brilliant, superb. I love you, baby. Everything is falling into place!'

'I phoned Seanie the hotel concierge guy in Ireland yesterday. We got a couple of stage side tables booked for a party of twenty in Symie's Bar in a place called Glengariff – '

'What makes you think the Ryder Cup dames will go?'

'I won't tell them where we're going until we're on the coach and everyone has had a few drinks. They'll think we're going to visit a stately castle or something – '

Mervyn laughed. 'They're in for one hell of a surprise – ' He paused. 'Wayne and the Ryder Cup top brass won't like it.'

Angie shrugged. 'So what? We've made it to the big-time, Mervyn. We can forget about Wayne and the Ryder Cup any time we like.'

Mervyn looked doubtful. 'Don't rush things, baby. Wayne is still big news. We still need him.'

'Sure we do. Why do you think I'm going to visit him in that training camp?'

A short while later Angie made her way down the narrow stairway from her agent's office and out into the bright Brooklyn sunshine. Mervyn watched as she hailed a cab and drove away. He returned to his desk, lifted the telephone. He waited while his secretary put him through to the Hollywood Reporter.

'Hello. Is that the news desk?'

'Yeah.' The male voice that answered sounded bored.

'I have a tip-off for you. About the actress Angie Wilde.'

'Who?' the bored voice asked.

'Angie Wilde. She's a movie star.'

'No kidding. How come I never heard of her?'

'Because she's just about to make her big break-through – '

'Look buddy, you're wasting my time. We get guys like

you phoning all the time with tip-offs about nobodies. There are a lot of dames out there willing to give a guy a good time if he gets their name in the Hollywood Reporter – '

Mervyn kept his cool. 'Ever hear of a director called Patrick Mannion. They say he's the next Tarantino?'

'Sure we heard of this guy Mannion. The little Irish guy is hot right now. What about him?'

'Mannion has just signed Angie Wilde up to star in his next movie 'Call Of The Dice'- '

At last there was a show of interest. 'Sure, I've heard of that movie. Now we're getting somewhere. So what's with your friend Angie?'

'Like I said she's gonna be a big name soon. But she has a past she'd like to keep hidden. She starred in a couple of porn flicks before she hit the big-time. You know the scene....'

'How long ago?'

'Four, five years maybe. She was a struggling stage actress at the time.'

'Do you know the name of these blue movies?'

'No. But you're a smart reporter. You got contacts. It won't take you long to find out...'

'Any other info you can give me?'

'Not much. They were shot in New York – and she used her own name - '

'Right. One more item. What's your name, buddy?' There was a click as the phone went dead.

Mervyn Lazlo leaned back in his swivel chair, took a pull at his cigar, smiled at the ceiling. Who was the smart ass that said there was no such thing as bad publicity.....

• • • •

Jeremy Walker turned the car in off the main road, drove a short distance along the rutted track until it disappeared beneath the overhanging branches. Then he and Katie alighted and walked the rest of the way through the sun-dappled trees towards the lake.

Katie felt his arm around her waist, warm and comforting. It was as though he was assuring her that everything would be alright, but that if she wanted to change her mind he would understand. She smiled up at him, a delicious tingle of excitement running through her body. Now that the moment had arrived she was feeling nervous. She had never taken off her clothes in front of a man before; not even for Benjy Duff during those dreadful nocturnal visits when he had sneaked into her room in the Loughduff Inn. Not even for her husband, who had never asked her to do so anyway…

Suddenly the trees ended and they were out into a clearing by the lakeside. The stillness was complete, save for the chirping of birds and the sigh of the slight breeze through the branches.

'What do you think?' Jeremy asked.

'It's beautiful. Peaceful too.'

'I discovered this spot not long after I moved into the cottage. I've done several canvases here. You'll recognise them when you see them in the exhibition.' He looked at her. 'You quite sure Katie, you don't want to change your mind?'

She shook her head and he bent down, kissed her lightly on the forehead, pressing her body to his. 'I'll go back to the car and bring the easel and the picnic basket.'

He disappeared through the trees. She looked across to the far side of the lake; the expanse of water was not great and she could make out birds flitting in and out of the branches. It seemed an ideal place for family picnics, but thankfully this being a weekday there was nobody in sight.

Jeremy returned with the picnic basket in one hand and a large, plaid rug under his arm. 'I'll fetch my easel later when we've had something to eat.' He spread the rug on the grass, undid the straps of the picnic basket and produced a bottle of red wine and two glasses.

He held up the bottle, smiling apologetically. 'This I'm afraid is the highlight. The rest consists of a couple of hard boiled eggs, a bowl of salad and some tomatoes. I'm not very good at this sort of thing.'

'I don't care. Just being here with you, on this beautiful afternoon...' They looked at each other for a moment, then melted into each other's arms, enjoying a long, lingering kiss. Katie felt the pressure of his arms; she allowed herself to be eased slowly down onto the rug, feeling the weight of Jeremy's body as he moved on top of her. His lips were on hers, his hand already toying with the buttons of her blouse...

Her hand moved over his. 'Please Jeremy. Later...'

His hand inside her blouse stopped caressing her braless breast. 'My God, Katie, you're so beautiful.' His voice was a whisper of passion. 'I do so want to put you on canvas, show you to the world – '

Katie laughed. 'I don't want the world to see me undressed. Only you, Jeremy.'

'Promise me you'll let me make love to you later. Here, before we leave – '

'I promise.' He withdrew his hand slowly, reluctantly. When they were sitting facing each other again he smiled and said, 'How about a glass of wine before we begin?'

She watched his strong hands uncork the bottle, his eyes on her all the time. The mid-afternoon sun was hot and Katie enjoyed the cool liquid as it coursed down her throat.

They were silent, enjoying the aloneness. Katie again found herself thinking how her life had changed so dramatically during the past few weeks. She was frightened that the happiness she had found might be snatched away as quickly as it had materialised. She was frightened also that she felt no remorse about her husband, lying in a hospital ward in Dublin, his body wasting away daily, his mind wandering. Meanwhile here she was by a lakeside in the sun, sipping wine and about to give herself to a man whom she did not even know had existed until a relatively short time ago.

Katie knew that what she was doing was wrong, but she was unable – or unwilling – to help herself. She had never known happiness like this before. And now that she had discovered it she was finding it impossible to walk away from it.

It explained why, as soon as Ben had driven off in his Mitsubishi Ranger to pick up whoever it was he planned to bring to Dublin to visit Travis, she had dashed upstairs, flung off the jeans and heavy plaid shirt which was her mode of dress on the farm, then had a bath and washed her hair, allowing herself the luxury of a shampoo to give it an extra sheen.

As she lay back in the bath in the silent house – Jack and Garret had started back in secondary school in Killarney after their summer break – Katie had experienced a mounting sense of excitement. It wasn't only that shortly she would be visiting Jeremy and showing him the drawings she had worked on during the past two weeks. It was more than that - today she was going to pose nude for him!

Katie had broken the news to him when she driven over to his cottage. Jeremy had received it calmly, his kiss expressing his gratitude. 'I know just the place,' he had confided, 'down by the lake – '

'Is it isolated?', she had asked anxiously. If someone from the locality saw them she would be mortified. The word would get back to Ben, to Travis. Katie knew she was putting her whole life, and that of her two sons, on the line.

'Yes, very. I'll bring a picnic, a bottle of wine. We can have a drink beforehand, celebrate the occasion. How's that?'

'Lovely.' He noticed her eyes were dancing with excitement. 'Before we go I want to show you some sketches I've done. Will you look at them, Jeremy, tell me honestly what you think of them.'

'Of course.'

'You will give me an honest opinion?', she had asked, her heart pounding.

'How can I resist anything you want, my darling Katie.'

She had fetched them from the car, spread them out on the big wooden table in the main room of the cottage. Jeremy had strolled around, peering from one sketch to another, evaluating each in turn, stroking his neatly trimmed beard in a thoughtful manner. Finally Katie couldn't contain herself any longer.

'For God's sake, Jeremy. Say something!'

He hadn't answered immediately. Finally he had lifted his eyes from the table.

'Well?' Katie felt weak, her heart was pounding. She realised she had been holding her breath.

'I'm very impressed, Katie. Very impressed indeed.' Jeremy's eyes too were shining with excitement. 'I think they're excellent. They certainly show potential. I may be wrong, of course, but I think that with a little more tuition and development you could earn a living as an artist.'

She felt so weak she had to sit down. 'Tell me you're not only saying that because it's me…'

'I wouldn't do that.' He turned from the drawing, looked at her. 'Like I said I could be wrong, Katie. I'd like somebody other than myself to judge your work. Henry Mackintosh, perhaps – '

'Henry Mackintosh!' Katie put her hand to her mouth with shock. 'Do you really think they're good enough to show to him?'

'Why not? He's more experienced at recognising and evaluating new talent than I am. Henry would look at them more critically, more commercially. If he thought them worthy enough he might even put them on show – '

'Do you honestly think they're that good?'

'Yes I do. Tell you what, I'm going to Dublin tomorrow to supervise the hanging of my paintings for the exhibition. You come along , Katie, and I'll ask Henry to have a look at them. How's that?'

That was over an hour ago. Now Katie was on her second glass of wine and she could feel the warm afternoon sun burning through her thin white blouse. She was feeling exhilarated, a little light-headed...

'Where would you like me to pose?' she asked.

Jeremy put his glass of wine down carefully, rose to his feet. He glanced around the clearing. 'See that rather inelegant tree over there? – ' he pointed to a tree with hanging yellow branches several metres from the water's edge. 'Come over and I'll show you what I have in mind...'

He helped Katie to her feet, picked up the rug, held her hand as they walked towards the tree. 'I want you to let your hair loose from the ponytail, Katie, and stand sideways like so – ' He demonstrated – 'glancing towards me – '

'You set up while I get ready.' Katie said, her voice barely above a whisper. Now that the big moment had arrived she felt very calm. She knew she had a good body thanks to the amount of active work she had to do around the farm. Even into her mid-30s she had never tended to put on weight. She was proud of her body; why should she not show her body off to Jeremy in an artistic manner?

He had spotted a small clearing through the trees. 'That looks like a good spot to prepare.' He handed her the rug. 'You might like to wrap this around you until I'm ready to start.'

Jeremy turned and walked back to where he had left the easel and canvas stool. Katie hesitated a few moments, then pushed her way through the overhanging branches. Alone in the sun dappled clearing, she disrobed quickly, folding her clothes neatly and placing them on the stump of a small tree. She shivered. It was cool beneath the branches. She pulled the plaid rug around her shoulders and stepped out into the sunlight, feeling the grass cool beneath her bare feet.

Jeremy was almost ready. He smiled encouragingly at her. He gestured to her to move towards the tree he had indicated earlier. 'You forgot to untie your hair,' he smiled.

'Oh, sorry – '

'Let me.' He reached behind her and undid the band. Katie's dark, lustrous hair fell loose around her shoulders. Then he slipped the rug from her shoulders.

He stood back, admired her. 'Perfect, he said. 'You look beautiful.' He arranged her stance, one half of her body in shade as she leaned back against the tree. He brought strands of her hair over her shoulder so that if fell across her right breast.

'Just one more thing – ' He walked a few paces to where some wild roses were growing. He pulled a stem loose and gave it to Katie. 'I want you to hold it and look at the rose, not at me. Just likes so…'

Katie nodded, took the rose. 'Is this okay?'

'Perfect. Think you can hold that pose for fifteen minutes at a time? Let me know when you get tired and we will take a short rest.' He kissed her gently. 'Thank you again, Katie.'

Jeremy crossed to his easel, sat down, and began to put her on canvas.

• • • •

Wayne Folen looked up in annoyance when he heard the light tap on the office door. 'Come in!' he shouted

Janet, the secretary lady who had been assigned to him by the training camp organisation, entered rather timidly, a sheet of paper in her hand.

'Excuse Mr. Folen, I know you said you weren't to be disturbed before the press conference but – ' She smiled apologetically.

Wayne didn't return her smile. 'So why the hell aren't my instructions being obeyed. I'm very busy right now – '

Janet was expecting a response like that. She knew things had not been going smoothly for the captain of the Ryder Cup team since the squad had arrived three days ago. So much media interest in what was going on between Wayne and his squad members inside the training camp. One had only to read the newspapers, watch the television, to see that information was being leaked to the eager media about the rigorous get fit regime which the captain had imposed on his players in the lead-up to the Ryder Cup.

'I'm sorry. This fax has just come through. I expect you'll want to see it – ' she paused. 'It's from the Washington – the White House.'

'You mean the President?'

'Yes.'

'Well, that's different. Sorry for that, you were right to bring it in. Thanks, Janet.' He took the sheet of paper from her, saw the famous insignia, waited until she had exited. Jeez, the White House! Wayne knew the President was a golf fanatic. Even the most powerful man in the world was caught up in the Ryder Cup clash.

He read the script. It confirmed that the President would host a farewell reception on the south lawn of the White House on Sunday afternoon next, prior to the Ryder Cup contingent departing for Europe. The fax stated that the ceremony would begin at 3pm and last an hour and that the |President was putting Air Force One at the team's disposal for a flight to New York. There they would connect with a luxury charter flight to Shannon in Ireland.

The final line of the fax message caught Wayne's eye. It

read: 'Telephone call will follow shortly. Good luck to you and your squad.' It bore the President's signature.

Wayne got up from behind his desk. What a boost to his morale – and it couldn't come at a better time. The team members were practically in revolt. His plan to get them physically and mentally fit in order to wrest the Ryder Cup back from the Europeans had backfired badly. Right from the first day the guys had grumbled about the fitness regime introduced by Al Gordon, Wayne's tough-as-teak ex-Marine buddy. The early morning five mile jog over the hilly terrain had several of the squad dropping out after the first couple of miles. Only the circuit training sessions, which Wayne had insisted on in addition to 18-holes of golf in the afternoon, were acceptable to the players, albeit reluctantly.

In the evening the rather prim lady sports psychologist – another Wayne innovation – had a tough time holding the attention of a group of guys who by then reckoned they were fit only for bed. To show their disinterest some team members had feigned falling asleep during the sessions; the lady psychologist was miffed and had threatened to quit. There were suggestions in the media that Wayne Folen was losing the confidence of his team.

Not even the arrival of the tailored outfits of jackets and creaseless slacks, the casual attire which the Ryder Cup members would wear at official functions, plus the sets of sports shirts, sweaters and customized golf bags, all with the Stars and Stripes and Ryder Cup insignia, had lifted the spirits within the training camp. The wives and girlfriends had also been togged out in smart jackets, skirt and blouses, including gloves. But as the ladies were not allowed into the training camp until the last night the menfolk had further cause to complain. Some sports writers had dubbed the luxury complex 'Folen's Folly'.

Reading and listening to newscasts of the unrest in the Catskills lead Wayne to suspect that one of his own team members had gone behind his back and broken his 'no speaking to the media' edict. The culprit, Wayne reckoned, was probably Casey Matthews, the 44 year-old veteran of the squad who had been elected spokesman for the players. Under pressure, Wayne had reluctantly agreed to hold a press conference to answer questions about the happenings at the training camp. Again under pressure he had agreed to allow Casey Matthews to share the top table with him and Cord McCallum at the press conference which was scheduled to get under way shortly. Wayne gritted his teeth; he was determined to stand his ground.

He read the White House fax over again. At least the President was on his side! The telephone on his desk shrilled into life. Wayne picked it up.

'Hello. Wayne Folen here - .'

'Hold on a moment, Mr. Folen. The President wishes to speak to you…' He almost let the receiver fall in surprise.

'Wayne, how are you? This is the President speaking – ' He recognised the voice.

'Mr. President – ' Wayne gulped. Jeez! 'Thank you for calling – '

'My pleasure. How are you making out?'

'Fine, fine, thank you, sir – '

'Under a little pressure right now, eh?' A short laugh.

'You could say that, sir. But don't worry, I'll be okay – '

'Sure you will. You've got balls, Wayne. Take my advice and hang in there. You'll be fine. I know what it takes to stick to one's principles – '

'Thank you, sir. I aim to hang in there. We U.S. Marines don't quit. When we start something we finish it. We get the job done – '

'That's the spirit! That's what I like to hear. And remember I'm right behind you, Wayne. I want you and your guys to bring back that Ryder Cup. I aim to be in Killarney on the last day to see you do it.'

'We'll do exactly that, sir. For you – and America. I appreciate your support, Mr. President.'

'You received the fax about the arrangements at the White House on Sunday?'

'Yes sir.'

'Everything okay? Anything else I can do for you and your squad?'

'No sir. Meeting you at the White House will boost our Ryder Cup hopes.'

'I want you to know, Wayne, that despite the duties of the office I'll be keeping in touch with the Ryder Cup battle here in the White House. I know you and your guys won't let America down – '

'We won't, sir. You can bet your life on that – '

'And Wayne - ?'

'Yes sir?'

The President adopted a conspiratorial tone 'You have my permission to go over there and kick some European ass! Within the rules and in an acceptable kind of way, of course!'

'Of course, sir!'

'You make sure to come back to America with that goddam trophy.'

'I take it that's an order, sir - .'

'You're damn right it's an order!'

'Don't worry, sir, I won't let myself be pushed around by anybody.

'Good. That's what I like to hear from our Ryder Cup captain. Oh, one last thing…'

'Yes sir?'

A slight pause. 'About your wife Marcia….' Another pause. 'My wife took the liberty of telephoning her today. The two ladies had a long talk…'

Wayne stalled. He wasn't sure quite what to say. He waited for the President to continue. 'I admire Marcia. She's a fine woman. Still standing by you, Wayne. You know that?'

'I was hoping she would, sir, despite what has happen- ed – ' He had telephoned Marcia at Shiralee's house a couple of times over the last few days but his daughter, outraged at her father's public humiliation of her mother, had refused to let her come to the telephone. In fact Shiralee was threatening to find a top agent to act for her mother so that Marcia could cash in on all the requests she was getting for interviews. Marcia had even received an offer to write a 'tell all' book about her life with America's errant Ryder Cup captain.

'You know deep down I still love my wife, Mr. President,' Wayne said. Did he mean that or was he just saying because it was the President on the other end of the line. He admired Marcia for the way she had conducted herself throughout this sorry mess. Never once had she come out and openly criticised him. The President was right. Marcia was a fine woman.

'Every man needs a good woman behind him Wayne, remember that. I hope I'm not interfering when I tell you that my wife has arranged for you to get a call from Marcia soon.'

'Thank you again, Mr. President. I look forward to that.'

'I'm told that you're going in right now and face some hostile question at a press conference?'

'That's right, sir.'

'I've had to face a few of those in my time!' Wayne heard the President chuckle. Then the tone of the voice hardened. 'Take my advice Wayne and take them on. Give them hell – don't take any bullshit from anybody. Remember I'm right behind you. In fact lots of Americans are right behind you. Good luck!'

The line went dead. Wayne rose to his feet, emotion welling up inside. He stood to his full height, felt like he was back in the Marines, standing to attention. He had an urge to salute his Commander-in-Chief. Instead he squared his shoulders, exited, and marched briskly past his wide-eyed secretary in the outer office. He strode down the corridor to the room where he was taking the press conference.

Give 'em hell! the President had ordered. Her aimed to give those interfering airheads in the media just that!

• • • •

'Tell me Donie, do you still have that shooting cottage up in the Gap of Dunloe?' Ben Gartland asked the question casually, studied the last of his Guinness as he swilled it around the end of his glass.

'I have,' Donie Dunhill replied, wondering what was behind the question. 'But as a place it's not exactly the lap of luxury. Just four walls, a roof and three rooms. No bathroom nor toilet like.'

'Not to worry. Fairly isolated isn't it?'

'To be sure. And a bit difficult to get to.' Donie caught the barman's eye, signalled for two more pints of Guinness. 'Grand spot for the snipe and the grouse, though – ' What the hell was Ben Gartland leading up to?

'Would you be using it over the next couple of weeks?'

Donie hesitated before replying. Ben was leading up to something. 'Probably not. We're busy with the harvest right now. Why do you ask?'

Ben looked directly at him. 'I might be wanting to use it for a few nights.'

'For who?'

'Never you mind. Someone very important.'

'Listen Ben, I don't mind giving it to you for a few nights, but I'd like to know what it's going to be used for,' Donie said as he paid for the drinks. They had stopped in a roadside hostelry halfway between Dublin and Killarney on the way back to Loughduff. A few hours ago they had exited from the Mater Hospital opposite Mountjoy Jail in Dublin after visiting Travis, Ben's brother. A Garda had stayed in the hospital room with them throughout the visit.

Donie had been shocked when he entered the room to which Travis had been moved from Mountjoy Jail. Travis was propped up on pillows, his face, under a black stubble of beard, drawn and haggard, his eyes dull and listless. A drip feed by the bedside was attached to his left arm and his condition was being monitored around the clock by a nurse.

Ben had done most of the talking, bringing his brother up to date on developments involving the farmers' protest, highlighting the huge interest from farmers around the world in Travis's hunger strike and the reason behind it. Travis seemed to understand but made no effort to talk. Donie noticed that neither of the brothers mentioned Katie or her boys. It was none of his business; maybe Ben didn't want to burden his brother with the rumours circulating locally about Katie and the handsome stranger in their midst.

They had only been allowed to stay ten minutes when the nurse requested them to leave. 'Your brother is very weak and it would not be good for him to be distressed further.' At the door she whispered to Ben: 'I'm afraid if he doesn't end his hunger strike soon he'll do permanent damage to his system – '

Outside the hospital Ben had been confronted by cameramen and reporters. They all wanted to know if he had requested Travis to come off his hunger strike.

'I have not. It would be a waste of time. If my brother dies I will hold the government responsible. His blood will be on their hands!'

Ben had not spoken much on the drive back and Donie, who saw himself as Ben's right-hand man on the farmers' protest group, had been glad when they had stopped for a drink. Now Ben was on about something and Donie was uneasy.

'Someone important you say, Ben. Like I've said that

place isn't exactly a hotel. If the person is that important you might do better looking for somewhere else. Myself and my lads are the only ones who go up there. And we're not very tidy – '

'There's a bed, isn't there?'

'Aye. Two.'

'Is there a stove?

'No. Only a fireplace. We bring up a gas ring for cooking.'

'Can the door be locked securely from the outside?' Ben paused. 'I mean would it be difficult for anyone to get out?'

'Get out? You mean escape?'

'That's exactly what I mean, Donie.' Ben lowered his voice, glanced around to make sure he was not overheard. 'Your place sounds ideal.' He grinned. 'Now all we've got to do is to get our man…'

Donie didn't like what he was hearing. He was a friend of Ben's but he knew that the man was dangerous, capable of stepping outside the law. And since Travis had been arrested the media attention that Ben was receiving as ringleader of the farmers' protest appeared to have gone to his head. Donie wanted to find out more about what he was letting himself in for.

'What are you on about Ben? You're surely not thinking of kidnapping someone?'

'Shut your big mouth!,' Ben hissed. 'Do you want everyone in the pub to hear you.' Ben's anger died quickly and he winked at Donie. 'It's something I've got in the back of my mind. I'll let you know what it is in good time.'

Ben studied his companion as they lowered their pints. Donie was about the same height and had the same build as Pauly Glynn. There should be no problem there. He would persuade Donie to step into Pauly's Garda uniform when the time came….

• • • •

Marty Kerrigan swung his leg over the saddle of his ancient bicycle, let it freewheel silently over the lush undergrowth, and when it came slowly to a halt he alighted and propped it up against a tree. Marty undid the straps of the carrier bag on the back of the bicycle, took out his camera and fitted the long range lens. Through the trees he could see the sun dancing off the lake. He looked forward to enjoying a couple of hours of his favourite hobby; studying and photographing the abundant wildlife on the lake.

As the local postman for Loughduff and the surrounding area, Marty enjoyed cycling along the winding roads of the locality, visiting the scattered farmhouses and stopping for a chat with the inhabitants, often calling back to take a photograph when something or someone with an interesting countenance caught his eye. He treasured the couple of days each week when, work finished, he took time off to pursue his hobby.

Widowed now for ten years, Marty shared a house in the village with his lone son, Cormac, who had himself inherited keen interest in photography from his father. Cormac worked as a photo/journalist with the local newspaper, The Kerry Herald, in Killarney. The newspaper occasionally used some of Marty's wildlife and portrait photographs and a gallery owner in Killarney had staged two exhibitions of the local postman's prints, many of which adorned his house in Loughduff.

Now he wended his way through the trees towards the lakeside, brushing aside the occasional overhanging branch that barred his way. Marty had almost reached the clearing when he saw the man on the far side of the lake, sitting in front of an easel. He recognised him immediately as Jeremy Walker, the Englishman who had moved into the area some months ago.

Ah, so someone else had discovered the beauty and solitude of the lakeside setting, Marty thought. He wasn't surprised that it had attracted an artist like Jeremy Walker.

Marty surmised that after viewing some of those very interesting paintings of the female form recently at Jeremy's invitation in his cottage, the young Englishman must now be entering a pastoral phase in his work!

The Loughduff postman was about to break cover and wave a greeting across the lake to the artist when something else caught his eye. It was a movement at a tree several yards from where Jeremy Walker was sitting. Jeremy had said something – Marty couldn't catch what it was – and somebody had moved from behind the tree.

When the figure emerged Marty saw it was a woman. He gulped, his Adam's apple sliding up and down his thin throat. Holy God – a naked woman!

Marty stared, dumfounded, wanting to take his eyes away yet unable to do so. He gulped again when he recognised who the naked lady was – Katie Gartland, nude as the day she was born! Her dark hair was hanging down provocatively over her breasts and Marty caught his breath at the sight of her long, slender body, the patch of dark pubic hair contrasting against the white of her skin. It struck him that the scene across the far side of the lake looked like something out of a ballet, or a painting.

He watched enthralled as Katie bent down, picked up a rug that had been lying on the grass, ran across the clearing towards Jeremy, her hair streaming out behind. The beauty of the scene was entrancing. Almost automatically Marty raised his camera and began shooting off some film....

He saw Katie pull the rug up around her shoulders. She laughed, held her arms and the rug open wide, said something to Jeremy.

Marty watched, his breath coming in short gasps, as the Englishman rose from his canvas seat, his eyes transfixed on the woman before him. He advanced slowly across the grass to where Katie was waiting, moved into her embrace. Katie's arms were now around the Englishman's neck, the rug shielding them both as they exchanged a passionate kiss....

From his vantage point through the opening of the overhanging branches Marty shot off some more film. People might call him a voyeur but he did not see it that way. If he ever had to recount what he had seen by the lakeside this sunny day his word could not be doubted; he had the evidence to prove it.

Then another thought struck him. Katie Gartland was in the news in a big way right now. She was being interviewed practically every day about her husband on hunger strike up in Dublin. Newspapers would pay handsomely for a picture of Travis Gartland's young wife frolicking naked by a lakeside in Loughduff with the handsome stranger whose name had been linked to hers by the local gossip.

The couple across the lake were still locked together in a passionate embrace. Marty would have given anything to have been able to photograph what was going on underneath that rug! The movements of the two bodies left little to the imagination!

Then what he had hoped would happen actually did. Losing herself to the moment, Katie released the rug and it slid slowly away, exposing her naked shoulders first, then her buttocks, until it fell around her ankles onto the grass. Neither she nor Jeremy made any attempt to retrieve it. Unencumbered now, Katie raised herself on her toes and locked her body into Jeremy Walker's....

Confident that the couple across the lake were entirely in a world of their own and that he would not be detected, Marty moved forward another few feet and began shooting film in slow, calculated movements. Just before the lovers of the lakeside finally broke apart, he stepped back into the cover of the trees, eased himself out of sight, and retraced his steps to where he had left his bicycle.

He could hardly wait to get home to the dark room in

the cottage to develop the film in his camera. This had been his lucky day! Cormac would know the right people in the media. The tabloids especially would pay a small fortune for the photographs he had just taken. And he would insist that his name did not appear in any of the newspapers. He was a respected member of the community and he wanted to remain so.

Marty Kerrigan was not interested in fame. But his postman's salary didn't amount to much – this was a God-given opportunity to get his hands on some useful money.

CHAPTER EIGHT.

'**B**ruce! Bruce! Where on earth are you? Come out here this minute. Did you know anything about this? It's – it's outrageous!'

Bruce Cartray sighed, rose reluctantly from his desk. What now, he wondered? He could tell by his wife's voice that she was annoyed. But then something was always getting up Sally's pert little nose these days. Ryder Cup syndrome – it was even getting to him.

Let the woman wait! He had more important things to do than listen to another of Sally's complaints. He studied his proposed Ryder Cup pairings on the computer screen once again. On the top of the list he had paired two Englishman Neil Naismith, Ryder Cup veteran and winner of the U.S. Masters and two other majors, with up-and-coming young star Ben Oswold, making his debut against the Americans. The elegant Naismith would relish being seen as the senior partner and the star of that pairing.

Bruce had broken with tradition a few days ago when he had telephoned Neil Naismith and paid him the compliment of asking him who on the team he would not like as his partner in the fourballs and the foursomes over the three days. Naismith's off the record reply had been brief and to the point:

'There are only two players in the squad I'd rather not partner. Lars Nyheim is tops because, to put it bluntly, I don't like the Swedish guy's attitude. He's a big hitter and a very fine golfer but he's erratic off the tee and when he gets into trouble he's inclined to lose his head. Frankly, he's not my type oft Ryder Cup partner. The other team member I'd rather not be paired with is our Irish friend Davy Cochran – ' Bruce remained silent; he had suspected a comment such as this. 'Davy finished in the top ten in his last three tournaments and was lucky to make the team,' Naismith continued unabashed. 'He's on a roll right now but he hasn't played in a Ryder Cup before and when the chips are down I can't see him handling the pressure. I like winners but I don't see Davy winning any points for us against the Americans in Killarney.'

Bruce stared at the list of 12 names comprising eight nationalities on the computer screen. Matching players from different countries and with different personalities was always a problem for the European captain. Past captains like Tony Jacklin and Bernard Gallacher had come out winners and were part of European Ryder Cup history. Bruce was anxious to win the trophy twice in succession and follow in their footsteps; should he captain a losing team in the Ryder Cup he'd carry that stigma around with him for the rest of his life.

There was less than a week to go before the opening ceremony when both he and Wayne Folen would officially announce the team pairings for the opening day. No doubt he would have to give a lot of thought to the pairings problem up to the very last moment. Right now, however, Sally had yet another problem that needed sorting out.

'Bruce! What on earth is keeping you? – ' His wife's shrill voice cut through his thoughts.

'Coming, darling – ' He walked down the carpeted hallway from his office, entered the spacious sitting room. Sally was waving a newspaper about furiously. 'Something wrong, my dear?' he asked superfluously.

'What do you think. Look at this - !' She thrust the

newspaper at him. 'Those Ryder Cup idiots have done it again. Look at the dreadful outfits they've had designed for my girls to wear.'

Bruce took the newspaper. Under the headline 'Ryder Cup Ladies Step Out In Style' The Times had published a series of photographs of the range of specially designed outfits which the wives and partners of the European team members would wear. A couple of models displayed the selection of sweaters, skirts with matching blouses, and trouser suits. The range also included shoes, scarves and even a cloche-style hat.

'Did you ever see such a selection of dreadful outfits?', Sally stormed. 'I resolutely refuse to allow my girls to wear such rubbish. Your Ryder Cup friends didn't even have the good grace to ask my opinion before they went ahead with these designs. I ask you – what would a bunch of grey-haired middle-aged men know about women's fashions?'

'But darling, read the report…those outfits were designed by one of the country's top couturiers. The lady is world famous – '

'I don't care how famous the lady is,' Sally stormed, 'those outfits look ghastly. Why wasn't I consulted beforehand? I'm not going to allow my girls appear in those rags!'

Bruce thought the ladies and their outfits looked pretty smart. He refrained, however, from voicing his opinion to Sally. She would accuse him of disloyalty, of not backing her judgement. He had enough problems to wrestle with right now.

'Why not leave well enough alone, darling. I doubt there's anything you can do about it now – ' If he had said that he hoped that America would win the Ryder Cup he would not have evoked such an angry response from his wife.

'Really!' She glared at him. 'You should speak your mind more often!' She grabbed the newspaper back from him, looked at it again.

'But darling, the outfits are already made,' Bruce tried to reason. 'The Ryder Cup is just over a week away. It's too late now for change – '

His wife was ranting again. 'I don't care. I'm going to telephone that Major Mackenzie, let him know I'm not happy with those those Ryder Cup outfits, that I want them changed – '

'Don't be silly, darling – '

'Silly am I? How are we supposed to look good against the Americans in those outfits? They'll make us look like schoolgirls!' Sally could visualise Angie Wilde strutting her stuff for the cameramen in top-of-the-range gear and shuddered.

'I'm sorry darling, but I haven't got time to get involved with what our girls will or will not be wearing,' Bruce felt he had to make a stand. Sally was taking things to far. 'My job is to motivate the squad, generate team spirit, get the pairings right –'

Sally was having none of it. 'Major Mackenzie assured me faithfully after the last Ryder Cup that I would be consulted on the designs this time around. Now they've chosen to ignore me again. I feel humiliated.' She knew how to play on her husband's sympathy.

Bruce was only half listening. He'd had a flash of inspiration. He would pair the Irishman Davy Cochran with Sweden's Lars Nyheim. The Swedish bad boy and the veteran Irishman – they would make an interesting combination. Or maybe he would pair the only Italian in the squad, Dominico Uragi, with Cochran in the first day foursomes and fourballs. They were both laid-back, happy-go-lucky characters who might just surprise the pundits by winning a point.

'Are you listening to what I'm saying, Bruce?' Sally's voice brought him back to the present.

'Er, yes. I'm right with you, darling.'

'Then you'll telephone Major Mackenzie, tell him

unless he does something about those outfits I will alert the media of my disappointment at not being consulted. I see it as a personal insult to myself and I am not standing for it.'

'You want me to telephone the Major?' Bruce groaned inwardly.

'Isn't that your duty as Ryder Cup captain? You're surely backing me all the way on this issue? –' Bruce couldn't believe what was happening. Here he was facing into a tough Ryder Cup battle with a European team comprised of eight nationalities as underdogs and his wife's only concern was would she and 'her girls' look good throughout the three days. No captain wanted to go down in the history books as a loser when it came to the Ryder Cup, yet here he was plagued with a wife who worried more about her own reputation than that her husband could be outsmarted by his American rival, make some wrong decisions under pressure, and forever have it thrown back in his face.

Wayne Folen was lucky, Bruce thought. Okay, so he was having his own problems with his wife, but at least they were self-inflicted and Marcia wasn't around every day badgering him about women's clothes! Since Angie Wilde had come on the scene Sally had become more edgy, conscious that she could find herself playing second fiddle to a publicity hungry bimbo actress. The fact that her husband was juggling with getting the team pairings right and trying hard to avoid bruising several inflated egos in a Ryder Cup squad comprising three Englishmen, two Scots, two Swedes, a Welshman, an Irishman, an Italian, a German and a Frenchman, seemed of no concern to Sally. Bruce reckoned it would take a U.N. Peace Commissioner to inject a spirit of harmony into that lot!

As he lifted the telephone Bruce prayed that Major Mackenzie would see his side of the argument and make a concession, however slight, that would appease Sally's bruised ego and make life easier for himself. Bruce felt he was ageing by the day – and the real Ryder Cup battle hadn't even begun.

● ● ● ●

The telephone rang just as Katie came downstairs into the hallway. 'Hello?' She hoped it wasn't another reporter looking for an interview.

'Katie!' It was Nell. 'I'm glad I caught you in. Have you seen the morning papers?'

'No.' A morning newspaper was a rarity in the household. 'Why are you asking, Nell?'

Nell took so long about replying that Katie thought her friend had been cut off. Then she heard Nell ask: 'Has Ben arrived for work yet?'

'No. I'm expecting him shortly. He probably went drinking last night after the protest in Killarney.' Why are you asking these questions, Nell? Is something wrong?'

'Katie, I think you should come over here to me before Ben does arrive. There's no telling what he'll do when he sees those pictures in the papers – '

'Pictures – in a newspaper?' Katie felt a sense of unease. She tried to keep her voice under control. 'What are you talking about, Nell? What pictures'

Her friend's next words came out with a rush. 'Photographs – of yourself and Jeremy. Taken at the lake yesterday – '

'Oh my God!' Katie was suddenly afraid. Her grip on the telephone tightened. 'Wh – what are they like?'

'Very – er – revealing.' Nell laughed shakily. 'I even got a bit of a shock myself!'

'What am I doing in them?'

'It says in the captions that you were posing for Jeremy. And by the looks of things you don't seem to have any clothes on – ' Nell paused, heard Katis gasp. 'I think you

had better come over and see them for yourself, Katie.'
Then she added, 'If it's any consolation, girl, you look
absolutely marvellous. You have a body to die for!'

Katie was so shocked by now that she was hardly
listening. Nell was right, Ben would be furious. There was
no way he would get through the town without someone
telling him about the photographs of her in the morning
papers. Ben usually stopped in the local newsagents every
morning to buy cigarettes.

Ben would not be the only one angry – the whole of
Loughduff would be outraged. The village had never had a
scandal on this scale before – and this one was now well
and truly out into the open. Katie wasn't worried about
herself – she had never mixed too much in the community
anyway – but she was anxious about Jeremy. He was an
outsider, a foreigner to the locals, and anger would be
turned towards him. Outsiders had been attacked and run
out of villages like Loughduff before, killed even, for
getting involved with a local woman. Ben Gartland wasn't
the only one likely to seek revenge on whoever it was who
had brought scandal to the community.

'Who took the photographs, Nell? Does it say? Jeremy
and I didn't see anybody by the lake yesterday – '

'The newspapers don't give any name – '

'How many photographs are there?'

'Four in the local newspaper, and a bit of a story
mentioning yourself, Jeremy and Travis and all that's been
happening here recently. I wouldn't be surprised if they're
in all the Irish nationals and the English tabloids too.'

'Oh my God!' Katie had heard enough. 'I'll be over
straightaway, Nell. I'll phone Jeremy first – '

'Right-o. Get over here quickly, Katie. I'll make a
strong pot of coffee!'

Katie dialled Jeremy's number. She was relieved when
he answered. 'Jeremy – ' she blurted out. 'Have you seen
any of the morning newspapers?'

'No. But I know why you've phoned, Katie. It's been on the local radio. I've had several reporters on to me already. I was just about to phone you – '

Katie felt herself go cold. 'What did they want.'

'The usual – a follow-up to the story. They sense a good scandal.'

'What did you tell them?'

'Absolutely nothing. I said I had no comment to make. I've taken the phone off the hook – ' Jeremy paused. 'Are you alright, Katie?' There was concern in his voice. Before she could reply he went on, 'I'm surprised they haven't been onto you already. Leave your phone off the hook. Is there some place you can go for a few hours?'

She told him about Nell's phone call. 'I'm going over to her place now.'

'Good. Hopefully the media won't trace you there. I'm sorry I got you into this mess, Katie.'

'Don't be sorry, Jeremy. I'm not. It brought us both together. That's all that matters.'

And it was too. But the gossip, the publicity – would they be able to handle it all? She had never been in a situation anything like this before. Her whole life had been transformed since she met Jeremy Walker. How often in the past had she looked out through her kitchen window at the drab, empty rain-sodden fields and wished for something to happen that would change her life forever, some sort of miracle that would release her from her loveless relationship with Travis. A miracle that would get her out of Loughduff forever and into a new world.

That miracle had happened and she was determined to grab it with both hands. She would accept the consequences if it meant being with Jeremy Walker. If Katie had ever harboured any doubts that she would lack the courage to leave her husband and leave Loughduff with her boys this recent happening had forced her hand. That decision had now been made for her.

'Katie, you know I have to go to Dublin today to work on my exhibition.' Jeremy's voice cut across her thoughts. 'Will you be alright while I'm away? I'll be back sometime tomorrow. We'll talk about our future, discuss all those things we plan to do together'

'I look forward to that, Jeremy. Phone me during the day. I'll be either here or in Nell's … '

'Just remember I love you, Katie. You know what I want you to do – come away with me somewhere. You and the boys. We can't remain in Loughduff, not after what has happened….Will you come away with me?'

'Of course. Where?'

'Somewhere. There are lots of places…Greece, Spain, Morocco maybe. Somewhere we can paint and be happy together. It will be a whole new beginning for both of us – ' He broke off. 'Look, I'm sorry, but I've got to go. We'll discuss it when I get back from Dublin. And Katie – ' his voice took on a serious tone – 'Be careful my darling. Try to stay out of Ben's way until I get back.'

Katie put down the telephone, stared at the wall, her heart pounding. Spain, Greece, Morocco – to her they were magical words, place-names on a map, places she had often seen featured on holiday programmes on television. Sun and sea…meals in the open air or on a beach. Bottles of wine, gaiety laughter…and Jeremy wanted her and the boys to go with him….

As she left the house she saw two cars driving in through the gates from the main road. They pulled up quickly when they saw her and several people alighted from each. When Katie saw the cameras she knew the media were on her trail. As she approached her own car the two groups converged on her.

'A moment please, Mrs. Gartland – ' a young girl shouted.

'I'm sorry,' she shouted to the girl – 'I'm on my way out right now.'

'It won't take long. I presume you've seen the photographs in this morning's papers – '

'No, I haven't. And I've nothing to say at present – ' Katie pulled open the door of her car. They were all around her now, and a hand-held tv camera was already whirring.

'Maybe you'd like to see them – ' The young girl was persistent. She was unfolding a newspaper. 'What is your relationship to Jeremy Walker?'

'I've already told you that I've nothing to say – '

'Does your husband know about the relationship with you and Jeremy Walker – ' This from a young man with the second group. 'Are you going to Dublin to see your husband?'

Katie pressed the accelerator and the car shot across the yard towards the roadway. She had to jam on the brakes when another car swung in from the road through the gateway. As she exited Katie saw it contained two people. The media hunt was really on.

She drove at speed to Nell's place. In the rear view mirror she could see the trio of cars following behind. She swung into Nell's driveway, slamming the door of her car behind her. As she was dashing up the steps Nell appeared in the doorway. Before her friend could say anything Katie dashed by her.

'I'm being chased by reporters, Nell. Tell them to go away. Order them off your property. Please!' As Katie went inside she heard Nell shouting at the newshounds, then closing the door behind her. In the hallway Katie leaned against the wall, breathless. They waited, listening, heard the cars drive off after a short while.

'They won't go away,' Nell said grimly, 'They'll wait outside on the roadway…'

They entered Nell's comfortable sitting-room. Katie noticed the newspapers, one spread out on the table, the other on the carpet. Without saying anything she picked up the one from the table, looked at the photographic spread on page three. She gasped in shock at what she saw.

• • • •

Ben Gartland was not feeling the best. He was suffering from a hangover the result of too many pints of Guinness with his cronies in the Loughduff Inn last night. Not that there was much to celebrate; the protest rally yesterday in Killarney had not enjoyed the same success as the previous one at the Parknasilla Palace Hotel. This time around the Gardai were out in force and, on orders from the Government, were aided by units of the Irish Army.

Barriers had been more efficiently manned and Ben and the protesting farmers, with their long lines of tractors and other farm vehicles, had not been allowed anywhere near the town. Only people on legitimate business were allowed through the barriers, patrolled by Army and Garda personnel, at the outskirts of Killarney and after a few hours of nothing dramatic happening the tv cameras had been withdrawn and the frustrated farmers had slowly dispersed.

Worse still, the protest had been mentioned only briefly on the tv newscasts last night to the disappointment of the big crowd watching in the Loughduff Inn.. Ben Gartland reflected on this as he drove through the town on his way out to the farm. Because of his hangover he was later than usual this morning. It was mid-morning now and he saw Pauly Glynn standing outside Loughduff's only newspaper shop. Pauly was in uniform and waved Ben down.

'Morning, Ben – or should I say good afternoon.'

Ben grunted a greeting out through the lowered car window. He was in no mood for Pauly's caustic remarks.

'Seen this morning's paper?' Pauly asked. He seemed to find the question amusing.

''Course not,' Ben growled. 'And get that smirk off your face. We're not finished with our protest yet'

'It's not the farmers' protest I'd be worried about if I were in your shoes,' Pauly grinned.

'What do you mean?' Ben didn't like the sly look on Pauly's face.

'Go in to the shop. Buy a copy of the Kerry Herald – and any of the other papers, for that matter. See for yourself.'

What the hell was this thickhead of a Garda on about? Ben got out of the car, slammed the door, brushed past Pauly. As he entered the shop two local women were coming out. They stopped, stared at him, they hurried past and scurried off down the street. Ben noticed them glancing back over their shoulders at him, whispering and laughing. Something was going on and he would have to find out what it was.

He ordered a packet of cigarettes then picked up a copy of The Kerry Herald from a pile on the counter. He was tendering a Euro note to the lady behind the counter when the picture on the front page caught his eye.

'Jaysus!' The word exploded from Ben's lips. He could hardly believe his eyes. It was Katie, lying back against a tree, naked, a leg strategically bent to obscure her pelvic area, her hair cascading down between her breasts. Ben read the caption. It had a reference to page three. Ben tore the newspaper open, another expletive escaping as he studied the other photographs displayed there. He crunched the newspaper into a ball, stormed out of the shop, Pauly was waiting on the pavement. The anger on Ben's face wiped the smile off Pauly's.

Ben cursed loudly. 'Who took them blasted photographs?'

'We don't know for sure. We're still making enquiries.' Pauly was enjoying the situation.

'What do you mean 'for sure'. Are you saying that stupid sergeant of yours suspects someone?'

Pauly shrugged. 'You'd better ask him, Ben. See if he'll tell you.'

'I will, I will. And if I ever find out who was behind that camera…..' Ben's face was contorted in anger.

Pauly stifled a grin. Of course Sergeant Gilhooly knew about Marty Kerrigan's interest in photography. The whole town knew about that. Weren't the sergeant and the postman good friends, and wasn't Marty's son a photo/journalist? Wasn't it entirely possible, the sergeant had reasoned with Pauly and his Garda colleague Jerry Carney earlier, that Marty in his pursuit of his hobby of photographing wildlife, had stumbled across the Englishman and Katie Gartland by the lake yesterday? Those photographs would have been worth a lot of money…

'I'm not sure it's an offence for someone to take pictures like those,' the sergeant had opined. 'It's certainly not an offence for a newspaper to publish them – the way standards are going these days they're not exactly earth shattering. We'll let things sit for a while, lads. Let events take their course, as we say in our business.'

Pauly watched as Ben looked at the pictures once more before crumpling The Kerry Herald into a ball, his face contorted with rage.

'Remember one thing, Ben. Whoever took those photos may not have committed a crime. Even if we do find out who was responsible it will be difficult to charge them with anything – '

Ben Gartland was barely listening. 'I blame the Englishman for this, ' His voice was low, as though he was speaking to himself. 'He's the one who's turning Katie's head against Travis. He should be run out of Loughduff – '

'Watch what you're saying, Ben. If somebody hears you - '

If Ben heard it didn't stop him. 'The Englishman will pay for this. Mark my words.'

With that Ben flung the newspaper into the back of his car, jumped into the driving seat, took at speed through the main street of Loughduff. He wasn't worried that Pauly had heard him make threats against Jeremy Walker. The thought of that Englishman cavorting with Katie, able to get her strip off like that, was enough to drive Ben almost insane.

Now he had gone too far. Jeremy Walker would not be the first outsider to come to Ireland and find out that it didn't pay to get too friendly with another man's wife.

• • • •

Nell entered the sitting-room and saw Katie staring at the photographs in the newspapers. She said nothing, waiting until Katie had put them aside.

'Oh God,' Katie's face mirrored the shock of the moment. 'They're worse than I thought, Nell. What am I going to do?'

'Have a cup of strong coffee, that's what,' her friend said pragmatically. 'The story is in all the newspapers and on the radio so there's very little you can do about it. I heard it mentioned on one of the talk shows just before you arrived. They were trying to contact you.'

'Are those reporters still hanging around?'

Nell went to the window, looked out. 'I'm afraid so. They're hanging around outside the gate.' Katie sat down, a worried look on her face, while Nell made the coffee. 'Do you have any idea who took the photographs?', Nell asked from the kitchen.

Katie shook her head. 'Neither Jeremy nor I saw anybody – '

'No, that's obvious,' Nell dry reply floated from the kitchen. 'I'd say everyone in the village has a good idea who took those photographs, but of course nobody will say anything. I believe Sergeant Gilhooly is making enquiries.'

'Oh God, Nell, all this publicity. I'm worried for the boys…'

Nell appeared with the tray, put it down on the table between them. 'Loughduff is such a small place,' she said as she poured. 'You don't need me to tell you that it'll be hard to live this down. Have you thought what you are going to do?'

'This has made up my mind for me, Katie. I'm going to leave Loughduff - ' She paused. Nell was her friend. She could confide in her, tell her everything. 'Jeremy has asked me to go away with him – myself and the boys. That's what I'm going to do.'

Nell's eyes lit up. This was straight out of the romantic novels she devoured every week. The heroine trapped in a humdrum existence, falling in love with a handsome stranger and being whisked off to live a fulfilling life of passion and endeavour in an exotic land where they lived happily ever after. But was she was hearing wasn't fiction. This was happening right on her doorstep – and to her best friend...

'Where would you and Jeremy go?' She hoped it wouldn't be back to England. That would be too humdrum by far.

'He's talking about Greece, or maybe Morocco in North Africa. Somewhere in the sun that has colour and life. Anywhere that will suit our work. Jeremy wants to forget the past, start a new life together!'

'Oh God!,' Nell said again. 'It's like something you read about – or see in those romantic films.' She sipped her coffee, forgetting for once to help herself to a chocolate biscuit. 'Tell me all about it.'

'There's not much more to tell.' Katie recounted the short conversation she had had on the telephone with Jeremy. Nell listened attentively, perched on the edge of the sofa, taking it all in. 'I suppose you think I'm out of my mind, Nell?'

'You'd be out of your mind if you didn't go, Katie.' She sighed. 'I only wish I were in your shoes right now. There you are, leaving this place behind, off on a romantic adventure with someone you're madly in love with while I'm left staring at the kitchen walls like Shirley Valentine!'

Katie looked puzzled. 'Shirley Valentine? Who is she?'

'Don't tell me you never heard of Shirley Valentine?', she asked incredulously. Then she understood…life with Travis Gartland wouldn't have included many visits to the cinema, or time for watching home videos.

'Shirley Valentine was a wife married to a not-very-nice husband,' Nell explained, picking her words carefully. 'She was so lonely she used to talk to her kitchen walls to make conversation. Then she went off to Greece and fell for this gorgeous local fisherman- ' Nell broke off. 'Oh Katie Gartland, I'm delighted for you.' A pause. 'Only….'

'Only what, Nell?'

Nell hesitated before replying. 'I'm still worried that you know Jeremy such a short time. You know so little about him. Of course tell me that it's none of my business and I'll shut up right now – '

'You're worried about his background. You mentioned it before…'

'Did I?'

'Yes.'

'I'm thinking only about you, Katie. I want you to find someone who will make you happy, believe me. You deserve it – ' she broke off, stirred her coffee. 'I'd like for you to know more about Jeremy. Like is he married, that sort of thing…'

'I don't know and I don't care whether he's married or not. I just know that I want to be with him.' Her gaze fell on the newspapers open on the carpet, taking in the spread of photographs. Jeremy had promised that the painting he was doing of her would be in good taste, and certainly the pictures which the unknown photographer had taken showed her in a good light. Katie had not realised that she could look so well.

Nell followed her friend's gaze. 'I hope Jeremy Walker

appreciates that he's a very lucky man.'

Katie smiled. She leaned over, took her friend's hand. 'Whatever I do in the future, and wherever I go, I want you to know thatk I'll miss you Nell. I'll miss you terribly.'

• • • •

The Irish Government Ministers, seated in their appropriate places according to their portfolio, ringed the large oak oval-shaped table in the spacious blue-carpeted room. Dossiers were spread out in front of every Minister in readiness for the weekly Friday morning Cabinet meeting at which matters of immediate importance were discussed and future strategy planned.

First item on the Government agenda today, underlined at the top of the order of business, was: 'Ryder Cup – Travis Gartland and the consequences of his hunger strike'.

Specially invited to this Cabinet meeting was Garda Commissioner Thomas Healy, tall, mid-50s, grey-hair brushed back, serious looking, resplendent in his light blue, gold-braided uniform.

The Ministers chatted animatedly among themselves as they awaited the arrival of their party leader, the Taoiseach. When the door opened and he swept in with his special advisor in tow the gathering, including the Cabinet's three female Minister, fell into a respectful silence. The Taoiseach was sixty-ish, medium height, grey thinning hair brushed sleekly back, his white shirt cuffs showing the regulation inch below the sleeves of his impeccably-cut suit. His heavily lidded eyes swept the room, passing swiftly over each Minister in turn. His face was impassive, unsmiling.

The Taoiseach sat down at the head of the table, glanced briefly at the agenda before him, and got straight to the point. 'What is the latest on the Ryder Cup scene?'

His eyes rested on Patrick McGlynn, the Minister for Tourism, Art and Sport.

McGlynn cleared his throat before answering. He had been rehearsing his opening sentence in his mind for the past half-hour. 'Taoiseach, ladies and gentlemen, without question the upcoming Ryder Cup clash between the superstar golfers of Europe and America is the biggest and, in terms of worldwide publicity, the most prestigious sporting event ever staged in Ireland - ' The Minister paused, pleased with his delivery. 'Upwards of seventy thousand people from all over the world, mainly Americans and Europeans, including team members, wives, officials and members of the international media, have been pouring into Killarney and the surrounding area during the past week. As you all know this prestigious event tees-off officially a week from today – The European and American teams arrive in Shannon on Sunday and will travel by road, heavily escorted, to their headquarters in Parknasilla. They will be helicoptered to the golf course and back to their hotel every day – '

McGlynn paused again, anxious to gain the maximum import for his next announcement. 'Thus far, television teams from over one hundred countries have arrived to broadcast the three-day Ryder Cup event to an estimated audience of one billion people. In tourist terms the spin-off for our country from the Ryder Cup is inestimable – '

The Taoiseach waved his hand impatiently, halting the Minister's eulogy in mid-sentence. 'Alright, Mr. McGlynn, we get the picture. All very laudable but let's skip the bullshit and get down to the real issue – ' He had everyone's attention. 'What about Travis Gartland? Are we going to allow the stupid bastard starve himself to death and ruin this whole marvellous set-up or are we going to do something about the situation?' The Taoiseach's gaze swept the table, settled on his Minister for Justice.

'Well, Joe?', the Taoiseach barked. 'Come on, man. We're waiting. Do you have a solution to this crisis? How are going to extricate ourselves from this mess?!'

Joseph Daly, portly, florid of countenance, appointed to his prestigious post in reward for whipping up crucial support for his boss in a tense leadership battle the year before, adjusted the spectacles on his rather large nose. This was a ploy he used to give himself a few extra seconds to gather his thoughts. He didn't relish what he was about to say.

'I'm afraid, Taoiseach, there's nothing new to report. This man Travis Gartland, the stupid bastard as you so rightly call him, is very weak and is still refusing to come off his hunger strike – '

He was frozen to silence by his leader's baleful glare. 'So how do you plan to overcome this problem, Joe? Have us all offer up a decade of the rosary to Saint Patrick?' The sarcasm was palpable and some Ministers smiled. Others looked uncomfortable. Poor old Joe, he was an easy target.

Joseph Daly cleared his throat. 'I had in mind asking Travis Gartland's wife to come to Mountjoy and try to persuade her husband – '

This time the Taoiseach brought his clenched fist down on the table in front of him. 'Jaysus Joe, have you no cop-on? Have you read this morning's papers – '

'I was just about to explain, Taoiseach – '

'Don't interrupt me, Joe!' An uncomfortable silence fell. All eyes were on An Taoiseach. Joe wished he had never entered politics. He should be back serving behind the bar in his pub in Sligo. 'Katie Gartland and her husband don't get on – ' The Taoiseach waved a morning newspaper – 'the woman is gallivanting around Loughduff with an English artist, posing nude for the bugger no less!….'

The Taoiseach paused. 'Katie Gartland is having the time of her life. Indeed, I'm confidentially informed, Joe, that she's the last person who would want this stupid bollix of a husband to give up his hunger strike!'

At the far end of the Cabinet table Alice Devlin, Junior Minister at the Department of Children, Religious and Social Affairs and a mother of six, joined her hands and offered up a silent prayer. Such foul language! She had once heard someone – probably a member of the Opposition - describe the present Taoiseach as a 'vile little man.' What an apt description!

'Commissioner!' The Taoiseach turned his gaze to the country's top police officer. 'Isn't there something we can do to get Gartland off his hunger strike? If the stupid bastard dies he'll become a martyr. The whole country will turn against the Government – '

' – and all the benefits of staging the Ryder Cup here will be lost,' Patrick McGlynn cut in. He was getting a lot of personal publicity from the big event and didn't want anything to mess it up.

'Well, Commissioner?' The Taoiseach glared at the Chief of Police, who didn't wilt under pressure.

'I agree with the Minister for Justice,' the Garda Commissioner said. 'There's very little we can do about Gartland. The hunger strike is his choice. The sale of that land to the Japanese has annoyed practically every farmer in the country. Of course we're monitoring Gartland's situation very closely,' the top Garda concluded, 'but I'm afraid there's very little we can do but sit and await developments – '.

'Hhmm...I don't find that very encouraging.' The Taoiseach let them know he wasn't impressed. His gaze again moved around the table. This time it settled on Seamus Conaty, Minister for Agriculture and Lands. A big farmer who ran an auctioneering business on the side, Seamus was a millionaire several times over, due mainly to insider information. He was presently under scrutiny by the Ethics Committee in Dail Eireann and could come under pressure to resign his Cabinet post in the near future.

'Mr. Conaty – '

'Yes, Taoiseach?'

'Your Department is responsible for selling the land to the Japanese – '

'As I recall, Taoiseach, it was a Cabinet decision - …' If he was being pushed to resign his Cabinet post, Seamus Conaty reckoned he might as well go out fighting.

'Thank you for reminding me, Mr. Conaty – ' There was no mistaking the sarcasm in the Taoiseach's voice. He fixed his Minister with a steely gaze. 'I want you to get those lands back from the Japanese consortium that bought them!'

Conaty swallowed. Jaysus, he thought to himself, the man has gone crazy, He's asking the impossible. Aloud he said: 'Pardon, Taoiseach?'

'You heard me, Mr. Conaty' the Taoiseach snapped. 'Get that land back.'

Cabinet members not directly involved in the discussion listened enthralled. This had the makings of real drama. Gut wrenching stuff.

Seamus Conaty kept his composure. 'How exactly do we get the land back, Taoiseach? The contract was signed months go.'

'That's not my problem, Mr. Conaty. I don't give a damn when the contract was signed, I want that land back for the local farmers.' The Taoiseach pursed his lips, a habit he had when he was thinking. 'There's a historic site on that land, isn't there?.'

'Yes, that was one of the things that attracted the Japanese – '

'Hhmm…' The Taoiseach rose slowly from his seat, conscious that every eye in the room was on him. He walked across the expanse of blue carpet, hands behind his back in his best Napoleonic pose, paused at the large window that gave a panoramic view of the well laid out gardens below. He gazed out, rocking backwards and forwards on his heels. After a few moments he turned, looked at the circle of curious faces.

'Anybody any idea how we can get ourselves out of this mess?' There was no response. 'A fine fucking bunch of deep thinkers you lot are!' Down the table Alice Devlin mentally started on another Act of Contrition. 'I suppose I'll have to do the thinking for the lot of you…'

The Cabinet members remained silent, watching their leader. The Taoiseach again addressed the Minister for Agriculture and Lands. 'I presume, Mr. Conaty, that we have an ancient castle somewhere that is being renovated at present?'

'Indeed we have, Taoiseach. Several in fact.' Conaty replied, relieved to have contributed something positive to the discussion..

'One surrounded by enough land to build a top class golf course and sports complex?'

Conaty nodded.'I think we can come up with such a specimen.'

'Good. Pick the best one you can find, get on to the Folklore Commission and have them concoct some historical happenings around the castle and the area in general, then offer it to the Japanese at half the price they've paid for the original 250 acres of Killarney land. If they play ball hint that I will consider doing them the honour of officially opening their golf complex when it's finished. Got that Mr. Conaty?'

A murmur of excited conversation broke out. The Taoiseach waited for it to subside, then he concluded. 'I think our Japanese friends will jump at that package, don't you?'

A chorus of agreement. Alice Devlin reckoned the Taoiseach was committing at lease a couple of sins – telling lies and cheating - but she remained silent, offering up a prayer of forgiveness instead. 'We tell the local farmers that they can have the Killarney land at a reasonable price, Travis Gartland comes off his hunger strike, and the Ryder Cup goes ahead without interruption. Ladies and gentlemen, problem solved.'

Again the buzz of conversation broke around the table. Smiles appeared on faces, heads nodded in admiration. Everyone looked happy except Seamus Conaty.

'May I say something Taoiseach?'

'Yes, Mr. Conaty?'

'Supposing - just supposing - that our Japanese friends don't go along with the new plan? What if they insist on holding us to the original contract?'

The Taoiseach sighed. 'That's what I admire about you, Seamus. You're an eternal optimist...' He walked slowly around the table, placed his hand on his Minister's shoulder. When he spoke he was smiling; always a danger sign. The tone was still threatening.

'Seamus, my old friend, somebody has coined the phrase 'Just Do It.' I see it on a lot on t-shirts lately. I want you to get one of those t-shirts, frame it, and hang it up behind your desk!' The Taoiseach basked in the laughter that followed.

• • • •

The sound of a car engine being revved woke Nell Flavin from a fitful sleep. Beside her in the bed Tom slept soundly. Nell pushed the bedclothes back and automatically eased her feet into her slippers in the darkness. As she did so she glanced at the bedside clock. The luminous face showed 2.25.am.

She was certain now that the sound she had heard earlier was of a window being smashed. She listened... were they muffled voices coming from the cottage across the way? Jeremy Walker returning from his trip to Dublin, perhaps? But Katie had told her that he would be away for a night, maybe two. Nell sat on the edge of the bed, listening, her ears primed for unusual sounds. It was a fairly isolated area and not many people passed by even on the main road at night.

Then she heard the dogs barking. Somebody was moving about outside. She knew she had not been imagining things when she saw the red blotch through the lace curtains of the bedroom. A fire!

'Tom! Wake up!' She shook her husband awake.

'What is it?' He sat up in bed, rubbing the sleep from his eyes.

'Get up. There's a fire. I think it's Jeremy Walker's place. I heard voices outside a few moments ago – '

Nell rushed to the window, pulled back the curtains. Yes, flames were showing through one of the ground floor windows of the cottage across the way. Outlined against the flames she saw the silhouettes of two men running towards the gateway. They disappeared from her view and a few moments later she heard the car, headlights off, roaring down the laneway leading onto the main road.

She grabbed her dressing gown off the chair. Tom was already pulling on a pair of trousers over his pyjamas. Nell switched on the light as Greg and Conor, their two teenage sons, exited from their bedroom.

'What's happening?', Greg, the eldest, asked.

'Put some clothes on and get downstairs quick,' Nell told them. 'The cottage across the way is on fire. Start filling some of the buckets from the pipe in the yard. Tom, you put on a jacket and get the fire extinguisher from under the stairs. I'll phone the fire brigade. Hurry! And be careful everyone!'

Nell scampered downstairs. After what seemed an age the late duty man in the Killarney Fire Station answered the telephone. She quickly gave him details of the location of the fire and asked him how long it would take for them to get to the scene.

'About fifteen minutes. Anyone inside the cottage?'

'I don't think so. As far as I know the owner is in Dublin at present.'

'Okay. Be careful. Nobody is to go inside. Heaters or canisters of gas have a nasty habit of exploding. We're on our way!'

Outside in the darkness, Nell dashed across the yard and ran the short distance to Jeremy Walker's cottage. Tom was already there and had the fire extinguisher working, spraying a jet through the broken front window. Greg and Conor were ferrying buckets of water across the yard and lining them up for their father when the fire extinguisher fluid ran out. The flames seemed to be dying down, certainly not getting any worse.

'I think we've saved the cottage,' Tom shouted to his wife.

'Thank heavens for that,' Nell shouted in return.

They were battling the blaze ten minutes later when they heard the klaxon of the fire engine in the distance. A couple of minutes later it had bumped its way along the rutted laneway and stopped outside the gate. In answer to a shouted question from one of the firefighters Nell pointed to a pipe in the yard. A hose was quickly fitted and the nozzle pushed in through the broken window to one of the crew who had smashed the rest of the frame and climbed inside. Another opened the front door. The others entered and inspected the interior with the aid of torches.

After a few minutes the senior fire officer came over to Tom, Nell and the boys who were huddled together looking on. 'Congratulations to you all. You did a fine job. You prevented the fire from getting a grip and destroying the whole place.' He paused. 'The man who owns it, he's an artist by the looks of things.'

'Yes,' Nell replied.

'I'm afraid some of his paintings have been damaged.' He went in through the front door, the beam of his torch lighting the way. Nell, Tom and the boys followed and gazed into the interior of the cottage. Downstairs was filled with smoke and there was a strong smell of burning. Water was everywhere and some framed paintings were showing damage. Otherwise things weren't too bad; the only real damage had occurred beneath the front window which was now devoid of every pane of glass.

The fire officer pointed to where his men were dampening down the remains of the fire. 'That's where it started. Looks like somebody smashed the window, threw in a bundle of straw or clothes and – ' his nose twitched – 'doused the lot with paraffin. We'll know for sure when we examine the scene fully tomorrow.'

Nell told him about hearing a window being smashed and seeing a couple of men running to a getaway car. 'I see, probably malicious then. I expect Sergeant Gilhooly in Loughduff will be interested in hearing that. I'll get in touch with him later today. He'll want to see the place for himself.'

Outside in the yard Nell told the two boys to go back to bed, which they did reluctantly. As he watched his men dampening down and cleaning up the debris the fire officer said, 'Am I right in saying that the artist who owns the cottage is that English fellow photographed painting those pictures of Travis Gartland's wife which appeared in the newspapers?'

Tom nodded and Fire Officer Dan Serling smiled grimly. 'Someone like that would certainly have made a few enemies in the area,' he remarked.

Back in her house later, when she heard the fire engine depart and she had made herself and Tom a pot of tea, Nell telephoned Katie. She hated getting her friend out of bed but Nell was worried. The violence had broken out already and she wanted to put Katie on the alert, check that she was unharmed.

She was relieved when Katie answered the phone. Nell broke the news as gently as she could, assuring Katie that no real damage had been done to the cottage.

'You said you saw some men running away, Nell. Did you recognise any them?' Katie

'No. It was too dark and I only saw them for a few seconds.' Nell paused. 'Do you know where Ben was last night?'

'No. I didn't see him all day.'

'I'm not surprised. He was probably off somewhere planning other things,' Nell replied.

Katie lowered her voice in case she woke the boys. 'Do you think he was involved, Nell?'

'Don't you? I'm sure Sergeant Gilhooly will be anxious to talk to Ben tomorrow. By the way, has the sergeant been over to see you yet about those photographs?'

'No. Why should he? I don't think anyone has broken the law.'

'Thank God you're safe anyway, Katie. You and Jeremy will have to be very careful from now on. Whoever tried to set Jeremy's cottage on fire did it as a warning. Don't ignore it, Katie.'

'I'll phone Jeremy at the gallery sometime today and tell him what has happened. Thanks for phoning, Nell. I'll be in touch.'

• • • •

The sun shone splendidly on the South Lawn of the White House as the cavalcade of limousines wended its way through the leafy surroundings and came to a stop at the designated tarmacadamed area. Secret Service agents stayed discreetly in the background as the members of the American Ryder Cup squad, resplendent in tailored blue blazers and pencil-slim white slacks with matching shirt and ties, alighted from the limos, helping their female partners out into the still air of a benign September Sunday afternoon in Washington.

White House officials came forward and escorted the

visitors, with Ryder Cup top brass and team captain Wayne Folen to the fore, towards the main entrance where a dais and a single microphone were mounted on the steps. The President and the First Lady had stressed that they wanted the occasion to be as relaxed and as informal as possible and the White House personnel were following their boss's orders to the limit.

And yet a degree of tension had already been introduced into what should have been a memorable occasion for the Ryder Cup party. As they had exited in cavalcade from their training camp in the Pokinawah Country Club in the Catskills this morning, heading for the airport to fly to Washington for the Presidential reception, they were greeted by the sight of a vociferous group of feminists from Women Together waving banners and chanting anti-Wayne Folen slogans.

As if that wasn't disturbing enough, just a few minutes ago as they approached the entrance gates of the White House the Ryder Cup party had run into another Women Together protest. Security guards had kept the angry feminists back at a safe distance from the convoy of limousines; nevertheless television cameras had captured angry scenes as tourists and passers-by had looked on with interest. Again, posters displaying captions condemning the captain of the U.S. Ryder Cup team were prominent.

Nothing like this had ever happened before to an American Ryder Cup squad and chairman Cord McCallum and his committee members had stared straight ahead as they passed the White House protesters, embarrassed and outraged nevertheless by the proceedings.

Now as Wayne Folen, his squad and their wives and partners stood around on the White House lawn making small talk, helping themselves to the glasses of chilled champagne being dispensed by bow-tied waiters, he could see McCallum talking animatedly to his fellow committee members. No prize for guessing what they were discussing!

'Has McCallum spoken to you at all since you arrived with the wives yesterday?'. Wayne whispered to Angie.

She gave him a sidelong glance. 'Are you kidding? The old stuffshirt has frozen me out. I feel like I got some kind of a disease!' Wayne looked grim but Angie laughed. 'Don't worry about me. I'm having a ball. And I'm sure looking forward to meeting the President!'

Wayne wasn't too surprised that Angie was being given a hard time by the top brass of the U.S. Golf Association. Right now her photograph was prominently displayed in all the Sunday newspapers. Yesterday's story from the Hollywood Reporter, prominently displayed on page one, had been followed up in a big way by the national press – accompanied by headlines like 'Ryder Cup Captain's Girlfriend Was Porn Movie Star!'

He too had been outraged when the story had broken yesterday. He had spent the day with his mobile phone switched off and had ordered reception at the Catskills camp not to put any telephone calls from newspapers through to him.

'Why the hell didn't you tell me you had appeared in blue movies?' Wayne had tackled Angie immediately after the story had appeared on the CNN early morning news.

'I'm sorry, honey. But it's no big deal. A lot of movie stars make porno movies before they hit the big time – '

'Yeah, maybe – ' Wayne had exploded. 'but I bet none of them have ever been involved with an American Ryder Cup captain! What the hell are you playing at, Angie?'

'I'm not playing at anything, Wayne. I'm sorry. I was going to tell you sometime. Honest.'

'You're giving Cord McCallum and his committee guys a helluva lot of ammunition to shoot at me. If the Ryder Cup wasn't coming up next week I'd be fired!'

Angie, putting on a performance that Patrick Mannion would have applauded, looked so crestfallen that Wayne had left it at that. He had taken a shellacking from

McCallum and being given a stern warning to keep Angie out of the spotlight.

That was easier said than done. Right now Wayne could see Angie posing happily for the posse of photographers covering the White House event. She was dressed in a stunning outfit that showed off her hour-glass figure to perfection. Wayne groaned. He hoped this would be the last hurrah for Angie as far as the media were concerned.

White wickerwork chairs, shaded by umbrellas, had been spread around the sun-dappled lawn fronting the colonnaded entrance, but not too many of the visitors took advantage. The Ryder Cup wives and girlfriends in particular, all of them looking like they had just stepped out of a fashion magazine, preferred to stand around in small groups, chatting and posing for photographs and the tv cameras.

A burst of applause erupted when the President and his wife exited from the building. They both waved to their guests, the First Lady looked absolutely stunning in a beautifully cut white lightweight linen suit and ruffled silk blouse, an ensemble which showed off her light tan and slim figure. She and her husband stood on the steps of the White House and acknowledged the applause.

The President held up his hand for silence and began his speech. 'Ladies and gentlemen, it's a pleasure and a privilege to welcome you, the members of the United States Ryder Cup squad, your captain Wayne Folen, committee members of the U.S. Golf Association led by the distinguished Mr. Cord McCallum, and your lovely wives and partners, to the White House – ' The President's words boomed out in the mild early afternoon air to his rapt audience.

'In a couple of hours from now you will be on your way to Killarney in Ireland where, over the three days from Friday next, you will do battle against the best golfers in

Europe for the famous trophy donated by Englishman Samuel Ryder which bears his name. The biennial battle for the Ryder Cup, although fiercely fought by the golfers themselves, had been contested with honour and the highest form of sportsmanship down through the years, and I know that, being American, you will maintain that tradition in the name of your country and do the nation proud in Ireland.'

The President paused, his next words awaited with interest by his adoring audience. 'As a keen golfer myself I aim to be in Killarney for the final day of the Ryder Cup' – he paused, waiting for the applause and cheering to die down – 'and I make no secret of the fact that I hope and pray that I will witness your captain, Wayne Folen, hoist the trophy aloft on your behalf, and for the honour of the United States of America!'

There was another burst of applause, this time more prolonged. The President continued in a more sober tone. 'I accept that in some recent Ryder Cup contests naked national feelings have surfaced during play and emotions have run exceptionally high. One has only to recall some of the unsavoury incidents and chants by groups of our over-zealous countrymen at Kiawah Island in 1991, and the invasion of the putting surface by our golfers and spectators in Brookline in 1999 – ' the President allowed himself a grin – 'although I am happy to recall that we won the prized trophy on both those occasions!'

This was greeted by a burst of laughter and applause from his audience. When the applause had finished the President continued, again in a sombre tone. 'I accept that leading up to the current Ryder Cup some American golf fans may have misinterpreted your captain Wayne Folen's burning desire to win, and that some fans are going to Killarney hoping to see our team, to quote the media, 'kick some European ass…'

A deathly silence fell over the White House lawn as

the President's next words rang out: 'I beg those fans to remember the sportsmanship of their forefathers when, before the first ever Ryder Cup contest in Massachusetts in 1927, our team sportingly offered to postpone the contest for a week to give their opponents adequate time to recover from the six day sailing across the Atlantic – '

The President's voice rose. 'That is the spirit of sportsmanship, friendship and conviviality in which I, and golfers around the world, want this Ryder Cup contest between our great country and Europe to be played. Good luck to captain Wayne Folen and all members of our Ryder Cup team in Killarney. May the best team win. God bless America!'

As one the assembled gathering rose from their seats and applauded the President. The clapping and cheering continued for a full two minutes as the President and the First Lady smiled their acknowledgement. Then it was time for time for them to move among their guests.

As his wife drifted over to where the ladies were gathered the President approached Wayne Folen. 'Hope you liked my speech, Wayne,' he smiled.

'Congratulations, sir. It was excellent, really superb – ' Wayne swilled the champagne around in his glass. Should he ask the question? Hell, why not – as one golfer to another. 'Did you really mean what you said just now – about not kicking European ass in Killarney?'

The President smiled. 'You're damn right I did. I was speaking as the President of the United States – ' the voice went down in tone. 'But speaking as a true-blue American Wayne, I want you to bring back that Ryder Cup. Go over there and do your darndest to win it for America!'

CHAPTER NINE.

Sergeant Gilhooly slowed his car, took careful note of the other vehicles parked in the road outside the entrance to the Gartland farm, then drove through the gateway and up to the house.

Reporters waiting to harass Katie Gartland as soon as she showed her face, he reckoned. Door-stepping they called it in the media. Thank heavens, in a backwater village like Loughduff, he had never had to deal with any real media pressure in his time. Not until nearby Killarney had been chosen to host the Ryder Cup that is. Now the area was saturated with snooping photographers and reporters, all eager to outdo each other and get that elusive world scoop.

He felt sorry for Katie Gartland. Like everyone else in Loughduff she was not used to this intense media scrutiny. Not that she hadn't brought it on herself; gallivanting with that English painter and her husband in jail, and posing for those scandalous pictures that had shown up in all the newspapers. What on earth had she been thinking off; was she losing the run of herself or what!

Now she was paying for her indiscretions in a big way. He had been strolling down the main street of the village as usual last Sunday after Mass and watched as herself and the two boys had come out of the church. All the locals had given her a wide berth, nobody making any effort to talk to her or her boys, heads lifting from the huddles of people as they passed, staring and unsmiling. Shunned in her own village. Sergeant Gilhooly reckoned that Katie Gartland would find it difficult to live with her past in Loughduff from now on.

She opened the door as he approached, an indication that she had been keeping an eye out for any unwanted callers.

''Morning, Katie.'

'Good morning, Sergeant. Come in.'

The kitchen was cosy and warm, shafts of he September sun lighting up the interior. Katie gestured for him to sit down and he took off his cap and placed on the faded blue tablecloth. He nodded when she offered a cup of tea. He'd had occasion to visit the Gartland household several times in the past, usually to question Travis or Ben about some fracas or other in the town the previous night. This was the first occasion he felt welcome.

'I see you've visitors outside.'

'Yes. They've been camping out there each day for the past week.'

'I'm not surprised,' the Sergeant said drily. 'You're big news, Katie. You're becoming even bigger news than the Ryder Cup!' He nodded his head towards the window. 'Are they a bother? I can tell them to push off when I'm leaving – '

She shook her head. 'Thanks, but I doubt that it will do much good. They'll just disappear for a short time and then come back again. I can't go anywhere without them following me.'

Katie poured tea for them both and sat opposite the Sergeant. 'I'm sorry, but I don't have much time,' she said apologetically. 'I'm catching the afternoon train to Dublin.'

'Oh. Going up to see Travis, I suppose?'

'Yes.' It was only half true. Katie's real purpose for going to Dublin was to meet up with Jeremy Walker, but she was not going to tell the sergeant that. Jeremy's exhibition had been a big success and, having been informed by Katie that the fire at his cottage had not been too serious, he had elected to stay in Dublin for a further day. Katie was pleased with the decision; she believed that he was safer in Dublin than he would be in Loughduff. Jeremy had informed her that he too was constantly being chased by the media.

'I'm looking for Ben,' Sergeant Gilhooly was speaking again. 'There are a few questions I want to ask him about that blaze at Jeremy Walker's cottage.'

'He's working in the top field with a couple of local men he's hired in,' Katie answered.

'Good.' Sergeant Gilhooly sipped his tea. 'How has he been behaving? Has he been giving you any trouble during the past few days?'

Katie knew he was referring not only to the blaze at Jeremy's cottage, but also to the photographs of her that had appeared in the newspapers. 'We did have a terrible row after he saw those photographs of me. He didn't get violent, but he did make threats against Jeremy. Ben and I don't talk much. He comes in with the men, eats whatever I've prepared for them, and leaves in the evening.'

'So he did threaten Jeremy Walker' the sergeant said. 'What exactly did he say?'

'Ben told me that he had blamed Jeremy for what was happening between the two of us. He said he told Jeremy to leave Loughduff or else - that if he didn't he – he would be run out.'

'Interesting. It's not the first time Ben has made those kind of threats to people.' Gilhooly leaned back in his chair. 'We came across some tyre tracks outside Jeremy Walker's cottage that looked like they had been made recently. They didn't match Jeremy Walker's car. I want to check them with Ben's Mitsubishi Ranger – '

'Ben's car is parked around the back.'

'Good. I'll check it out before I walk up the fields and talk to Ben. Of course even if the tyre tracks match up to Ben's Mitsubishi it's not conclusive evidence that he was responsible for the fire – '

'Have you talked to Nell and Tom Flavin?'

'Yes. But they weren't much help. They saw only a couple of shadowy figures on the night. They don't think they would be able to identify anybody.'

The Sergeant drained his cup and stood up. Katie rose too, went to the window and looked out. Gilhooly studied her in profile; yes, she was indeed a fine looking woman. The hard life on the farm, married to someone as unappreciative and as uncouth as Travis Gartland, had done her no harm at all. On the contrary Katie Gartland seemed to be blossoming of late; in the past few weeks she had being paying more attention to her appearance. Her dark hair, tied in a pony tail at the back, was glistening and gave her a very elegant appearance. Even the very ordinary white cotton shirt she had tucked into what appeared to be a new pair of slimline jeans failed to hide the fact that she had a figure that men would notice and women would envy.

'I'll be off then. You'll have to hurry if you're to catch that train to Dublin, Katie – ' He paused in the doorway, his big frame almost filling the space. 'I hope you don't mind my asking, Katie, but how are things between yourself and Travis?'

She could have told him that her domestic problems were none of his business but she knew there was genuine concern behind the question, the sergeant had had his difficult times with both Ben and Travis over the years. Pity she had not confided in him all those years ago when she was being abused as a teenager in Loughduff.

'It wasn't very pleasant the last time I visited Travis in Mountjoy,' Katie replied in a low voice. 'I'd rather not go into detail if you don't mind, sergeant. I hope I'm wrong but I don't expect things will improved this time either.'

'Well, good luck anyway. If there's anything I can do let me know. And give Jeremy Walker my regards.'

• • • •

Attired in his trademark pinstripe pants and dark jacket Norman Spencer, manager of the Parknasilla Palace Hotel, was fussing about, ascertaining that everything was spot-on for the scheduled midday press conference of the rival Ryder Cup captains. An air of expectancy hung over the large gathering of international journalists seated in half-circles in the Dunloe ballroom, all of them hoping this first press conference of the week leading up to the big event would throw up its share of controversy.

The American and European Ryder Cup teams and their officials had jetted separately into Shannon Airport yesterday and, under strict security, had been driven by luxury coach to their base in the Parknasilla Palace Hotel. The hotel itself and its expansive grounds were also under strict security, with a large force of Gardai deployed. They were aided by a hundred burly members of a private security firm, dressed in dark sweaters and each with the regulation thick neck and bullet shaped head, patrolling inside and outside the complex. The Government also put on call a squad from the country's Armed Response Unit. It was vitally important from a national point of view that the Ryder Cup extravaganza should be staged without serious incident. Nothing was being left to chance.

From his vantage point on the dais Norman Spencer surveyed the plethora of Ballygowan bottles of fresh spring water, the array of empty glasses and the quartet of microphones laid out on the green baize-covered table. His gaze swept over the rows of seated journalists and the banked masses of tv cameras. He smiled in satisfaction, congratulating himself on having arranged for the hotel's name to be prominently displayed in the background.

The only cloud on Norman's horizon right now was yet another protest being staged outside the hotel entrance. The Women Together movement, Irish-style, were determined to show solidarity with their American sisters, their posters highlighting the disdain in which they held American Ryder Cup captain Wayne Folen and the cruel manner in which he had treated his faithful wife. The women's protest was being monitored discreetly by the Gardai. As a confirmed bachelor Norman Spencer deplored strident women. And to make matters worse they were getting an outrageous share of coverage from the ever-present media.

Norman moved quickly from view as an officious-looking young man in dark blazer and slacks advanced from the other stage of the stage and stood in front of the main microphone. Behind him a quartet of solemn looking men entered from the side and took appropriate seats according to their respective printed names. An expectant silence fell in the packed ballroom.

'Ladies and gentlemen,' the young man began in a pronounced American accent, 'the first of the daily press conferences leading up to the tee-off in the Ryder Cup on Friday next is about to begin. The press conference is scheduled to last approximately one hour. Allow me to introduce – on my right - Major David Mackenzie, chairman of the European Ryder Cup committee... European team captain Bruce Cartray. On my left are their American counterparts Mr. Cord McCallum, chairman of the U.S. Ryder Cup committee, and U.S. Ryder Cup team captain Wayne Folen....' The announcer turned to his audience. 'Thank you for you attention, ladies and gentlemen. You may now begin to ask questions ' The young man exited quickly from the stage.

The four men, their unsmiling faces mirroring the

gravity of the occasion, duly acknowledged the muted applause. Their sombre demeanour indicated that they were not enjoying the experience of facing the members of the media. The questions were soon coming thick and fast. Initially they were fairly innocuous, mainly to do with the how both squads were coping with the switch to a new hotel set-up and the security problems it posed, also about the two 'wild card' selections which each captain had selected for his team. Then it was down to rather more serious matters.

A man in the second row raised his hand. 'I have a question for the American captain…Are you still confident that America will win the Ryder Cup. And if you think so, why are you so confident?' The accent indicated the questioner was a European..

'Sure I'm still confident we'll win,' Wayne's answered in his usual clipped tone. 'As to why it's fairly simple. We have the stronger team – eight of my squad are in the top twenty in the current world rankings. There are only three members of the European team listed in that category.'

The Swedish reporter was not to be put off. 'Leading up to the Ryder Cup the United States, on paper, invariably seems to have the stronger squad. Yet in recent years the Europeans have had more than their share of victories. Why should the same not happen this time?'

'I'll give it to you straight – ' Wayne seemed to be relishing the challenge. 'The reason Europe won't win this time is because my guys are members of the best prepared U.S. Ryder Cup team ever to come out of America. Both physically and mentally I'd bet my life that right now, man for man, they are way ahead of their European opponents – ' This outspoken comment evoked a buzz from the audience.

'Are you saying the European golfers are, physically and mentally, below par?' someone asked.

'I'm saying we put a lot of hard work in place in our

training camp in the Catskills. I'm confident the pay-off will result in us taking the Ryder Cup back to America.'

Cord McCallum, sitting beside Wayne, began to feel uneasy. Not only at his captain's over-confidence about regaining the Ryder Cup, but about mentioning the training camp in the Catskills. No Ryder Cup captain had ever demanded such a commitment from his squad before, the players had objected to it, and it had attracted some adverse publicity. McCallum's worse fears were confirmed when the next question came up from the floor.

'Didn't some of your squad stage a revolt against your training regime in the Catskills?'

'Revolt?', Wayne barked. 'There was no revolt. Sure, some of the guys found it tough, but they agreed it was something they needed. It toughened them up. We had a discussion and sorted things out - '

'A question for Bruce Cartway –' an American voice cut in. 'You didn't see fit to bring the European squad to a training camp in the mountains for physical and mental toughening-up. Do you think the Americans are better prepared this time than ever before and are going into the Ryder Cup with a big advantage?'

Europe's captain was too experienced to fall into the trap of criticising an America Ryder Cup supremo. Nevertheless he did want to take the opportunity to score over Wayne Folen.

'I had my squad follow exactly the same routine I employed two years ago when I was in charge and we won the Ryder Cup. True, we didn't go to a training camp to prepare like the Americans. Frankly I don't think that kind of approach is necessary. I have every confidence that my fellows have prepared themselves both physically and mentally for the upcoming contest and that we will retain the trophy.' To Wayne Folen's annoyance this measured reply evoked applause from what were obviously European journalists in the audience.

'Anything to say to that, Wayne?' a voice asked.

'We'll see who is right over the three days of the Ryder Cup. Physically and mentally my men are in great shape. We can't wait to go to war against Europe.'

'And hopefully kick some European ass. Is that what you mean, Wayne ?' someone shouted up.

'Call it what you will,' Wayne replied. 'We'll do whatever we have to do to win.' Beside him Cord McCallum groaned inwardly. Things were getting slightly out of hand. His fear was that Wayne would be walked into saying something inflammatory.

'What about that Women's Together protest outside the hotel, Wayne? Do you feel that the protest is aimed directly at you? And what exactly is the state of the relationship right now between yourself and your wife Marcia?'

Wayne gave the female reporter who had asked the question a withering look. 'I'm here to answer questions about America's participation in the Ryder Cup. I will not answer questions relating to my personal life. I hope I am making myself clear'

At the other end of the table Bruce Cartray was enjoying the press conference no end. He thanked his lucky stars for being married to a wife like Sally. Yes, she was a bit of a bossy-boots and gloried in the spotlight of her husband being Ryder Cup captain – and a winning one at that, but at least she had a bit of class. Sally would do all she could to make sure he would repeat his triumph of two years ago. Wayne Folen had brought all this on himself by ditching his wife Marcia for a high-flyer like Angie Wilde.

The next question was again directed at the American captain. 'What have you to say to the thousands of American golf fans who, probably due to your comments some time ago, are right now crowding into Killarney with various objectional slogans on their t-shirts?'

Cord McCallum held his breath as he waited for his

captain to reply. 'I value the fans' support and I appeal to them to display a sense sportsmanship and fair play to both teams during the Ryder Cup,' Wayne said evenly. 'I ask them not to adhere to the sentiments displayed on their T-shirts and to treat the Ryder Cup and the European players with respect.' Beside him Cord McCallum breathed a sigh of relief. Was his captain at last learning the art of diplomacy?

The next question, again addressed to Wayne, was the now almost standard one about the course on which the Ryder Cup was being played and if it had been 'doctored' to suit the home team.

'Is it true Wayne, that you have some criticism of the Killeen course in Killarney? That you are not happy with some of the work done on the course during the past year and that you think that the course has been set up specially to favour the Europeans?'

The American captain was forthright. 'Yeah, I'm unhappy with the way the Killeen course has been set up – and my team members agree with me on this.'

The forthright answer created a bizz of excitement. The only sound to break the silence was the whirring of the tv cameras. 'What exactly are you unhappy with, Wayne?' someone asked.

'Quite a few new bunkers have been put in around the three hundred yard area from the tee. These are obviously put there to intimidate the big hitters on my team, guys like Joey O'Hara for instance. A glance at the current driving statistics will show that few of the European golfers are driving the ball three hundred yards or more off the tee. It's obvious why those new bunkers have been put in.'

'Anything else about the course you're not happy with?'

'You bet there is – ' Wayne seemed pleased to have been given the opportunity to sound off. 'A lot of the fairways have been narrowed and the rough has been allowed to grow to long. I reckon during this Ryder Cup spectators will see a lot of cautious rather than exciting golf. My guys would have liked wider fairways. American fans like to see big-hitters in action. It makes for more spectacular golf. The Killeen Course as it stands now definitely favours the Europeans -.' Wayne paused briefly, then finished defiantly, 'But I'm not worried, we're still gonna win the Ryder Cup!'

A mixture of loud cheering from members of the American media, countered by whistles from their European counterparts, erupted in the gathering. Now the verbal battle was really hotting up! This was what the members of the media wanted to hear!

'Did you make your views about the set-up of the course known?' Before Wayne could reply another reporter shouted out: 'Is it true you asked your chairman Mr. McCallum to make an official protest about how the course has been prepared but that he refused to back you up?'

Another deathly silence. A smile played around the American captain's lips. 'I think you should direct that question at Mr. McCallum,' he replied.

'Any comment, Mr. McCallum?' the same reporter asked.

All eyes switched to the American Ryder Cup chairman. He cleared his throat, his bronzed, lined face impassive. 'It's true that Wayne did ask me to make an official protest. But I refused to do so as no rules were broken and I didn't consider a protest necessary. Wayne accepted my decision and there is no conflict between us.'

'Is that correct, Wayne?'

'You've got your answer from Mr. McCallum. But I would like to add that in recent Ryder Cup clashes, the American captain in my opinion has been – and I'm trying to be diplomatic here - talked into making too many concessions to the Europeans. I reckon that's why some of America's top golfers haven't performed as well as they should have in previous Ryder Cup contests - ' Wayne thumped the table. 'It's time the American captain stopped being nice and we Americans became winners again! That's all I have to say on that subject.'

Bruce Cartray felt it was time he garnered some of the spotlight. 'With all due respect to Wayne and the American players, I think that their accusations about the course being 'doctored' to suit us is total and utter rubbish! – '

A gasp went up from the packed audience at the strong language used by the usually discreet European Ryder Cup captain. Bruce Cartray seemed unconcerned at the excitement his comment had created. 'It seems to be that Wayne Folen is already looking for an excuse for what I and my chaps aim to bring about - an American defeat in the Ryder Cup!'

Wayne Folen clenched his hands on the table until the knuckles showed white. He was breathing deeply, evidence that he was trying to control his feelings. Was the clash between the two captains that the media believed inevitable about to happen? A journalist kept the pot boiling by asking if there was acrimony, not only between the two captains, but also between the European and American squads in general.

'Is this the reason why the Americans and Europeans are domiciled in separate ends of the hotel and are also using separate dining-rooms? Is there a ban on members of both teams mixing socially?' the journalist probed.

Major Mackenzie was seen to hold a whispered conversation down the table to his American counterpart Cord McCallum. When Cord McCallum nodded his head in agreement Major Mackenzie rose to his feet.

'Ladies and gentlemen may I have your attention please. Mr. McCallum and I feel it appropriate to terminate today's press conference as of now. We have covered a range of subjects and perhaps it is appropriate to have a cooling off period. Tomorrow's press conference will be held here at the same time – '

There was a murmur of surprise from the audience. The Major waited for it to die down. 'I want, however, to make one thing clear. Regarding rumours and innuendo in the media alleging that the American and European players and officials are not fraternising, Mr. McCallum and I want to deny that emphatically.' He smiled benignly. 'In fact members of both teams and their wives are attending a formal dinner in the hotel tonight to honour the captains of European and U.S. Ryder Cup squads of the past. Rest assured that everyone will enjoy themselves at tonight's function. Thank you!'

With that the four principals at the green baize table rose to their feet and exited the stage. The members of the media slowly filed out of the press conference conversing among themselves. It had been a lively enough opening session. The gut feeling was that there would be one or more sensational happenings before this Ryder Cup got under way.

• • • •

Ben Gartland punched the numbers on his mobile phone and waited. He glanced over shoulder, made sure the two hired farmhands were out of earshot further down the field.

'That you, Pauly?'

He heard Pauly swear softly. 'Jaysus Ben, I told you never to phone me here at the station. What the hell are you on about – '

'Relax, will you. I know Gilhooly's not there. The stupid bastard has been up here at the farm asking me a few questions. He's just left.'

'Yes – and he'll probably be back.'

'What makes you so sure?'

'Because, Ben, he suspects you're behind the fire at the Englishman's cottage.

'Does he now? He'll have to prove it, won't he?' Pauly heard Ben laugh.

'What is it you want Ben,' Pauly asked impatiently.

'I want you to do me a little favour, Pauly. I want to borrow your uniform for a few hours tomorrow night.'

'What!' Pauly was stunned.

'You heard me. It'll be only a few hours – '

'Are you off your head, Ben! A Garda can't give his uniform out on loan - '

'Nobody's going to know. Like I said it'll be just for a few hours - '

Pauly cursed silently. What sort of a moron was Ben Gartland? 'I can't do it, Ben. It's against regulations, that's why – '

'I told you before not to spout regulations at me!' Ben's voice was low, angry. 'Isn't it against regulations for a Garda to take backhanders? Or for a crooked cop to take payola to look the other way...' A sneering laugh. 'You could go to jail for that, Pauly.'

Pauly hesitated, thankful there was nobody else but himself in the station right now. He cursed himself for having gotten involved with this power crazy lout. 'What do you want a Garda uniform for anyway, Ben?' Pauly had a fair idea what Ben Gartland had in mind. He hoped he was wrong.

'You don't worry about that - '

'Has it anything to do with what we talked about the other night....Joey O'Hara, that young American golfer. I want to know, Ben.'

'Alright, alright, so it does involve Joey – '. Ben was getting impatient.

'Go on.'

'I want to take him out of circulation for a few days.'

'Out of circulation.....you mean kidnap him?'

'Call it what you like.'

'Holy God Ben, you're not still thinking of going through with that crazy plan, are you?'

'Why not?'

'Because it's mad, crazy. What if you're caught, or if something goes wrong and something happens to that young American fella, there'll be hell to pay – '

'Nothing will happen to him. And don't worry, we won't be caught – '

'Like I said, it's mad, crazy. I don't like it, Ben – '

Ben gritted his teeth in anger. The yellow bastard was getting cold feet. 'I don't give a fuck what you like or don't like, Pauly. I want a loan of that uniform…' There was a silence. 'Are you still there?'

'Who else is in on this?' Pauly asked. Ben couldn't do this job on his own. 'And what happens if whoever is wearing my uniform is arrested - '

'Nobody will get arrested. I have it all worked out – '

'But Ben, that hotel where the golfers are staying is crawling with security. Gardai, Special Branch officers, private minders – Honest. I've been in the Parknasilla Palace. You can't turn around without bumping into someone in uniform – '

'Do you think I don't know that. I'm not stupid,' Ben shouted into his mobile. He looked over his shoulder; the two hired men were busy bailing hay. 'Look Pauly, no one will question someone dressed as a Garda. O'Hara will be told that we've suddenly discovered a couple of his long-lost relatives, that he can be taken off for a private visit to them without any reporters snooping around. How's that?'

Paul still wasn't convinced. 'What happens then?'

Ben hesitated. He was reluctant to tell Pauly too much. But if he didn't his drinking companion might not play ball, he was wary enough already. 'We stop the car at a fairly isolated spot – I'm not saying where. You get your uniform back in a couple of hours. We blindfold Joey, take him to a hideout in the Black Valley mountains, alert the newspapers and the television and hold the bastard there until after the Ryder Cup is over.' Ben paused, waiting for Pauly's reaction. None was forthcoming. 'It'll create huge publicity for us, Pauly.' Ben's voice had a triumphant ring. 'The Government will be only too anxious to give us what we want!'

Pauly still didn't like what he was hearing. If Joey was kidnapped there would be hell to pay. Was there any way he could put Ben off?

'You've forgotten one thing, Ben – '

'Have I now. And what's that, Pauly?' Ben wasn't too pleased.

'I was the one who contacted Joey O'Hara about his Irish ancestors when he was here a couple of weeks ago, remember? Won't he be expecting to see me again? He'll be suspicious of anyone else – '

'Don't worry about that,' Ben brushed the objection aside. 'These big-shots meet so many people the young fella will probably have forgotten what you looked like. I bet Joey doesn't even remember your name. Anyway, if he does ask, my fella will say you're busy on another job, or maybe not on duty. Simple eh?'

Silence while Pauly pondered this. 'I still don't like it Ben. It's too risky if you ask me – '

'I'm not asking you, Pauly – ' Ben's voice had hardened. 'I want that uniform. Don't push me to hard or I'll turn nasty. I mean that. I have enough on you to get you drummed out of the Garda and into jail. I want you to bring your uniform to my place after the station closes as usual tomorrow evening. Got that?'

Pauly decided on one more throw of the dice. 'Listen Ben, I'm going to tell you something that's top secret. Gilhooly has heard on the grapevine that the Government is doing a deal with the Japanese for another site to build their golf course. You know what that means?'

'Tell me.'

'It means the land will go to the local farmers after all. The protest will end – '

He could almost hear Ben's brain grappling with the new information. 'And you believe that, Pauly, do you? More fucking fool you. The Government is trying to get off the hook. They're putting out that fairy tale hoping I'll get the farmers to back off – ',

'Why not wait Ben. See what happens – '

'No!' Ben's roar cut Pauly short. 'I don't trust them fuckers in Dublin! They think we're thick farmers, that we'll believe anything they say. As soon as the Ryder Cup is out of the way I can see the deal with the Japs will be back on. They'll get what they want - our land. The fields that are rightfully ours - '

Pauly groaned inwardly. It was no use. Ben Gartland was power crazy, so much so that he was determined to go along with his madcap plan, make more headlines, appear on television. Pauly knew he would have to play along; otherwise Ben would carry out his threat about those favours from the past…

'Alright Ben. Have it your way. You'll have the uniform tomorrow evening.'

'Good. You're a pal, Pauly.'

'That fire at the Englishman's cottage…?'

'What about it?'

'Did you have anything to do with it?'

He heard Ben's laugh. 'Even if I did, d'you think I'd be telling it to an upright member of the force like yourself, Pauly?' Ben laughed again before his mobile phone went dead.

● ● ● ●

When Katie Gartland alighted from the train at Dublin's Heuston Station almost the first person she saw on the platform was Jeremy. He came towards her, took her hand in his and kissed her lightly on the cheek.

'Katie, my love, great to see you....'

'Lovely to see you too, Jeremy.' They linked arms and looked into each other's eyes, oblivious to the other passengers hurrying past. Katie scanned the crowd as they exited from the train station and walked towards the car park. Thank God nobody was pointing a camera at them. It was beginning to rain and Dublin in early evening looked somewhat uninviting.

They sat in the car for a few moments, enjoying the closeness, Katie trembling with excitement at the prospect of what might lie ahead. She put those kind of thoughts out of her mind. 'I'm sorry about your cottage.'

'Not to worry. You're here, Katie, that's all that matters. And I have some good news for you' His eyes were alive with excitement.

'You have! What is it?'

'I'll tell you in a moment. It wonderful.'

They were out into the traffic now, driving through Dublin's northside towards Mountjoy Jail. Katie's heart beat faster. She could do with some good news; she was not looking forward to visiting Travis.

Jeremy spoke, his eyes still on the lines of traffic. 'Those drawings of yours that I brought along for Henry to see...He says they show promise – real promise. He reckons if they were in colour he could put them on show in his gallery. Mind you it'll mean some work - '

Katie's heart leaped. She could hardly believe it. This was even better news than she had dared hope for. The very idea of people admiring her work and paying money for her paintings was exciting. Who knows...maybe in time she could become a fully fledged artist. It was something she had dreamed of when she was young.

'Jeremy, what can I say...I owe everything to you.' Katie smiled at him. They had stopped at a traffic light and she leaned over and kissed him lightly on the cheek. It seemed such a natural thing to do and yet she was conscious that, during all their years together, she had never had occasion to show such warmth to Travis. Things were happening so quickly. If only she were free to go away with Jeremy Walker tomorrow, take the boys with her, not have to worry about her husband or his brother. Oh God, what was she wishing for…that Travis might die on hunger strike? No, she didn't want that to happen, but she was determined to get out of her loveless marriage. To get away from Loughduff and leave those dreadful memories of the place behind…

Jeremy must have been reading her thoughts. 'What about Travis?', he asked. 'Are you going to tell him about us – if he doesn't already know, that is.'

Katie shook her head. 'I don't think so. It wouldn't help Travis in his condition. And it would give Ben an excuse to think up something, do something violent – '

'Yes, you're right. It's too big a risk. I don't want anything to happen to you, Katie.' He thought for a moment. 'Why don't we just slip quietly away together, you, me and the boys. Nobody would need to know until we were gone. And by then we could be somewhere in Greece or North Africa. It would be difficult for them to find us…'

'Whatever it is you want, Jeremy. Myself and the boys will go along with you. But we must be careful. Everywhere I turn there seems to be reporters following me, asking questions. They're parked outside the house all day, watching and waiting for something to happen.'

'Let's hope we can escape them today,' Jeremy replied. 'I want us to have time alone, together.' He was smiling to himself as he guided the car through the traffic, and Katie soon found out why. 'Henry has offered us the use of his apartment tonight -…'

She glanced sideways at him. 'Why did he do that?'

'Because I asked him to. Hope you don't mind…'

They parked the car in a quiet street of small, red-brick two-storied houses a few minutes walk from Mountjoy Jail and the adjacent Mater Hospital. Before she got out of the I car Jeremy gave her a long, lingering kiss that had Katie wishing for more.

'I'll wait for you here, Katie,' Jeremy let go her hand. 'Good luck my love.'

She had barely turned the corner when she saw the reporters. They were lying in wait, lounging on the stone steps of the main hospital entrance, some with cameras at the ready. Katie kept her head lowered, avoiding their gaze as she approached. As she came within earshot they began firing questions.

'Will you be discussing those controversial photographs of yourself with your husband?'

'What exactly is your relationship with Jeremy Walker, Mrs Gartland? Are you seeing him regularly?'

'Have you any idea who took those pictures of yourself and Jeremy?'

'Are you and your husband splitting up? Why won't he end the hunger strike for the sake of you and the children?'

'What do you know about Jeremy Walker? Has he been married before – and if he was would that make any difference to your relationship?'

Katie ignored the barrage of questions as she went quickly up the stone steps of the hospital entrance. She had often seen celebrities on television, or people who were on trial coming out of court, being pursued by members of the media and had felt pity for the person being bombarded with questions. Now it was happening to her.

She entered the hospital reception area and was making her way towards the stairs when she heard her name being called. Turning, she saw a man of about her own age approaching. He wore a doctor's white coat.

'A moment please, Mrs. Gartland – '

'Yes?' Oh God, had something terrible happened to Travis?

'I'm Doctor Thornton. Noel Thornton. I'm one of the team attending your husband.'

'How is Travis?' He saw the anxiety in her eyes.

'He's as well as can be expected under the circumstances.' Dr. Thornton paused, looked rather grave. 'To be honest, your husband is a very ill man. He's doing immense damage to his system and unless he comes off his hunger strike soon – and I mean very soon - I'm afraid the damage could be permanent. Perhaps something worse….' He left the rest to her imagination.

'I'll talk to my husband. But I'm not sure it will do any good. He – he's a very stubborn man – '

He looked into her eyes. 'I'm afraid that may be impossible – talking to your husband, I mean.'

Katie's heart missed a beat. 'Why not? Is he…' The words would not come.

'Like I said, Mrs. Gartland, your husband's condition is serious, but he's conscious and mentally he is reasonably strong. It's just that…' Dr. Thornton paused, looked uncomfortable. 'I'm afraid, Mrs. Gartland, that your husband does not want to see or talk to you right now – '

Katie was stunned. 'Those photographs in the newspapers….' Doctor Thornton broke off. 'He is angry and has given us instructions…I'm sorry. There is nothing we can do.'

'But I must see Travis - '

'I'm sorry. A visit right now might not be the best thing for him. If you went up now it would not do him more harm than good.'

The words were like a death sentence. Katie felt embarrassed. Her husband banning her from visiting – the shame of it all! When the media got hold of the story, as no doubt they would…! She dare not think about it.

'But I'm his wife. I have a right to see my husband – '

Dr. Thornton studied the woman standing before him. He shared her embarrassment. She was not what one would judge to be fashionable dressed, and she was certainly not one of those pushy women coming to visit who knew what was good for her son or husband and with whom medics had to deal with occasionally. Katie Gartland looked much younger than her husband; even her demeanour was different to his. She was soft-spoken, shy almost. Dr. Thornton saw before him a striking young woman, with her dark hair brushed back, accentuating her high cheekbones.

Travis Gartland had been a difficult patient from the moment he had been admitted to the hospital; surly, uncouth and unpleasant. Hard to believe that this attractive young woman was his wife; even more difficult to believe that he was turning his back on her.

'I accept that you have a right to see your husband, Mrs. Gartland. But take my advice and leave things be for the present. It would be very difficult for you in front of the medical staff at his bedside.'

Katie looked at him with eyes that were brimming with tears. 'Yes, I understand. Thank you, doctor.'

'Your husband is in no immediate danger, I assure you – '

She nodded her head, turned away silently towards the exit. Dr. Thornton watched her walk across the polished floor until she disappeared out through the large swing doors, sensed her humiliation. He sighed, turned and walked up the stairway, his thoughts still with the woman whose life he had touched so briefly.

For Katie Gartland the huge hospital doors closing behind her symbolised the sealing into the past the twenty years she had been chained to Travis Gartland. She felt rejected, yet at the same time she a new chapter of her life that was opening up before her. She had wasted valuable years of her life in Loughduff, trapped in a marriage to man whom she had neither loved nor respected. Now he had turned his back on her, given her the freedom she so earnestly desired. Katie was determined to grasp the opportunity with both hands.

Outside the hospital the media scrum had formed again. The journalists were taken by surprise at the shortness of Katie's visit and sensed that something dramatic had happened. Despite her obvious distress they began firing questions at her once more. Again Katie steeled herself to ignore them as tears began to stream down her cheeks.

She almost ran down the street. Two television cameramen got in front of her and began filming her progress. When they had got what they wanted they walked back towards their colleagues. Katie took a circuitous route back to where Jeremy was parked, making sure none of the media were following her. As she slid into the seat beside him he could tell that something was wrong.

When she recounted what had happened in the hospital he took his hand in hers, tried to comfort her. They sat in silence for a while, watching some children playing games in the street, both of them lost in thought.

Finally Jeremy said, 'Tell you what, let's go to the gallery, talk to Henry. He'll discuss with you what he has in mind for your painting. That should cheer you up, Katie.' He squeezed her hand. 'After that we'll stroll around Temple Bar – you might like to do some shopping – and then we'll have a romantic candlelit dinner in a nice restaurant. How about that?'

'And afterwards?' Katie smiled, the memory of what had happened in the hospital fading by the minute. 'What exactly do you have in mind, Jeremy Walker?'

It was his turn to smile. 'How about we leave that in the lap of the gods? Remember Henry has offered us his apartment if we need it.' He paused. 'Do you have to go back to Loughduff tonight?'

She turned in the seat, faced him. 'No – and I don't think I want to,' Katie replied softly. She could feel her heart thumping. What on earth was she saying? What was she allowing herself to be lead into? Never in her wildest dreams, crying softly in her bed at night, isolated from an uncaring husband, had she ever imagined that life would offer her another another opportunity to find love and happiness.

'What is it you want, Katie?'

'I want to stay tonight in Dublin with you.'

'I was hoping you'd say that.' He leaned over kissed her. 'Henry has arranged to stay with friends. I got him to fix that before I met you today!'

'Did you now...' Katie could feel her mood lightening still further.

'What about the boys. You'll have to telephone them.'

'I don't think that will be necessary.'

He looked surprised. 'Why not?'

'Because I told Garret and Jack before I left that I might have to stay overnight in Dublin – to talk to someone who is interested in my sketches!' Katie blushed slightly at her admission.

'You cunning little vixen!' Jeremy laughed out loud. He started the car, headed for the city centre. After a while he said, 'Tomorrow before we return to Loughduff I'll make enquiries about the car ferry sailings to France. It's time we started making plans for the future, Katie.' She nodded in acquiescence. Was all this a dream from which she would rudely awake?

Henry Mackintosh welcomed them warmly when they entered his art gallery a short while later. He gave Katie a peck on the cheek, exchanged some small talk with Jeremy, then said to Katie, 'My dear, has Jeremy said anything to you about those drawings you did for me?'

'He said that you were pleased with them – '

'Pleased? – ' Henry's eyebrows shot up – 'Katie darling I adored them!. You have a talent, make no mistake about that. But that talent needs to be nurtured. You've a lot of hard work ahead of you. You need tuition – and I must warn you that you won't get that in a place like Loughduff – '

'What would you suggest?' Katie was clinging on to Henry's every word.

'You need to travel, my precious. Travel stimulates the mind, opens up new vistas to the artist. You must experience life to the full - ' he was waving his hands about expressively. 'Find and explore those new vistas, new styles, mix and work with people who will stretch you without interfering with your natural ability – ' Henry broke off, smiled mischievously, 'In my opinion, my dear, you need to be taken under another painter's wing, someone with experience who will offer criticism, constructive criticism, bring out your best attributes as an artist – ' . He paused again 'I suspect you know who I have in mind, my dear....'

'Katie and I have already discussed some of those issues, Henry,' Jeremy cut in quickly.

'Good.' Henry turned to Katie again.'Take my advice, my dear, and grab this opportunity with both hands. It will mean you making sacrifices, changing your whole life. Rise to that challenge. Life is too short to spend day after day in drudgery and boredom – ' Katie suspected Jeremy had been filling her benefactor in on her background. 'I'll do all I can to help you, Katie, but ultimately the decision to grasp the opportunity lies with you.'

'I understand what you're saying, Henry. And thank you for everything. You're very kind – ' She paused, lost for words, slightly overwhelmed by it all.

'Kindness has nothing to do with it, my dear,' Henry said imperiously. 'I pride myself on my ability to spot genuine talent, make a little money for myself in the process. That's why I brought Jeremy over from England.

He is already on his way up the ladder, and I am confident you can follow in his footsteps.'

Henry broke off suddenly. 'And now if you'll both excuse me I must close the gallery and depart into the night – ' He looked into a convenient mirror, straightened his bow tie, adjusted the silk handkerchief in the top pocket of well-cut jacket. 'My presence here, I suspect, is no longer neither required nor desired…'

'Thanks for everything, Henry. We appreciate it, don't we, Katie?'

'I'm sorry if we're putting you out of your apartment – ' Katie sought to apologise.

'Worry not,' Henry had a twinkle in his eye. 'I too once enjoyed the passion of a woman's love…' He sighed, looked wistful. Katie would loved for him to continue, but Henry decided whatever he was going to divulge about his past would remain a secret – for the present at least. 'Oh, I left a bottle of my best wine in the fridge for when you both return later tonight. Do help yourselves.' He waved and was gone.

Jeremy and Katie strolled around Temple Bar, choosing the restaurant where they would eat with care. Dinner was delicious, one to remember. Afterwards they walked arm-in-arm through this, the city's cosmopolitan area, taking in the sights, talking and giggling like a honeymoon couple. It was getting on for midnight when they made their way back to Henry's apartment and let themselves in. Henry's third floor abode comprised a spacious livingroom, two bedrooms, a kitchen and a bathroom. It also had a tiny balcony which overlooked the busy street below. Jeremy opened the bottle of wine that Henry had left. They enjoyed it sitting out on the tiny balcony, watching the crowds below bustling about and admiring the lights glowing on the waters of the Liffey.

Inside again, curtains drawn, they embraced without saying a word, sharing passionate kisses, enjoying the closeness of each other's body. Katie felt Jeremy's hand searching for the zip on the back of her dress. He moved it downwards tantalisingly slowly. Katie felt hot passion coursing through her lower body. She had never experienced anything like it before. Her whole being was trembling and she was completely powerless to his touch...

'Have you ever been soaped all over and made love to in a hot shower?', Jeremy asked huskily.

'Never.' It had not been one of her husband's favourite pastimes!

'Would you like to be initiated?' The answer was in her eyes.

First, they undressed each other slowly, letting items of their clothing nestle on the floor at their feet. When they were both naked Jeremy took her hand, lead her to the spacious marble tiled bathroom with its separate bath and shower unit. He gave her a baptism under a delicious spray of hot water, both of them taking it in turn to use liberal amounts of their host's scented bath fluid with which to soap each other's body. Then they locked their arms around each other, each of them conscious of the arousal within themselves. Katie could feel Jeremy's lips on hers, passionate and demanding. Pinned against the warm tiles, eyes closed in ecstasy, arms clasped tightly around Jeremy's neck, Katie arched her body and moaned softly as he entered her.

Later he carried her to the large bed where, throughout the night, they made leisurely love again. Outside they could hear the revellers making their way home through the streets of Temple Bar. Dawn was not too far away when sleep finally claimed them both.

● ● ● ●

Angie Wilde was bored. And when Angie Wilde was bored she craved action. She was looking forward to tonight when she aimed to provide some real fun during her Girls' Night Out!

Only a few days back in Ireland and already she had it up to here with the goddam Emerald Isle. If that female guide assigned to American ladies by the Tourist Ireland brought herself and her girls to view another ancient Irish monument, ushered them into another craft shop, or had them sit through another session of high-kicking, heel clicking Riverdance-style jigs and reels, Angie figured she would go crazy!

Those deadly functions might be okay for upmarket Sally Cartray and her European ladies, but jeez enough was enough. Before she hit the road to Hollywood Angie reckoned on showing some real action to her red-blooded American girls!

She had seen enough ancient Irish ruins in the last few days to last her a lifetime! What she wanted right now was to be where the real action is. That place was America – Hollywood to be precise. She was anxious to start filming 'Roll Of The Dice' with the little dynamo that was Patrick Mannion. She couldn't wait to be invited to all those A-list parties, have a choice of getting laid occasionally by some handsome movie hunk. She looked forward to seeing her picture in the showbiz pages, appearing on the late night talk shows, being in demand for interviews, getting chauffeured around in limos - that's the type of action she wanted.

Instead, here she was stuck in Ireland, attending boring dinners where she and the other girls had to listen to boring speeches or stifle yawns during endless golf talk.

All her girls were playing their parts in attending the various official functions with their partners. But secretly most of them agreed that there was too much formality surrounding the Ryder Cup schmozzle. So many angst-ridden press conferences, followed by interviews and then more practice sessions in Killarney. Fine for the men but rather tedious for the girls. Then there were those formal dinners at night, hosted in turn by the respective golf associations and by Government backed organisations like Tourism Ireland. These functions invariably included a host of grey-haired VIPs and various Irish Government dignatories with middle-aged wives in tow. Not exactly the type of activity guaranteed to get one onto the front page or into the gossip columns of the international press the following day.

Angie reckoned that attending fashion shows and gazing at ancient monuments was okay up to a point. But it wasn't what she wanted right now. It was a long way from Hollywood.

Since the Ryder Cup team had arrived in Ireland Angie hardly ever had Wayne to herself. Not that she particularly wanted to continue to act like his luvey-duvey girlfriend.. Now that her mission had been accomplished – and tonight's stage show at Symie's Bar in Glengariff would surely hit the headlines - she had gone off Wayne big time. She wanted out of the relationship, and if her plan of suddenly ditching America's Ryder Cup captain meant more publicity and pictures of herself in the newspapers, so much the better.

She showered, wrapped herself in a bathrobe and rummaged through the wardrobe of clothes she had brought over for the Ryder Cup. To hell with those formal evening dresses, she needed something eye-catching to wear tonight, something that would knock the eyes out of those Celtic Tiger guys! She selected a pair of black lycra toreador pants and a red blouse with ruffled sleeves and a cleavage that finished just short of her navel. When Angie had finished dressing and fixing her hair she surveyed herself in the mirror. Jeez! She hoped Wayne would not return early from Killarney and see her in this outfit…!

She had not told the girls about Symie's Bar and the Celtic Tigers. Instead she had informed they were going on a 'mystery tour' into the Irish countryside with a promise of something special en route. Were they in for a big surprise!

Whatever about her finding the lead-up to the Ryder Cup rather boring, Angie had to admit was that the event was some crowd-puller. The wives had seen it for themselves any time they had been taken on a scenic tour of Kerry. Once outside the private and heavily guarded grounds of the Parknasilla Palace they had witnessed some of the rivalry between the thousands of golf fans from Europe and America who crowded into Ireland's most famous scenic area to see the eagerly awaited clash of the world's golf superstars.

For security reasons it had been agreed that only 35,000 ticket holders would be allowed onto the Killeen course on each of the three days of the Ryder Cup. There would be no alcohol on sale on the course. Thousands of fans had been unable to get tickets but that had not stopped them from coming to Killarney anyway.

She had arranged to meet the girls downstairs for a drink before they embarked on the coach for Glengarriff and Symie's Bar. On impulse she decided to phone Mervyn before leaving. Now that she planned on flying the coop it was up to Mervyn get busy back home and handle the publicity there. Time for him to earn his ten per cent.

She lifted the telephone in the room, dialled. 'That you, Mervyn?'

'Angie baby! What a pleasant surprise. I was just thinking about you. How are you?'

'Bored, Mervyn,'

'No kidding?' The tone had come down a notch. 'So what else is new?'

Angie let that pass. 'I'm through with this Ryder Cup lark, Mervyn. I've had it up to my ears. We've achieved what we wanted to achieve and now I want out – fast!'

Mervyn was no fool. He could sense when one of his clients needed help. 'Hey, hold on, honey. I thought you were enjoying yourself – '

'So you got it wrong. Look, back home I've got a movie lined up with a hot director. My big break – what I've worked my ass off for. We're almost ready to roll, that right? So what am I doing here in the Emerald Isle staring at ancient monuments and trying to look interested! I want with the real action, Mervyn. Got that?'

'I'm with you, baby. Your wish is my command – '

'Stop talking in clichés then, baby.I want action. What do you aim to do?'

'I'll do anything you say. What have you got in mind?'

'Phone Patrick Mannion for a start. Tell him I'm through here with Wayne Folen and the Ryder Cup, that I'm catching the first plane out tomorrow – '

'Tomorrow. Hey, hold on baby. You can't do that – '

'Wrong, Mervyn. I can and I'm doing it!'

'Sure, baby, sure.' Mervyn's tone was soothing. Angie was really fired up. Maybe her new found fame was going to her head. But quitting just when things were looking good? Was she crazy? Then the headline flashed up before Mervyn: 'Angie Wilde Walks Out On Ryder Cup Captain Wayne – ' As a headline that one was a whopper. Maybe the dumb broad wasn't so dumb after all.

' Okay Angie, I'm right behind you. When are you planning on flying out?'

'I aim on getting a plane out of Shannon tomorrow.'

' Does Wayne Folen know anything about this?'

''Course not!' Angie hissed. 'Do you think I'm crazy.' He let that pass. 'Let's face it, Mervyn, Wayne and I are never going to be an item. The guy reminds me of my father for chrissake! He's no use to us anymore. Time for him to crawl back to his little wife – '

'I have news for you, honey,' Mervyn cut in. 'He may not have to do that. Marcia is standing by him. The word is the President's wife has been in touch with Marcia. She has snubbed the Woman Together crowd and she's quoted as saying that all she wants is her husband back home – with the Ryder Cup – ' Mervyn paused. 'Wayne is supposed to have been in touch with his wife thanking her for her support'

'So what. I don't give a shit. I just want out of here.'

'Okay, Angie, leave everything to me. I'll get in touch with Mannion in Hollywood, tell him you're on your way ready for when he starts shooting – ' He stopped. 'Hey, what about that night out you were supposed to have with the girls over there? You going to pass on that?'

'Relax, darling. That little shindig is tonight. We're about to hit the road – '

'Fantastic, baby, fantastic - !'

'One more thing, Mervyn…'

'What's that?'

'Do you know how the hell those newspapers got hold of the story about those blue movies I acted in – '

'I don't know, baby. Honest. Cross my heart - '

'You haven't got one Mervyn you asshole!' She slammed the phone down.

Mervyn smiled to himself. Everything was going according to plan. That night out that Angie had planned sounded interesting. She probably had the shindig covered from a publicity point of view. But like a good agent he was taking no chances. He lifted the telephone, began to dial…

Angie had arranged to meet the girls in the bar off the foyer. As she exited from the elevator she saw her friendly porter smiling at her. 'Your luxury coach is waiting for you and the ladies, Miss Wilde – '

'Fine. We'll have a quick drink then we'll be on our way.'

'Hope you all enjoy the night.' He gave her a cute smile. 'I think you will…'

Angie thanked him. 'You'll tip off the news guys after we leave?' she whispered.

'Of course. I've got the phone numbers of the various hotels where they're staying –' He touched his cap in gratitude when she slipped him some folding money.

Angie entered the bar and saw her girls sipping drinks and chatting in small groups. She saw that some of the European wives and girlfriends had joined them. As she entered Sharon Dougherty, Joey O'Hara's stunning looking girlfriend, approached.

'Hey Angie, some of the European girls want to know if they can come along with us tonight. That alright with you?'

'Sure. Doesn't Sally Cartray had something lined up for them?'

'She has – a visit to an exhibition of ancient Irish art.' Sharon rolled her beautiful eyes. 'I don't think the girls are interested.'

Angie smiled. 'Can't say I blame them - ' Having some of the European wives on board was a bonus. This was getting better by the minute!

She ordered a double vodka martini. Nothing like getting into the mood of the evening. When Sharon asked where they were headed for their night out Angie was evasive. 'One thing for sure – they won't be studying ancient Irish art where we're going!'

'Hmmm, sounds like you have something very interesting lined.up,' Sharon smiled.

Angie took her drink from the barman and lowered half of it. 'We've got to get the girls on the coach before Wayne, Cord McCallum and the others arrive back from Killarney. I don't want them asking questions. I'll tell the girls where we're going when we're on our way'

Half-an-hour into the journey, as the driver of the luxury coach wended his way through the town of Kenmare, the singing started. The young man in bow tie attending the mini-bar at the rear of the vehicle had been kept busy serving drinks since they set out. The gathering was getting more exuberant with every mile, and when Angie called for silence and announced where that they were on their way to see a group of male strippers called the Celtic Tigers in action, the news was greeted with screeches of delight from the ladies.

Dusk was descending when the coach pulled into the large car park adjacent to Symie's Bar in Glengariff. The area was already packed with cars and there were also four other touring coaches besides their own. Judging by the crowd – most of them females – making their way through the entrance it looked like the 'House Full' sign would be going up outside Symie's place tonight.

The driver got out first and helped his female passengers alight. Some of them did so rather unsteadily, watched by a group of leering locals men who showed up to eye the visiting female clientele whenever the Celtic Tigers hit town. A man who had obviously been waiting for the coach's arrival came out from the entrance. He wore an old-style dress suit which, on his thick-set, middle-aged frame, looked at least a size too small for him. His steel grey hair was thick and curly and as he approached his pale blue eyes were dancing with devilment..

'Good evening ladies. Welcome to Symie's Bar,' he announced in a loud Irish brogue, his smile lighting up the night. 'I'm Symie Reynolds, your host for the evening.'

Outside the coach, the group of stylishly dressed women gazed in awe at Symie's place. It didn't look very imposing. There were two entrances, one with 'Bar' and the other with 'Lounge' signs over the doors. The outside of the establishment was painted bright blue, the paint faded and peeling in places. The gold lettering on the windows was in Gaelic and gave an antiquated look to the place.

'Not exactly The Sands in Las Vegas, is it?' Angie heard someone behind her whisper. There were girlish giggles. Nobody seemed too concerned; the ladies just wanted to get inside.

'Hi. I'm Angie Wilde. I'm the lady in charge.'

Symie feasted his eyes on Angie, trying hard not to stare at her cleavage. He shook her proferred hand, disappointed she didn't offer an embrace . Jesus!, if she gets up on stage with the Celtic Tigers in that outfit there'll be a riot!

Symie had never seen so many good-looking women in his car park before. 'Cead Mile Failte, ladies,' he shouted. 'Ye're all very welcome. Inside with ye now and enjoy yourself. We've something very special lined up for ye tonight!' His eyes followed them admiringly as they sashayed across the tarmac towards the lounge entrance.

'Where's the powder room, Symie?' Angie asked. 'Some of the girls want to freshen up.'

Symie looked puzzled for a moment. 'Powder room?...' Enlightenment dawned. 'Oh, you mean the toilet. Shure I have as fine a lavatory as you'll ever see across the yard out the back. Didn't I clean it out myself with disinfectant specially for ye tonight! – ' He added in a loud voice. 'If any of ye find the chain a bit hard to pull give a shout and me or any of the lads will help out!...!' There was more girlish laughter. Angie and Sharon looked at each other. This promised to be some night!

On the way in there were shrieks of laughter when the two posters advertising the Celtic Tigers were spotted. Gasps of appreciation went up as the new arrivals feasted their eyes on the gleaming, manicured bodies of Dec, Pat, Billy Boy and Sean, a quartet of Dubliners currently the rage of the Irish cabaret scene.

Symie saw their admiring stares. 'I'm telling' ye ladies, ye won't see four finer specimens of Irish manhood than these four young fellas. Shure the women can't get enough of them!'

Looking every inch the proud entrepreneur, Symie lead them through an outer lounge area where the mainly male clientele sitting on stools momentarily forgot their pints of liquid as they ogled the line of expensively dressed women swaying through their domain. There were nudges and winks and whispered remarks as the procession passed.

The ladies trooped into the large cabaret room. Huge wooden beams crisis-crossed the ceiling and around the walls were old framed photographs and relics of farm implements of the Irish farm past, including rakes of all descriptions, bridles, turf cutting slanes, an assortment of horse shoes, crosscut saws, hay knives and roof thatching tools. The almost all-female audience, in groups of four or more, were already seated at tables littered with glasses and bottles, waiting for proceedings to start.

The American contingent gazed in awe. 'Hey, isn't this quaint. I love it,' one of the party giggled.

' It certainly is ladies' night out,' another exclaimed, surveying the sea of female faces turned in their direction.

Symie overheard and as he lead the way through the tables towards the front he shouted over his shoulder, 'I had these four lads on last month for the first time and, God's me judge ladies, I could have sold the place out twice over. The women went wild for them. Ye'll feel the same when ye see them in action.'

He lead them to a semi-circle of small tables covered in white linen at the front of the stage. Symie summoned two young waitresses to take their orders before disappearing. Seconds later he exited from the side of the stage and addressed the audience.

'Good evening, everybody. Ye're all very welcome to Symie's Bar in beautiful Glengariff. We have some very special guests here tonight, a group of ladies from Europe and America, wives and girlfriends of the mighty men playing in the Ryder Cup – ' He paused briefly. 'I want ye to give them a big Irish welcome…'

He gestured to the ladies from Europe and America to stand up and take a bow. Angie wished Symie would get on with it. She and the rest of her party groaned when, after the applause had died down, their host announced grandly: 'In their honour, and at considerable expense, I have brought along a local tenor, Liamy Hogan, who will render some famous Irish airs, starting with the loveliest of them all – Danny Boy – '

This was greeted by a loud groan from the audience. Then the slow hand clapping started, followed by chants of 'We want the Celtic Tigers….' 'Bring on the Celtic Tigers…' Soon every female in the room followed suit. When Symie saw Angie and her girls also joining in he realised he could have a female riot on his hands. He quickly waved the Irish tenor back into the wings and announced that the Celtic Tigers would go into action immediately. Loud cheers greeted the announcement..

Soon afterwards the house lights dimmed, two spotlights pierced the darkness, and into the glare leaped the four muscular Dubliners. Dec, Pat, Billy Boy and Sean were dressed in top hats, white tie and tails, each with a Fred Astaire-type silver-top cane in his hand.

Their entrance was greeted with shouts and screams from the audience. This increased in volume when the Tigers went into a snappy dance routine. The screaming rose to deafening heights when the quartet began to divest themselves of the various items of dress. The sequence ended with the Celtic Tigers being revealed in all their sun tanned and well-oiled glory, clad only in shiny black leather thongs that left little to the imagination.

By then the audience was going wild, with women at the back of the cabaret room standing up on chairs to get a better view of the stage, waving their drinks in the air and screaming out for more action .

Angie glanced around the room. The lights had come

up during the short interval between acts and she could see several people with cameras. The press had arrived! In the mayhem and excitement nobody seemed to notice. All eyes were on the stage.

The photographers didn't have long to wait for some sensational shots. For their next routine the Celtic Tigers came out dressed as old-style sailors, in striped vests, bell-bottom slacks and with little white hats on their heads. Once again during a very active dance number items of clothing were divested one by one to the ecstatic screams of the audience until all that was left was their white hats and thongs covering their private parts. This time, however, the Celtic Tigers jumped down from the stage, all set to continue their act among the audience.

The four guys had obviously been alerted to the fact that there were some very important females at the front tables. The quartet of scantily-clad, well-muscled males descended on the Ryder Cup women, cavorting suggestively and pulling several to their feet. They made for the best-looking women among the group, and that included Angie and Sharon Dougherty. The music on the tape deck throbbed out a sexy Julio Iglesias number while camera flashes popped to record the scene.

After several minutes dancing with the ladies the Celtic Tigers retreated, went back up on stage, and gestured to any of the Ryder Cup group who dared to join them there. Sharon Dougherty, strands of her tawny shoulder-length hair framing a face that had graced many magazine covers, was the first to accept, followed closely by Angie.

'Come on girls,' Angie called out to the others, 'It's disco time, let's have a ball. – everyone on stage!'.She set an example by kicking off her high-heeled shoes. The rest of the party jumped to their feet and followed Angie's example before invading the stage. What followed was one of the wildest and most enjoyable nights ever witnessed in

Symie's Bar in Glengariff – and photographers from the world's press were there to prove it!

Over two hours later, after a rousing twenty-minute finale that saw the Celtic Tigers whip the female audience into a frenzy of singing, dancing and general mayhem, the show ended. Soon afterwards groups of tired and emotional females were departing in coaches and cars from Glengariff. Slowly the car park emptied until the only vehicle that remained was the luxury coach of the Ryder Cup ladies. Inside the now silent cabaret room Symie Reynolds, tuxedo cast aside and with his shirtsleeves rolled up, was uncorking several bottles of champagne and pouring a farewell drink for his special guests. It was a time for celebration; Symie reckoned his bar was about to make headlines all over the world.

'A toast to yourselves, ladies. As fine a bunch of wimmin as I'm ever likely to see. You're all welcome back to Symie's Bar anytime.' The Celtic Tigers quartet of Dec, Pat, Billy Boy and Sean, their well-muscled torsos now hidden beneath tee shirts and slacks, had joined the Ryder Cup ladies in a flirting session and everyone was having a good time as glasses were filled, emptied and filled again.

Symie had just burst into a rendition of a rousing Irish rebel ballad to entertain his audience when the large uniformed figure of Garda Sergeant Manus McManus loomed in the doorway and began to make his way through the sward of tables towards the revellers. Symie's song died in his throat. The sergeant paused and surveyed the scene before him.

'Evening, sergeant,' Symie said, a trifle uneasily. He sensed what was coming.

The sergeant made a great play of looking at his watch. 'More like morning, Symie,' he remarked ominously.

'Would ye care for a little drink? A celebration like with our special lady guests – '

'No thanks. I'm on duty.' Sergeant McManus looked at

the array of bottles and glasses. 'Ye know you're breaking the licensing laws, Symie. These premises should have been cleared two hours ago.'

'Is that right?' Symie looked innocent. 'Two hours ago, bedad.' He grinned at the ladies. 'Doesn't time fly when ye're having a good time – '

'Aye'. The sergeant reached into his top pocket, took out a notebook. 'I'm afraid I'm going to have to book the lot of ye.'

Symie almost choked. 'Book us be damned, sergeant! These ladies are my guests. Do ye know who they are?'

Sergeant McManus ran his eyes over the lovely ladies before him; some of them looking slightly the worse for wear. 'I accept that the ladies are a class above your unusual clientele, Symie, but they're breaking the law by drinking after hours – '

'Does this mean we're going to spend the night in your jail, sergeant?', Angie asked, to a chorus of girlish giggles.

'No, but ye will all have to pay a fine.' The sergeant gestured to the grinning Celtic Tigers. 'Mind you if I had my way I'd put these boyos in jail for indecent exposure. – ' This observation brought forth more giggles from the ladies.

The sergeant waited until the laughter had died down before clearing his throat and saying sternly, 'Now ladies, your names and addresses please. One at a time.' He pointed to Angie. 'You first, young lady!'

'Would you like my telephone number also?' Angie asked coyly. Some of the ladies volunteered theirs also. The sergeant was not amused.

Twenty minutes later, when all the formalities with the law had been completed, the ladies of the Ryder Cup were making the most of the opportunity of kissing goodbye to the Celtic Tigers - and a beaming Symie Reynolds – in the car park. Then it was into the coach for the drive back in the early hours to the Parknasilla Palace Hotel. Running repairs to make-up were made during the drive, nevertheless when they trooped into the foyer of the hotel quite a few members of the party were showing signs of the long night's hectic activity.

As they entered the hotel the ladies were confronted by a stern faced delegation of American and European golf officials, Wayne Folen and Bruce Cartray among them. Sally Cartray, looking elegant despite the lateness of the hour in a flowing silk dressing gown, was also an interested spectator. She suspected what was coming and knew it would be worth losing some sleep to witness it. She tried not to look too pleased.

Cord McCallum stepped forward, said sternly for all to hear. 'Miss Wilde, it's almost three a.m. I want you to know that your behaviour in keeping these ladies out so late on your excursion is a breach of security and has sparked off an all-out alert – '

'We're very sorry, aren't we, ladies?' Angie managed to look contrite.

'Why didn't you telephone to let us know where you were. You have been highly irresponsible,' McCallum thundered.

'We were having such a good time we didn't realise – '

'Major Mackenzie and I will not take that as an excuse. This is a serious breach of Ryder Cup protocol and we are holding you responsible.'

'I really am sorry, Mr. McCallum – ' Angie called on all her acting prowess to plead her case. 'I was trying to help, showing the girls a good time – '

'We thought you and the ladies had had an accident, that the coach had gone over a cliff, something dreadful like that,' Major Mackenzie brushed her excuse aside.

Angie saw Wayne in the background, glowering at her. She yawned. 'Like I've said, I'm sorry. Now if you gentlemen don't mind, we're all very tired. We could do with some sleep. I'm going to bed. Goodnight all!'

With that Angie turned on her heel and made her way towards the elevator. Sally Cartray was the only person in the hotel foyer with a smile on her face. She had a feeling she had seen the last of Angie Wilde.

CHAPTER TEN.

Angie finished writing her goodbye note to Wayne Folen. She had kept it short and to the point. Now that she was quitting the scene she saw no reason to go into any great detail about their brief affair. Last evening's boozy encounter with the Celtic Tigers in Symie's Bar – and the resultant angry reception on their return to the hotel - had given her the ideal opportunity to exit stage left. For Angie it was a clear case of goodbye Wayne Folen, hello Hollywood.

She read the note over to herself one more time:

> Goodbye Wayne honey. Sorry to have to say goodbye like this but I guess you and I have reached the end of our relationship. I'm going to Hollywood and maybe you should go back to your wife. Apologies for last night and all those pictures in this morning's newspapers. As you can see, myself and the girls really had a fun time. Hope you bring back that Ryder Cup.
>
> > Nice meeting you,
> > Angie.

She propped the sheet of hotel notepaper up against the mirror of the dressing table. Then she finished the rest of her packing and picked up the telephone.

'Hello…Reception? This is Angie Wilde in room two-one-three. I'm checking out right now. Send someone up please to collect my bags. Also, I want you to find out the time of the next flight to New York or Los Angeles from Shannon Airport. Book me a seat on it and also book me a cab to take me to the airport. I'll pay for the flight when I arrive at Shannon. Got all that? Thank you.'

The young lady at reception replaced the receiver, instructed a uniformed young man in the foyer to go up to room two-one-three and bring down the luggage of the lady occupant who was checking-out. 'The lady's name is Miss Angie Wilde…'

The two young men reading newspapers within earshot of the reception desk looked at each other.

'Hey, did you hear that?' the one with a couple of cameras nestling at his feet remarked in an American accent.

'Yeah…Wayne's girl. Checking out,' his buddy remarked. 'Interesting.'

'You bet. Looks to me like she's walking out on Wayne – before the Ryder Cup.'

'Sure does. You reckon it has something to do with last night's shindig?

'You bet it has. Wonder does Wayne know Angie is taking off?'

'Let's find out. Wayne left with his squad over an hour ago for a practice round in Killarney. How about we try to contact him there by phone?'

'Good idea.' His companion took out his contact book, found the right number, began dialling on his mobile…

Upstairs in her room Angie Wilde was gazing with satisfaction at the huge spread of stories and pictures which the international press had given to the visit of Ryder Cup wives to Symie's Bar in Glengariff last night. She smiled triumphantly. She was finally finished with this Ryder Cup caper – and hallelujah! – she was exiting in a glaze of glory!

The headlines in heavy black type across several

columns in all the newspapers were eye-catching. 'Ryder Cup Women Let Their Hair Down During Wilde Night In Symie's Bar', screamed one. 'Angie's Girls' Have Sexy Romp With The Celtic Tigers,' and 'The Wilde Wild Women Meet The Celtic Tigers' were two more that grabbed readers' attention.

And the pictures – wow! The photographers had certainly done their job well; the racy stories were accompanied by equally racy photographs of several of the wives and girlfriends of American Ryder Cup stars cavorting with bare-torsoed members of the Irish male strippers group. If the newspaper stories were racy in detail the pictures left little to the reader's imagination.

Wayne Folen had been fuming when he had followed Angie up to their room in the early hours. He had obviously been given one hell of a shellacking from Cord McCallum and his colleagues on the Ryder Cup committee – not to mention some of the angry husbands!

'You'd better believe it, Angie, what you did tonight, bringing the ladies out to a place like that, will certainly make my job a helluva lot more difficult than it is already,' Wayne had fumed at her. 'How the hell are my guys supposed to concentrate on the Ryder Cup with you bringing their wives to a place like that?'

Angie let Wayne rant on, playing her little innocent girl role to perfection. She didn't care about the Ryder Cup. She wanted out and that was it. She hadn't tried to smooth things over with Wayne when he undressed and climbed between the sheets last night. She reckoned that he would be in no mood to kiss and make up – not that she wanted to do so either.

The arrival of the morning newspapers to the Parknasilla Palace had added fuel to the flaming rows that seemed to be flaring up everywhere in the hotel. The carry-on in Symie's Bar was also featuring prominently on all the tv news channels on both sides of the Atlantic. All the Ryder Cup ladies, European and American, had been given strict orders not to discuss the episode with anyone, especially members of the media.

When Angie had entered the dining room to have breakfast – alone, Wayne having pointedly preceded her – the hum of conversation had noticeably died and she had taken her seat at Wayne's table in deathly silence. Nobody had spoken to her since, not even her female companions of last night. No Ryder Cup wives had ever stepped out of line like that before in the history of the event and they obviously felt they had let their menfolk down.

Well, to hell with them all! Angie had consoled herself as she finished writing the note. She had just about had enough. Wayne had left immediately after breakfast with his Ryder Cup men for Killarney for yet another practice round of golf. He had barely spoken to her before he left and he had such an angry look on his face that no member of the media dared approach him.

Angie didn't let the mood in the hotel get to her. Why should she, after all she had achieved what she had set out to do. If Wayne thought he was going to find her twiddling her thumbs on his return later this evening he was making a big mistake. She could hardly wait to shake the remnants of the Emerald Isle, its ancient monuments and its forty shades of green, off her elegant shoes.

She heard the knock on the door, a call to tell her that her cab was waiting. Before answering it she folded a couple of the newspapers, put them in her holdall bag. She would read them on the aeroplane. Also, Mervyn would be interested in putting them on his file.

Angie was following the uniformed young man with her bags across the hotel foyer when she heard a camera click. She paused, smiled at the guy who obligingly clicked the shutter again.

'You leaving, Miss Wilde' the cameraman's companion observed.

'What does it look like I'm doing – going on a picnic!' Angie smile took the sting out of her reply.

'Mind telling us where you're off to?'

'I'm on my way to Los Angeles. You know I've got a film lined up. Patrick Mannion, my director, wants me on the set of 'Roll Of The Dice' immediately. He phoned me a couple of hours ago – ' It was a little white lie but it sounded good.

'And Wayne Folen? Does he know you're leaving?'

Angie shrugged. 'Why don't you ask him?'

'You mean you're not staying for the Ryder Cup?'

Angie shrugged again, gave them her Marilyn Monroe smile. 'Ryder Cup? Who the hell cares about the Ryder Cup? I'm an actress. I got more important business to attend to – '

'Does this mean it's all over between yourself and Wayne?'

'You want me to spell it out for you? Let's just way it was nice while it lasted – and you can quote me on that! Give my regards to Wayne next time you see him.

She paused, waved. 'Bye bye, boys....' The photographer shot off several more photos of Angie Wilde as she got into the waiting taxicab and waved goodbye.

● ● ● ●

At midday on Wednesday, two days before the Ryder Cup was due to tee-off, the Irish Government called a press conference at which it was announced that there had been a major breakthrough in the negotiations with the Japanese consortium planning to build a major golf and leisure complex in the Killarney area.

'In view of the on-going opposition to this major project from a minority of local farmers, one of whom has been on a life-threatening hunger strike during the past few weeks, the Government has been negotiating with the

Japanese businessmen involved in a bid to have the project moved to an equally suitable and historic site in Donegal.

'In recent weeks, protests have been staged which have threatened the smooth staging of the Ryder Cup in Killarney. The Government has decided that a disruption of the biggest international sporting event ever to be held in this country would not be allowed to happen.

'Accordingly, a satisfactory outcome to the talks between the Government and the Japanese consortium has been reached. This major Japanese project, which will provide hundreds of jobs and will be of enormous benefit to the local community, will now be sited in Donegal.

'The Taoiseach is grateful to the members of Japanese consortium for their co-operation. He is confident that the outcome to the negotiations will allow the Ryder Cup contest between Europe and America to take place without any further interruptions or protests.'

Katie and Jeremy heard the Government press statement being read out on the radio as they were about to leave Henry Mackintosh's apartment to drive back to Loughduff. They both remained silent for a few moments, lost in thought, thinking how this latest development might impact on their lives and the plans they had been making during the night, in between their bouts of passionate lovemaking.

'You know what this means, Katie? – that Travis will probably call a halt to his hunger strike,' Jeremy said. He paused, not wanting to put the question that he knew would have to be answered.

'I don't care. It makes no difference to me, or our plans,' Katie responded. 'I'm not going back to him or to live on the farm. That part of my life is over.'

He crossed the room, put his arms around her. 'I was hoping you would say that. I was afraid to ask, afraid that you might want to change your mind....'

Katie slid her arms around his neck, kissed him

tenderly. 'Never! Nothing can come between us now, Jeremy, and especially not after last night. I want to spend all my nights – and the rest of my days, with you. You have changed my whole life. How can I ever repay you for that?'

'I could think of one way straight off!' Jeremy laughed. 'But I know you're anxious to get back to Loughduff and the boys.' When they broke apart he looked serious. 'What will you do now, Katie? I mean immediately. Do you wish to see Travis before we drive back?'

She shook her head. 'No. Certainly not. What's the point? He refused to see me yesterday and he'd probably refuse to see me again today. I don't care if I never see my husband again.'

'You sure that's what you want, Katie?'

'Certain. I know what I'm saying, Jeremy. Travis and I are finished. But I'm anxious to see Garret and Jack, tell them what's going on, ask them if they wish to come with us or remain in Loughduff with their father – '

'Okay, we'll say goodbye to Henry first, thank him for the loan of his apartment. I want to get back to Loughduff also as quickly as possible. I'd like to see the cottage, check out how much damage that fire caused, arrange for it to be put up for sale....'

The office of Irish Ferries was within walking distance of the apartment. Before starting on the drive back to Kerry, Jeremy and Katie went in and booked a family cabin for a Sunday sailing from Rosslare, a port in the south-east coast, to Cherbourg in northern France. Katie's heart beat faster as she listened to Jeremy making all the arrangements for the sea voyage. It would be her first time to travel outside of Ireland. There was surely no turning back now

An hour later they were well on their way back to Kerry. Although it was a long trip Katie enjoyed the journey. She was beginning to feel more secure in Jeremy's company; he had a way of making her feel special. She found him easy to talk to and now that he had rekindled her interest in painting they had a lot in common.

They arrived back in Loughduff in the late afternoon and drove straight to Jeremy's place. The fire damage didn't look too bad from the outside and Katie assumed that Nell had been over to clean away some of the debris left in the wake of the firemen. Katie and Jeremy were inspecting the downstairs area, which had suffered most of the damage, when Nell poked her head around the door.

'Hello you two. Welcome home. No need to ask if you enjoyed your trip to Dublin!' She saw Jeremy and Katie smile at each other. Katie looked a bit embarrassed, so Nell went on quickly, 'Tom and the boys cleaned out most of the burnt rubble, and I've mopped up a lot of the water that the firemen used.'

'Thanks Nell,' Jeremy said gratefully. 'If it hadn't been for you and Tom the whole place would probably have burned to the ground.'

Nell brushed his thanks aside. 'Unfortunately some of your paintings have been destroyed – including some of your female nudes!'

Jeremy surveyed the scene. 'I'll have words with Sergeant Gilhooly as soon as possible, see if he has any idea of the identity of the men you saw running away after the fire –. For your information, Nell, I'll be putting the cottage up for sale shortly.'

Nell glanced at Katie. She would have loved to ask about Travis and what was happening there but thought better of it. She did, however, bring up the topic of the Government's recent statement outlining the plan to bring peace before the Ryder Cup got under way and she asked Katie if this meant that Travis would be giving up his hunger strike. Katie told her friend that she didn't know what her husband's plans were but that she expected the hospital would be in touch with her shortly.

Katie felt tired. She had really enjoyed the last two days

with Jeremy but she was glad when he suggested that he drop her home before he got down to cleaning up the remains of the fire damage. She wanted to talk to her two boys; it was time for them to know about Jeremy Walker and how their relationship had developed. She would have to explain to them sensitively and carefully that she planned to leave their father, the farm and Loughduff forever and to start a new life away from Ireland. She was hoping with all her heart that they too would want to be part of that new life...

Jack and Garret came to the door to welcome her home as the car drove into the yard. She did not broach the subject immediately; instead she set about cooking a meal for them all. She told them of her visit to the hospital and why she had been unable to visit their father.

'Is he alright? When will he be coming home?' Jack, the younger of the two, asked.

'Your father will probably end his hunger strike shortly, if he hasn't already done so by now so he should be fine,' Katie answered. Then she said, 'I don't know when he is coming home – ' she paused, 'When he does I may not be here.'

Jack and Garret looked at each other, uncomprehending. 'Why not? Are you going somewhere, Mom?', Garret asked.

'Yes, but don't worry, I'm not leaving you and Jack behind. I'm hoping you will both come with me, that we can still be together.' She was choosing her words carefully; despite her tiredness she knew she had to continue. 'Now listen carefully, there is something important I have to tell you both. It concerns myself and Jeremy Walker...'

They listened silently as she outlined delicately, sometimes close to tears, what had happened between herself and Jeremy Walker since they had met briefly that Sunday night at the farmers' meeting in the local hall. Katie didn't have to go into detail about how unhappy her life had been up to then; her boys were young adults; she was sure they had sensed that something was wrong in the relationship between their mother and father.

She had barely finished when Garret blurted out; 'We don't want to stay in Loughduff either. We want to go wherever you go, Mom.' He looked at his younger brother. 'Don't we, Jack?'

'Yes. I don't want to stay here, on the farm with Dad. Take us with you, Mom,' Jack pleaded. 'We want to be with you – '

Katie rose, hugged them both, tears in her eyes. She said a silent prayer of thanksgiving that the boys had agreed to come with Jeremy and herself. She was certain now that she was doing the right thing, for their sakes as much as hers. Over the years Travis Gartland had been neither a good husband nor a good father to the boys; she felt no remorse at them all leaving him.

She warned the boys not to say a word to anyone about what was happening. They were about to retire to their room when Jack suddenly remarked to his brother…'You forgot to tell Mom about the lady who telephoned when she was away – '

Katie looked at her son quizzically, 'Lady? What lady?'

Garret looked guilty. 'Sorry, it slipped my mind…Last night before Jack and I went to bed, the phone rang. When I answered it there was a lady on who said she wished to speak to you. She sounded disappointed when I told her you weren't here – '

Katie felt uneasy at the news. Possibly it was because not many people, other than her friend Nell Flavin, had reason to get in touch with the Gartland household. Maybe it was a reporter looking for yet another interview. Or could it have been one of the nurses in the hospital in Dublin? Maybe something had happened to Travis? But surely someone would have phoned back, been in touch with her since if that was the case?

'Did she leave her name, or a number to ring back? Did she say why she was telephoning me?'

Garret shook his head. 'I asked for her name or if she would like to leave a number. She said she would telephone again soon. She asked me who I was and when I told her she said she wanted to speak to you specially – ' Garret paused. 'She didn't sound like anyone local. She had a funny accent.'

Katie felt frustrated, and not a little frightened. But she didn't want the boys to notice. 'Did she say where she was phoning from?' Katie persisted, forcing a laugh. 'Come on Garret, she must have given you some information – '

'Well, she did say she was calling from somewhere in England – '

'Whereabouts in England?'

Her son's face puckered in thought. 'A place called Norfolk, I think it was. Who do we know over there, Mom?'

Katie didn't answer. She was too busy with her own thoughts. Norfolk! Wasn't that the place Jeremy had told her he was from that first night they had met? It was about the only bit of real information he had revealed about himself since then. Not that she had ever pressed him about his background; maybe she was afraid what he would reveal. What connection had this woman to Jeremy Walker, the man she had pledged herself to, the man with whom she was planning to spend the rest of her life with?

Was she someone from Jeremy's past.... a wife maybe, or someone he had had a relationship with? Should she telephone Jeremy or drive over to his place and tell him about the phone call from the lady with a foreign accent? Perhaps she would be better waiting until the lady called again before mentioning anything to Jeremy? She decided on the latter course of action.

'Something wrong, Mom?' Jack's anxious voice brought

Katie back to the present. 'You look kind of serious. And you didn't finish your tea…'

Katie smiled at her youngest son, hiding her anxiety. Now she had something else to worry about apart from her husband. It was a problem she knew she would have to confront very shortly.

● ● ● ●

Ben Gartland listened to the Government's press release being read out on the car radio. It was late evening now but the news of the agreement between the Irish Government and the Japanese consortium to move the planned golf course and leisure complex away from Killarney had been broadcast on TV and radio throughout the day.

'Do you think there's any truth in what the Government is saying, Ben?' one of the two men sitting in the car with him asked.

Ben stared straight ahead. 'The hell I do! I don't trust the slimy bastards up in Dublin. It's a trick to get us to back off until the Ryder Cup is out of the way.' He glanced anxiously down the deserted stretch of road 'Our kidnap plan goes ahead.'

The two men with Ben exchanged glances. They would rather be back in the Loughduff Inn drinking pints instead of indulging in this dangerous business. They had hoped that Ben would change his mind and call off this kidnap of the American golfer. But Ben Gartland was a dour individual, not one to be crossed. You did his bidding or else you made a bad enemy.

Ben and his two companions were parked on a lonely stretch of road leading to the Black Valley area, about ten miles from Killarney. They were waiting here for the arrival of Donie Dunhill and his quarry, Joey O'Hara, the world's No.1 golfer and a key member of the U.S. Ryder Cup squad.

The area was wild and rugged, not much travelled by locals but favoured by the adventurous tourist for its desolate grandeur. Houses dotted the mountainside here and there, some of them deserted completely, others turned into holiday homes. There was good fishing in the various small lakes that nestled in the area known as the Black Valley. Donie Dunhill was one of the local farmers who had converted a deserted house in the valley into a shooting and fishing lodge, which he used occasionally. Ben reckoned it was an ideal place to keep somebody prisoner for a few days...

Ben's mobile phone had rung a short while ago, Donie on the other end, under instructions what to say in case anyone was within earshot or listening in. 'Just checking with you, sergeant. Everything is going according to plan. I'm about to leave the hotel now with our guest. Expect us within the hour...'

'Ye hear that, lads', Ben's voice had a note of triumph. 'That was Donie. He's on the way with our man. You know what the plan is. We'll rough this young fella up a bit, show him we mean business, then we'll take him to Donie's place up in the valley....'

Earlier, Donie Dunhill had experienced no difficulty driving in through the gates of the Parknasilla Palace Hotel. The Garda uniform, borrowed from a reluctant Pauly Glynn under pressure from Ben Gartland, was the passport. It fitted Donie adequately enough and he had been waved through with only a cursory glance by the private security men on duty.

Inside the hotel itself there was heavy security. Donie kept out of the way as much as possible, noting the large number of uniformed Gardai roaming around; their numbers matched by bulky men whom he reckoned were undercover minders brought over specially from America. Donie strolled around casually, his eyes searching for the superstar young American golfer whose picture had been prominently featured in newspapers and on TV all week.

He spotted his quarry sitting in a corner of the lounge by himself, relaxing and reading a newspaper. As he approached Donie noticed that Joey was reading the report, photographs included, of last night's adventures of the Ryder Cup ladies in Symie's Bar in Glengariff. The news media had certainly gone to town on the coverage of Angie Wilde and her girls' night out.

Donie strolled over, introduced himself to the young American, using a false name. As they shook hands he saw Joey studying him carefully. Probably expecting me to ask for an autograph, Donie thought. Instead he went into his prepared script, 'I've good news for you, young fella. Remember those Irish ancestors you asked us to trace? Well, we've found some who seen to fit the bill.'

'The young American's eyes lit up. 'No kidding? That's great news. You guys must have got lucky - when I was here last time your colleague didn't seem to hold out much hope - '

Donie smiled, tried to look a lot more relaxed than he felt. 'There are so many O'Haras in this neck of the woods. We had to check everything out, make sure we had the right family – '

'What makes you so sure you have found the right one?' Donie was a bit taken aback by Joey's suspicious nature. Jaysus the young fella's supposed to be delighted with the news, not look like I'm telling him a lie, which I am.

'We've found an O'Hara family whose great-grandfather emigrated to Boston. We think these are almost certainly the ancestors you're looking for, Joey. We'd like you to come and meet them, ask them a few questions'

Joey still looked a bit doubtful. 'With respect officer, you still haven't answered the question. What makes you so sure these O'Haras are ancestors of ours?'

Donie was beginning to wish he hadn't let himself in for this caper. He was getting into deeper water by the minute. Blast Ben Gartland anyway – he should have stood up to Ben, told him to get someone else to do his dirty work. Ben was so puffed up by his own image nowadays he wasn't thinking straight.

'We can't be one hundred per cent sure, of course. But this family informed us their ancestor went into the building business in a big way, sent his sons to university. A couple went into politics, like the Kennedys – ' Donie was desperately making it up as he went along. It worked! The young American was nodding his head, looking interested.

'Hey, that ties in with what my father found out about us when he did some research – Okay. I suppose it's worth a try. When can I meet these O'Haras?'

Donie felt like cheering. He'd done it! 'Right now. Tonight. They live on a farm, it's only about half-an-hour's drive from here - ' He stopped. Joey was shaking his head.

'Sorry. No can do. Not tonight. I've got to attend a special Ryder Cup dinner in the hotel tonight. It starts in a couple of hours time – '

Donie was desperate. So near - and now this. He couldn't let Joey escape. He'd play one more card.

'Shure that's just fine. No problem. I have a fast car outside. I can have you there and back in plenty of time for that dinner. Have a few words with your ancestors now, tell them you and your father will return in a few days, Maybe next week when the Ryder Cup is out of the way. They'll be only too delighted to see you, Joey – '

Joey was looking doubtful again. 'I'm not supposed to leave the hotel. None of the team members are. Those crazy farmers and their protest have everyone scared – '

'But haven't you heard? – that's all over. The Government has sorted everything out with the – the Japanese – ' Or should that be Chinese? Donie wasn't sure.

He didn't care. He was jabbering on now like a fool. Anything to get Joey O'Hara outside and into that car! Anything not to have to face an angry Ben Gartland...

He could see that Joey was weakening. 'I'd sure like to meet those folks, talk to them. Dad would be delighted.' Joey glanced around, leaned forward, whispered. 'You sure we can be there and back in – ' he glanced at his Rolex - 'a couple of hours?'

'No problem,' Donie lied. 'I know the area like the back of my hand.

Joey knew it was risky, but the idea of meeting some of his distant Irish relatives was too much. 'Okay, I'm with you!' He looked around furtively. 'You go outside first officer, wait for me. I'll come just as I am. It'll save time and won't look suspicious...' What the hell, Joey thought. He'd never stepped out of line before, never broken the rules. But this was something special...

Outside on the steps of the hotel while he waited for Joey O'Hara to join him, Donie Dunhill reached for his mobile phone, dialled. Ben Gartland answered. 'We're on our way, sergeant - ' Donie began.

There was one more near miss. When Joey came outside he halted momentarily. 'Hey officer, what's with the car? Where are the flashing lights, the police signs – '

'This is top security. It's an unmarked vehicle. On loan from the Special Branch – that's our Undercover Unit - ' Donie was running out of police speak. 'Get in!'

At the front gates the same two security men who had earlier waved Donie through saw the uniform and repeated the exercise. Donie doubted that they even knew who his passenger was. Once on the main road he pressed his foot hard on the accelerator. Within a few minutes of leaving the hotel they had passed through the town of Sneem and were out into open country.

Dusk was beginning to fall as they skirted Lough Brin, one of the many picturesque lakes in this part of Kerry.

Soon he would be at the crossroads where Ben and his men were waiting.

Joey had been chatting away all the time they were driving. He was relaxed now and seemed to be looking forward to the family reunion which he assumed lay ahead. 'You know my old man is gonna be really surprised when I phone and tell him I'm on my way to meet his Irish forebears.'

Donie was so busy concentrating on negotiating the narrow, winding roads that he was barely listening to what Joey was saying. The September shadows were closing in and it would be dark soon. Not long to go now. He hoped there would be no violence, although you could never be sure when Ben Gartland was involved. Ben was hyped up to the gills with the aggro and the publicity his campaign was generating…

Suddenly Joey's last words sunk in. 'What do you mean, phoning your father to tell him? – ' Out of the corner of his eye Donie saw Joey reach into the pocket of the lightweight golf jacket he was wearing. He took out a mobile phone, began to punch in some numbers.

'Wait a minute, young fella…What are you up to?' Donie asked, alarmed.

'I'm putting through a call to Dad in Washington. Gotta tell him the news, ' Joey replied as nonchalantly as if were about to order his favourite pizza from the local takeaway.

Donie almost let go of the wheel with alarm. 'Wait a minute! You can't do that!' he shouted.

'Why not? What's the problem?' Joey replied. He had finished dialling now and had put the mobile to his ear.

'It – it's against regulations!' Donie stuttered lamely. He could hardly inform the young fella what he was being kidnapped! Not for the first time Donie felt real panic. This was unbelievable. Here he was approaching the kidnap site, with the unsuspecting victim sitting beside him, and the young idiot was telephoning his father in Washington!

Jaysus! If he didn't stop Joey O'Hara making that telephone call there was a strong possibility the FBI, the CIA, the U.S. Army and maybe even the U.S. Marines would be on their tail before Ben and the lads even got Joey into the getaway car!

'Now wait a minute, Joey. Hold your horses – '

He was too late. Already Joey had made the connection and was speaking to someone, several thousand of miles away. Donie cursed the advance of communications technology under his breath.

'Hello, is that the Senate building in Washington?... I wanna speak to Senator John O'Hara.... This is his son Joey here – ' A pause. He turned to Donie – 'Where exactly are we right now?'

Donie Dunhill nearly exploded. This was getting more bizarre by the minute! If Joey O'Hara wasn't silenced soon there would be big trouble. Luckily they were almost at the kidnap spot. Donie slammed his foot down on the accelerator and the car shot forward. It had the effect of taking his passenger's mind momentarily off the Senate in Washington!

'Hey, what's the hurry, officer? Do all you Irish cops drive this fast? Are you crazy or something? What the hell is going on? – '

Donie didn't answer. Instead he pressed even harder on the accelerator. If only he could get to Ben and the boys before big mouth Joey blew the kidnap plan sky high!

Too late! – Joey was already in touch with father's office...!

'Hi Dad, how are you? Joey here. You won't believe this but I'm on my way right now to meet our Irish ancestors – '

Donie saw the car in the distance. It was parked sideways, blocking the narrow the road almost completely. He maintained his speed, then jammed on the brakes and brought his car to a screeching halt. Three figures dressed in dark, bulky jackets jumped from the other car. Each person had a balaclava pulled down over their faces. Two of them carried what looked like baseball bats, while the third, the bigger of the trio whom Donie recognised as Ben, carried what looked like a canvas sack.

The three came towards Donie's car, the two with the baseball bats at the ready approaching the passenger side. 'What the hell – What's going on here?' Joey reacted quickly. He raised his mobile to his mouth, shouted into it, 'Dad, something's happening. Looks like a kidnap! Alert the cops, quick!'

One of the balaclava-clad figures pulled open Joey's door, reached in and began hauling him out.'Come on. Out!' He shouted. 'Make it fast – and no trouble!'

Joey stumbled onto the roadway. The trio of kidnappers gathered around him. One of the men grabbed Joey's mobile phone and was about to fling it over the hedge into a field when the one who seemed to be the leader shouted, 'Hold onto that!'

The big man muttered something to the other two who pinioned Joey's arms by his side. The leader flung the sack over Joey's head, pulled it down as far as it would go, then passed a stout strap over it and pulled it tight around the captive's body.

'Get him into the car. Put him in the back and try to keep him out of sight. If he gives any trouble you both know what to do…'

Donie watched as the duo with the baseball bats manhandled Joey O'Hara into the back seat of the kidnap vehicle which had the registration plates blacked out and which Donie reckoned had been stolen. As Ben was removing his balaclava Donie beckoned him to one side.

'Ben, the young buck was onto his father in Washington on his mobile just before I got here – '

He saw the anger on Ben's face. 'Why didn't you fucking stop him!'

'How could I, and me driving?'

Ben swore loudly. 'We can't talk here,' He was edgy, afraid another car would come on the scene. 'You get that uniform back to Pauly. He'll alert us to what's happening on the Garda side. I'll be in touch with you later. Now get going Donie.'

Ben turned on his heel, ran back to the other car, got behind the wheel. The car took off with a screech of burning rubber towards the MacGillycuddy Reeks, the mountain range towering dark and forbidding into the night sky. Donie Dunhill opened the boot of his car, took out the clothes that were there and began to change out of the Garda uniform in the back seat. A few minutes later he took the right hand turn onto the main road that would bring him back towards Loughduff.

Meanwhile, at his desk in Washington, Senator John O'Hara stared at the dead telephone in his hand. 'Jennifer! Jennifer!' he shouted out through the open door to his secretary.

A young, smartly dressed woman came into the room. 'Yes Senator?'

'Get me the police – quickly. My son Joey's just been on his mobile from Ireland. He shouted something about being kidnapped'

'Kidnapped! Oh my God, Senator! Are you sure?'

'I'm certain that's what he said. He managed to get a message to me on his mobile. He said he was in a car being taken somewhere – shouted something about a kidnap before the phone went dead.'

'I'll contact security immediately. They'll get help – ' The young lady reached for the telephone on the Senator's desk.

Senator O'Hara jumped to his feet.. 'The President must be alerted immediately!'

• • • •

The telephone in the newsroom of the Kerry Herald tinkled. Con Sharkey, one of the newspaper's most experienced reporters, picked it up. 'Hello?'

He automatically glanced at the wall clock. 10.10pm; he had been on duty for just over four hours, working on some less than earth-shattering stories. Con was bored and looking forward to a colleague coming back on duty to allow him to slip into the pub next door for his usual couple of drinks.

'Is that the newsroom?'

'Yes.'

'Am I talking to a reporter?' The tone was pure Kerry, aggressive into the bargain.

'You're talking to Con Sharkey, chief reporter.'

'Am I now? Then listen carefully chief reporter, this is important. I'm only going to say it once, so write it down – '

Con groaned inwardly. Another late night crank full of his own importance. No doubt about to report a missing dog or cat, or a traffic light not working somewhere. Con didn't bother switching on the tape recorder on the desk. The next words had him regretting his error.

'We've kidnapped the famous American golfer Joey O'Hara and we're holding him until after the Ryder Cup is over. Got that?'

'Jaysus!' Con jerked upright, almost let the telephone fall out of hand. 'What's that you just said? Could you repeat it please.' He reached over, switched on the tape recorder.

'You heard me chief reporter. I told you I was only going to say it once. We've kidnapped Joey O'Hara. That's all you need to know.'

'Hey wait! Don't hang up. Is this a joke? What's your name?'

'Fuck off. What class of a fool d'you think I am!'

'Wait, wait!' Con was desperate. There was only himself and the editor on duty right now, the latter out of earshot in the cubby hold he called his office. 'How do I know this isn't a hoax?'

'It's no hoax. Check it out – phone the |Parknasilla Palace if you don't believe me.' The line went dead.

Con stared at the dead instrument in his hand. He thought about informing the editor. Surely it was a hoax, a head-banger alone somewhere with nothing better to do than stir things up? Late duty reporters knew how to deal with this type of thing; no sense in alerting his editor just yet. He would check it out first.

Con dialled the Parknasilla Palace, asked if he could speak to Joey O'Hara. He was requested to hold on.

After a long delay a man who introduced himself as Cord McCallum came on the line. He identified himself as chairman of the U.S Ryder Cup committee, then asked, 'Who am I speaking to and why do you want to talk to Joey O'Hara?'

'I'm Con Sharkey, chief reporter with the Kerry Herald newspaper. It's important that I speak to Joey O'Hara - '

A pause. 'I'm afraid that's not possible right now,' Cord McCallum cut in.

'Why not?'

Another pause. Con could sense the other's brain ticking over seeking an excuse. He began to feel excited. It was looking like he was on to something.

'The members of both teams are at a private dinner and it's not desirable to disturb them. Perhaps I can help?'

Con was long enough in journalism to know when someone, as they say in the business, was being 'economical with the truth'. Time for shock tactics.

'Listen carefully, Mr. McCord. I've just had a telephone call from a man who claims that Joey O'Hara has been kidnapped. I'm checking to find out if it's true or if the phone call is a hoax. Now you had better come up with some answers or else I'll be getting touch with the police to check it out – '

Yet another pause. 'Hold on a moment.' Cord McCallum was obviously discussing the situation with someone. Con was getting more excited by the second. He sensed he had hit the target. Eventually the line became alive again and Cord McCallum said, 'Mr. Sharkey, I'm putting you on to one of your own high-ranking police officers…'

This time the voice was crisp, authoritative, a touch friendly. 'Hello Con. Chief Superintendent Kieran Clarke here. How are you – ' Con recognised the voice. He had had dealings with the local Super on many occasions over the years. Now he was getting somewhere.

'I'm fine, Super. Just checking out a story – '

'So I'm told. Now listen carefully to what I'm going to tell you, Con. It's dynamite and highly confidential. After I finish speaking to you I want to talk to your editor. Got that?'

'This sounds serious, Super….'

'It is. Very serious. Something nasty has happened. I emphasise that what I'm about to tell you is completely off the record. If you go against my orders, Con, I'll throw the book at you and your newspaper. Got that?'

Holy God! He had never been threatened like that by a member of the Gardai before. 'Of course, Super. '

'Okay. Now listen carefully. I can confirm that Joey O'Hara, the American Ryder Cup golfer, is not in the hotel at present. I can also confirm that he has been kidnapped – '

'Jaysus! – '

'It happened at approximately six forty-five this evening at a location unknown. Joey O'Hara was last seen leaving the hotel in a car with someone wearing a Garda uniform. We are presuming at this moment that that person was a bogus Garda – '

Con could hardly believe what he was hearing. No wonder the Super was acting up. A world exclusive – and it had fallen right into his lap! He hoped that the tape recorder was in working order. Without it he'd have difficulty convincing his editor the story was genuine.

'How do you know all this, Super?'

'The person behind the kidnap was in touch with us. Very briefly I might add.'

'What else can you tell me, Superintendent?'

'Fortunately, by an amazing coincidence, at the precise moment of the kidnap, Joey was speaking on his mobile phone to his father, Senator John O'Hara, in Washington. Unfortunately the young fellow was unable to give his father any details before he was overpowered – '

'Joey was actually talking to his father at the time of the kidnap? – '

'That's what I said.'

What a story! This was getting better by the minute! Con could hardly believe his luck.

The Super's next words sounded a death knell to Con's vision of enduring fame. 'Unfortunately for you and your newspaper Con, it's a story neither the Kerry Herald or any other newspaper will be able to publish – '

'What's that again, Super?'

'You heard me. No details of the kidnap are to be published by the media.'

'A sensational story like this? You're joking Super? Why not?'

'Because by doing so you would be putting Joey O'Hara's life in danger. Also if this story got out it would enormous damage to the country. The Taoiseach and his government have been informed of what has happened and they have imposed a ban on all information relating to the Joey O'Hara kidnap. That ban includes the media, newspapers, radio and television.'

'But they can't do that – !'

'They've just done it, Con. The Taoiseach is appealing to all editors in radio, tv and the newspapers not to publish anything about the kidnap for at least twenty-four hours. By then we expect to have Joey O'Hara released and the kidnappers arrested.'

'What makes you so confident of that?'

Superintendent Clarke paused a moment. Just how much could he divulge to a newspaperman? Could he trust the local newspaper? He reckoned he didn't have much choice. He would have to buy time.

He didn't need reminding what would happen if the members of the international media thronging Killarney for the big sporting event got a sniff of the story of the kidnap of the world's Number One golfer. They would work themselves into a frenzy, chasing the story and getting in the way. Mercifully right now they were preoccupied covering Angie Wilde's sudden departure for Hollywood and the embarrassment it was causing to America's Ryder Cup captain.

'All I can say at the moment, Con, is that we are confident of rescuing Joey O'Hara within the next twenty-four hours. We've a good idea who is behind this kidnap operation. Also there's another factor in our favour. It's a very important factor which I am not at liberty to divulge at present – '

'Ah come on now, Super. Could you not tell me what that is? Just between the two of us like – '

'Dammit man we're wasting time! I wouldn't be talking to you at all only you've been tipped off, probably by the man behind the kidnap', the Super shouted down the line. 'I've told you enough already. Now put me on to your editor immediately!'

• • • •

The weak early morning sun filtering in through the tiny window of the wooden shack, which Donie Dunhill euphemistically described to would-be clients as a 'shooting and fishing' lodge, woke Joey O'Hara. He came back to consciousness slowly, his eyes wandering around the unfamiliar surrounds as the events of last night began to register

He eased his large, athletic frame into a more comfortable position on the narrow bunk bed. The chain on his left leg which was clamped firmly to the bunk didn't help matters. He was still dressed in the casual tracksuit bottoms and lightweight golf jacket which he had been wearing when he left the hotel last evening.

Joey pushed back the rough blanket, sat upright and took note of his surroundings. He was in a small, dingy room that looked like had not been cleaned or the floor swept in ages. Two tiny windows – too small for him to squeeze through should he contemplate an escape – allowed in just the right quantity of light. He could hear mumbled voices coming through the wall from another room of the shack. Slowly the events of last night began to take shape....

After he had been bundled into the car with the sack over his head by the three men wearing balaclavas, the car had been driven off at speed. A short while the car had stopped and he had been transferred to another vehicle. That drive had lasted about an hour he reckoned, and a lot of it was uphill – he could tell from the sound of the engine – and along winding roads. He reckoned they were in a very isolated area because he did not hear the sound of many other cars passing. The men rarely spoke and when they did they avoided using names.

Eventually they had reached their destination. Joey had been taken roughly from the car and the sack had been removed. By then darkness had fallen and he could see nothing of his surroundings in the pitch blackness. He had been bundled quickly inside what looked like a shack and told to sit down. He had not been impressed by his surroundings; rough wooden walls, equally rough, sparse furniture and no electricity. A gas ring in the corner looked like the only means of cooking. One of the men put a match to two oil lamps, throwing up towering shadows on the walls which made the place look even more forbidding.

'What the hell is going on? Who are you and what do you want?' Joey had asked his captors. The trio, who were again wearing balaclavas, looked from to the other.

Eventually the bigger of the trio who had earlier been giving all the orders and who seemed to be the boss, answered roughly, 'Shut up and don't ask questions. And don't try any funny business like trying to escape. That way you won't get hurt.' He had turned to the other two, 'Take him inside. You know what to do.'

Joey had been brought into the other room, thrown roughly on the bed, and had his leg manacled to the sturdy frame. An hour later he had been brought a mug of tea and afterwards given an opportunity to go outside to the toilet – watched by two of the men. After that it was back to the darkness of his small prison. He lay down on the bed, the muffled voices from the other room eventually lulling him into a fitful sleep.

Now the door was pulled open and a balaclaved head was thrust into the room. 'He's awake,' the hooded one called over his shoulder. 'Want me to bring him in?' There was a muffled reply.

Joey's chain was unlocked and he was brought into the other room, pushed roughly onto a chair at the table. The big man, also wearing a balaclava, was busy over the gas ring in the corner. His accomplice – the third member seemed to have left – watched Joey closely.

The big man turned from the stove and thrust a tin plate in front of his captor. Joey looked at the four sausages and a couple of fried eggs beside them. swimming in grease. He decided to do without breakfast.

Instead Joey said, 'I suppose you guys know who I am?'

A pause. The smaller of the men answered. 'We're not fuckin' thick. You bet your life we know who you are.' Joey guessed he was younger than the big man, about his own age, he reckoned.

'How long are you going to keep me here? You know I'm playing in the Ryder Cup. It begins the day after tomorrow – '

The younger one gave a muffled laugh. 'You mean you're supposed to be playing in the Ryder Cup, Joey....'

They stood, staring.'What do you guys want...Money? Take my advice - let me go before the cops catch up with you. We'll call it quits. How about it?'

'Don't answer him,' the big man growled.

Joey was getting desperate. He wondered if his father had understood his garbled message before he had been overpowered. He had got out the word 'kidnap'. That was vital. He was almost certain that a rescue bid was already under way.But he couldn't be sure.

The anti-kidnap microchip embedded on his person.... Should he tell his captors about it? That would really surprise them, scare them into letting him go maybe. He decided against the idea. The anti-kidnap device was embedded in the lobe of his ear, invisible to the human eye. If he told them they might decide to perform some amateur surgery. Joey shuddered at the thought.

'Scared, are you?' the big man laughed harshly. 'This is a lonely area. Nobody will find us up here. If you try to escape – ' He was interrupted by his mobile phone ringing.

Joey watched him unhook it from the belt around his midriff. Before answering it he gave instructions to his companion. 'Watch him carefully and if he tries anything give him a few whacks of that - ' he nodded towards the baseball bat. The big man opened the door and went outside. It was early morning and the air was cool. A hazy rain was falling.

Ben pulled his balaclava up onto his forehead. 'Yeah? Who is it?'

'Ben! Is that you? This is Pauly – ' He sounded frightened. 'Where are you?'

'Where the hell do you think I am – up at Donie's in the Black Valley – '

'You've got Joey O'Hara? Where is he?'

'He's inside. Fonsie is keeping an eye on him.'

'Is he alright? Not injured - ?'

'He's okay so far. If he gives any trouble Fonsie will take care of him.'

'Ben, get the hell out of there – fast! They're on to you!'

'What's that?' There was static on the line. Ben swore, the blasted mountains…

'I said get out of there, Ben. Quickly. They're closing in on you right now., The Army – and the Emergency Response Unit, and the Special Branch. Get out Ben. Let Joey O'Hara go and run for it!'

'What are you talking about. How do you know all this?'

'I'm on duty here at the station. I've just heard it on the Garda waveband – '

Ben swore again. 'How did they get on to us so quickly?'

'Joey O'Hara has a microchip in his ear!'

'A what?'

'A microchip.'

A pause while Ben's brain grappled with the new technology. 'What the hell is that?'

'A gadget, like a magnet – ' Pauly's reply came in a rush of words. 'It can track people anywhere by satellite – like when they've been kidnapped. All the big shots have them nowadays, pop stars, big businessmen, top sports stars. Joey has one in his ear – '

Pauly stopped, groaned. He knew he wasn't making sense, not to Ben Gartland. Pigs, cows, farm talk…..they were Ben's subjects.

'You say it's in his ear. How come I didn't notice it?'

'You're not supposed to!', Pauly shouted. Ben Gartland was an idiot. 'I'm telling you Ben to get out of there. They're tracking you by helicopter. They'll be there soon – '

'A helicopter! – ' Ben paused, listened, looked skywards, saw a dot in the sky. 'Jaysus, they're here already!'

In the Garda station Pauly slammed down the phone. As far as he was concerned Ben Gartland could look out for himself from here on in.

Ben burst back into the shack. Fonsie Blake, the young farm labourer who Ben had recruited to help in the kidnap, saw the panic on his face.

'Something wrong?' Fonsie asked.

'We're getting out – and we're taking our friend with us!' Ben pulled Joey O'Hara to his feet.

'Why? What's happened – ?' Fonsie looked puzzled. Reacting quickly to a situation wasn't his forte.

'Shut up and do as I say!', Ben shouted. 'We're making a run for it.' He nodded towards Joey.. 'Watch him. I'll bring the jeep around – '

'It might be better if we left him here – '

'Bring him I said!' Ben snarled. 'Use that baseball bat if necessary – '

Ben ran out. Fonsie picked up the baseball bat. 'Get up,' he shouted at Joey O'Hara. 'Outside quickly – ' He waved the baseball bat threateningly. Outside he could hear Ben revving the Mitsubishi Ranger. He followed Joey O'Hara out. It was then that Fonsie saw the helicopter. It swooped low over the house, turned.

'You and him in the back!', Ben shouted from the car.

Fonsie grabbed Joey, pulled him towards the jeep. Joey wrenched himself free, waved at the 'copter overhead.

'Stop that you bastard!', Fonsie raised the baseball bat but Joey was too quick for him. Before Fonsie could deliver the blow the world's top golfer stepped forward and swung a punch, catching Fonsie on the side of the face and sending him sprawling on the grass. Joey turned, took off as fast as he could towards the belt of woodland that bordered the shack where he had been held captive.

Fonsie shook his head to clear it, scrambled to his feet

and prepared to set off in pursuit. He was stopped by a roar from Ben. 'Leave the fucker Fonsie! Get into the car - '

Fonsie barely made it into the Mitsubishi before Ben had it moving at speed down the rutted path towards the gate which lead onto the narrow roadway. Fonsie followed Ben's example and removed his balaclava, feeling his jaw gingerly.

He stared. 'Look!', Fonsie shouted, pointing. 'Soldiers and Gardai. Gangs of them!'

Ben was too busy guiding the jeep down the rutted track to turn his head. Instead he pressed his foot on the accelerator, the Mitsubishi shot forward, smashed through the closed wooden gate, sending shafts of wood flying right and left. Fonsie took time out from rubbing his aching jaw to grin delightedly. This was more exciting than anything he had seen on telly!

They hit the road with tyres screeching just as two Garda cars, with signals flashing, roared around the bend of the road a couple of hundred metres behind. The squad cars were followed by an army jeep. Up above the helicopter swung away from the house, came on fast and swooped low over the Mitsubishi, the noise from its whirling blades rising above the roar of the Mitsubishi's engine. The chase was on!

Ben decided against taking the main route leading to Killarney. Instead he gunned the Mitsubishi along a narrow secondary road that lead into the MacGillycuddy Reeks. Soon they were speeding into the shadow of Carrauntouhil, Ireland's tallest mountain, with the sirens of the two Garda pursuit cars going full blast. Tyres screeching, engines roaring, the chase continued along the narrow, twisting road that climbed the side of the mountain. Fonsie, frightened now, glanced nervously to his left, got an unwelcome view of what seemed a bottomless gorge.

'Jaysus Ben be careful!' he pleaded. 'Maybe we should stop and give ourselves up?'

He was answered by a roar of laughter, a demonic sound that did nothing to allay the fear that had the hairs standing up on the back of his neck. 'Give ourselves up!', Ben roared, 'and spend the next ten years behind bars! The bastards will have to catch us first!'

The hazy rain had ceased and the sun was shining, its morning rays low in the sky, a blinding hazard whenever the Mitsubishi swung away from the shadow of the mountain. Ben kept glancing in his mirror and swearing loudly, and every time he did so Fonsie offered up a silent prayer, something he had not done for a long time. He turned and glanced out through the rear window; maybe it was due to the narrow, winding mountain roads, but their pursuers did not seem to be gaining on them. Fonsie was thankful that not too many tourists took their cars along this route because of the hazards. He could still hear the helicopter hovering around.

They were now skirting one of Killarney's famous lakes and speeding down towards the Gap of Dunloe, the area's famous beauty spot. Ben slowed the Mitsubishi momentarily only when they met other cars coming the opposite direction. Fonsie had fleeting glances of frightened passenger faces and heard other drivers sound their car horns in warning. They went through the Gap of Dunloe at a speed never experienced in the area before, the Garda sirens scattering tourists and causing the owners of the horses and donkeys, the usual mode of transport through the Gap, to grab the bridles of the frightened animals.

Fonsie breathed a sigh of relief when they left Killarney's scenic area behind and hit the relatively straight stretch of road heading into Killorglin. But his relief was short lived; no sooner had Ben taken the right hand turn to Killorglin at the t-junction than the two powerful Garda cars began to close on them. Ben glanced in the mirror before hitting the accelerator. The needle shot up to 100 mph and was still climbing. Fonsie began to pray again.

Ben drove at speed through the winding, hilly main street of Killorglin, missing parked vehicles by inches. Shops and houses went by in a blur and any of the local inhabitants unfortunate enough to be crossing the road had to leap for safety.

As they reached the outskirts of the town a Garda car loomed up, parked sideways across the road, endeavouring to block it to traffic. Two uniformed officers were standing at either end of the vehicle. 'What the – ' Ben swore.

'They must have radioed ahead – ' Fonsie shouted the obvious. Fear had long since replaced the excitement in his eyes. At last it looked like their pursuit was coming to an end.

He was mistaken. They were now on the main road to Glenbeigh and fortunately for Ben the Garda car was not big enough to block the road completely. There were gaps on either side of the vehicle.

'Hold on tight, Fonsie!', Ben shouted, pressing his foot down. 'We're going through!'

Fonsie closed his eyes, put his hands to his face. There was a loud bang and he was thrown forward by the impact. Then he felt the Mitsubishi shoot forward again. He heard Ben's demonic laugh at the same time as he looked back through the rear window. The police car was slewed completely around, its boot burst open by the collision. The two Gardai were picking themselves up from the side of the road where they had dived for safety.

'Stupid bastards if they thought that Ben Gartland was going to stop!'

The Mitsubishi roared on, the three cars behind still doggedly in pursuit, the Gardai cars with their sirens blaring and the roof signals flashing. The noise of the helicopter added to the din.

'We're never going to throw them off, Ben,' Fonsie wailed.

'Think not? Just watch me, Fonsie. I'll show them stupid bastards what driving is all about!'

Through Glenbeigh and out the other side of the town, with the huge expanse of Dingle Bay glistening in the distance. The Mitsubishi was now speeding towards the area known as King's Head, along the scenic but dangerous coast road. Fonsie was frozen with fear, his knuckles showing white so tightly did he grip the sides of his seat. Maybe next time they hit a straight stretch of road with fields on either side he would wrestle the wheel from Ben and take a chance of crashing the vehicle. Anything was better than sitting beside the madman that was Ben Gartland with the Atlantic beckoning below...

'Jaysus Ben, watch out!' Fonsie cried out in fear.

Too late! The large shadow of a tourist coach loomed around a curve in the road. Ben braked, turned the steering wheel sideways to avoid hitting the oncoming vehicle head-on, fought desperately to regain control as the tyres screeched towards the edge of the cliff road.....

Fonsie Blake screamed, a terrible, frightened sound that was more animal than human. The coach driver was also battling desperately to avoid the inevitable crash. He managed to turn his heavy vehicle in towards the grass margin. The Mitsubishi hit the coach a glancing blow before disappearing over the side of the cliff road. Halfway down it hit the rock face and bounced outwards. It entered the blue waters of Dingle Bay roof first, throwing spray high into the air.

By then the pursuing Garda cars and the Army jeep had pulled to a stop at the side of the road, their occupants watching helplessly as in the sea, the Mitsubishi Ranger sank slowly below the Atlantic waves.....

CHAPTER ELEVEN

Friday morning in Killarney dawned bright and sunny, with a teasing wind blowing in off Lough Leane. All roads leading to the Killarney Golf and Fishing Club were alive with long lines of cars and fans on foot making their way to the Killeen course. Many of them had their faces painted in national colours; others in noisy groups waved flags and banners, while lots of rival fans were wearing T-shirts bearing the Stars and Stripes or the ringed emblem of Europe. As if to emphasise the intense rivalry generated by the occasion, and despite the appeals of both Ryder Cup bodies, many fans on both sides were wearing T-shirts with provocative slogans on them.

It was the opening day of the Ryder Cup and thousands of golf fans were already on the course, vying for vantage points around the first tee, eager to see the opening shots of the morning foursomes in what promised to be a high voltage clash between the golfer superstars of Europe and America.

The official starter, resplendent in blazer, gleaming white shirt and slacks, and sporting a Ryder Cup tie, consulted his time sheet. He tested his hand-held microphone for sound then stepped forward, conscious of the phalanx of television camera focused on him.

'On the first tee, representing the United States of America –' the rising volume of cheering from the American fans began to drown out his words – 'K.C Matthews and Joey O'Hara – '

The cheering and shouting around the first tee continued, both the U.S. players waving and acknowledging the support. Despite the last-minute pleas from both camps for spectators to show respect for the Ryder Cup and good sportsmanship towards the players, the crowd was going wild even before a ball was struck. For anxious officials watching the scene the spectre of past fiery Ryder Cup clashes was already surfacing....

'Go get them our guys!', a spectator waving a star-spangled banner shouted above the din. An equally loud male European voice answered, imploring his multinational team to 'Come on Europe – let's spank the Yanks!' It was obvious that despite the pleadings of officialdom, national passions were going to be given full vent over the next three days.

'Just listen to that great reception for young Joey O'Hara,' the CBS commentator, seated in a cabin overlooking the first tee, enthused. 'Twenty-four hours ago the world's Number One golfer was the victim of a kidnap that, sadly, ended tragically in the deaths of two local men. Joey was held captive in a hunting lodge in the mountains near here but made a dramatic escape during a police and army raid yesterday. Against all medical advice American captain Wayne Folen has picked him to lead off the foursomes this morning. It's an amazing decision by Wayne Folen, one that has been criticised in many quarters, including by some members of the American squad itself....'

Yesterday afternoon the traditional Ryder Cup opening ceremony had been held in front of the clubhouse before a distinguished gathering that included the President of Ireland, the Taoiseach, government dignitaries and members of the American and European Ryder Cup teams and officials. The world's top golfer, Joey O'Hara, was prominent by his absence.

Hours earlier, after he had made his dramatic escape from his kidnappers, Joey had been helicoptered back to the safety of the Parknasilla Palace Hotel. At a hastily convened press conference details of the kidnap, Joey's escape and the high-speed pursuit leading to the death plunge of the two kidnappers into Dingle Bay had been released to an astonished world media.

At the conference Cord McCallum had announced that Joey O'Hara would not be taking part in the opening ceremony as he was undergoing medical tests and was under observation after his traumatic experience. Answering questions, the U.S. Ryder Cup chairman hinted that the young golf superstar would probably not be selected to play during the opening day of the contest.

Last night television viewers around the world had seen Joey O'Hara, in an emotional link-up with his father in Washington, tell of his ordeal at the hands of members of the breakaway Irish farming group, two of whom had later died in the car plunge into the waters of Dingle Bay.

'I guess you could say I'm lucky to be alive,' an obviously still shaken Joey had told his father in the telelecast. 'If I hadn't knocked that guy over and decided to make a run for it I would have been in that car that went over the cliff.' Now as the Ryder Cup got under way those same tv viewers could scarcely believe that the young fellow had been sent out to play in the highly-charged opening foursomes.

Wayne Folen had brushed aside all warnings that his top player needed more time to recover from his ordeal. 'The members of my Ryder Cup squad are mentally and physically tough. I'm very happy that I had my guys up in the Catskills for a week in that training camp. I know I'm taking a risk, going against the opinion of my Ryder Cup committee members. But I know what I'm doing. You watch, Joey will respond to my picking him. He'll handle the pressure. – '

As he sat in the golf buggy alongside the first tee Wayne Folen fervently hoped he was right. In selection young Joey he had overruled the team doctor and angered Cord McCallum among others. Wayne knew he was taking a big chance with Joey; but he was anxious to get some early points on the board.

A deathly silence momentarily descended on the Killarney Golf and Fishing Club as K.C. Matthews prepared to hit the opening drive of the contest. In the commentary boxes television pundits were explaining to audiences around the world the intricacies of foursomes golf, in which two players in each partnership play alternate shots with the same ball. With four morning foursomes and four afternoon fourballs to be played, it means that there were eight vital points to be won on this first day.

Standing on the first tee Joey saw his partner smash a 3-wood straight as an arrow and into the ideal position on the fairway, 270 yards distant. The first hole on the Killeen course is only 434 yards, not long by today's standards with most pros now regularly hitting drives around the 300 yards mark. But at Killeen the lake cuts into the fairway all the way down the right side. K.C's good play had left his partner with a straightforward shot to the green, setting up a possible birdie chance.

Wild applause and cheers broke out from the American fans at K.C. Matthews' effort. As he walked slowly past the two European golfers he made a point of glancing at them, smiling confidently. K.C's body language said it all: 'Hello guys. We're gonna rub your noses in it today!'

Neil Naismith, the veteran who had represented Europe with distinction in eight Ryder Cup encounters, then stepped up and hit his tee-shot straight down the middle, the ball finishing several yards past that of his rival. More wild applause and shouting. Naismith was happy; he had used his influence as the senior member of the squad to pressure his captain Bruce Cartway to allow him to play with fellow Englishman and Ryder Cup rookie

Gary Formby. Naismith reckoned he would be the star of this partnership....

As he walked down the fairway to where his partner's ball had landed, Joey O'Hara felt the perspiration break out on his forehead. Jeez! What was happening to him? He had been warned about the fierce tension attached to playing in the Ryder Cup, but this wasn't only nervousness, this was something else. He felt unfocused, slightly dizzy, like a rookie who had never played at this level before. As he walked down the fairway Joey took a few deep breaths, tried to clear his head...

Joey reached the ball. It was lying perfectly on the fairway. He studied the line to the green, 165 yards distant. After a short consultation with his caddie he picked a 7-iron from the bag. As he stood over the ball he could feel the breeze coming over his right shoulder. That would help in keeping the ball away from the water. The water! Why was he thinking about the water on the right. It was a straightforward shot. Think positive - he'd knock it close to the flag, give his partner a good chance of a birdie, put pressure on the Europeans.

Joey swung the club smoothly. He heard the huge gallery gasp. As his head came up on the follow-through he could hardly believe what he was seeing – his ball was heading straight for the lake! In his buggy Wayne Folen watched stone-faced as Joey's ball disappeared beneath the surface and the ripples began to spread.

● ● ● ●

A shout from the head of the Garda Sub Aqua Squad below at the water's edge interrupted the conversation taking place between Sergeant Gilhooly and Chief Superintendent Kieran Clarke.

'Looks like they've located the car, Superintendent. It shouldn't be long now before we have it on dry land'.

'Aye'. The Super waved an acknowledgement to the Gardai. He looked at his watch, muttered beneath his breath. He had planned on being in Killarney this morning to see the start of the Ryder Cup, but now his visit would have to wait until the afternoon. He would check on how the battle was progressing later...

A buzz of anticipation rose from the various groups of people gathered along the foreshore, including photographers and a couple of tv camera crews. The latter moved into position, readying their equipment. About twenty yards offshore the dredger that had steamed down the coast from Castlemaine was anchored, the chains from the on-board crane sunk beneath the surface of the water. It is doubtful if the King's Head area of Dingle Bay, where yesterday the Mitsubishi Ranger with Ben Gartland and Fonsie Blake on board had gone out of control and plunged over the cliff, had ever before witnessed such activity. Now the real drama was about to begin.

Superintendent Clarke looked at the wisps of white cloud drifting lazily across the blue sky, whipped by a light breeze. Ideal weather for golf. He had been in Parknasilla earlier when the European and American squads had been helicoptered to the course. In the wake of yesterday car chase tragedy the farmers' protest had fizzled out, and even the numbers of feminists picketing outside the hotel gates in Parknasilla had seemed smaller than usual.

It was now accepted that Ben Gartland and his unfortunate passenger had not survived the car plunge into the sea. Drowned probably, if they had survived the cliff plunge and the subsequent crash into the mass of jutting rock before hitting the water. Surely nobody could have survived that horrific happening.

Below, there was still no sign of the vehicle breaking the surface. 'How are your inquiries proceeding, sergeant? You're confident Ben Gartland is one of the men in that car?' the Super asked.

Gilhooly squinted against the sun, surveyed the activity on the dredger from the elevated area where they were standing. 'Yes. We suspected it all along.. It's Ben Gartland alright. We checked and he didn't return to his place last night –'

'And the other person?'

'Probably young Fonsie Blake, a local farm labourer.'

'Hmmm. That Garda uniform that the man who spoke to Joey O'Hara in the hotel was wearing. Any idea where that came from?'

'Nothing definite as yet,' the Sergeant replied guardedly. 'We're still working on that.' He had good idea where the uniform had come from but he wasn't saying anything. Not yet, anyway. He had to check with Pauly Glynn. Pauly had not shown up for duty this morning and the landlady at the house where he lodged didn't have any idea of his whereabouts. It would be difficult to pin anything on wily Pauly.

As for Donie Dunhill, he had been brought to the Garda station and questioned about his lodge in the Black Valley having been used for the Joey O'Hara kidnap. Donie had protested his innocence; yes, he had given Ben Gartland the key, but he had assumed that Ben had merely wanted to look over the place with a view to hiring it for a weekend of fishing in the area. He had never suspected that Ben Gartland would be using it for any other purpose.

Sergeant Gilhooly was glad that his superior didn't pursue the questioning. Instead the Super took to pacing up and down the grassy knoll from where they were observing the action on the foreshore below. Another ten minutes passed before the clanking of the chains indicated that something was being brought up. Then slowly the rear bumper of the Mitsubishi Ranger broke the surface.

When the vehicle was halfway out of the water the crane operator halted the operation to allow some of the sea water drain off. Again the crane was set in motion and slowly the rest of the dark blue vehicle cleared the surface. The damage to the front of the Mitsubishi where it had bounced off the rock face before plunging into the sea was plainly visible. As it was lowered towards the deck of the dredger, eager hands reached out to steady it. Four wooden chocks were placed under the wheels and then it was surrounded by Gardai in white overalls.

The Super and Sergeant Gilhooly made their way down onto the foreshore as the men on the dredger struggled to get the door on the driver's side open. It had been pushed back off line by the impact with the cliff face. When it was finally prised opened a body was removed from the vehicle and laid out on the deck. The action was repeated on the front passenger door and a second body was removed and placed beside the first. Both bodies were quickly covered with white sheets.

The crowd watched as the two bodies were secured on stretchers and lowered into a motor launch. The launch roared into life and made the short journey to the shore. As television cameras whirred the bodies were taken from the boat and carried to a waiting ambulance, en route to the hospital in Killarney where an autopsy would be performed.

Before the bodies were put into the ambulance Sergeant Gilhooly moved in, lifted the covers on both the bodies. He sighed, said to his superior, 'I always suspected that Ben Gartland was heading for big trouble, but I never thought he would end up like this.'

He turned, saw that the Super wasn't interested. He was listening intently to someone talking on his mobile again, asking a question now and again. A broad grin slowly broke across his face at whatever he was hearing.

'What's the word from the Ryder Cup?' Gilhooly asked as they crunched their way up towards the road towards the waiting Garda car. He wasn't particularly interested in golf but he wanted to keep on the right side of the Super.

'I've just checked on the morning play. And guess what? – ' Gilhooly shook his head, tried to look interested. Gaelic football, his native Kerry winning the All-Ireland, now that got his heart racing. But men hitting a small stationary ball into a hole – he could take it or leave it!

'We've whitewashed the Yanks in the morning foursomes!' the Super said excitedly. 'The European crowds at Killeen are going wild.'

• • • •

Wayne Folen stood on the edge of the 18th green, felt the pent-up emotion of the crowd about to explode as soon as Kurt Mason stroked the ball towards the hole twelve feet away. Wayne stared fixated as the ball left Mason's putter, heard the crescendo of American cheers trying to will the ball into the hole….

Mason grimaced in agony as his ball horseshoed around the rim and stayed out. Wayne, sensing that the tv cameras were on him, forced a rather grim smile – the Europeans had whitewashed his guys in the morning foursomes! As captain of a U.S. side not to register a single point on the opening morning's play he had made Ryder Cup history – but for all the wrong reasons!

Five hours ago he had got an inkling that he was in for a tough morning when Joey O'Hara had unbelievably shanked his opening shot on the first fairway into the lake. The world's top golfer wasn't supposed to do things like that. That one bad shot been an omen for what was to follow; it set the trend for the other team members in action during the morning. Wayne had watched helplessly as every member of his squad in the morning foursomes had played below form. His guys seemed to have the jitters; how else could he explain the catalogue of poor shots leading to disaster after disaster that had befallen eight of his most experienced players during the morning's play?

Earlier Wayne had stood on the edge of the 13th green and witnessed Joey O'Hara missing a putt from four feet that would have kept the match between himself and K.C. Matthews against the European pairing of Naismith and Formby alive. When Joey's ball had failed to drop it meant that in the top match of the morning foursomes the crack American partnership had been emphatically walloped 6 & 5. That result had sent shock waves through the other three American pairings playing behind.

At that point in time the portends for the Stars and Stripes were not good. At the halfway mark in the other three matches the American pairings were behind in all of them. The thousands of American fans who had crossed the Atlantic to cheer on their team were experiencing a nightmare opening morning. The European supporters were ecstatic and in full cry.

As he flitted from match to match in his buggy keeping up with the action, Wayne occasionally caught sight of Cord McCallum and his fellow committee members on the fringes of the fairways. The grim look on their faces told its own story; Wayne knew what they were thinking – that he had made a big mistake in going against their wishes, playing Joey O'Hara so soon after the young guy's kidnap ordeal.

They were right, of course. Wayne realised that now. He had gone against the team doctor's advice, gambled and lost. He knew that as captain the buck stopped with him.

'Sorry skipper for letting you and the guys down – ' a disconsolate Joey had murmured as he walked off the 13th green.

Wayne had put his arm around Joey's shoulders, tried to hide his disappointment. 'Don't apologise Joey. I reckon it was my fault. I shouldn't have put you into the action so soon after what happened.

'Yeah, Joey just wasn't himself out there today,' K.C

Matthews cut in. 'He should not have been asked to go out there.' The senior member of the squad, unbeaten in three other Ryder Cup clashes until this morning, didn't believe in hiding his feelings. Matthews hated being beaten and was laying the blame where it belonged – with his captain.

Wayne didn't reply. He didn't want to start an argument with any of his players. Besides, this wasn't the only disaster of the morning foursomes. He had watched speechless as his next two foursomes pairing lost to the Europeans, albeit on the final green on each occasion. That had made it 3 – 0 to the Europeans. Then had come the final ignominy – Kurt Mason and Larry Maleski losing their contest, also on the 18th . It was almost too much to bear. Shortly he and Bruce Cartray would face the media and there was no doubt in Wayne's mind which captain was going to take most of the flak!

Four points to zero down – the media would crucify him. Cord McCallum was at his elbow, eyes as cold as steel. 'I hope, Wayne, you won't be stupid enough to go against our advice again and risk playing young O'Hara this afternoon?'

Wayne made a supreme effort to keep calm. 'That'll be my decision, Mr. McCallum,' he replied levelly. 'For your information my pairings are already decided.' He waved a sheet of paper that he would shortly be having photocopied and, following the rules, showing it to his European rival Bruce Cartray, then releasing it to the media. He was outraged that McCallum had challenged him within earshot of a group of spectators.

In the press tent the rows of reporters were lined up like members of a jury. Wayne took his seat behind the microphone, several feet from where a beaming Bruce Cartray was sitting. The first question was directed at him.

'Your guys have just been whitewashed in the foursomes, Wayne. First time ever in the history of the Ryder Cup. What happened out there?'

'What the hell do you think happened?' Wayne snapped. 'My guys underperformed. We got beat. No excuses.'

'Was it a mistake playing Joey O'Hara against the doctor's wishes?'

Might as well bite the bullet, he thought. 'Yeah. Looks like in hindsight I made a mistake. I take full responsibility.'

'Your medic claims he warned you last night that Joey wasn't fit to play, yet you ignored him. Is that true?'

'I just admitted that, didn't I?'

'What was your reason for playing Joey?'

'Because I wanted an early American point on the board. I wanted us to win that first match out. That's very important. It gives a side a great psychological boost.'

'So you pitched in a player who had gone through a kidnap ordeal and who you were told was probably suffering from post traumatic stress disorder – '

Post traumatic stress disorder – rubbish! Wayne wanted to shout out. In Vietnam me and the guys and went out every day not knowing if we were going to come back alive or badly wounded. Nobody asked us if we suffered from post traumatic stress disorder. We did our job and we got on with it. Young sports guys today are too soft, can't stand the pressure. Guys who play golf especially. Too many college wimps with limited talent who within a few years of turning pro are millionaires. Hell, now they're even wearing a gadget in their ears in case they get kidnapped!

Instead Wayne said, 'Lots of people do jobs that bring on stress. Pro golfers are no different. Maybe some of them think they are but they're not!' That last bit was out before he could stop himself.

'Have you lost the confidence of your squad, Mr. Folen? There's talk that Angie Wilde walking out has undermined your authority - '

The question brought a deathly silence in the media

centre. Wayne fixed the young lady reporter who had asked the question with a baleful glare.

'What do you think, Miss?'

'I'm asking you the question, Mr. Folen.'

'You'll have to ask the members of my squad that question. I have no comment whatsoever to make about Miss Wilde. Next question please…' Wayne was fuming inside. Had that question, and the smart remark about Angie Wilde, been put forward by a male member of the media he'd have gone down and belted him one for sure!

Down the table Bruce Cartray hid a satisfied smile. He was secretly enjoying seeing Wayne Folen on the retreat so early. Only halfway through the first day of the Ryder Cup clash and already advantage Europe big time! The next few questions were directed at him and Bruce fielded them expertly.

'You spanked the Yanks this morning, Bruce. Are you confident, even though this only the opening session, of retaining the Ryder Cup?'

'Far too early to say,' Bruce replied easily. 'My fellows did everything I asked of them and I'm very happy right now. But there are still two and a half days to go and a lot of points to be won – or lost. I expect the Americans to fight back strongly in the afternoon fourballs'

The end of the press conference couldn't come soon enough for Wayne Folen. As the questions came thick and fast he was very much on the defensive. Nobody mentioned Angie Wilde by name again, but someone half-jokingly asked, in the light of what was happening away from the golf course, if Wayne himself was maybe suffering from a form of post traumatic stress disorder! To his credit Wayne responded in a light hearted manner, although he was fervently wishing the session to be over.

He was glad when not long afterwards one of the Ryder Cup officials called a halt. The two captains rose to their feet, exchanged a few brief words and an equally brief handshake, and exited at different ends of the long table. There was no doubt that there was no love lost between the two men. The members of the media rose to their feet as one and hurried to the exits, hoping to grab a quick lunch before heading out to see the afternoon action.

• • • •

The telephone shrilled just as Katie entered the kitchen. Probably Sergeant Gilhooly, she surmised, telephoning with further details of Ben Gartland's fatal car plunge into Dingle Bay. By now they would have recovered the bodies, made positive identification.

The sergeant had called yesterday evening to break the news about a Mitsubishi going over the cliffs and into Dingle Bay. Katie and the boys had listened in silence as he had outlined details of what had happened following the kidnap of the young American star golfer. Katie had listened in silence, her face expressionless. She felt no sorrow, no emotion. So what if it was Ben's Mitsubishi that had gone over the cliff – and she assumed that it was his vehicle because he had not been around the farm at all yesterday. She had never liked her brother-in-law, had hated his awkward and lewd advances to her over the years whenever Travis was not around.

Ben Gartland's death, unfortunate as it was, meant nothing to her. Already she had consigned to the past. In two days time she and the boys would be on their way to either Morocco or Greece, and a new life with Jeremy. The dreary farmhouse where she had spent so many unhappy years with a husband she despised would soon be erased from her memory.

It wasn't Sergeant Gilhooly's voice that came over the telephone. A woman's voice answered. She sounded young, twenties perhaps, Katie surmised. With a hint of a foreign accent.

'allo?'

'Yes?'

'Mrs Katie Gartland?'

'That's right. Who's speaking?' She knew instinctively whom it was – the young woman who had telephoned two days ago when she and Jeremy were in Dublin. Katie suddenly felt uneasy.

'Ah yes…You do not know me. My name is Juliette. I am telephoning from England, from Norfolk – '

The placename made Katie go cold. 'You telephoned before. Two days ago. I was away – '

'That is right. I spoke with one of your boys – '

'Yes, he told me. I was – er – hoping you would ring back – ' Katie bit her lip. That wasn't quite true; she had been dreading this call.

'Of course. I am sorry. I have been busy…'

There was an awkward pause, each waiting for the other to proceed. Katie was reluctant to do so, afraid of what she conversation might lead to. But she knew she must find out the truth. 'What is it you wish to speak to me about?'

'I wish to talk to you about Jeremy….and Serge our baby!'

This time Katie's heart did miss a beat. 'A baby. You and Jeremy…'

'Yes. He did not tell you?'

'No. But - I'm sure he would have told me had I asked,' Katie replied lamely.

'Of course.' They both knew that wasn't true.

'You and Jeremy…..you obviously knew each other very well…'

'Oui, very well indeed. Before he went to Ireland – ' Juliette paused, said, 'I'm sorry, this must be very difficult for you…'

'How did you know where to contact me?'

'The photographs of Jeremy painting you by the lake…. They were in all the English newspapers. It was easy – '

'Yes, of course.' Jeremy had never talked much about his background, but Katie had always suspected there must be other women. Those nude portraits...

'Were you and Jeremy – ' Katie paused, 'married?'

'Married?' She heard Juliette laugh. 'No, of course not. Jeremy did not want that. We were not man and wife. We were lovers.'

Lovers! The word was like a dagger to the heart, even if it did sound very sophisticated. Katie felt herself at a loss for words. Juliette may be younger but she sounded assured beyond her age.. Of course she was French; that explained it.

'How did you meet Jeremy?' Katie heard herself asking. 'You're French, aren't you?'

'Yes. From Rouen – ' Katie had never neard of the place. She hadn't the faintest idea where Rouen was in France. 'I come to England three – no four – years ago when I was nineteen, to work – '

Heavens! Juliette was only twenty-three. A mere girl.

'I am an expert cook, a Cordon Bleu – ' she was speaking again. 'Soon after I arrive in England I get work in a restaurant in Norfolk, a beautiful place, plenty of tourists...You ask me how I meet Jeremy...He comes in one night when I am finished in the kitchen and I am having a drink with friends at the bar. We get talking. I find him very charming. He buys me a drink...' Juliette broke off.

'Yes....Do continue. What happened then?'

'Please! You want to hear all the details!' Juliette's tinkling laugh came over the phone. Katie waited, remained silent. 'Jeremy comes into the bar the next night, and the next night after that. He asks me back to his apartment and, well, we become lovers.'

'I see.'

'I hope you are not angry, Katie...' A pause. 'Please, may I call you Katie.'

'Yes. Of course.' Might as well be friends with Juliette, Katie reasoned. They had a lot in common. 'What happened next – between you and Jeremy?'

'I leave my work in the restaurant and I help in his studio. He asks me to pose for him and I become his model. He tells me I am his favourite model – ' She paused, obviously expecting Katie to say something. When she remained silent Juliette continued... 'I wouuld to speak to him, to tell him about Serge, his baby – '

'Didn't Jeremy know you had a baby?'

'No, Jeremy did not know – '

'But I don't understand – ' Katie's mind was in a whirl.

'Before I found out that I was pregnant Jeremy decided to go away. I could not stop him. Like every artist he is selfish. He thinks only of his work. His painting comes first. Always – '

'You mean he left you?'

'Yes. He went away.' Juliette was certainly forthright.

'Where did he go?' Katie paused momentarily. 'Was it to Greece? Somewhere like that?'

'Yes. To Greece. How did you know? Did he tell you?'

'No. It – it was a guess.'

'He promised me that he would write, get in touch with me. But he never did.'

'Why didn't you get in touch with him?'

'How could I? I did not know where he was. He did not write or telephone. Jeremy vanished. I thought maybe he was still in Greece until I saw those photographs in the newspapers – '

'Yes, of course.' Katie fell silent. Hearing of Jeremy's past like this was quite a shock. Now she knew why had he been so secretive with her, giving only the merest details about his background. Why had he not told her about Juliette? Perhaps there had been other women. Was he afraid that if he revealed too much to her that she would have nothing to do with him? What did all this matter…she was in love with Jeremy Walker and he had asked her to go away with him. She had made a decision and there was no going back now.

What would he say if she told him that she knew about Juliette – and that he had a son. Would that make a difference, drive a wedge between them? Would he still love her, still want to go to away with her and her two boys? She did not have to tell Jeremy that she knew about Juliette. Not immediately anyway. Why spoil things between them, throw away the chance of a new life?

'I'm sorry, but I'm afraid you can't speak to Jeremy,' Katie said.

'Why not?' Juliette sounded annoyed. 'Ah yes of course. His telephone is out of order. I am told that there was a fire at his cottage. That is why I am phoning you, Katie. You must tell him that I am coming to Ireland shortly to see him, with Serge – '

'No Julietee, you mustn't – ' Katie shouted into the telephone.

'Why must I not see Jeremy?'

'Because I don't want you to. Don't you understand, Jeremy is in love with me now. He told me so. And I'm in love with him. We have plans – ' Katie stopped. She must not tell this French girl too much. It was now Friday afternoon; in two days time herself and Jeremy would be on their way to Greece with the boys. A new life was opening up for her, nothing must interfere with that. This was her chance to finish with Loughduff, and the farm – and Travis. Forever. She would never get an opportunity like this again.

'But you are married, Katie. What about your husband, the newspaper story said he is in jail – '

'He is out now, recovering in hospital. He will be back home soon.'

'You and Jeremy....You are lovers. No? Does your husband -?' The voice trailed off

'You don't understand, Juliette. I don't love my husband! I don't care what he thinks. All I know is that Jeremy Walker loves me now and I want to be with him. You must not interfere, Juliette – '

'Wait!' Juliette must have sensed that Katie was about to put down the phone.'What does it matter that we are both in love with the same man. It has happened before – '

'You are still in love with Jeremy?'

'Of course. Why should I not be?'

'He abandoned you and your baby – '

'Abandon no. I do not think that Jeremy meant for us to be apart forever. I know he did not want that. I remember some things he say…beautiful things. I know he would want to see me again – and Serge also – '

'Goodbye Juliette. Please, you must try to find someone else….'

Katie replaced the phone, took it off its stand. She walked to the kitchen window, gazed out of the afternoon sunshine. No, she would not drive over to see Jeremy. She would not divulge to him the conversation she had had with a young woman called Juliette. She would not question him about his former lover, not tell him about the baby he had never seen. Like her, Jeremy Walker had a past that she assumed he wanted to forget. Why should she spoil their future together by confronting him with it now?

She accepted that it was not what most women would do given the same circumstances, but she was determined to go down that road. She was passionately in love with Jeremy Walker and nothing she had heard over the telephone in the last few minutes would alter that. She did not care what Jeremy had done in the past, it was their future together that was important. He had opened up a new life for her, a life she had never thought possible until she had met him. She was not going to jeopardise their future together for the sake of a young French woman and her baby.

Juliette would show up in Loughduff soon, of that Katie was certain. But she would be too late; by then herself, Jeremy and her two boys would be gone, on their way to a new life together.

What would she do if sometime in the future Juliette discovered where they were in Greece and walked back into their life? How would Jeremy react then? Katie turned from the kitchen window, banished the vision from her thoughts. That was a gamble she must take. She had made up her mind, committed herself totally. There was no turning back now.

• • • •

The Irish weather was on its best behaviour for the second day of the Ryder Cup clash on the picturesque Killeen course in Killarney. As with yesterday, a testing breeze blew across the fairways from Lough Leane, the lake bordering the course, and intermittent sunshine broke through the white scudding clouds. Once again, from an early hour, thousands of golf fans descended on the course, packing the roads leading to it and causing chaos in the famous town of Killarney a mile distant.

'What a magnificent setting,' the CBS Sports commentator enthused as he surveyed the colourful scene from his elevated position bordering the first tee. Cameras panned to take in the banks of eager fans waiting for the action to start, the expanse of Lough Leane, and the majestic blue-tinted mountains in the near distance.

'In this beautiful south-west corner of Ireland the battle for the Ryder Cup continues, and let me tell you folks, Wayne Folen is a worried man today,' the American commentator went on. 'Yesterday was a disastrous day for our guys, and make no mistake, if they play as badly today as they did yesterday this clash of golf's superstars could go down in Ryder Cup history – using Irish terminology – as The Wake By The Lake!'

This reference to the mournful prelude to an Irish funeral was appropriate as far as the American fans were concerned. The first day of the Ryder Cup clash had seen their team overwhelmed by the rampant golfers from Europe. After the unprecedented 4pts to zero whitewash of the morning foursomes, things had improved only marginally in the afternoon for the United States squad, with Wayne Folen's men managing to share two of the fourballs and losing the other two matches played. It meant the Europeans held a whopping 7pts to 1pt lead after the first day – the biggest ever first day lead since the Ryder Cup was first contested way back in 1927.

'Last night after dinner Wayne Folen locked himself and his team members away in his room for a two hour talk-in,' the CBS commentator continued. 'I have it on good authority that it was one tough session. The captain faced criticism from the senior members of the squad about at least one of his team selections, and also about his own personal problems during the run-up to this Ryder Cup. Several of the players claimed that their captain's domestic problems and his obsession with a certain blonde actress – who departed the scene very rapidly a couple of days ago – has taken his mind off the real job in hand – that of winning the Ryder Cup for America.' The commentator paused. 'In particular Wayne came in for criticism from squad members for selecting Joey O'Hara to play in yesterday morning's foresomes so soon after Joey's traumatic kidnap.

'I'm reliably informed that Wayne accepted the criticism from the squad members,' the CBS man told his early morning audience back in the United States. 'But no way did he back off....as soon as the talk-in was finished he had his guys out in the hotel corridor practising their putting on the carpet for a couple of hours!

'Today the thousands of American fans here in Killarney are hoping for better things from their team. The other big news here at the Ryder Cup is that the President will definitely fly into Killarney before tee-off tomorrow morning. He will be accompanied by Senator John O'Hara, father of Joey O'Hara. The arrival of the President is bound to boost the morale of the squad on the final day – if our guys are still in with a chance!', the CBS man added ominously.

Below on the first tee the television cameras zoomed in on Wayne Folen chatting to the top American pairing of K.C. Matthews and his new partner Harley Coots. They were set to face Europe's Neil Naismith and his young partner Gary Formby in the day's top foursomes. At 7pts. to 1 down Wayne knew that a win was vital in the first match off; his fervent hope was that Matthews and Coots would do the business.

This time he had listened to the team doctor and, under pressure, had left Joey O'Hara out of the day's action. But whatever mental condition Joey was in, Wayne had told him that he would have to play in tomorrow's twelve vital singles matches. With twelve points at stake on the Sunday, and given America's Ryder Cup tradition of fighting back on the final day, Wayne was hopeful that all was not yet lost.

He knew it would be, though, if the Europeans hit form today like they did yesterday. A repeat of Friday's result would mean that the contest would be over after only two days play – a feat never achieved before by either side in Ryder Cup history. Cord McCallum and his fellow committee members were hoping they would not have to face that kind of humiliation with the President flying in.

Half an hour past midday, after almost four hours of play, and with the first match of the morning foursomes drawing to a close, the spectre of that nightmare becoming a reality was looming ever larger for the American captain and his struggling squad members. .

Early on in the morning play there had been hopes of an American revival when K.C. Matthews and his partner had taken a three hole lead at the halfway mark in the top match against the European pairing of Naismith and Formby. But the Europeans had fought back and, cheered on by legions of vociferous supporters, had won the last hole to claim an unexpected victory.

The match had developed into a dour battle, ending in acrimonious circumstances on the final green amid controversy leading to the two disgruntled Americans walking off without the traditional handshake with their opponents. The American duo had been outraged when Naismith for the Europeans called a penalty on his opponent Matthews for picking up his ball after he had putted up to twelve inches of the hole. The American had taken it for granted that the putt was conceded but Naismith had disputed this. The referee had no option but to award the hole – and the match – to the Europeans. The rival fans gathered around the eighteenth green had gone wild and several fistfights had broken out among the crowd. These had been quickly quelled by Garda and security personnel.

The two captains had also become embroiled in the controversy and were caught on camera by millions of tv viewers around the world arguing and gesticulating wildly at each other. Once again the usually sedate game of golf had succumbed to Ryder Cup mania.

Wayne Folen, a lone figure whizzing around in his golf cart offering encouragement and endeavouring to inspire his players, was to suffer more agony before the other three morning matches were completed. In the next two games both of the American pairings were leading playing the final hole, but inexplicably let their advantage slip and in the end had to be satisfied with finishing all square with their European opponents in both games.

The last foursome pairing of the morning was one that would haunt the American captain for all time. For fifteen holes Wayne saw two of his players, Denny Holgado and Val Perkins, both appearing in their first ever Ryder Cup, play superb golf to be two up with only three holes to play against the European duo of veteran Irishman Davy Cochran and the big-hitting Swede Lars Nyheim. At last it looked like the Yanks were going to claim a vital point from the remaining morning foursome.

Then the kind of tension that golfers experience only when they are playing for their country in the Ryder Cup hit the American partnership. On the par-5 sixteenth hole, a hole playing the easiest of the eighteen at Killeen, Denny Holgado, reckoned one of the straightest drivers on the U.S. tour, hit his tee shot into the gorse on the right of the fairway. His partner Perkins, following the flight of the ball, looked grim. He looked even more grim when Davy Cochran hit his tee shot for Europe straight down the middle.

Perkins did well to chop an 8-iron out of the gorse and onto the fairway, albeit still 200 yards from the green. When the big Swede hit a 5-wood second shot pin high onto the fringe of the green it looked good for the Europeans. That was until Denny Holgado, making up for his earlier mistake, hit a superb 4-iron third shot that finished a mere two feet from the flag. Thunderous cheers echoed around the course from the American fans and it looked certain that the U.S. would get a birdie-4, halve the hole with their opponents and move closer to victory in the match.

The delirious American fans reckoned without the veteran Irishman. Davy Cochran sized up his shot carefully from the side of the green. He and his caddy had a discussion that lasted a full minute before Davy took out a 7-iron from his bag. He had decided on a chip and run shot, one of his favourite ploys that had paid off many times in his long career.

Thousands of pairs of eyes followed the ball as it began its journey, the first couple of feet in the air, then landing and moving across the green. The cheering increased in volume as the ball rolled across the green sward – and it rose to a crescendo as the ball slowed but reached the hole with just enough momentum to topple in.

The Europeans had made an eagle-3 to win the hole and be only one down with two to play. They were back in the match!

Later, at the evening media conference, Wayne Folen conceded that was the shot that wrecked American hopes of a single outright win in the morning foursomes. With no past Ryder Cup experience to call on, Holgado and Perkins felt the pressure increasing over the next two holes and struggled with their game. On the other hand the European pair grew in confidence and began to play and look like winners.

When the Americans lost the par-4 17th hole to another European birdie the match was all square with one hole to play. The treacherous 18th hole at Killeen is not for the faint hearted, especially when there is Ryder Cup pressure involved. The Americans struggled from the tee and after three shots were on the green but a long way from the hole. They finally had their fate sealed when Davy Cochran sank a big putt for the third European birdie in a row to win a match the Americans looked to have had in the bag.

Rampant Europe had won the morning foursomes on the second day by 3pts. to1.The overall score now stood, unbelievably, at Europe 10pts, America 2pts. Standing at the side of the green waiting to greet the disconsolate twosome of Holgado and Perkins, Wayne Folen forced a smile. Inwardly he felt like a man who was facing a hanging.

He and the other members of the squad gathered around to console Perkins and Holgado on their loss. 'Just look at that circle of grim faces,' the CBS commentator said. 'Nobody in that squad looks happy. This Ryder Cup is turning into a nightmare for the American captain and his men. They just don't seem capable of raising their game to match the Europeans.'

Down below Wayne walked quickly towards the clubhouse entrance, staring straight ahead and ignoring the questions fired at him by some members of the pursuing media. He had reached the sanctity of the clubhouse entrance when a grim-faced Cord McCallum caught up with him.

'I'd like a word with you, Wayne,' McCallum said. Without waiting for a reply he walked into the clubhouse lounge, found a quite corner and sat down in a leather chair, waiting for Wayne to join him.

McCallum came straight to the point. 'My committee members and I are very disappointed with the team's performance so far, Wayne. What the hell is happening out there? As a golfing nation we are being humiliated. The Europeans are kicking American ass! You do realise, I suppose, that we have yet to win a match in this Ryder Cup?'

'I know what the score is,' Wayne replied levelly.

'Then what the hell to you propose to do about it?'

'What the hell do you expect me to do about it?'

'That's your problem. That's why my committee and I appointed you captain. – ' Cord McCallum broke off. 'We expect a better performance for the fourballs in the afternoon. '

'You'll get it, Mr. McCallum, don't worry.'

'What the hell to you mean don't worry,' McCallum exploded. 'I am worried! Every goddam American spectator out on the course is worried. The millions of Americans watching this Ryder Cup back home are worried!' He glanced around, made sure he was not being overheard. 'Do realise the President is flying in tomorrow and that before he arrives the Ryder Cup could be all over – with Europe the runaway winners!'

Wayne sighed. 'Sure I realise that, Mr. McCallum – '

. 'We need four wins in the afternoon to put us back into contention. I expect you to deliver, Wayne.'

'It's not impossible. My guys and I are as disappointed as you are. I just can't figure what's gone wrong – '

'I'll tell you what's gone wrong, Wayne ' McCallum was really fired up now. 'You've allowed too many things in your private life to go wrong, that's what. Your troubles started with that blonde bimbo you picked up a couple of months ago.Your mind just wasn't on the job, Wayne – and by that I mean winning the Ryder Cup for America! You have to get yourself back on track and do just that. As Americans we can accept defeat in the Ryder Cup with good grace. But we will not accept himiliation. Do I make myself clear?'

Wayne sat with his guys over lunch and endeavoured to boost their flagging morale. He was careful not to be critical of any individual's play in particular. He could sense they were as disappointed as he was. He hammered home the point that although Europe had a commanding lead of eight points the Ryder Cup had only reached the halfway mark 'With four points up for grabs in the afternoon fourballs and twelve matches to be played tomorrow there is still all to play for,' he emphasised.

'Come on, you guys. Show me some American grit. We can do it!' Wayne thumped the table to emphasise his point. 'Now glet out there and kick ass!' He knew he sounded desperate and he was. The prospect of flying back to New York on Monday after a humiliating defeat, without the Ryder Cup, facing a hostile media all to keen to grill him over the Angie Wilde affair, was not one he would look forward to.

Midway through the quartet of afternoon fourballs it looked like Wayne's lunchtime pep talk was having the desired effect. In desperation he had split up the experienced duo of K.C. Matthews and Harley Coots and paired each with Ryder Cup rookies Denny Holgado and Val Perkins – and it worked a dream!

Matthews and Perkins played some spectacular golf in the first game off and after nine holes were four up on the European pairing of Germany's Oscar Freidling and Scotland's Andrew Tier. The Americans, with Perkins sinking some outrageous putts, finished off the match on the 13th green for a morale-boosting 5 & 4 win. It was the first full point that the U.S. team had won in this Ryder Cup and as the winning putt rolled into the cup it was greeted by some boisterous exhibitions of support from the American fans and with shouts of derision from their European rivals.

Back on the course the new pairing of Harley Coots and his new partner Denny Holgado was also doing the business. They had not lost a hole by the halfway mark in their match and were four up at the turn. They lost the 10th hole to go back to just three up with eight to play, but they stifled any hope of a European fight-back by halving the next three holes, winning the 14th with a birdie, then safely halving the next to win by 4 & 3.

Once again the American fans celebrated noisily and the smile was back on Wayne Folen's face. 10pts to 4. Okay, the margin was still big but the fight-back was on and his guys were looking good. If his men could win the last two games of the afternoon and pull the European lead back to a mere four points going into the final day he would look forward to confronting Cord McCallum and his committee members over dinner!

It was not to be. The American captain had his dream

shattered when the Europeans staged a comeback and won the last two games of the afternoon. Wayne was bitterly disappointed and showed it at the media conference later when he took on any reporter who suggested that at 12pts.to 4, and needing only to win two of tomorrow's twelve matches to retain the trophy, that the Ryder Cup was practically in European hands once again.

It didn't help his mood when, shortly after taking on the media, he was confronted by an unsmiling Cord McCallum.

'That fight back you promised didn't last very long, did it, Wayne?' McCallum asked sourly. 'We're in trouble again. Big trouble.'

'For Chrissake! You think I don't know that! But I'm not throwing in the towel. This Ryder Cup is not won yetk, not with twelve points to be won out there tomorrow. We're still thinking about winning.'

'Glad to hear it. But as I see it we need a miracle, Wayne. I don't believe in miracles and I have no faith in any Ryder Cup captain that does.' The thin lips tightened. 'Maybe I should phone the President, advise him not to come tomorrow – '

'Don't you dare do that, Mr. McCallum,' Wayne exploded. 'Having the President fly in to see my guys play is a great honour for the squad. One sure way to inspire them is having their President here tomorrow. Request him to say a few words to them before they tee-off. It's been done before in the Ryder Cup – '

'Sure it has. But we were never so far behind as we are now – ' McCallum was twisting the knife. 'If you can't get every member of your squad to perform well in the singles matches tomorrow and we suffer a humiliating defeat you'll go down in Ryder Cup history as the worse American captain ever. How would you like that?'

Wayne brushed past his tormentor and entered the clubhouse, fighting to control his anger. He could do with a drink – a stiff one. He went upstairs, ordered one from room service, took it over to the window and stared out across the boat lake at the back of the hotel.

The old guy McCallum was right, he had to admit that. Things had started to go wrong from the night he had met Angie Wilde at the bar, spilled that drink over her. Of course he had been set up, he knew that now. The newspapers were already running stories that Angie had used her time with the U.S. Ryder Cup captain to get publicity and boost her acting career. Ditching his wife for Angie had not been a smart move. How he would love to have Marcia here now, to confide in, give him the encouragement he needed at this time. Should he risk a phone call – or was it too late?

He was not looking forward to the gala Ryder Cup dinner tonight, which many former Ryder Cup players and captains had flown in to attend. In ordinary circumstances he would have enjoyed the occasion, especially with Marcia by his side. Bruce Cartray would be there with his wife, smiling, trying not to be too condescending about the almost certain European victory tomorrow.

The worst American captain in Ryder Cup history…Wayne grimaced as he recalled Cord McCallum's words. No, he was certainly not looking forward to that dinner tonight…..

Cord McCallum had watched Wayne go up to his room. He was worried. Despite his captain's fighting spirit Wayne Folen looked like a beaten man. And his team looked beaten too. How could a captain who had suffered so many setbacks be expected to face the members of his squad, inspire them to reach untold heights? Wayne Folen wasn't capable of that right now. He needed a lift, something to get him going again.

Action had to be taken quickly to save situation and it was up to him, Cord McCallum, chairman of the U.S. Ryder Cup committee, to take it. He looked at his watch.

5.30pm – Saturday midday in Washington. An appropriate time to make a telephone call to the White House....

• • • •

About the same time that Cord McCallum was making his telephone call to America, Katie Gartland and her two sons were putting the finishing touches to packing their suitcases for the trip abroad that would change their whole lives.

Katie had the final plan in place. Tomorrow morning she and the boys would drive into Loughduff and attend eleven o'clock Mass in the local church as usual. No doubt after the recent happenings they would be the centre of prying eyes, not to mention the wagging tongues of the village gossips. Her husband's hunger strike, the scandal of her affair with Jeremy Walker, those photographs by the lake, and Ben Gartland's kidnap of the young American golfer followed by his death plunge into sea two days ago...all those happenings had made world headlines and brought her into the spotlight.

Her husband was still in hospital and was not expected home for another few days, hopefully in time for the funeral of his brother. The death of Ben Gartland and the Japanese consortium's acceptance of a new site for their golf complex from the Irish Government had effectively ended the strike by the local farmers. By the time Travis was fit enough to return home she and the boys would be long gone from Loughduff, settling in to a new life in the sun with Jeremy Walker.

Best to stick to the routine she had followed every Sunday morning so as not to arouse suspicion. It was the normal routine for her to drive into the village for Mass with Garret and Jack while her husband slept off the hangover from his usual Saturday night drinking session.

She usually had an after-Mass chat with Nell Flavin and Tom. Katie doubted that tomorrow any of the locals would approach her for a friendly chat.

With only Jeremy's car available there was a premium on what they could take with them abroad. It suited Katie; she had entered the Gartland abode as a young girl with practically nothing, and she intended leaving it the same way. She was resolved to bring as little as possible with her from the past.

The Irish Ferries sailing to Cherbourg in the north of France departed Sunday at 6pm from Rosslare, a two hour-plus drive from Loughduff. Jeremy would pick her and the boys up at the house around 2pm; this would give them adequate time to catch the ferry sailing. Katie was placing the last of her clothes in her suitcase on the bed when she heard Jack calling out from downstairs:

'Mom, a Garda car has just driven in. I think it's Sergeant Gilhooly – '

She hurried downstairs, looked out of the window, saw the Sergeant get out of the car and approach the house. She felt a sense of unease; did the Sergeant suspect something – that she was leaving...? If he did was it within his authority to stop her? 'Go upstairs to your bedroom, Jack. Help Garret with the last of the packing.' She was afraid her youngest son might let out some vital bit of information in front of Gilhooly..

Katie opened the front door, ushered her visitor in. The Sergeant nodded a greeting, removed his cap, sat down at the table but refused the offer of tea. His eyes were everywhere, taking in everything.

'I called briefly to tell you, Katie, that the hospital won't release Ben's body until Tuesday. I presume you'll want to make arrangements for the burial?'

Katie sighed with relief. 'Yes. I suppose I'll have to start thinking about, maybe talk to Travis.' Someone would have to look after Ben's funeral, thankfully it wouldn't be her. Right now she couldn't care when or where Ben Gartland was buried.

The Sergeant was talking again, glancing around. 'A sad happening...' He paused. 'I don't suppose your husband will be well enough to attend?'

'I – I can't say right now. I haven't spoken to Travis lately.'

'Oh...I see. Any idea when he's coming home?'

'No.'

'Hhmmm....Oh well... Everything alright with you, Katie?'

'Yes, of course.'

Another pause. 'I'm informed that Jeremy Walker is putting his cottage up for sale. You know about that, I suppose – '

'Yes. He told me.'

'Any idea what his plans are? It appears like he's leaving Loughduff. Can't say I blame him...'

Katie shrugged. 'Why don't you ask Jeremy himself...'

'Aye, I will, I will. Just thought maybe you would know.' He was staring directly at her, watching for her reaction. What was his real reason for visiting? Katie felt uncomfortable under his scrutiny. She had to say something.

'Any progress in your inquiries as to who tried to set fire to Jeremy's cottage?'

'That investigation is still proceeding. I was hoping to question Ben Gartland again. I've no doubt that Ben was involved in that. But the way things have turned out we may never find out who started that fire. Sometimes things work out for the best. Would you agree with me, Katie?'

'Yes, Sergeant, I would.'

A silence. 'You sure, Katie, that you don't have something to tell me?'

'Like what for instance, Sergeant?'

'Oh, anything at all. I have to ask these questions, Katie. You understand. It's part of the job.'

'Yes. I understand.'

'Will I be seeing you and the boys at Mass tomorrow?'

'You will of course. Why shouldn't you?'

'Good, good.' He rose to his feet. ' Ah well, I'd better be going....'

'Sure you won't stay for some tea?'

He shook his head. 'No thanks. I've a feeling you're busy.' What exactly did he mean by that she wondered? He turned as he opened the door. 'You're kquite certain you don't know anything more about Jeremy Walker's plans, Katie? – '

There was something afoot, he could sense it. Katie Gartland wasn't telling him everything. He liked this young woman, pitied her sometimes with the husband she was tied to, would like to help her in any way he could. She'd made a bad marriage with Travis Gartland, it had been the talk of the town for years. He had not been too surprised that she had taken to Jeremy Walker. Given her circumstances he could believe it was happening. What he found it hard to believe was that Katie was now waiting patiently for her husband to return to the farm, knowing what was bound to happen when Travis did so. Sometimes it was better not to probe too deeply into personal matters. Still, the law is the law, and he had a job to do.

Sergeant Gilhooly paused in the doorway. 'We both know Katie, that while Travis doesn't have a lot of friends in Loughduff some people are in sympathy with him after what happened between you and the Englishman. I can understand if Jeremy Walker wants to leave, he probably feels threatened. But it's my duty to warn you that if whatever Jeremy Walker plans involves you taking the boys away without their father's consent...' he left the sentence unfinished.

'What Jeremy Walker and I do is the business of nobody around here,' Katie replied sharply. 'It's my life, Sergeant'

'It may be your life, Katie, but the law is the law. I'm

reminding you that you can't take the boys outside the jurisdiction without your husband's consent, no matter how badly he has treated you in the past. You understand that, Katie?'

'Thank you for your advice, Sergeant. I'll remember that.'

'Good.' He smiled. 'Where are the young rascals, anyway? Out on the farm somewhere, I suppose....'

He made it sound an innocent query, although Katie knew it wasn't. 'Actually they're upstairs in their bedroom with their Playstation – ' She prayed he wouldn't find a reason to go up to talk to them.

It looked for a moment that might be his intention. She was relieved when he said, 'I'll leave them to it. Goodbye, Katie. Take care of yourself.'

'I will, Sergeant. Thanks for calling...' Katie watched until he got into the car, drove it down the gravel path and out onto the road. She breathed another sign of relief.

• • • •

The bedside telephone rang in Wayne Folen's hotel room. He looked at his watch, groaned. It was past 2am. Having just gone to bed after yet another formal Ryder Cup dinner, Wayne had been looking forward to several hours undisturbed sleep before tomorrow's final day Ryder Cup battle.

The last thing he wanted right now was a nosy newshound on the trail of another damaging exclusive. He lifted the receiver, said cautiously, 'Hello?'

'Wayne...?' He recognised the female voice immediately. It was one he had not heard in a long time. His heart leaped. 'Marcia!'

'Hello Wayne. How are you?'

' I'm fine, fine. How are you, Marcia? – '

'I'm fine too, Wayne. You sound tired. I probably woke you up – '

'You did. But it doesn't matter. Hey honey, I'm glad you phoned, great to hear your voice, – ' He paused, asked. 'Is everything alright? I hope there's nothing wrong?'

'No, no.' She paused, 'I – I just wanted to phone you. Say hello. You're having a tough time right now. I wanted to check how you are, make sure you are alright.'

'That's real good of you, Marcia. I'm fine, fine. Honest,' he lied. 'How is your hip?'

'Still a bit stiff. But I manage – '

'Of course you will, honey. It'll take time…'.

A pause. Wayne waited. Marcia of all people! He couldn't believe it. He wished he could reach out, touch her hand. Maybe he should tell her that… 'I didn't expect you to phone, Marcia, after all I did on you. But I'm glad you did…'

'Thank you, Wayne. That's what I wanted to hear. Shiralee and I have been watching you a lot on television these past few days. You don't look like you're enjoying yourself over there Wayne.'

He laughed grimly. 'I'm not. It's tough. We're all struggling, the guys, myself…'

'You hang in there honey, you hear. There's still tomorrow – '

Honey! She had called him honey! Was Marcia giving him another chance? He couldn't believe his luck.

'I wish you were over here with me right now, Marcia – '

'You really mean that, Wayne?'

'Sure I do. I'm sorry for all the pain I caused you. I was a fool. I realise that now – ' The words were tumbling out; he couldn't help himself. 'I still love you, honey. Always have. I want you to know that - '

'I know you do. But tell it to me again, Wayne…'

He did so. 'I made a terrible mistake. I only wish you were here beside me so that I could make it up to you – '

He heard her laugh. He could hear people talking in

the background. Was Marcia at a party or something? She was talking again. 'Shiralee sends her love too. She's forgiven you for all the trouble you caused. And I do too.'

'You don't know how good it is to hear you say that, Marcia.. I can hardly wait to get home to see you again. Only problem is the way things are over here right now I guess I may not be bringing the Ryder Cup back with me – '

'Don't say that!' she admonished him. 'That's not like you, Wayne. You and the boys can still do it – '

'You really believe so?'

'Of course I do. You go out there tomorrow and do the job, you hear me, Wayne – show them what you're made of, that you're one of the best American Ryder Cup captains ever. I believe in you, Wayne.' It was the real Marcia talking.

'You know the President is flying in to morrow?'

Marcia gave a short laugh. 'Course I do. It's in all the newspapers, on the television. You make sure you give the President something to cheer about –'

'I'd sure love to have you over here with me in Killarney, honey. How about you hitching a ride on Air force One?'

He heard her laugh again. If only he knew! 'I guess it's after midnight over in Ireland right now. You get back to sleep, Wayne honey. Can't wait to see you soon.'

'Goodnight Marcia. Thanks for the call. Remember I love you.'

'Goodnight Wayne. I love you too.'

The line went dead. Wayne replaced the receiver, stared at it. What a marvellous surprise! Marcia calling out of the blue – just when he needed her. He felt so elated he wanted to throw his door open and run up and down the corridor letting everyone know that Marcia, his wife, still believed in him.

Instead Wayne lay back on the pillow. He felt good,

really good. Maybe Marcia phoning him was a good open. Suddenly he got the feeling that a miracle was possible tomorrow. He would make the final day of the Ryder Cup a memorable one!

CHAPTER TWELVE

The sound of a sharp but discreet knocking on his door brought Wayne Folen out of the bathroom where he had been shaving. Who the hell wanted to see him at this time of the morning? It seemed no time at all since he had dropped back to sleep after Marcia's phone call. As he moved to open the door he glance automatically at his watch. It showed 6.15am. He had planned an early walk down by the lake, alone, relishing the peace before the tension of the day began to kick in. The knock on the door sounded again. Jeez! not another crisis – he hadn't even had breakfast yet!

Wayne opened the door to find a fully-dressed Joey O'Hara outside. He groaned inwardly. What now with Joey? Hadn't the guy had given him enough problems already!

'Sorry for the early morning call, Wayne,' Joey smiled apologetically. 'Mind if I come in?'

'Sure.' Wayne closed the door. 'Like some coffee – ?' He switched on the bedside coffee maker.

'No thanks. I've just had some.'

'Sit down then. What's on your mind?' Joey didn't look at all worried. Maybe the guy just couldn't sleep, worrying about having to go into battle in the Ryder Cup today. Wayne wouldn't have been surprised if a lot of his guys had spent the night pacing up and down their hotel rooms!

Joey sat down facing his captain. 'About today's singles matches, Wayne….

'What about them?'

'You have me down at number four in the order...'

So that's it. Joey is worried about the final day. Probably still suffering from the effects of his kidnap ordeal and reckons he's not up to the pressure, wants to be put lower down the list of today's play.

'That's right. You're teeing-off against one of the Swedes, Olle Nordquist at ten-forty. I'm counting on you for a win. I know you've been through a tough time, Joey, and maybe you're worried about today – '

He broke off when he saw that Joey was shaking his head. 'I don't want to play that Swedish guy today. I want to go off in the top match, Wayne. Against their number one Neil Naismith.'

Now it was Wayne's turn to shake his head. 'Sorry, Joey – ' He had already gotten into big trouble with the world's top golfer, putting too much pressure on the young guy. Now he wanted to be put out in the top singles! If Joey lost to Naismith, which Wayne reckoned he probably would, it would have a demoralising effect on the rest of the team and be seen as another big mistake by the captain.

'Please, Wayne – '

'I said I'm sorry, Joey.' He saw the young man's disappointment. 'You know the media are labelling this Ryder Cup The Wake By The Lake because of our poor showing. I can't take a chance with you, Joey – not after what you've been through – '

Joey leaned forward, spoke rapidly. 'I know I can beat Naismith and put that first important point on the board. It's vital we win the first match today. It will inspire the other guys – ' He sounded like his life depended on it. 'Trust me, Wayne, please – '

Wayne sighed. 'Look Joey, Europe need only two points to tie this series and retain the Ryder Cup....One win and a couple of halved games will do. Bruce Cartray is sending out his big guns in the top matches to get it over early. Sam

Torrance did the same as European captain at the Belfry and it paid off. Hell, it could be all over by lunchtime if we don't come out firing on all cylinders. We've got to win that top match. If I take a chance and put you out against Naismith – and you lose – it's practically all over for us – '

Joey jumped to his feet, agitated. 'But that's just it, Wayne, I won't lose! I know I won't. I'll beat Naismith handsomely. Give me the chance. Please. I won't let America down!'

Wayne paced up and down the room, pondering. After a while he said, 'I'll give it to you straight, Joey. I wouldn't be playing you at all today only I have to.' He stopped pacing, looked directly at the world's No.1 golfer. 'What makes you so certain you'll win. How do I know you're not still suffering from post traumatic stress. Our medic is still not convinced that your mind is focused – '

Joey waved his captain's doubts aside. 'Bullshit! That's just medical talk. I know how I feel. I'm up for this one, Wayne, believe me – ' Joey's eyes were blazing with hyped-up emotion. 'Imagine what will happen when I destroy that guy Naismith out there. Our fans will go wild and our guys will be on a high. Hell, it'll be Brookline all over again!'. He was pleading now. 'Come on, Wayne. Take that chance. What have you got to lose? Let's be honest…Right now your rating as a Ryder Cup captain back home is shit! Pull this one out of the fire and you'll be a hero! They might even give us a ticker-tape reception down Fifth Avenue – '

Wayne laughed. 'Yeah?'

'Yeah!

'I don't want any ticker-tape parade. All I want to do is win the Ryder Cup for America! – ' Wayne ran his fingers through his close cropped hair. 'Trouble is, Joey, I don't think I could play you in the top match against Naismith even if I wanted to – '.

'What d'you mean?'

'Last night Bruce Cartray and I agreed to select our teams for today. I've already given him my selection – and you're No.4 on my list. I doubt I can change that now. It's against Ryder Cup rules. Not unless Cartray agrees to the switch.'

'Try him, Wayne. That guy is so sure of winning he'll probably agree – '

'You think so?'

'Yeah. And when I whip Naismith and our guys are inspired to make the greatest comeback in the history of the Ryder Cup, you'll really have put one over on the European captain. The Europeans have done it to us a couple of times. How about it?'

Wayne's eyes glinted. He liked what he was hearing. A chance to kick Bruce Cartray's ass. Better still, stepping off the aeroplane in New York tomorrow holding the Ryder Cup aloft, the crowd cheering, cameras flashing, Marcia by his side…What had he to lose? Nothing. His rival already had one hand on the Ryder Cup. But it wasn't over yet! The Fat Lady hadn't finished singing. In fact she was only warming up!

'Goddam it Joey – I'll do it! I'll meet Cartray, talk him into making the switch. You can take it, Joey, that you're in at Number One and playing Naismith!'

'Yippee!' Joey jumped a couple of feet into the air. 'You won't regret it, Wayne, I promise!'

'And I promise if you do let me down I'll kick your butt all the way back across the Atlantic. Now get out!'

Joey was exiting when Wayne called out. 'One more thing. How am I going to explain to K.C. Matthews that instead of him playing No.1 he's now back down to No.4?'

Joey grinned. 'You don't have to explain to him, Wayne. I already told K.C. myself!'

• • • •

'Ladies and gentlemen….a big Irish welcome please for the President of the United States!'

The huge crowd of golf fans and dignitaries gathered in the immediate area in front of the clubhouse at the Killarney Golf and Fishing Club applauded loudly and waved miniature American and Irish flags as the military helicopter descended out of the sky and landed gently on the recently cut green sward. The Guard of Honour of members of the Irish Army stood stiffly to attention along both sides of the red carpet which trailed from the ceremonial platform all the way to the clubhouse steps.

All eyes were on the door of the helicopter as the rotor blades died. A short flight of steps were rolled into place. The members of the No.1 Irish Army Band were at the ready, set to render the Presidential salute whenever the President of the United States appeared.

Lined up also facing each other were the members of the European and American Ryder Cup teams and officials, the players already attired for the tee-off on this tense final day.

Once again Killarney was bathed in bright morning sunlight, reflecting off the waters of Lough Leane and beaming down in a blue haze on the mountains in the distance. Camera crews from many countries were on hand to record the U.S. Presidential Ryder Cup visit. Above the almost cloudless sky the Goodyear Blimp gave an aerial view of the proceedings to millions of tv viewers in America and through the rest of the world.

'Any moment now those helicopter doors will open and the President of the United States, a big golf fan himself, will make an historic visit to a Ryder Cup in Europe,' the CBS newscaster intoned reverently. 'With the President will be Senator John O'Hara, anxious no doubt to see his son Joey, a kidnap victim in Ireland earlier in the week, play a vitral role in keeping America's slim hopes alive today.' A camera panned to pick up Joey in the line-up with the U.S. Ryder Cup squad….

'The big news this morning is that in a desperate effort to boost America's fading hopes of winning this Ryder Cup, much criticised team captain Wayne Folen requested and has been given permission to move young Joey O'Hara up from number four in the original singles to the top match. Joey will now take on Europe's top golfer Neil Naismith. Wayne Folen has taken a big gamble and the outcome of that clash will be vital to American hopes – '

The newscaster broke off suddenly as the helicopter doors opened and a quartet of burly men in suits stepped out onto the platform and descended the steps, their eyes roaming over the assembled crowd.

'And here is the President!' The CBS man shouted excitedly into the microphone as the tall, athletic figure with the coiffed steel-grey hair stepped into view. Casually dressed in a windcheater, sports shirt and slacks, the President stepped forward and waved to the crowd as a sea of miniature American flags were waved skywards. Behind the President the figure of Senator O'Hara also appeared as the Irish Army band gave forth a stirring rendition of the American national anthem.

To the surprise of the waiting dignitaries when the national anthem was finished the President did not decent the helicopter steps. Both men seemed to be waiting for somebody else in the 'copter to join them.

A few moments later a third figure appeared in the 'copter entrance. It was a woman, dressed in a smartly cut crème coloured suit, her blonde hair, turning grey, neatly coiffed and framing her pert, smiling face. She was supporting herself with a dark walnut silver-topped walking stick in her right hand.

'Ladies and gentlemen,' the President addressed the teams and officials lined up directly below him, 'allow me to introduce to you a very courageous lady…Marcia Folen, wife of our Ryder Cup captain! Marcia has flown all the way from San Diego to be by her husband's side on this very important day...'

There was another prolonged burst of applause from the massed crowd. Everyone realised the significance of the appearance in Killarney of Marcia Folen, the lady who for the past couple of months had been featured on television and in the newspapers as the wronged wife of America's Ryder Cup captain. Now here she was arriving just when he needed her most.

Wayne Folen, looking like a man who could hardly believe what he was seeing, stepped forward as the President helped his wife down the short flight of steps.

'Marcia,' Wayne said, extending his two hands towards her.'What a marvellous surprise. Why didn't you tell me when we were talking on the phone – '

'Shush, will you –' his wife smiled. 'I'll explain everything later,' They embraced as cameras flashed and the huge crowd burst into a spontaneous round of applause.

'Thank you, Mr. President – ' Wayne shook the President's proffered hand. 'You don't know how much having Marcia here means to me. Thank you on behalf of myself and the members of the U.S. Ryder Cup team.' A beaming Wayne stood holding his wife's hand as photographers scrambled to record the scene.

'What a surprise, and what a memorable heart-warming occasion,' the CBS man told his American viewers. 'Let's see if it will help Wayne and his men perform a near-miracle and get their hands on that Ryder Cup.'

Silence settled over the gathering as the President moved to a dais on which a battery of microphones were in place. He paused for a few moments then began his speech.

'Ladies and gentlemen,' the U.S. President began, 'let me start by saying how delighted I am to be back here in Ireland, in beautiful Killarney, for the final day of the

Ryder Cup contest. As we have seen over the years, and indeed as we have just witnessed, the Ryder Cup is one of those great occasions that stirs the emotions of people and brings two great golfing rivals into sporting conflict.' The President paused, smiled. 'On a personal level, let me say that being here in Killarney this morning sure beats sitting in the Oval office wrestling with the problems of the world – and right now I don't mind admitting our guys are having one hell of a battle trying to win the Ryder Cup war against their talented European rivals!'

The President paused to allow the loud burst of laughter mixed with applause to die down. When he continued his tone was more sombre. 'Away back in 1927, when that far-seeing Englishman Samuel Ryder founded this great biennial contest, he did so to foster goodwill and comradeship between golfers from both sides of the Atlantic – and with the express desire that the only real winner would be the game of golf itself. I am supremely confident that at the end of play today, Samuel Ryder's wishes will be respected, and that this Ryder Cup contest will be fought out in a very sporting manner by themembers of two great sides, free of any animosity and rancour.'

These last remarks raised a few eyebrows. Not for the first time the Ryder Cup contest was putting to the test the fostering of the sportsmanship, companionship and friendly rivalry which old Sam Ryder had had in mind all those years ago. The verbal confrontations and animosity between the two captains had seen to that!

As if mindful of this, the President concluded his short speech by wishing both teams and their respective captains good luck throughout this final day. 'The first singles match is due to tee-off within the hour and I hope I won't be accused of being bi-partisan if I tell you that, at the behest of Marcia Folen, I will spend a short period of that time talking to Wayne Folen and his team members in the hope that I can inspire them on to great heights today. Thank you all.'

'So you asked the President to give us a pep talk?' Wayne whispered to his wife as the applause rang out and the Irish Army band struck up again.

'Yes honey. Reading the newspapers about how the Ryder Cup was going over here I reckon your boys needed it. Hope it's okay with you?'

He patted her arm. 'Sure it is. It could just be what is needed to get the guys fired up. Now tell me, how come you hitched a ride on Airforce One? You never mentioned that to me when you were on the telephone.'

'I wasn't supposed to! Cord McCallum telephoned the White House yesterday after the second day's play had finished here. He told the President that you and the squad members needed a boost. He suggested to the President that he should bring me along with Senator O'Hara on Airforce One. The President thought it was a good idea – and so did I! I got the call from the White House yesterday afternoon. I was picked up by limo and flown from San Diego to Washington in a U.S. Navy jet. In fact I was on my way to Washington to pick up Airforce One when I telephoned you during the night!'

Wayne smiled. So Cord McCallum had done him a big favour. It had not stopped the old guy from accosting Wayne just after breakfast and warning him that if his gamble with playing Joey O'Hara in the top singles today didn't come off 'there will be hell to pay when we get back home!'

Wayne was reminded of that as he looked to where Senator O'Hara, joined by Cord McCallum, was having an emotional re-union with his son. The President was also in the group, adding his congratulations to Joey on his escape from kidnap. The world press, and particularly the various camera crews, were having a field day recording the happy occasion.

After a suitable period of time the President lead the way into the clubhouse, followed by Wayne and the members of his Ryder Cup squad. Upstairs they were shown into the specially reserved room where the most powerful man in the world would give them his pep talk. Everyone else was excluded – even Cord McCallum! Half a dozen Secret Service men stood outside to make sure the session was not interrupted.

Twenty minutes later the door opened and a smiling President exited, followed by Wayne Folen and the members of his team. Before they went downstairs again the President shook with each man in turn, had a final few words of encouragement. The guys, resplendent in their Stars and Stripes outfits, headed to the practice area where they would loosen up before the first match teed off.

'On the tee, contesting the first match of the day's singles – Neil Naismith representing Europe, versus Joey O'Hara of the United States of America…'

It was the moment the massive crowd had been waiting for. The official starter's voice was drowned out by the roars of the excited fans gathered around the first tee and lining the fairway four deep all the way down to the first green. Those closest to the tee saw Ryder Cup veteran Naismith exchange a handshake with his youthful American opponent, both men managing a smile and exchanging a few words. The crowd fell silent and the tension was almost unbearable as Joey O'Hara pressed a tee into the turf, straightened up, and squinted into the sun down the fairway of the 395-yard opening hole.

Midway down the fairway the U.S. President, now sporting an official American Ryder Cup windcheater and sun visor, was seated beside Wayne Folen in the electric buggy. Two other buggies carrying burly security men were in close attendance.

Later at a packed press conference Joey O'Hara was to confess that he was so nervous hitting that first tee shot that he was certain he had shut his eyes on the downswing. If the unthinkable was true it made no difference to the execution of the shot; Joey's 3-wood, chosen for safety rather than distance, propelled the ball like a bullet fired from a gun straight down the middle of the fairway, finishing 280 yards distant. It would leave him with a short iron second shot to the green, difficult because he had to fly the ball over a green side bunker. But the Americans in the crowd cheered. At least he wasn't in the lake!

Neil Naismith made a great show of taking his No.3 wood out of his bag. He was tempted to take his driver, smash a drive beyond that of his young American rival, stamp his authority on the match. But this was no time for bravado. Plenty of time to put pressure on Joey O'Hara later. A ripple of excitement went through the crowd as Naismith prepared to drive off. He sensed it and his mouth set in a determined line. Joey O'Hara might be he world's No.1 according to the computers, but for the past five years Naismith had topped the European Order of Merit and one didn't achieve that by buckling under pressure.

He addressed the ball and almost nonchalantly swung the club. He barely acknowledged the cheers as it flew in the wake of his opponent's ball, finishing a couple of yards behind that of the American. The Europeans in the crowd gave vent to their feelings as both golfers strode determinedly down the fairway, staring straight ahead.

As the Englishman's ball had finished fractionally behind his opponent's he would be first to play his second shot. Naismith, coolness personified, studied the line to the green, took his stance and swung smoothly with an 8-iron. He watched his ball as it arched, landing past the flag. It took the backspin, zipped past the cup, finishing about four feet from the hole. Tumultuous cheers from the European fans, which Naismith acknowledge by a languid wave of his hand. He and thousands of pairs of eyes watched as Joey O'Hara stood over his ball, eyeing up his second shot to the green. A 9-iron for Joey. To the right the blue waters of Lough Leane beckoned .

Would the young American repeat his performance of the first day and hit his shot into the water? Sitting in the golf buggy beside the President, Wayne Folen clench his hands with nervous tension. The crowd were silent. Joey blanked the memory of that disaster two days ago out of his mind as he placed the 9-iron carefully behind the ball. His back swing was smooth, the contact perfect. The ball zoomed high into the air, arched, came down and hit the green two inches short of the cup, jumped forward and came to rest eight inches from the hole.

The American fans cheered lustily.The President jumped to his feet in the golf buggy and was seen to applaud Joey's shot wildly. At the wheel of the vehicle Wayne Folen allowed himself a rare smile.

The crowd watched as Neil Naismith walked onto the green, his face impassive, picked up Joey ball and handed it to him, conceding the putt. Then he set about studying his short putt to halve the hole.

Naismith knew the importance of this four-footer. Sink it and he would show his opponent – and the American supporters – what he was made of. It would be a huge psychological blow, albeit there were still another seventeen holes to go. If he missed…The Englishman shut out that negative thought almost before it took hold.

The deathly silence descended again on the scene as Naismith hunkered down and studied the putt for a full minute. He rose and conversed briefly with his caddy. The spectators saw him make a gesture with his hand, as though indicating his ball would break slightly left. The caddy nodded in agreement. The tall Englishman took his stance over the ball, hesitated briefly, then stroked it gently towards the left side of the cup, allowing for a slight borrow. European groans of dismay and disbelief clashed with American yells of delight as the ball, hit just a touch too hard, went through the borrow and finished up a couple of inches directly behind the hole.

Neil Naismith stared at the ball as though he could not believe it was still above ground. But it was; he had lost the first hole of the match and was one down. The Americans had their noses in front on this final day and Joey O'Hara was leading the charge.

'Go for it, Joey! Kick some European ass and show our guys the way!' The world No.1 ignored the shouts as he made his way to the second tee. As a teenager he had watched the 1999 Ryder Cup clash at Brookline in America, cheered madly at the great fight back of the U.S. players on that final day. Was this the start of a repeat? He must keep his cool, ignore the shouts from the excited spectators.

Even the most optimistic of American supporters could hardly have believed how this top match would work out in their favour over the next three hours. In that period of time supporters of both teams watched in almost disbelief as the young American hit some of the best golf shots ever seen on the famous Killeen course in Killarney. Added to his immaculate play off the tee and fairway, Joey O'Hara displayed a magic touch on the greens and in the process inflicted the heaviest ever match play defeat on Europe's No.1 golfer.

Incredibly, Neil Naismith had to wait for six holes to be completed before he could snatch even a half in his match. He did so on Killeen's famous island par-3, but by then he was five down and the dazed look on his face said it all. The punishment was to continue. Unbelievably he was walking off the par-4 twelfth before he heard the match referee declare that he had actually won a hole. In between Naismith had shot four birdies and two pars, but so brilliant was Joey O'Hara's play that all those holes had been halved.

As the two top golfers in Europe and America stood on

the 13th tee the result of the Naismith versus O'Hara match was a foregone conclusion. Emphasising his superiority yet again, the American split the fairway with his tee shot, hit yet another magnificent second shot to the par-4 hole to set up yet another birdie chance. After a shattered Naismith had missed his putt from six feet for a birdie, Joey rolled in his short putt to inflict a 6 and 5 win and send American hopes soaring. The overall score was now Europe 12pts; America 5pts.

That win in the top match, the manner in which it had been achieved, and the massive spurt of inspiration it sent through the other members of the American team playing behind made the nightmare of Brookline in 1999 a reality for the Europeans. It seem to unnerve the other members of Bruce Cartray's squad, none of whom appeared to be able to capture the form of the previous two days. Indeed in all of the other games many of the Europeans got off to poor starts and by halfay in their matches were engaged in survival battles against the now rampant American golfers.

As Joey O'Hara walked off the 13th green to a hero's welcome from the wildly excited U.S. fans he saw his President awaiting him. Standing by the President's side was Joey's beaming father and also a very happy looking Wayne Folen.

The President extended his hand as a mass of photographers scrambled around. 'Congratulations, young man. A superb display. The Senator here can be very proud of you.'

Joey shook the outstretched hand. 'Thank you, sir. Your pep talk really got us going. On behalf of the team thank you for stopping over in Killarney.'

While Senator O'Hara embraced his son in front of the tv cameras, Wayne stole a glance at the giant scoreboard at the back of the 13th green. He could hardly believe what he saw.

Every one of the final eleven games were now out on

the course and his men were leading in six of them, including the next four matches to be decided. Of the other five games the Europeans were leading in only one, with the remainder all square. Wayne reckoned that there was still all to play for in this Ryder Cup!

'Come on, Wayne, back into that buggy,' the President ordered. 'Our men are on a roll right now and I want to be there to see all the action!'

• • • •

Katie Gartland exited from the 11am Sunday Mass in Loughduff's Church of the Redeemer and waited with her two boys, as was her custom, until the crowd had thinned and she could spot her friend Nell. She knew Nell and her husband Tom always attended the same mid-morning Mass with their two offspring and she was anxious to have a chat with her near neighbour. It would probably be the last after-Mass chat they would enjoy for a long time.

She had not as yet spoken to Nell about the phone call she had received from the young woman called Juliette. She wanted to do so before she left Loughduff. Looking down the main street of the town, with its faded shop fronts and the pub that brought back so many unhappy memories for her, Katie was sure she never wanted to see the place ever again.

As she waited to see Nell she was conscious of the furtive glances being cast her way by the townspeople as they traversed the open space outside the church, making their way down the stone stops onto the sidewalk. Nobody stopped for a chat or to exchange a greeting. Since those photograph of her posing seductively for Jeremy by the lakeside had appeared in the newspapers she had been ostracised. Nobody was prepared to put their reputation on the line by being seen talking to her. Except her friend Nell, of course.

At the Mass ceremony the priest had requested the

congregation to pray for the soul of the late Ben Gartland
and the young man who had died so tragically with him in
the cliff plunge two days ago. But as she stood outside the
church nobody approached her to offer condolences.

Despite the feeling of loneliness Katie smiled to herself.
No doubt after Mass next Sunday she would be the main
topic of conversation! She wondered what parish priest
Father McGarry would say about her then. Probably
denounce her from the pulpit and ask the congregation to
pray that the adulterous young wife would return to her
husband. Lighted candles and votive lamps would be
offered up in the hope that that miracle might happen.

Nell spotted Katie and came over. She glanced around,
made sure there was nobody within earshot. 'Well, Katie, I
suppose you're all set. Everything packed and ready to
go…'

Katie nodded, smiled. 'I can't wait to get going, Nell. I
keep thinking that something will happen…'

'God Katie, how I envy you! Heading off to the
unknown. All that sun, and the wine – and gorgeous
Jeremy – ' Nell sighed wistfully. Then she noticed the
rather sombre look on her friend's face. 'Something
wrong?'

Katie hesitated. She just had to tell Nell about that
telephone call from the called Juliette.

'Yes, something has happened. I'd like to talk to you
about it…'

Nell saw the serious look on her friend's face. What was
it, she wondered. Surely Katie hadn't changed her mind?
Had it something to do with Jeremy?; Nell had had a
suspicion from the very beginning that he was hiding
something, a secret from his past. She was dying to know
what it was but there were too many people about
watching, eyes lowered.

'We can't talk here, Katie. I sometimes think the trees
in Loughduff have ears!' Nell gave several passing women

within earshot a withering look. 'Why don't we drive back
to your place. We can talk there. Do you have time?'

'Yes. Just about.'

'Good. Tom stays in Loughduff after Mass every Sunday
to have a few drinks with his pals. I can leave my boys here
and pick them up later. How's that?'

'Fine.'

Nell tapped her bag as they moved away from the
church. 'I have a bottle of wine in here that I bought
before going into Mass. Tom and I treat ourselves to a few
glasses on Sunday evening while we're watching
television.' She giggled. 'I've a feeling he won't be getting
much tonight!'

Katie called to her two boys, drove back to her house,
Nell following behind in her car. A few minutes later they
were sitting across the table from each other in the
kitchen, the sun shining in through the window, glasses of
wine already poured.

Nell raised her glass. 'A toast – to you and Jeremy.' She
hoped she wasn't saying the wrong thing. What if the
whole thing has fallen through? Surely that couldn't
happen. Not at this stage…

They drank. 'Thanks Nell. This is a lovely surprise.' She
saw her friend looking at her intently, waiting.

'Well…' The tension was getting too much for Nell.
'What is it you want to talk about, Katie? You're not
looking too happy if I may say so. You're still going away
with Jeremy, aren't you?' She would die if the whole thing
had fallen through.

'Yes, of course we're still going away together –

'What on earth is it then? Out with it girl. For God's
sake – '

Katie told her friend about the unexpected telephone
call from the girl called Juliette, the conversation that
followed, and about the French girl's baby.

'Jeremy's'? Nell asked.

'Juliette says so.'

'Oh....' A worried look flitted across Nell's rounded face. 'Here, you need another drink – ' She poured for them both. 'What are you going to do, Katie? Have you told Jeremy about his former girlfriend – that she's had his baby and that she's anxious to contact him?'

'No, I haven't. And I don't think I will. It doesn't make any difference as far as I'm concerned. I love Jeremy, Nell. He says he loves me and I believe him. I want to go away with him. I can't let anything come between us now.'

Nell looked at her, thought briefly before replying. 'I think you're doing the right thing, Katie. I know it's hard on that girl Juliette, but if he left her like that he couldn't have really been madly in love with her anyway. You're prepared to take a chance and go away with Jeremy. I would too if I were in your shoes. You have an opportunity to start a new life. What have you got to lose? For heaven's sake take it Katie! You deserve it – '

Katie rose from her chair, went around the other side of the table and hugged her friend. 'Thanks again, Nell. I was hoping you would say something like that.' She laughed despite her moist eyes. 'I was determined to go away with Jeremy anyway! – '

'I knew you were – and I can't say I blame you! Sure I'd do the same myself if I had half a chance!'

They talked some more, lingering over the bottle of wine, neither of them wanting the conversation to end. Over the years they had spent a lot of time in each other's kitchen, discussing their lives, arguing, complaining, sorting out problems, finding solace in each other's company usually during the many drab, dreary days of winter. Now that aspect of their relationship was about to end, maybe forever. It was time to say their goodbyes.

'I hate to say it Katie but it's time I was going . Tom and

the boys will be waiting. Anyway, you probably still have a few things to do before Jeremy calls...'

'We're practically ready to go.' Katie glanced around her kitchen. 'I supposeI I'll miss this place, despite everything. Right now I can't wait to see the last of it. Honestly, Nell I hope I never have to come back.'

'And why would you want to come back. You were never happy here. Now you're about to leave it all behind, take off to a faraway place, maybe a romantic island, with someone you love. Very few women get a chance like that, Katie.'

'I know what you're saying is right, Nell. Pray that nothing will go wrong for myself and Jeremy.'

The words had dried up and they were both silent. Now that they moment had arrived neither of them wanted to say the dreaded word 'goodbye'. When they were standing in the open doorway Nell paused.

'Promise me you'll write, Katie, that you'll keep in touch. I won't tell anyone, including Sergeant Gilhooly, where you are. Honest.'

'Of course I'll keep in touch with you, Nell. I'll never forget all you've done for me over the years....the advice, the encouragement you gave me when I needed it most. You made me laugh in the darkest moments...'

They fell into each other's arms, clung together. When they finally broke apart tears were streaming down Nell's broad face.

'Oh Nell, for heaven's sake – ' Katie was fighting back her own tears.

'I'll miss you, Katie. I know I will – terribly.'

'I'll miss you too, Nell.'

Nell smiled through her tears. 'I'm so happy for you.'

'I know you are – but heavens you don't look it!' Katie forced a laugh. 'Now stop crying or I'll change my mind!'

'You won't ever return to Loughduff, Katie. I just know you won't,' Nell said through her tears. 'Don't be like

Shirley Valentine. She made the mistake of going back to Liverpool. It was the wrong thing to do.'

'Goodbye, Nell.' They hugged each other again. Then Nell broke away, walked quickly out to her car. Katie watched as she turned, gave one last wave, got in. The engine roared into life.

Katie dabbed at her tear-stained eyes as the car disappeared from view out through the gateway and onto the road. When the sound of the engine at last died away she went back indoors.

• • • •

As the September sun began to decend behind the MacGillycuddy Reeks the noise level emanating from the Killarney Golf and Fishing Club rose to unprecedented heights.

Amid mounting excitement, golf fans scrambled from match to match, hanging onto every shot as the Americans staged the greatest fight back ever in the chequered history of Samuel Ryder's exalted trophy.

By five pm., ten of the twelve singles matches between Europe and America had been completed. Unbelievably the two sides were now level at 13 points each. The giant scoreboards dotted around the course told the whole incredible story: America had achieved the almost impossible by winning the first eight matches played, the next two had been halved, and with the final two games of the contest now nearing completion the destination of the most prized trophy in world team golf hung delicately in the balance.

Standing on the 17th tee, veteran Irish golfer Davy Cochran was perspiring profusely and growing increasingly nervous. Three hours ago he had reckoned on this being the greatest day in his long golfing life, instead it was turning into a nightmare.

Davy had a terrible feeling in the pit of his stomach that the outcome of this titanic Ryder Cup battle was going to hinge on the last match on the course – which would be the encounter between himself and the ice-cool Texan Tyrone Oates. Davy wasn't too happy with the scenario; despite the coolness creeping into the September evening he was beginning to feel uncomfortably hot and sticky.

He stole a glance at the nearby scoreboard to see how his Italian team-mate Dominicio Uragi was doing in his match against that other tough American competitor Wes Daal. Davy didn't like what he saw. Having been in command early on in his match, the Italian had lost the last two holes and was now walking up the 18th fairway level with his American opponent. Obviously the pressure during the last hour or so had got to him and his game had deteriorated. With his teammate Uragi unlikely to win the final hole in his match it was probable that the outcome of the Ryder Cup would depend on the final pairing. Davy Cochran had the terrible feeling that Doomsday was approaching!

Hard to believe that just over an hour ago, two up with only four holes to play, he had been cruising to victory, looking set for a stroll up the final hole, waving to the crowds, all set to give Europe the vital point for a dramatic Ryder Cup win. Davy had visions of himself emulating those other Irish Ryder Cup heroes of the past... Darcy defying the odds to defeat Crenshaw at Muirfield Village in 1987; O'Connor Jr.'s great 2-iron shot to the heart of the 18th green at The Belfry in '89 to destroy Fred Couples; Walton keeping his nerve for that vital last hole win at Oak Hill in Rochester in '95 against Jay Haas, and McGinley's unforgettable putt on the last green at The Belfry in 2002 to halve with Jim Furyk, a putt that had secured Europe's win. Irish heroes all.

Unfortunately events had taken an unexpected turn.

Now it looked like he, Davy Cochran, was about to ruin that proud Irish winning record!

Back on the 15th tee, well in command, Davy had committed the cardinal sin in golf of thinking too far ahead. Stupid! His opponent Oates had remained calm, focused, refusing to get ruffled even though defeat was staring him in the face. With thousands of fans screaming him on, and fired up by the President of the United States cheering and waving the Stars and Stripes from the buggy which Wayne Folen was driving like a madman over the fairways, Tyrone Oates had play some inspired golf over those final holes and had deservedly narrowed the gap.

The slimline American had won the dogleg par-four 15th hole after Davy had pushed his second shot into the bunker on the left of the green. The Irishman had splashed out short and, under intense pressure, missed a putt of six feet for a half. It was a bad mistake and Davy Cochran knew it. Now he was only one up with three holes to play....

'Take it easy, Davy. Slow down a little,' Bruce Cartray had whispered to him as he was making his way to the 16th tee. 'You're still one up and he's running out of holes. Play for pars and hope you'll make birdies, make him feel the pressure. You can do it.'

Davy nodded, noting at the same time that his captain's smile of assurance looked a bit strained. Davy cursed that late night drinking session he had enjoyed with a group of Irish supporters last night that had progressed into the early hours. He had always enjoyed a drink or two on tour – the pundits reckoned that was why he had never made it bigtime as a pro; now he was suffering for celebrating too soon!

After the team dinner last night Bruce Cartray had taken Davy and his Italian team-mate Dominicio Uragi aside and confided to them that he would be playing them both in the last two singles games on Sunday. Davy and

Domenicio had been expecting this. They accepted that, despite their good showings over the first two days, they were acknowledged as the two weakest players in the European squad. They knew that on the final day the captain planned on playing his best players first, winning early matches to secure the necessary paltry two points and get the Ryder Cup match over as soon as possible.

'You two chaps have performed exceptionally well so far and deserve a reward,' Bruce Cartray had said. 'By the time you get to play we'll almost certainly have delivered the coup de grace to the Yanks and retained the Ryder Cup. You two fellows probably won't even have to play the last few holes. I expect we'll have scalped the Yanks by then.'

Davy had grasped the opportunity. 'Does that mean we can relax, enjoy a couple of drinks with our friends tonight?' he asked.

Bruce had hesitated. He knew Davy Cochran's barroom reputation on tour. 'That's not quite what I had in mind, Davy old boy.'

'I don't mean going out on the town,' Davy had assured his captain piously. 'Just a couple of beers with the wife and a few friends – '

'And for me, maybe I share a bottle of wine tonight with my wife and some friends also,' Dominicio Uragi had cut in.

Bruce Cartray had relented, albeit somewhat reluctantly. His two veterans had surprised everyone – himself included – by their performances so far in the tournament. They deserved an easy draw in the singles he reckoned, a victory stroll up the eighteenth fairway, basking in the applause of the huge crowd, the Ryder Cup already in European hands...

It wasn't turning out quite like that. The Europoean captain's plan had misfired. The Americans had come out on the final day with all guns blazing and Joey O'Hara's huge win against Neil Naismith in the top singles match had sparked off a succession of American victories that had brought the United States right back into contention.

As the Americand won match after match Bruce Cartray began to feel like a man condemned. He could see certain victory slipping from his grasp. His fate now rested on how the two weakest members of his team would perform over the next hour – and both of them were probably nursing hangovers! The media would crucify him for losing the Ryder Cup – and Sally would give him the tongue lashing of all time!

On the par-five 16th hole, named the MacGillycuddy Reeks after the famous mountain range, Tyrone Oates hit a massive drive down the middle of the fairway. Davy Cochran, really rattled now, hooked his ball left into the gorse. Minutes later the Irishman tramped through the rough and surveyed the damage; his ball was lying in close proximity to a gorse bush and he could only hack his second shot back onto the fairway. It was still his turn to play and he raised European cheers when he hit his third shot – a fairway wood – onto the small green. Davy breathed a sigh of relief; despite his bad drive he still had a chance of a birdie putt.

There were groans from the home supporters when the Tyrone Oates followed the Irishman onto the green with only his second shot. The big Texan looked very determined as he strode down the fairway. And he proved his will to win when, after carefully surveying the line of his putt, he calmly stroked the ball in from twenty feet for an eagle three to win the hole. A sea of flags bearing the Stars and Stripes waved to the heavens.

The Irishman's two shot lead of a couple of holes ago had now evaporated. The match was all square. The thousands of American spectators, sensing the most unlikely Ryder Cup win ever, were cheering madly, stampeding from green to the next tee in a manner that put life and limb in danger.

Standing on the 17th tee Davy Cochran offered up a silent prayer.'Please God, help me. Don't let me be the player to lose the Ryder Cup for Europe. I'll do anything you ask of me. I'll even give up the drink!' He couldn't remember an occasion in the past when he had been driven to make such a rash promise!

The 17th hole at Killeen is a 410-yard par-4 with water and thick gorse on the right. Not a long hole by today's standards and a definite birdie chance if the golfer can drive it straight from the tee and hit the fairway. Oates hit an excellent 3-wood tee shot that split the fairway and avoided the lake – a perfect shot. Halfway down the fairway Wayne Folen punched the air and his distinguished buggy passenger stood up and applauded. Even the Secret Service men in the two accompanying buggies were looking excited.

On the tee Davy Cochran was hoping his prayer had been heard by the Almighty. He adjusted his grip slightly and swung his 3-wood, hoping to fade his ball from left to right. But a touch of tension had crept into his backswing and the clubhead came into the impact area just a shade off line. As the ball sailed through the air Davy knew it was going to stay left and miss the fairway. It did just that. The groan from the Europeans in the crowd could be heard a mile away.

As the ball landed amid a cluster of grass and pine needles Sally Cartray turned to her husband in the golf buggy they were sharing.. 'Can your friend Davy reach the green from there with his next shot?' she asked.

The strain was now showing on the face of Europe's captain. Bruce Cartray had long since lost that confident look he had shown standing by the first tee this morning when play had started. ' It depends on how the ball is lying. It doesn't look very good from here.'

Sally could sense that her prestige as the wife of a

winning Ryder Cup captain was in jeopardy. All that dreadful publicity; the knives would really be out for her husband if he lost the Ryder Cup now from such a commanding position. She could see all those after-dinner talks to women's clubs she had planned disappearing...

'That stupid man!' she fumed. 'Calls himself a professional golfer, does he? The man can't hit a ball straight! He's going to lose us the Ryder Cup!'

Other members of the European team who had finished their matches, wives and girlfriends in close proximity, were following the remaining two games and lending support. Those who were not following the fortunes of Davy Cochran were grouped around the 18th green which Dominicio Uragi had failed to find with his second shot. The European players watched anxiously as the Italian lined up his third shot, a chip from just off the green . Wes Daal was already on the 18th putting surface, about twelve feet from the flag in two shots. A birdie - probably to win the hole – looked odds-on for the American...

At the same moment in time Davy Cochran arrived at his ball and grimaced when he saw where it had landed. It was lying on a nest of pine needles and there were also two small stones lying in close proximity to the ball, near enough to prevent him from striking it cleanly. Like every professional golfer Davy was conversant with the rules of the game; he knew he could remove those stones without penalty – as long as his ball did not move in the process. He bent down and carefully, very carefully, removed the two stones. Then he started the more delicate job of moving some of the pine needles...

• • • •

Sergeant Gilhooly sensed that the house was deserted, as distinct from nobody being at home, as he drove in through the gateway and approached up the gravel path. He could always tell from little things, like the curtains not moving as someone glanced out to see who the caller was when they heard the car. Or Katie Gartland or one of the boys opening the front door in welcome before he rang the bell.

The real giveaway was no smoke coming from the chimney. Katie Gartland had never known the luxury of central heating and would have had a fire going at this time of year when the September sun had lost its warmth. He wondered if the bird had flown.

The Sergeant knew he could have called earlier. But then maybe he had not wanted to. Sometimes routine police work had to go by the board when one was dealing with a person in certain circumstances. He had seen Katie Gartland coming out of the church this morning, saw her talking to her friend Nell Flavin, watched as the two of them, and Katie's two boys, had driven off in their cars. It had looked like a normal Sunday morning in Loughduff, although he had sensed it wasn't quite so. He had a suspicion that Katie Gartland planned to flee the country with her two offspring. The question was – did he plan to do anything to stop them?

He had telephoned the Irish Ferries office in Dublin yesterday afternoon, identified himself and asked them to check their passenger list to see if a Jeremy Walker had made a booking on the car ferry from Rosslare to Cherbourg anytime within the next few days. The nice young lady had confirmed within minutes that a man of that name had, a few days previously, reserved and paid for a car space plus two adjoining cabins on the 6pm sailing from Rosslare on Sunday, due to arrive in Cherbourg at approximately 1pm the following day.

'Did he say how many people were travelling with him?'

'His wife and their two teenage sons…'

'Hmmm…I don't suppose he gave any details of where they might be heading after Cherbourg?' The Sergeant knew it was a long shot, but sometimes long shots paid off.

'I'm sorry, sergeant. We wouldn't have that information. Our job is to get our passengers safely to Cherbourg. What they do after that is entirely up to them.'

'Of course. Much obliged. Thank you.'

Sergeant Gilhooly got out of his car, went over and inspected the other vehicle parked outside the house. So Katie had left the family car behind. Obviously they had only used Jeremy Walker's. They were travelling light. Was that a sign that they intended to return to Loughduff? He doubted it.

He looked at his watch. 5.20pm. Still plenty of time to stop them if he wished. He could drive back to the station, telephone his colleagues in Rosslare, inform them of what was happening and get them to board the car ferry and detain Jeremy Walker, Katie, and her two boys. It would only take about ten minutes...

Dan Gilhooly knew he wasn't going to make that telephone call. Not today anyway. Maybe tomorrow or later in the week – Tuesday, when she didn't show up to Ben Gartland's funeral – he would start making enquiries. Luckily Travis Gartland was still too ill after his hunger strike to travel to Loughduff and attend his brother's funeral. Had Travis been able to travel, returning home to find his house empty and his wife and two sons missing, the game would have been up for Katie.

Why should he hunt down a young woman like Katie Gartland who, as far as he knew, had never done harm to anyone. Why ruin her chance of a fresh start in life, condemn her to years of misery with an uncouth, uncaring and violent husband like Travis Gartland? Katie had been dealt a bad hand in life. He had known her from the time when, as an naive teenager, she had come out of the convent orphanage and gone to work behind the bar in Bengy Duff's pub. The Sergeant had heard the whispers of the abuse allegedly inflicted on her, but the young Katie had been either too naïve or too afraid to complain. Marriage to Travis Gartland had presented her with a way out. It was a high price for any young woman to have to pay.

Sergeant Gilhooly doubted if Katie Gartland had ever really enjoyed a good day in her entire life. Not until she had met Jeremy Walker that is. Was she doing the right thing in running away with the flamboyant Englishman? It was not for him to judge. If that was what she wanted he certainly was not going to drag her back to a life of misery. He had warned her how she could end up breaking the law so he had done his duty. Life had dealt Katie a second hand of cards and not many people got that kind of opportunity.

The Sergeant approached the front door, saw the key that Katie had left dangling there. He went inside, looked around the room before entering the kitchen. Everything was neatly in its place. No unwashed cups or plates lying around. The sink was empty, a clean tea towel hanging nearby. He looked around for a written note on the table, on the dresser maybe. There was none.

He went upstairs, glanced into what was obviously the boys' bedroom. It was sparsely furnished with two beds, both neat and tidy, a table with a mirror, a couple of chairs and pictures of sports and pop stars on the walls. He opened the wardrobe doors; it was empty save for a row of coat hangers.

As soon as he entered Travis and Katie's bedroom he saw the note. It was attached to the mirror of the old-fashioned wardrobe by a piece of Sellotape. The words were in block letters, the message stark in its simplicity. It was unsigned.

> The boys and I have left you. We are not coming back. Do not try to find us. Our marriage is finished and I do not want to see you again.
>
> Katie

The Sergeant read it twice without removing it from its position. It said it all. Katie Gartland was gone, a woman who had made her mind up to swap the past for the future. She had probably even dropped the Gartland name by now. He doubted he would ever see her again.

Outside again Sergeant Gilhooly got into the police car, stared back at the house. 'Wherever you are heading, Katie,' he said aloud, 'God bless you and good luck to you and the boys.'

He started the engine, drove out through the gate, took the road to Killarney instead of the one to Loughduff. He wasn't a big golf fan, but he hoped to be in time to catch the finish of the Ryder Cup battle.

• • • •

Under the close scrutiny of the match referee and his opponent Tyrone Oates, and with the lenses of several tv cameras monitoring his every move, Davy Cochran very carefully eased away the couple of pebbles and several pine needles from the immediate area of his ball in the light rough where it was nestling. He knew that if he inadvertently touched his ball, causing it to move, he would be penalised a shot under the strict laws of the game.

Out on the fairway Bruce Cartray and his American counterpart Wayne Folen were also following the proceedings. Bruce decided to keep his distance from Davy Cochran, he would let the player handle the delicate operation with the pine needles. He did not want to put any more pressure than was necessary on the veteran Irishman right now.

Bruce Cartray surveyed the scene from the fairway, having left Sally sitting in the golf buggy. He looked into the distance, saw the huge crowd around the 18th green. All was not yet lost. Communicating on his two-way radio a couple of minutes go he had learned that Dominicio Uragi was preparing to play his third shot from just off the 18th green, with his American opponent Daal already on the putting surface but a distance from the cup. Maybe the Italian would chip in and win the hole with a birdie, get that vital point that would win the Ryder Cup for Europe. Bruce Cartray reckoned he could do with a bit of good fortune right now!

There were still several pine needles resting almost under his ball in the rough, and Davy Cochran reckoned it was too risky to remove them. He straightened up, walked back onto the fairway to survey his shot to the green – a ploy to gain time, calm himself down. This was no time to get flustered and make a wrong decision. He must endeavour to look calm, exude confidence, be in control. He could feel his heart pounding. Jeez! – what if he had a heart attack, in front of all these people, and millions watching on tv!

As he walked back towards his ball an almighty roar rent the heavens. It drifted down from the area of the 18th green. Something dramatic had happened up ahead, Davy reckoned. He asked his caddie for the bottle of Ballygowan water to relieve his parched throat. He prayed that Domenicio Uragi had not been defeated. Suppose he had won…it would take all the pressure of him!

Davy glanced sideways, saw Bruce Cartray on his walkie-talkie, his face showing the strain as he checked out what was happening at the 18th. Suddenly the usually staid European captain raised his hands in triumph, punching the air like a lager lout. Davy saw Cartray pull a surprised Sally from the golf buggy and hug her. They were jumping about like two kids.

'What the hell is happening?' Davy asked his caddie.

Bruce Cartray was striding across the fairway towards them, his face wreathed in a smile. 'Davy lad, would you believe it – Domenicio chipped in from off the green for a birdie! He has left Daal with a tricky twelve footer to halve the hole. If the Yank doesn't hole it we'll have the 14 points needed to retain the Ryder Cup!'

A wave of relief swept over Davy. He said a swift, silent prayer for his teammate. Well done Domenicio. It was just what he needed to hear. If the American missed his putt for a birdie Europe would win that match and the overall score would be 14pts to 13 in Europe's favour. Davy would have that nice easy walk up the 18th fairway, knowing he could afford to lose his match against Tyrone Oates and Europe would still be champions. Phew!

'Sshhh…! Cartray held his hand up for silence. 'Daal is about to putt…the ball is on its way – ' Davy held his breath. Another thunderous roar rolled down the fairway from the18th green. He watched Bruce Cartray's facial expression, saw it change from exultation to concern. Across the fairway Davy saw Wayne Folen and the American President punching the air with delight. He knew what it meant.

'Daal sank the putt!,' Bruce Cartray was looking grim again. 'That game is halved. You know what that means, Davy. We still need you to get half a point. You can do it!'

Davy made an effort to smile. The news from the 18th green was like a death sentence to him. He couldn't have devised a worse scenario for himself had he tried. He was in trouble at this 17th hole. Should he lose it he would go the 18th hoping for a half against an upbeat Tyrone Oates. The prospect didn't appeal to Davy Cochran. No doubt right now Domenicio Uragi was being congratulated by his ecstatic teammates. Davy wished he was walking off the 18th green right now.

He stood over his ball again, surveyed the shot to the green. It was a tough one. Oates's ball was twenty five yards ahead of him, lying nicely on the fairway. Davy was roughly 160 yards from the pin, hitting off a bad lie into a narrow green that sloped away on all sides. If he hit it short he would probably land in the small bunker at the front; anything hit too firmly was in danger of rolling down the slope past the pin and leaving a tricky chip shot back.

Thousands of anxious pairs of European eyes watched as the Irishman swung a 7-iron and the tiny white orb rose into the evening sky. The ball arched in flight, hit the green behind the pin, spun back towards the hole. It finished about ten feet away. An awkward distance, but at least the putt was uphill.

It was a good shot under the circumstances and the applause was generous. 'Well done, Davy,' his captain shouted. The veteran Irishman breathed a sigh of relief.

Then it was Tyrone Oates's turn. Huge cheers burst from thousands of American throats as the 9-iron shot rose high into the air, plopped onto the green, took backspin and finishing three feet from the pin. Advantage U.S.A., albeit Oates faced a tricky downhill putt.

The wall of noise that accompanied the two protagonists all the way to the 17th green was unnerving. Both men stared straight ahead, a look of deep concentration etched on their faces. If anything the tall Texan looked more relaxed. He walk was the unhurried gait of a man who knew he held the advantage. The buggy containing Wayne Folen and the U.S. President was guided through a corridor of stewards to a prominent greenside position where they could see the action. Wayne's eyes searched out and spotted Marcia across the other side of the green with the other American wives. He gave her a thumbs up sign and she waved. His team had made a magnificent comeback. Ryder Cup glory was still within his grasp.

The President leaned over, whispered to Wayne: 'Do you think your guys can pull it off, Wayne?'

'Yes sir. The Irish guy Cochran looks shattered to me. He's just lost two holes in succession. Don't be surprised if he misses his putt and Tyrone holes his.' Wayne grinned, asked.'You enjoying yourself Mr. President?'

'Hell, there's more tension out here today than at any time since I've been President!'

On the green Davy Cochran was fighting to calm the inner turmoil that was threatening to turn his legs to jelly. Never in a long and distinguished pro golf career had he experienced this sort of pressure. He felt like he wanted to be sick. And the noise – it only subsided whenever either himself of his opponent were standing over a shot.

Making a superhuman effort to look calm he stalked his putt from all angles. Thank God it was uphill. He would have to be careful and not leave it short. It was late evening now and he knew a slight moisture was possibly beginning to form. But he didn't want to hit it too hard past the cup and leave him with knee-trembler on the way back.That didn't bear thinking about! Davy knew that Tyrone Oates would concede him nothing at this stage...

Davy stood over the putt, stroked it, kept his head still. He heard a crescendo of noise from the supporters and when he glanced sideways he saw the ball about four feet from the hole, heading for the centre of the cup. He watched it disappear from view. What an unlikely birdie after that dreadful tee shot!

'Good on yeh!, Davy lad. Show the Yank how it's done!' he heard an Irish voice amid the din.

Davy bent down and retrived his ball. He stood back, held up his hand to the crowd for silence while his opponent studied his putt. Inwardly he hoped that Tyrone Oates would miss. One up playing the 18th, knowing that he needed only a half to retain the Ryder Cup for Europe. The pressure would be off him and on the American.... No such luxury – Oates rolled in his tricky putt to a burst of prolonged applause.

The official marker's voice rang out over the din: 'The 17th hole is halved in birdie. The match remains all square with the 18th and final hole to play...'

Davy Cochran was to state in the press room afterwards where he faced the world media that he did not remember the short walk to the 18th tee. It was as though he was in a trance. He was oblivious of the thousands of spectators stampeding across the Killarney links to gain vantage points along both sides of the fairway. He did remember glancing at Tyrone Oates on the tee and thinking how cool, calm and collected his opponent looked. Davy felt drained himself and just wanted to play this final hole and get this whole damn Ryder Cup thing over with.

The final hole on Killarney's Killeen course is a treacherous 450-yard par four, with gorse and a stream down the left hand side, at the end of which is a large lake. This in turn feeds a smaller lake that eats into the front and side of the green, making it a difficult target to hit from the fairway. Bunkers, a cluster of bushes and a stream are the hazards to be avoided on the right side of the fairway. Some cynic had named the hole Slan Abaile which, in Gaelic, means Safe Home.

Davy cursed that person under his breath as he looked down the final fairway. He had just seen Tyrone Oates effortlessly hit yet another screamer of a drive straight down the middle. Didn't the guy ever smash one into the rough? Oates looked so calm it was like he was playing a friendly round of golf with his best buddy instead of battling it out in the deciding game of a Ryder Cup battle!

Selecting his 3-wood for safety – he didn't care if his drive ended up well behind his opponent as long as he was down the middle – Davy swung as smoothly as his nerves would allow at the ball. He followed the flight, watching in horror as his ball careered through the air off to the right, sailed over the heads of the spectators lining the fairway, and disappeared behind a cluster of small bushes. It was the worst drive he had hit all day. A groan of despair rose from the throats of the European supporters.

From his vantage point halfway down the left side of

the fairway Bruce Cartray also groaned. Beside him he heard his wife use a swear word and mutter something uncomplimentary about the antecedents of the Irishman. In his lofty perch in the commentary box behind the 18th green the duo of CBS Sports broadcasters tried to stay impartial as they commentated to the millions of American tv viewers back home.

'That is a very poor tee shot from Davy Cochran. What do you think of the situation in this game right now, Jack?', the commentator asked the famous veteran golfer.

'That was indeed a poor drive from the Irishman,' the veteran of many Ryder Cup battles agreed. 'Right now the United States are favourites to win. That was the shot of a man under real pressure. Cochran has lost his game completely over the last four or five holes and it looks like he's going to lose the Ryder Cup for Europe. I wouldn't be surprised if that ball is unplayable...'

'We'll get a camera onto that ball and let you see exactly how difficult a situation the Irishman is in on this last hole....'

A host of tv cameras zoomed in on a grim faced Cochran as he walked up the fairway. The next camera shot switched to the area in the rough where the Irishman's ball had landed. The ball was in an almost unplayable position, resting lightly on a patch of grass under the overhanging branch of a small tree.

'This is going to be a really tough shot,' one of the CBS man intoned. 'What do you think, Jack?' Audiences awaited the voice of the world renowned former player who now brought his knowledge of the game to tv audiences at all major tournaments.

'That overhanging branch makes it a risky shot,' Jack opined. 'I really don't think he has a clear view of the green from there. I won't be surprised if Davy opts to drop out and take a one shot penalty. We'll know a lot more soon when Cochran sizes up the situation, takes a couple of practice swings, and decides if that branch is impeding his shot…'

'If he has to take a penalty drop it would really put Oates in the driving seat. It will mean the Irishman will be playing his third shot to the green – '

'Yes, it looks grim for Europe even though Cochran needs only to halve this hole for Europe to retain the Ryder Cup. Look at Tyrone's ball right in the middle of the fairway. He has a straightforward second shot to the green.'

'Yeahl, an easy second shot for a guy of Tyrone Oates's calibre,' the CBS man intoned.

'There are no easy shots in a Ryder Cup,' Jack cautioned. 'Right now Tyrone looks a dead cert for a par, maybe even a birdie. Let's see what happens – '.

Their conversation was interrupted as the camera picked up the Irishman staring down at his ball. He shook his head, turned and said something to his caddie. Then he took a club from his bag, stepped close, made a couple of very careful practice swings.

'Is Cochran aiming on taking on the shot, Jack?' the CBS commentator asked.

'Right now he's sussing out if he can commit himself to a full swing without that overhanging branch interfere with his shot,' the former U.S. Ryder Cup captain said. 'See, he's trying it again. The ball is in there somewhere. Hey, be careful, Davy – ' Jack warned. 'Those practice swings look a bit wild to me. He's got to be careful he doesn't disturb the ball or even a leaf from that bush. That could be interpreted as improving how his ball lies. If he does that he's in trouble – '

Jack broke off suddenly. Something was happening down there. Davy Cochran was shaking his head, pointing to his ball, saying something to his caddie. He turned and called the match referee over. His opponent Tyrone Oates was in close attendance. They were all looking very serious. The two team captains, sensing something unusual had happened, climbed out of their respective buggies and joined the group. The referee and Davy Cochran bent down and peered at the half-hidden ball under the bush. Television cameramen were jostling each other to get a fix on it.

The CBS commentator cut to his on course reporter. 'What the hell is happening down there, Sam?' he asked.

The camera picked up on course reporter Sam. 'This is a disaster for Europe,' Sam replied in reverential tones. 'Davy Cochran's ball moved slightly while he was making those practice swings. I don't think anybody else saw the ball move except Davy. He's reported it to the referee and to Tyrone Oates. The word is that the Irishman has called a penalty shot on himself. That could well cost him the hole – and Europe the Ryder Cup. This is sensational!'

TV viewers around the world tuned into the Ryder Cup clash saw Bruce Cartray and Wayne Folen join the group before the camera switched back to the match referee. The latter cleared his throat then announced in a loud voice: 'Davy Cochran's ball moved while he was taking a practice swing and he has called a penalty shot on himself. He will replace his ball in the original spot where it landed off the tee and now be playing his third shot to the green!'

In the CBS commentary box Jack was shaking his head, smiling wryly. 'What a disaster for Europe – and what a sporting gesture from the Irishman. Davy could have been the only person to see that ball move and he might have tried to get away with it. Instead he's done the honourable thing. I've played in many Ryder Cup contests in my time but, for sportsmanship, that sure beats everything – '

Down below Tyrone Oates was seen to give his opponent a consoling pat on the back, offer what were obviously words of commiseration. The crowd saw the gesture and showed its appreciation with cheers and applause.. The two captains also seemed to have forgotten their past differences as Wayne Folen chatted to Bruce Cartray. Davy Cochran and his European teammates looked disheartened. They knew that unless Davy did something spectacular now the Ryder Cup was bound for America.

As he prepared to play what was now his third shot out of the thick rough, Sam the CBS reporter on the course, came back briefly on screen.

'I've just grabbed a quick word with our President,' he told his audience. 'The President reckons that Davy Cochran's action on calling that penalty shot on himself was the greatest sporting gesture in the history of the Ryder Cup. And Wayne Folen was in full agreement. But it's still now over yet, folks. The Europeans could still win this great event on the 18th green. Remember all that's needed is for Davy Cochran to halve this hole. They still have all to play for… '

The camera returned just in time to the Irishman's attempt to hit a 5-iron shot from his very difficult lie. It was a huge gamble to take but Davy reckoned at this stage he had nothing to lose. It was all or nothing…

Davy knew he had a great shot as soon as the club made contact with the ball. The crowd watched in awe as it took off on a low trajectory and headed straight as an arrow towards the distant green. An ocean of expectant faces followed its progress. Roars of acclaim died in thousands of throats as the ball appeared to be heading for the yawning greenside bunker…

The ball cleared the back of the bunker by inches and took off across the green at speed. The cheering grew in volume as the ball, slowing down now, was seen to be rolling straight for the flagstick at the back of the green. On the fairway 170 yards away Davy heard the thunderous roar of the crowd and thought for one glorious moment that his ball had hit the flagstick and disappeared into the hole.

Sadly it had not – but it was close, finishing just four feet above the hole. The spectators applauded what many reckoned was the best shot of this titanic battle. When the Irishman strolled onto the green, doffing his cap as the cheers rang out, he stared at his ball and knew his troubles were far from over. He had left himself with a tricky downhill putt that would break sharply to the right. He would probably need to hole that for a par to halve the hole and retain the Ryder Cup for Europe. It was not a task that Davy Cochran was looking forward to.

The expression on Tyrone Oates's face had not changed. He remained focused, impervious to the noise rolling around the 18th green. A couple of minutes ago he had been extremely confident of winning the Ryder Cup for America. Now the balance had swung again in Europe's favour. That wonder shot by Cochran had put the pressure back on the Texan. Oates knew he had to at least get a par, hope his adversary would miss his short, tricky putt that, with the penalty shot he had incurred, would mean the Irishman taking a bogey 5 to lose the hole. First though, the American knew he had to hit the green with his second shot.

Like many before him over the years the tall Texan succumbed to Ryder Cup tension. He had played immaculately all day, now he pulled a 6-iron shot out to the right, missing the green by several yards. The tv caught him with a look of disbelief on his face. Once again the crowd erupted, sensing the match wasn't over yet – not by a long shot! The army of course stewards fought valiantly to contain the crowd as thousands of spectators stampeded down the fairway behind the two protagonists and their caddies. Some were even clamouring up into the trees surround the 18th green.

Oates had been lucky. His ball had missed the trees on the right of the green and was lying perfectly, pin high, in the fringe grass. The Texan had one of the best short games around the green on the U.S. tour and indeed was currently leading the tour statistics for chipping into the hole. It was his specialty. Tyrone Oates was confident he could get a par at least on this final hole and leave his opponent with a knee-trembling short downhill putt to keep the Ryder Cup in Europe. He must get his third it close to the pin then sink the putt.

The spectators went silent as Oates strode to and fro from the flagstick, judging the texture of the grass on the green and studying the subtle undulations between his ball and the hole. He decided on the exact spot where he wanted his ball to land so that it would run up close to the hole – maybe even go in for a birdie 3 and a Ryder Cup win for America! As he studied the shot he kept reminding himself that he had holed much more difficult chip and run shots than the one facing him right now.

The television cameras were also focusing on Wayne Folen. He was seen to say something to the President, then leave his seat in the golf buggy and approach to where he could get a better view of what was happening. Silence reigned around the green as Tyrone Oates took his favourite pitching wedge out of his golf bag, stepped back slightly from his ball and took a few practice swings. The only sound to be heard in the deathly silence was the lapping of the water on nearby Lough Leane…

Oates stepped forward over the ball, hit a short crisp shot. The ball popped into the air, landed exactly the right distance from the cup, began its journey towards the hole. The crowd broke silence to cheer and roar. The noise grew in volume as the ball rolled across the smooth surface. It was right on line – but did it have enough momentum to reach the cup? It did – but the cheers died in thousands of American throats as the ball stopped agonisingly on the lip of the hole, hung there, but refused to drop.

For a few seconds Tyrone Oates stared at the ball, then he began to walk very slowly towards it, staring it, willing it to tumble into the hole of its own accord. It did not drop – and he tapped it in for a par-4. Davy Cochran heaved a sigh of relief. He still had a chance of halving the hole, but he had some work to do. His mouth felt dry and the palms of his hands were sweaty.

'To halve this match, and for Europe to retain the Ryder Cup, Davy Cochran must hole this very tricky short putt for a par.' the CBS sports commentator told his audience in hushed tones. 'It's almost like history is repeating itself. In 1991 Germany's Bernard Langer had a putt of six feet on the 18th green in the final game against Hale Irwin at Kiawah Island to win the Ryder Cup for Europe. Langer missed . Will Cochran suffer the same fate? He knows that if he misses he'll go down in Ryder Cup history as the man who lost it for Europe - '

The American commentator broke off. 'Hey, what's happening now...Look at this! - Wayne Folen is coming onto the green...'

The camera picked up the U.S. Ryder Cup captain striding purposefully towards Tyrone Oates. The latter seemed just as surprised as everyone else at his captain's intrusion. Thousands of spectators ringing the green, and millions enjoying the drama on television, saw Wayne Folen say something to Tyrone Oates. They saw the look of astonishment on the American golfer's face as listened to what his captain was saying.

'What the hell is happening out there?' The commentator's voice trailed off again. 'Hey, what the - I don't believe it! Tyrone Oates is picking up Davy Cochran's ball! They're shaking hands – ' The commentator's voice was rising with excitement. 'This is incredible. Oates has conceded that difficult little putt to the Irishman – and I reckon he did so on his captain's orders. The score is 14 points each and Europe has retained the Ryder Cup! What a sensation!'

There was pandemonium on the 18th green,

reminiscent of other controversial Ryder Cup encounters, as team members from both sides, officials and hundreds of spectators brushed aside security personnel and invaded the green sward. Confusion reigned at first as many were unsure of the significance of Tyrone Oates's sporting gesture, and whether or not he had made it at the behest of his captain. The match official tried to make himself heard above the din.

'Ladies and gentlemen, Tyrone Oates has conceded the putt of his European opponent Davy Cochran. The final match has finished all square. This means that the overall result is that Europe and America finish even on fourteen points each. As holders, Europe retains the Ryder Cup!'

As the announcement ended his teemmates hoisted a still dazed Davy Cochran onto their shoulders and paraded him around the 18th green in front of the tv cameras. The rest of the ecstatic European golfers, the tension of the past few hours disappearing from their faces, were being congratulated by their captain Bruce Cartray. Members of the American squad, some looking bewildered, others bitterly disappointed at having possible victory snatched from their grasp, were nevertheless applauding and congratulating their opponents. It was an incredible finale to a memorable Ryder Cup.

Amid the chaos Wayne Folen found himself surrounded by tv cameras and newsmen thrusting microphones into his face, each of them seeking the answer to the burning question: Had he instructed Tyrone Oates to concede that vital putt on the 18th green?

'Yes I did.'

'But why, Wayne? That was a tricky putt. Davy Cochran could so easily have missed - '

'- and if he had you'd be bringing the Ryder Cup back to America tomorrow – ' another newsman cut in.

'You think I didn't know that,' Wayne snapped. He was almost disappearing under a wave of microphones.

'Then why on earth didn't you let Cochran putt?'

A deathly silence decended as America's captain took a deep breath. Suddenly he smiled and the anger disappeared from his eyes.

'I'll tell you why I told Tyrone Oakes to pick up his ball and concede....' The crush became almost unbearable as those with microphones pushed forward to capture what was going to be said next. 'A few minutes earlier while playing the 17th hole, Davy Cochran, under severe pressure to win, had called a penalty shot on himself. He did that knowing he would probably go down in history, and be remembered forever, as the guy who lost the Ryder Cup for Europe. Then, again under severe pressure on the 18th, he played one of the greatest recovery shot to the green that I've ever seen -'. Wayne broke off. The hundreds of people within earshot were hanging onto every word.

'For me those two incidents epitomise everything that this magnificent biennial golf tournament between Europe and America is all about, great sportsmanship and great shotmaking, a lot of it under severe pressure. No way was I going to have those two great incidents overshadowed by the indignity of a guy missing a short putt on the final green.

'Besides – ' those crowding around and millions of tv viewere worldwide saw a rare smile from the American captain – 'who's to say that Davy Cochran wouldn't have knocked that putt in anyway? I reckon he would have holed it – but after that great sporting gesture of his I wasn't going to let him suffer the indignity of maybe missing that putt. Thank you, ladies and gentlemen. I've nothing more to say right now!'

As Wayne turned away he found Marcia standing behind him. There were tears of joy in her eyes. She threw her arms around him, whispered in his ear: 'I'm so proud of you...'

On the clubhouse steps, surrounded by the members of

the U.S team and their officials, the President of America was endorsing Wayne Folen's sporting gesture.

'I expect a lot of Americans will be disappointed that our guys will not be bringing the Ryder Cup home. You all know how we Americans love to win. But I would appeal to those disappointed fans to look at the big picture. Earlier today we saw American golfers display the kind of grit and determination that has made our country great. And Wayne Folen's unforgetable sporting gesture on the final green in the last match, when the result hung in the balance, was in the best Ryder Cup tradition. I think Wayne Folen did the right thing. America should be very proud of him.

'We didn't regain the Ryder Cup today and I warmly congratulate the European golfers on their maginficent display over the three days – ' The President paused, smiled. 'But watch out Europe – I want to see Wayne Folen again appointed captain when you come to America two years hence – and this time I've no doubt the Ryder Cup will remain on our side of the Atlantic.' The President waved goodbye. 'God bless America and God bless you all!'

After the dramatic ending to the contest it took over an hour before the excitement peaked and died down. By then the American President had been helicoptered to Shannon en route to Berlin for the summit of world finance leaders. Meanwhile, supporters from both sides had found their way to the area where a stage had been erected, fronted by rows of seats in preparation for the presentation of the Ryder Cup trophy . With Lough Leane providing a magnificent backdrop, members of both teams and their respective captains took their seats on the flag-bedecked platform to be introduced individually to the cheering crowd. In the triumph of victory and the bitter-sweet taste of honourable defeat, animosities of the past week were forgotten as one-time rivals and their spouses paid gracious compliments to each other.

The biggest cheer of the afternoon occurred when the Ryder Cup was presented to Europe's smiling captain Bruce Cartray who, before making his winning speech, insisted on his rival Wayne Folen coming forward and joining him at the microphone. Together the European and American captains hoisted the Ryder Cup aloft for all to see. It was claimed later that at that precise moment the thunderous applause could be heard back in Killarney!

Later that night the huge ballroom of the Parknasilla Palace Hotel witnessed a glittering finale to what the media had already labelled 'the most dramatic and exciting Ryder Cup ever.' Members of both teams, spouses and officials gathered for a sumptuous dinner, followed later by a cabaret of singing and dancing featuring internationally famous Irish acts. This time the speeches were mercifully short; although not so the festivities which carried on well into the early hours.

• • • •

It was midday on Monday when the specially chartered airliner with the American Ryder Cup contingent on board took off from Shannon and headed westwards across the Atlantic to New York.

Despite the fact that the famous trophy was not on board the mood on the luxury aircraft was light-hearted and jovial. The newspapers strewn around the executive class cabin highlighted the extraordinary exploits that had taken place in the Ryder Cup venue in Killarney yesterday. Top of the list and vying for equal attention were the magnificent sporting gestures of local hero Davy Cochran and the American captain Wayne Folen. Headlines like 'Everyone A Winner in Ryder Cup Battle', 'Hail The Ryder Cup Heroes', 'Wonderful Wayne Avoids A Wake By The Lake' and 'Davy Does Us Proud,' (this latter in one of the Irish newspapers) abounded. The early morning tv newscasts had been loud in their praise for the battling U.S. squad and their tough-talking captain. 'They may have lost the battle, but they've won the respect of sportsmen and women around the world,' one commentator trumpeted.

Marcia Folen raised her glass of champagne. 'Here's to you, dear. You heard what your old friend Cord McCallum said at the dinner last night – he called you a true-blue American, praised your sportsmanship - even said you would go down in Ryder Cup history!'

Wayne grunted. 'The old guy doesn't fool me. Cord McCallum was as disappointed as I was that we didn't kick European ass – '

'Nonsense, Wayne. Everyone in America is proud of you today.'

'You reckon so?' Marcia squeezed her husband's hand in reply 'It still bugs me that I didn't bring back that darned trophy. It should be sitting right between the both of us – '

Marcia glanced sideways at her husband. 'There's always the next time – '

Wayne shook his head. 'Not for me there isn't. I got one bite of the cherry and failed. That's it I reckon - '

'No it isn't. Something in her voice made him glance at his wife. She was smiling.

'You heard what the President said yesterday. He hinted that he'd like to see you back as captain…'

Wayne smiled grimly. 'Not if Cord McCallum has his way – '

'Cord McCallum was proud of you also. He said so in his speech. Why do you think he told me that he'd like you back as captain in two years time?'

. 'What! You're kidding. Did he really tell you that?'

'Yes. And he sounded like he meant it.'

'The old guy must have broken out and knocked back too much champagne – '

'You know Mr. McCallum doesn't touch alcohol. He

was speaking off the record, of course. And this time there'll be no Angie around to mess things up for you. Promise?'

Wayne touched his champagne glass to hers. 'That's a promise.' He relaxed back in the luxurious lounger as the airliner eat up the miles across the Atlantic. Ryder Cup captain again. Another chance to make good, and on home soil too!

Wayne's eyes glinted. He had paid his dues to the Ryder Cup with that sporting gesture yesterday. He would always be revered for that. But what he firmly believed had come to pass – nice guys don't win! He would keep that in mind in two years time....

● ● ● ●

Meanwhile thousands of miles away, on another stretch of sea, the passenger ferry Normandy had ploughed its way around the tip of Land's End in southern England and had entered the English Channel on course for Cherbourg in northern France. It was due to dock there in just over an hour's time in the early afternoon.

Jeremy Walker stood at the rail, a lone figure, the strong wind tearing at his beard and his shock of russet hair. He narrowed his eyes against the spray and peered into the distance, saw the first sign of land beginning to appear on the horizon.

The overnight crossing from Rosslare in southeast Ireland, down through St. George's Channel, had been memorable in more ways than one; a storm had blown up just after midnight which meant that many of the passengers had retired early to their cabins, Jeremy, Katie and the boys included. The boys had succumbed to sleep quickly after a long day. In their cosy cabin behind closed doors, Jeremy and Katie had lain ensconced in each other's arms, discussing their future together, kissing, making love at intervals throughout the night as the Normandy ploughed through the high seas. It was near to dawn before Katie had finally fallen asleep in her lover's arms.

Soon they would be docking in Cherbourg. The four of them would pile into the car, drive across France, into Germany and Austria, down the length of the former Yugoslavia and into Greece. They would find a house near the sea, perhaps on one of the islands, or maybe move across to North Africa. He and Katie would set up home, sell their paintings, educate the boys, eat, sleep, drink wine and be happy together, grow old looking into the golden sunsets....

Jeremy heard his name being called out. He turned, saw her approaching along the deck, her dark hair streaming across her face, the wind catching, outlining it against her trim figure. She looked like a Raphaelite portrait, beautiful, sensuous, her dark halo of hair flowing wild, a smile playing about her lips, her eyes on him.

She had come up from below, having left Garret and Jack enthralled in the safety of the computer games salon. He smiled at her and straightened up from the rail. She melted in close and he encircled her in his arms.

'I estimate we'll be in Cherbourg in less than an hour,' he said.

'I can't wait. Imagine, we'll be together, every day – '

He looked into her eyes. 'Are you happy, Katie Gartland?' he asked.

She shook her head. 'I am not Katie Gartland, not any more. Katie Gartland is dead, buried in a place called Loughduff. Promise me you won't ever use that surname again?'

She turned her face to his. He lowered his head, put his lips to hers. The kiss was soft and lingering. 'Does that answer your question?', he asked when they finally broke apart.

Katie smiled a reply, turned back and gazed over the

rail. The storm of last night had passed and the sea was now relatively calm. She felt the warmth of Jeremy's body, the comfort of his arms around her. She leaned back, rested her head on his shoulder and together they gazed towards the advancing shore.

OPERATION BIRDIE

If you enjoyed *All To Play For* perhaps you might also like to read 'Operation Birdie', a romantic/thriller by William Rocke also set in the world of big-time golf.

The scene: Turnberry, the famous golf course on Scotland's rugged west coast.

The prize: The Open championship, the most prize in world golf.

The players: 150 of the game's top stars, battling over four days in front of thousands of spectators and a television audience of millions, with fame and fortune awaiting the winner.

OPERATION BIRDIE takes the reader behind the scenes of big-time professional golf. We meet the jet-setting superstars from around the world, along with those struggling to make it to the top, some obsessed with winning at any cost....

The action off the course is every bit as exciting as the battles on it; rich, bored wives seeking attention, mistresses and groupies looking for action, plus the hard-nosed members of the media looking for a story.

Mingling with thousands of spectators are Martin Dignam and Marie Kird, members of the Real IRA sent over from Belfast on Operation Birdie to disrupt the Open. The original plan was to blow up the war memorial on the course with no loss of life, but hard man Dignam has other ideas....

OPERATION BIRDIE is a fast-paced thriller that golf fans - and readers seeking sheer entertainment - will find difficult to put down.

Available from: William Rocke,
Rocphil Publishing,
3 Hazelwood Drive,
Artane, 1 Dublin 5, Republic of Ireland.

€10 (postage paid)
Stg£6 do.
US$15 do.